The Assassin of Verona

ALSO BY BENET BRANDRETH

The Spy of Venice

Benet Brandreth

PEGASUS CRIME
NEW YORK LONDON

THE ASSASSIN OF VERONA

Pegasus Crime is an imprint of
Pegasus Books Ltd.
148 West 37th Street, 13th Floor
New York, NY 10018

First Pegasus Books hardcover edition May 2019

ISBN: 978-1-68177-876-1

10 9 8 7 6 5 4 3 2 1

Printed in the United States of America
Distributed by W. W. Norton & Company, Inc.

To my mother:

If you had been the wife of Hercules,
Six of his labours you'd have done, and saved
Your husband so much sweat.

To my father:

Good my lord,
You have begot me, bred me, loved me: I
Return those duties back as are right fit,
Obey you, love you, and most honour you.

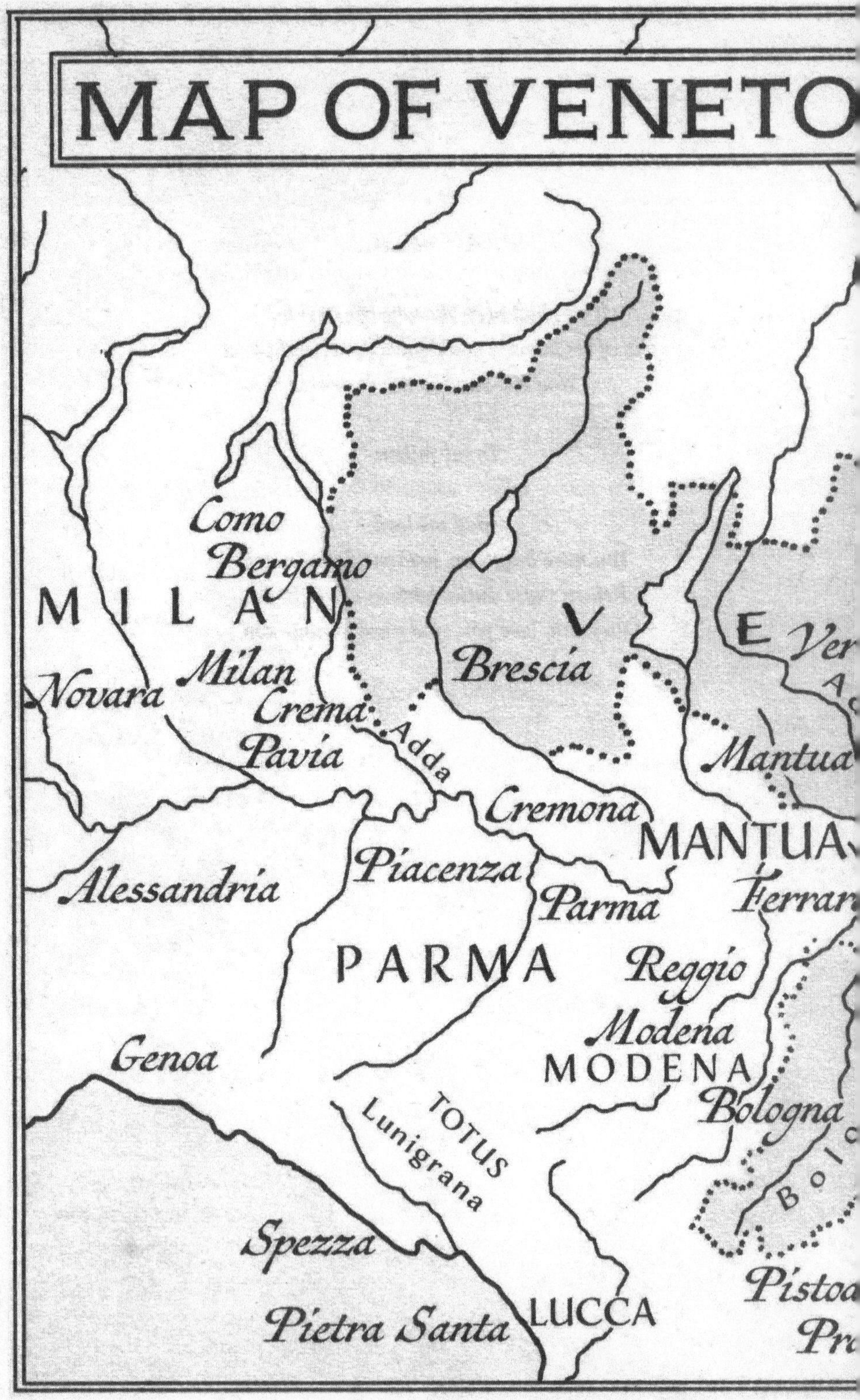
MAP OF VENETO
MILAN
Como
Bergamo
Milan
Novara
Crema
Pavia
Adda
V
Brescia
E
Ver
Mantua
Cremona
MANTUA
Alessandria
Piacenza
Parma
Ferrar
PARMA
Reggio
Modena
MODENA
Genoa
Bologna
TOTUS
Lunigrana
Spezza
Pistoa
Pietra Santa
LUCCA

Aquileia
Trieste
Venice
ISTRIA
Padua
Rovigo
Ponte Lagoscuro
RRARA
Comacchio
Ravenna
Faenza
Forlí
Romagna
STATE
N
W
E
S

Dramatis Personae

Rome

Pope Sixtus V — The former Cardinal Montalto, a man of strong will and stronger action, a pope of whom it is said that he has m spies than other Italian princes have soldiers.

Father John Thornhill — An English priest.

Cardinal Decio Azzolini — Papal Secretary.

Arrigo — A soldier in the army of the Republic of St Peter.

Venice

William Shakespeare — Player disguised as William Fallow, steward to the English Ambassador to Venice, Sir Henry Carr.

Nicholas Oldcastle — Player disguised as Sir Henry Carr, English Ambassador to Venice.

John Hemminges — Player and friend to the former.

Isabella Lisarro — Pœt, courtesan and wonder of an age.

Marco Venier — Nobleman of Venice, wealthy patron of the arts provided they be profitable.

Cosimo Tiepolo — Younger brother to Francesco Tiepolo – an attainted traitor to the Republic of Venice and an exile.

Monsignor Cesare Costa — Nuncio to the Holy See.

Isabella Andreini — Player and mistress of the most famous troupe in all of Italy, I Gelosi.

Verona

Duke Leonardo Barbaro	A proud and intemperate nobleman, ruler of a portion of the Veneto.
Aemilia Barbaro	His daughter.
Valentine Vicentino	A distant cousin to the Duke.
Rodrigo	The Duke's steward.
Dionisio	Servant of the Duke's household.

Outlaws

Orlando	Leader of the vagabond fellowship.
Luca	An outlaw and brother to Tommasso.
Zago	Cook to the outlaws.
Petro	Priest and minister to the outlaws.
Ludovico	An outlaw.
Tommasso	An outlaw and brother to Luca.
Jacopo	An outlaw.

Scenes

Prologue	Rome, August 1585
Act One	Venice and Verona, November 1585 to February 1586
Act Two	Verona and woods in the Veneto, February to March 1586
Act Three	Verona and woods in the Veneto, March 1586
Act Four	Verona and woods in the Veneto, March 1586
Act Five	Woods in the Veneto, March 1586
Epilogue	Woods in the Veneto, March 1586

Prologue

Rome, August 1585

The small group gathered before the wooden statue of the Christ. It was a plain and simple thing, no great master's work. Yet it was the reason for their journey. The statue stood at the centre of a private chapel on an estate two leagues outside Rome. At the centre of the group stood the Pope with his Secretary beside him. Behind them stood four men in the robes of various orders and with faces whose skin bore the colouring of several nations. The four men, each of whom had been loyal to the Pope even when he had been merely the Cardinal Montalto, had been called to the estate for conference, each making a journey far longer and more arduous than that of the Pope and his Secretary. None understood why they were to meet here, so far from the comforts of the Vatican Palace, until the Pope began to speak – and then the value of this secluded meeting place and its seeming other purpose in the statue became clear.

The little group of priests stood alone in the chapel save for the owner of the estate, who stood nearby shifting from foot to foot. The man's delight at the great honour of the Pope's visit had been transformed. Pride had turned to concern and concern to fear. He did not understand all that passed between the Pope and his confederates, but he understood enough to know that this was discourse on matters political, not wise or safe for one such as him to hear, and it frightened him that none seemed to care that he did hear it.

Outside, beyond earshot, held back by the Pontifical Guard, were pilgrims. They had come in their hundreds this past month, paying the owner of the estate well for food, for water, for beds. They came to view the miraculous statue that wept tears of blood. The statue that the Pope now stood gazing upon. The pilgrims had left rich offerings to be washed by those tears, the stain of whose path could be seen on the statue's roughly carved face, which now was dry. Their excitement to have arrived at the same time as His Holiness was great. Would the Pope witness the miracle himself?

The Pope turned back from contemplation of the statue to the four men behind him.

'You understand the importance that I place on your mission?' he asked.

All four men bowed their heads.

'Have you any questions?'

'Does your Holiness have a description of the English agents?' asked the tall, gaunt priest who stood a little apart from the others.

Cardinal Azzolini answered for his master.

'Little more than that they are English, Father Thornhill. Of the Embassy there are two: an old man, tall and round, the Ambassador, and a younger one, who plays at poet and lover in Venice. These two may be innocents who serve to distract us from the true agents of the English crown. There is a third that we know of also, of middle years, a true killer if rumour be believed. Three at least, yet all must be taken. How many English can there be in Venice?'

'Do not concern yourself overmuch with the Ambassador and his men, Father Thornhill,' said the Pope to the tall priest. The Pope turned to the pink-faced man that stood next to the priest. 'It will be your task, Monsignor Costa, to deal with the English Embassy while it remains in Venice. Your roles,' he gestured to the other three, 'are in the north. You, Father Thornhill, to Verona, you, Father Montanio, to Padua, and you, Father Fiorucci, to Mantua. There is a disease in the north that must be cut out before it rots the healthy body. Root out heresy where you find it, purge it with fire. I must have quiet if France and Spain are not to be diverted from their path to fruitless battle in the northern duchies. If in your mission you find any messenger that may have evaded Monsignor Costa in Venice, well then, I trust that you will attend to it with—'

His speech was interrupted by a shout from the pilgrims at the door. It was echoed by a sigh that went up from the four men facing the Pope. Cardinal Azzolini placed a hand upon the Pope's arm to draw his gaze back round to the statue, from whose eyes there now dripped bloody tears. The owner of the chapel and the statue fell to his knees and began praying loudly for the mercy of Christ the Redeemer. The Pope stared at the statue for several moments until he realised that only he and the gaunt priest, Father Thornhill, were not kneeling. Thornhill's pale eyes were not fixed on the statue as the others' were but on the praying figure of the owner of the chapel.

The Pope turned and called to his guards' commander at the chapel's door. The man ran to him.

'Your sword,' the Pope commanded.

'Your Holiness?' his captain asked, eyes flicking to the statue, unsure what the Pope sought.

'Give me your sword, Captain,' the Pope demanded again, his irritation clear.

The captain hurried to pull the long sword from its scabbard and placed it in the Pope's hand. The Pope now strode to the statue and crossed himself.

'As Christ, I worship you,' he proclaimed loudly. Then, lifting the sword above his head with both hands, 'But as wood, I break you.'

Cardinal Azzolini watched in horror as the Pope brought the sword crashing down on the miraculous statue, which split asunder with a loud snap. A hush entered the chapel followed by a moan of disbelief from the crowd pushing at the door. Then the Pope held out the sword to his captain, shaking it to grab the attention of the stunned man. Just as the captain reached out to take it, the Pope snatched it back to move the wooden pieces with the blade's tip.

'You see?'

The captain bent forward. The head of the statue was hollow and within it sat a sponge soaked in blood. Wrapped round the sponge was a thread that, drawn, pulled tight about the sponge. The trail of the thread led to the rear of the nave. The captain strode to the back and dashed aside a curtain that hung there to reveal a cowering woman, one end of the thread grasped in her hand. She dropped it as if it had become hot and fell to her knees imploring forgiveness and pointing at her husband, the owner of the estate.

The Pope gestured to the owner of the estate with the sword he still held.

'Seize them. Take them to Piazza di Ponte. Take his head as a warning to others not to abuse Christ's name by preying on the credulous. Her flog.'

Ignoring the couple's cries for lenience the Pope turned back to the four men.

'The names of our agents must not reach England. The heretic Queen Elizabeth must be deposed. Without England there is no Philip, without Philip there is no Jerusalem. Our plans turn on our men in England. They must not be exposed. You understand? Cast mercy from you. Do whatever must be done to keep them secret.'

Act One

Venice and Verona, November 1585 to February 1586

And will this brothers' wager frankly play

Venice

It came, as so many deaths do, as the result of a wager.

William took Isabella's hand and kissed it, receiving only a warning look in return. He strode to the balcony and stripped off his doublet, to the general applause of the gathered guests. William bowed in acknowledgement; Isabella rolled her eyes. Then William turned to Cosimo Tiepolo who stood similarly shorn of all clothing save that which modesty required.

'You see, Tiepolo, we English have nothing to hide.'

Cosimo Tiepolo gestured to his own state of undress in answer. William put on a face of great sadness.

'Oh, you are merely exposed, Tiepolo.'

The young man curled his lip at William's barb. Let the Englishman battle with words, Cosimo thought, I have weapons that leave more lasting wounds. He pointed out across the balcony to the city of Venice. Below, the Canal Grande curved away, a glittering road of silver in the light of the full moon. Beyond, the buildings were dark shadows, studded here and there with gold from the light of lamps at the shrines, the *ancone*, that were placed throughout the city. In the silence of the night it seemed as if those at the Ca' Venier were the only people awake. Even the Canal Grande was still, no breeze lifted its waters, no gondola travelled upon it.

'To the statue of the Hunchback at Rialto and back,' declared Cosimo.

'And the loser quits Venice this very night?'

'I swear it.'

'As do I.'

Cosimo nodded, smiled, then leapt to the parapet and dived. William waited only long enough to cast a smile in Isabella's direction before he too bounded to the balcony's edge and sprang high, turning his body in the air to strike like an arrow into the water below.

Isabella strode to the balcony and looked out to the canal. She picked out the two heads cleaving their way through the waters of the Canal

Grande, already some distance from the Ca' Venier. Headstrong youth, she thought, her fingers fretfully dancing on the balcony rail. Had William so quickly forgotten the enemies they had made, the dangers that surrounded them, the need to guard themselves and venture forth only in company, among friends? Marco Venier approached and placed his hand over her own where it clutched at the parapet. After a moment she took it back.

'Foolish man,' she said.

'Perhaps he is, but I think your Will will win his wager,' Marco answered, 'and better such a wager than the duel that was threatened.'

'When I spoke of fools, I was not speaking of that headstrong boy but of you, Marco. Why did you invite Cosimo Tiepolo to the feast knowing that William would be here too?'

'I am a neutral, Isabella. I oppose none, at least not openly. Cosimo's brother Francesco may have been attainted traitor but his family's power is not to be dismissed, nor its scions ignored.'

'Be that so, still, where lay the wisdom in bringing together two avowed enemies?'

Marco gestured to his guests, now pulled together in knots of heads, all bent in delighted gossip.

'Little wisdom,' said Marco, 'but much entertainment.'

Isabella looked at those gathered at the feast. She could see more than one that shook hands and joined their wagers to that of William Shakespeare and Cosimo Tiepolo. She looked back at their host, Marco Venier, her friend, whose thin lips now carried a wicked smile. Almighty God, let not William lose, thought Isabella, or I will be alone among these crocodiles.

Why, your dolphin is not lustier

For a moment, when he struck the water and its cold clutched at his sides, William regretted the fretful mood that had provoked him to the wager. Then his head pierced the water's surface, he saw his quarry ahead and he felt the thrill of the chase upon him. All thought of consequence was banished, for a young man longs to feel his strength and William felt his now. His arms cleaving the water of the canal like an oar's blade, he struck out and, steadily, he gained on Cosimo Tiepolo.

The moon shone fair on the water of the Canal Grande, showing William a path of slippery onyx. Even had it not, in the four months that had passed since William's arrival in Venice, he had learned the city's ways well enough to know his route now. The Canal Grande curved away in a great arch ahead and beyond that bend, out of sight, lay the statue of the Hunchback by the Campo Erberia, which he or Cosimo must reach and return from. The straightest path lay along the Canal Grande. Cosimo took that course. William knew another route, crooked but shorter. He might cut across the bend of the Canal Grande by turning down one of the canals that stemmed from it and gain minutes on his opponent.

It was just such a boastful claim to knowledge of the city that had been the prompt to argument at the Ca' Venier. Though William was not a year older than when he had left his home in Stratford, the months that had passed since then had been rich in experience. The company of his friends Hemminges and Oldcastle and their players' lessons in London had become the dangers and disasters of the fateful embassy to Venice. How had fortune twisted and turned then, the Ambassador's murder compelling Oldcastle and him to disguise themselves as the English Ambassador, Sir Henry Carr, and his steward, William Fallow. A disguise that they still wore and whose comforts they had grown accustomed to but not before it had exposed them to the hate of the Pope's assassin, Giovanni Prospero, snatching Hemminges from them, and then giving him back just in time to save Vittoria Accoramboni, the Duchess of Bracciano, from Prospero's murderous game. William himself marvelled at the difference between his greener days and those he mastered now. Above all else, the love of Isabella Lisarro, a woman he considered matchless, fierce in intellect, against whom he could find no worthy comparison, had given him confidence in his own abilities and judgement. So, when the discourse had turned to questions of England's newly begun war with Spain, William had ventured his opinion.

'It would serve Venice well to aid our English cause in the Netherlands. Philip of Spain is no friend of Venice. It is his ships that have cut the vein of Venice's trade with the East. Yet by England's defiance he is made distract, turns his thoughts northwards and away from those places most dear to the Republic's interest.'

'How can Venice align itself with England? England is a heretic state, her Queen excommunicate, her navy little more than pirates.'

It was a thin-lipped man that spoke, his voice carrying an accent from outside Venice, though from where William could not say. His dress severe in cut and colour, he was a poor guest at a celebration such as this. William and Isabella had noted him earlier precisely for how he stood out, dour amongst the joy. The more so since he kept company with far gaudier fellows whose rich dress marked them as members of the *Compagnia della Calza*, a society of the wealthy youth of Venice. This man was a crow among peacocks, his voice as devoid of emotion as his clothing of colour.

William frowned. 'Venice trades with the Turk, with the Jews, with the Russians. Venice is commerce and commerce knows no religion. Besides, Venice loves a victor and England will be victorious.'

A new voice spoke in answer. 'Your Earl of Leicester will be crushed within the month, William Fallow. England is a child, at war with men full grown.'

William had not expected to see Cosimo Tiepolo at Marco Venier's feast. Still less to see him so proud, dressed in the flame-coloured stockings of the *Compagnia della Calza*.

'England is an insect, a beetle, next to the power of Spain. It will be crushed like one.'

William caught Isabella's cautioning look but paid it no heed. He could see well enough that Cosimo sought to provoke him but, so, he had succeeded.

'There is a difference between a grub and a butterfly. So England was a grub but is now grown. You think Spain's eye will pass over Venice without pause because it did not aid England? Think rather that Spain will take each, one by one, that fought alone when together they might have held out till the end of time. I say again, an alliance is as much in Venice's interest as England's.'

'You claim to speak in Venice's interest?' Cosimo's voice rose.

William cut across him. 'I do. It is not the first time I have spoken in Venice's interest when those born to that interest have counselled against.'

Green-blue Murano glass shattered across the mosaic floor of the Ca' Venier's great room. The sound brought silence to the guests gathered in the Palazzo as all turned to look first at the angry young man who had hurled it and then at the young man whose shrewd eyes briefly gazed on the broken remnants at his feet before turning to look again on the hurler.

'That was my grandfather's,' observed Marco Venier.

'Your arrogance is unbearable.' Cosimo Tiepolo spoke from a face hot with choler. He felt the eyes of the silent guests on him and fought for composure.

'You claim to know this city but you are a cuckoo, no more,' said Cosimo.

'I am not born of the city, true, but I know its mood better than you do, peacock. And if a cuckoo, then all I have done is push out a basilisk egg that, left untouched, would have devoured the whole brood.'

A low, delighted muttering was running round the crowded guests for William's words were well aimed. All understood that this William Fallow, the English Ambassador's man, spoke of Cosimo's brother Francesco Tiepolo, so recently declared traitor by the Council of Ten of the Signoria of Venice and fled the city under sentence of death. If rumour were to be believed – and when was it not – this William was responsible for the charges. His jibe at the brother seemingly confirming it. Only William and Isabella among the guests knew that the charge of treachery against Francesco Tiepolo was false. Or that William had arranged it to see justice done against Francesco for what William thought a far greater, far fouler crime against Isabella that would otherwise have gone unpunished.

'All you will know of this city is two strides' length of it and one stone,' answered Cosimo, stepping forward, his hand moving to the dagger at his belt.

Marco Venier stepped in front of him. 'Gentlemen, calm.'

The thin-lipped Crow spoke up: 'Perhaps these two would consider a contest and a wager on it?'

'Capital conceit,' said Marco Venier, his hand on Cosimo Tiepolo's arm, feeling the tension in him.

'What stakes could this man offer that would make me shift?' sneered Cosimo.

'I have a thought,' said the Crow.

William saw the gleam of the lamp on the corner of the Canal Grande and San Maurizio and struck out north along the smaller canal. In moments he could no longer hear the sound of the other man swimming. There was an instant when he thought he heard the sound of feet running, but then silence fell. William was alone.

The time may have all shadow and silence in it

William hauled himself from the water and looked about.

He had re-entered the Canal Grande by the Palazzo Lando. A glance to his right showed him the Campo Erberia, empty at this hour, to his left revealed no sight of Cosimo Tiepolo. Either William had pulled far ahead of his challenger or the man was already out of the canal and making for the Hunchback. Haste was called for whatever the answer.

William ran across the Campo and past the great brick edifice of the Church of San Giacomo di Rialto. Ahead, opposite the church, was the statue of the Hunchback, crouched in the shadow of the steps that ran up its back. William touched it, as those about to embark on a voyage did for luck. He spun about, listening. Where was Cosimo? In front of him the great clock on the front of the church pointed to the eleventh hour. The Campo was silent. William understood in that moment that he had been a fool: there was a reason that Cosimo Tiepolo was nowhere to be seen. When Cosimo had realised William no longer followed hard behind he had simply stopped and waited. If Cosimo vouchsafed that it was he had touched the Hunchback first and then returned, what judge would gainsay him?

Cursing himself for a foolish honest man and the Tiepolos for their treacherous nature, William turned and ran back to the Canal Grande. His only hope now lay in Cosimo's need to guess a plausible gap of time in which to have reached Rialto and returned. The only way to be certain of that was for Cosimo to sit and wait where he might see William returning and then, full-fresh from his rest, dive in and finish the race, ahead of William. William met the canal's edge and once again dived into the water and pulled hard.

His strokes no longer cut cleanly through the water, anger made them shake and shudder. He turned once more from the Canal Grande at the Palazzo Lando. His strong intent was all bent on speed, on remembering his route, and he did not hear the footsteps again running beside the canal nor the splash of another diving into the water. The first he knew of the danger was when an arm pulled him beneath the waters.

Then is sin struck down like an ox

The hand grasped William's leg and heaved. His head dipped and he took in a draught of the foul canal water. Hands grappled his body and dragged him down. William kicked furiously up to reach the surface. He coughed and drew a hasty breath before he was pulled back down below. He twisted in the murk of the canal and wrestled for the arms of the creature holding him. Heat built in his lungs and he fought with all his will not to open his mouth.

Hands pressed against his throat; though what need there was to strangle him when the waters of the canal would drown him he could not think. He almost laughed at the absurdity of it, of his double murder, strangled and then drowned. At last his hands found the arms that held him and felt their way up with an urgent angry caressing that reached shoulder, then neck, then jaw until they came to embrace the face of whatever man it was held him. He dug his thumbs into the eye sockets. At once the waters thrashed about him and he was released, thrust away. William kicked for the surface.

The two men burst from water into air at almost the same instant. The still night was rent with the sound of deep heaves and flailing arms. William drove for the canal's bank and pulled himself on to the street, coughing, heaving, hacking for breath. He had risen to one knee when the boot caught him in the ribs and lifted him away. He rolled with the blow and cracked into the wall of a building. He looked up to see the sole of a boot, water cascading from it, driving at his head. He kicked hard at his attacker's rear foot. Planted as it was, that leg, when William's foot caught the shin, toppled back and the kick that would have dashed William's brains from him skittered off against the cobbles instead, to the music of a howl of pain from his assailant.

William rolled to one side and gained his feet, grasping a loose stone from the ground as he did so. His ribs ached but the pain was not so sharp as to make him think them broken. Two yards from him a figure, as sodden as William, limped around to face him.

'Francesco Tiepolo.'

'The same, William Fallow, the same Francesco Tiepolo that you have slandered and driven into exile.'

The proud youth who had once strutted before him and threatened vile deeds against Isabella Lisarro now cut a pathetic figure. It was not just that his former finery was gone, replaced with plain weeds besmirched with mud, a matted and sodden hood to hide his golden mane. His hollow cheek and haunted eyes spoke of the price of failure. William revelled in the signs of the punishment that he had brought on Francesco's head. There was no mercy in him for this one, this man who had threatened his beloved Isabella. Francesco's eyes held the fixed look that spoke of courage taken by the glass. How had he returned to Venice? The Signoria should have taken him before this moment.

Francesco drew a knife. William's breath still came in heaves and he looked about for a refuge that might buy him a moment to recover. 'Will you add to your capital crimes, Francesco?'

'I have been exiled from Venice. Do I fear death now?'

As he spoke Francesco advanced on William. He brandished the knife before him and William watched it snap back and forth like a flag in a strong wind.

Francesco lunged but William was ready. He had seen in Francesco's wafting blade a fighter in want of experience. William blessed his friend Hemminges, who had trained him to fight, for a hard taskmaster and a shrewd one. William let his arm drift in front of him as bait. Francesco lunged to cut it and as he did, William struck. He pushed aside Tiepolo's blade and swung the stone from the street to crack into Francesco's temple, felling him like an ox.

For a moment William stood over the senseless figure. Then he put his foot on the villain's side and made to roll him into the canal. A hand gripped his arm.

'You are not turned executioner yet, William.'

William did not look round at Hemminges' voice. He took his foot from Francesco's side.

'You were watching?'

'Always, but lost you when you turned aside from the Canal Grande. As must this one have done.'

'What will you do with him now?' William asked.

'Time's wasting, Will,' was all Hemminges' answer.

William tore his eyes from the prone man before him to look on Hemminges' face. He grinned at his friend, then turned and ran to the end of the street and dove again into the murky waters of Venice.

There is a plot against my life

William now swam cleanly again. It was as though the desperate battling in the waters had let the anger from his blood. Thoughts congealed in the cool of his mind.

Cosimo Tiepolo had known of the feast at the Ca' Venier and that William would be there as a guest. The Tiepolo brothers must have laid their plans accordingly, Cosimo provoking William, threatening a duel that became the prompt to a wager that drew William out, alone into the dark and silent canals of Venice. Yet, wait, was it not the Crow that suggested the wager? Who was he to the Tiepolos? A chance taken or an actor in their scheme? William thought back to when he had first strayed from the Canal Grande to take the crooked route to Rialto. Had he not heard footsteps running? The sound of Francesco forced to alter the place of his ambuscade.

It was a bold plot. Why not the hired villain's dagger in the dark? No, that was not Francesco's way, William realised. He wanted to be in at the kill, to taunt and to boast, as he had sought to do when he threatened Isabella. It was that selfish desire to gloat that had drawn Francesco Tiepolo back to Venice, in defiance of the order of exile. How our character exposes us, William thought.

What followed? What followed? William's stroke slowed. A hundred yards ahead he could see the buildings part and the moment when his path would take him from the smaller side canals back on to the Canal Grande. He slowed more and let his strokes become shallower and the more silent for it. William was no longer thinking of haste to return to the Ca' Venier. He knew now how it was that Cosimo intended to gauge the right time: he waited for his brother's report of a murder achieved.

Wrath, envy, treason, rape, and murder's rages

Cosimo crouched on the jetty ahead like a raven on his perch, shrouded even from the moon's light by the shadow of the Palazzo behind. In the quiet of the night William's movement through the water carried out to the crouching man.

'Is it done?' Cosimo's voice came back across the night in a harsh whisper. William made no answer.

'Is it done, Francesco?'

Still William made no reply other than to draw closer, stroke by stroke.

'Francesco, are you injured? Why don't you answer?'

Cosimo's voice now had a note of fear in it. William carried on with a steady, even pull. He drew alongside, then past the jetty where Cosimo waited and on. His path took him from the shadow of the buildings. He heard the gasp of recognition and the shout that followed.

'Fallow!'

Over his shoulder William called back, 'Too late, Cosimo. The course is run, the victory won.'

'Where is Francesco?' his brother cried.

'Where?' William stopped his motion and turned to where Cosimo now stood on the jetty. He trod the water and called out, 'Behind. By Campo Sant'Anzolo will you find him, or at least his body, his soul may already be in Hell. Yet, he was not dead when I left him, if you hurry you might save him yet.'

Cosimo let out a cry of rage and William laughed.

'Of course, if you do, you will certainly lose this wager and then it follows, lose Venice too. Which will it be, Cosimo? A brother's love or a mother's embrace?'

William turned and set out again for the Ca' Venier. He had a lead of twenty yards and there was a chance, a chance at least, that Cosimo would look to save his brother rather than himself. An angry cry and the sound of Cosimo hurling himself into the water put an end to that hope. To think of others was not the Tiepolo way. Now, for victory against the weight of his tired and bruised limbs, William had to count on his small lead and on Cosimo's own joints being stiff from an hour of cramped waiting, wet and cold.

The two men swam towards the light of the balcony. A hundred yards from it they heard a watcher's shout go up and then a babble of voices.

'They are returned!'

'Who leads?'

'Nothing either way.'

Cheers rang up and William heard his name and that of Cosimo Tiepolo hurled into the night air by the excited guests. William's lead was cut to nothing. His arms swung like dead men from a noose, wrung out of life. He could see Isabella and Marco Venier press their way to the front of the crowd on the balcony. Isabella clutched the rail with both hands.

The last was to climb the walls to the balcony. He and Cosimo reached the stones of the Ca' Venier at the same instant. William reached up to the lip of one of the corner stones and hauled himself from the water. In sudden motion of his own, Cosimo struck out and latched on to William's waist and heaved. William was thrown back, the two men spun in the water, Cosimo pushed down on William's shoulders, driving him deep into the canal's water, even as he thrust away. William burst back above the water to see Cosimo already at the wall, the guests above crying their delight at the battle below. His head was a hammering drum of pain. He reached the wall and began to climb but Cosimo was a body's length from him and already reaching for the base of the balcony. William sprang up and caught Cosimo's leg. Cosimo kicked back but William clung on as a drowning man to a rock. William unhooked one arm and clutched at the wall, planted his feet and pulled up. Now they perched, face to face, each clinging to the imperfections of the wall by a single hand, the other hand locked in battle with their enemy.

William felt his strength gone: that last surge of heat having propelled him forward had left naught behind for further contest. Cosimo's eyes held William's and gleamed his triumph. He bent William's arm and, groaning out at his victory 'gainst the frustrations of the night, began to force William away from the wall. William felt his fingers slipping.

Then Cosimo's face and voice transposed from a cry of triumph to a scream of agony. The sharp heel of a woman's chopine peeped through the balcony's pillars and pressed down upon the back of Cosimo's hand. He let go his hold on the base of the balcony and plunged away into the canal. William did not pause to reckon at redemption's cause. His fingers cramped and the shoulder of that arm Cosimo had wrestled with was a twisted rope of agony, torn as it was wrenched from Cosimo's grip as he fell. He hauled himself up in agonised movements and more fell than climbed over the parapet. He rolled on to the floor and from his back looked up at the guests gathered about him.

'Am I the first?'

Marco Venier looked down at him and then out over the parapet. 'And the last by the look of it. It seems Cosimo sets course for new worlds.'

'In that at least, he shows honour,' said William, and then burst into laughter that became in turn a fit of coughing and hacking that drove the other guests from the balcony back into the warmer comforts of the Ca' Venier. The last but one to turn and leave was the Crow. His eyes on William's prone body glittered with malice and there was a moment when William thought he might find another stamping foot descending on him to add to Francesco Tiepolo's at the canal. Isabella's voice sprang up.

'Your name, sir?'

The Crow looked up from William to Isabella and the malice in his eye flared brighter and promised violence but the moment passed and with it, but without answer to Isabella, the Crow turned and left. William pushed himself to his knees.

'Your shoes, Isabella,' he said from his bent stance, 'become you well.'

William stood up.

'I have been very foolish, Isabella.'

'As always. Foolish and brave at the same time. The sin of youth.' Isabella ran her hand across William's forearm. A long gash lay open in the sodden linen, stained with blood. 'I take it there was more to this race than swimming.'

'So it played out,' said William. 'If it had not been for you and Hemminges . . .'

He left the rest unsaid for Isabella had grasped him in a sudden embrace. She clung to him and whispered in his ear. 'I was so afraid, William. So afraid, to be alone. If you had lost . . .'

He felt her tears fall on to his shoulder and he brushed her hair with his hand, not caring that he spoiled its delicate arrangement with his damp caress. She pulled back and, putting her own hands to his face, drew him to her, granting him a fierce kiss that thrilled with the passions and terrors of the night.

'Come. No more foolishness tonight,' she said. 'Let us make our excuses to our host and be gone. You must rest and recover your strength.'

'Willingly, for I hope I shall need it.'

Isabella rolled her eyes once more but she did not contradict him.

The fields are fragrant, and the woods are green

Verona

Aemilia put her hands over her heart and sighed.

'You like it?' asked Valentine.

'Oh Valentine, would that we too could live as the lovers in your verse do, freely.'

Valentine came and sat beside her on the stone bench. She looked at the pure pleasure on his face at her praise and returned that look with pleasure of her own. His words were as beautiful as he. She had feared that she was to spend her whole life in her father's palace surrounded only by the old, the martial and the stern, with their dry talk of livestock, politics, or the disciplines of war. Now Valentine was here and Valentine was wonder and the promise of a different future. His long blond hair was gathered back from the fine bones of his face and the morning's light gave his blue eyes the lustre of gemstones. He dared to take her hand in his. The two youths were as close together as they had ever been, closeted from the cold of winter and the prying eyes of maids within an arbour in the palace gardens.

'Your poem,' Aemilia said, letting her hand remain in his and joying at its bold touch, 'speaks to me of your great soul.'

'It speaks of yours, Aemilia, for you are its inspiration.'

'I think a little of the inspiration lies with Catullus,' she answered.

'There was some of Catullus in it, true,' he said, his face turned from hers to gaze out across the garden. She had meant only a gentle jibe, and to mind him that she too knew her poets and their verses, but his hurt frown and hand withdrawn told her she had struck deeper than she meant.

'Don't pout, Valentine. It makes you frown and that mars your beautiful brow and you know it is chiefly for your looks that I dare my father's wrath.'

'You sport with me,' answered Valentine, hurt look still perched upon him like a bruise on an apple.

'I do. Oh, Valentine,' she said, 'I spoke only in wonder at your art. To see you take a master's words and turn them to a greater purpose still.'

A tilt of his chin told her that whatever hurt her first words had caused him, these new ones had been a balm, that he saw she did not mean to slight him for wearing borrowed garb but praise him as an heir to greatness. She reached out and took his hand to draw him back. He was so delicate a soul, as all great poets are, she thought, and she must not forget that she, lacking a mother, had sensibilities formed by the blunter company of her father and his soldiers.

'I am still honing it,' said Valentine. Aemilia nodded and concealed a little smile to see her flattery win him round to her again.

'What gave you its conceit?' she asked to draw him out.

'I thought on the news of outlaws in the woods outside the city. How they grow in number and of how some talk of their villainy, their cruelty, and their lawless lives. I hear these tales and think only of how they live far from the cares and constraints of our gentler world. Sometimes these palace walls seem to me a prison.'

He threw out an arm to gesture at an unseen place beyond the garden's walls.

'There are they free to live as they wish, to love as they wish, wanting only soft grass for a bed, sweet water from the stream to drink and the sun to warm them.'

Valentine's fair brow was furrowed with fierce desire as he spoke. Aemilia thrilled to hear his passion. The following pressure of her hand on his brought his look back to her. He put his other hand on hers to hold it closer.

'I would that we were there, Aemilia. I would that my poverty did not keep me from your father's favour.'

Aemilia sighed again. 'You would give up all comfort?'

'What comfort is there, Aemilia, to sleep on soft sheets and drink sweet wine, if it means you and I may not be together? Rather old bread and the nettle bower and you. Sometimes love demands a sacrifice and for your love I would sacrifice all.'

His face was close to hers and she could smell his sweet breath, oranges and cloves mingling with her own scent of roses. The world seemed very still in that moment, no leaf whispering in the wind, no bird's song breaking the silence, just Valentine, his hands around hers and the trembling beat of her heart. Oh what a wonder it would be, to cast off duty, to take a lover and to live freely in the woods.

Gravel crunched underfoot. Aemilia snatched back her hand at the sound of her maid's approach but she could not take her eyes from Valentine as he hurried to stand at a more seemly distance from the Duke's daughter. His look was full of promises as it held her own and her thoughts lingered on the freedoms of the forest even as her maid led her away to dress for dinner.

Let's not confound the time with conference harsh

Venice

'We must leave,' Hemminges said again.

'No. I'll not hear of it,' William answered. 'There is little pleasure in such a course and much travail.'

William sprawled across a long bench beneath the window. One arm, wrenched by Cosimo Tiepolo's fall, he held stiff against his chest. The other, bandaged from the cut received two nights before, held an apple. He had yet to take a bite from it, but played with it instead, making it spin. His mind seemed all held in that game though he, Hemminges and Oldcastle sat in conference on matters of great moment.

They were in the main room of the House of the White Lion where the English Embassy was lodged. Hemminges had moved into the rooms that William and Oldcastle had once shared, now that William had found another, more convivial, lodging with Isabella. He was still a frequent visitor, for the food was better and Oldcastle's company greatly to be enjoyed. Hemminges was out in the city almost as often as William himself and they saw each other seldom, save that twice a week Hemminges kept up his lessons with William in fencing and fighting, which William endured because he had grown to like Isabella's appreciation for their effect on his frame.

William had questioned Oldcastle where their friend went and was told that Hemminges had made friends with a fencer of the Niccoletti, one of the factions of Venice that engaged in sportive battles on the Ponte dei Pugni, the Bridge of Fists. 'Made his friendship in the traditional manner of men, my boy, by beating him in an arm-wrestle. And hence the two exchanged martial talk as if dear John were not a player now but a soldier still. He tells me that these Venetian fencers have an art with the single stick that is much to be admired. Judging by his own cracked knuckles and bruises, that is the kind of admiration John feels they have earned. He prattles some nonsense to me about bridges and galleys being alike narrow and demanding a special skill at fighting, an art with the sword that is suited to the small space of battle. I confess he lost me early but I did not like to look uninterested for fear he'd turn his talk to demonstration.'

William thought Oldcastle wise for it explained many a cruel new trick that Hemminges had shown him in their lessons. The owner of the House of the White Lion and their host, Salarino, still looked on Hemminges with a fearful eye, which William thought wise also. It was not just that Hemminges' solid frame could be made to move with a deadly grace, but that Hemminges held up a moral line more straight and unswerving than any builder's plumb. Wisdom or fear be Salarino's motive, in the result it meant for the Englishmen great comfort at little cost, as Salarino bustled to keep Hemminges happy.

To this incentive Salarino had added one of his own. He had set himself the task of converting Oldcastle from doubter to proselytiser for the food of Venice. As the three Englishmen argued, small dishes of fish, balls of rice fried in spiced oil, unknown vegetables dressed in vinegar, were laid before the throne of Oldcastle's liking. To these offerings Oldcastle would respond with a regal nod. He consumed all that was put before him with a noisy relish, save only the onions in vinegar, at the sight of which he curled his lip and pushed that plate from him.

'There is little to please in a knife 'tween the ribs either, Will,' said Hemminges.

'Or in hanging 'tween the columns on the Piazette di San Marco,' added Oldcastle through a full mouth. The unfamiliar Italian words caused a foam of food to form across his lips.

'You overplay the dangers, both,' said William, smiling at Hemminges' worried look and Oldcastle's unhappy one. 'Our guise as England's Embassy has withstood the Signoria's scrutiny. If they or the Council of Ten know we are not who we claim to be then they have chosen not to act on that knowledge. Why should that change? As for knives in the dark, who is left to wield them? By your own report, Francesco Tiepolo is mortal wounded and he and his brother are fled Venice. They should thank God for your merciful nature, Hemminges, for I would have called their crimes capital. And for the Pope's assassin, Prospero, he is passed into the Doge's prisons.'

'That is the safety of days, not weeks. God's blood, Will, but the dangers gather. You think the Tiepolo will forgive you when Francesco dies? Nor will the Pope sit idle. By your own report there is the question of how Francesco came back to Venice and the Signoria all unknowing of it, and the mystery of this Crow you spoke of at Venier's feast. Even if we do not see the Pope's hand in this, since the news that England is now in open war with Spain at Antwerp has reached Venice, to be securely fitted to our disguise as England's Embassy but increases the danger to us, does not prevent it.'

Hemminges planted his fists on the table top. 'If we have bought a space of time in which we are secure then we are best advised to use that time wisely and make for home.'

William sprang from his seat and plucked the wine glass from a protesting Oldcastle's hands and held it out to Hemminges.

'Wine, Hemminges, food beyond measure.' He gestured at the window beyond which could be seen the Canal Grande. 'A city of golden wonders beyond these walls. Leave this for England? We were a ragged crew there, Hemminges, or have you forgot? You'd have us fly from paradise to purgatory. That is not the normal order of things.'

'This is not paradise, William.' Hemminges shook his head. 'This is Eden and that business with the Tiepolo brothers is the eviction notice already posted on the gate. Our time here cannot last. The only way to stay here forever is to be buried here.'

'Better dead in Venice than half-life in England.'

'Boastful words. Have we not received word from England that we must return and explanation make? Do we not owe a duty? Does our pardon not lie in safely bringing back our intelligence? Have you forgot that we must take back to England the names of the papal spies?'

'I have not.'

'Those names were bought at a high price, William.'

'You think I have forgot it?'

'I do wonder at it.'

Oldcastle reached up and took his wine glass back. He took a long swallow in the silence that followed while William and Hemminges glowered at each other. Oldcastle tapped the back of William's hand to signal that he should pass the wine jug.

'It surprises me that you should be so reluctant to return home, to wife, to family,' Oldcastle said.

William sat back down. He did not look at either Oldcastle or Hemminges but out of the window at the city. 'I cannot leave.'

'She will understand,' said Oldcastle. His voice was soft. He filled another glass and pushed it over to William. 'In her occupation, the passing of men is as inevitable as the passing of years.'

William looked up, lightning in his eyes, thunder in his tightening jaw. 'This is not business, Oldcastle.'

'I did not say it was, Will. I remind you only that the lady thrived before your coming and will survive after your going.'

'It is not for her sake that I cannot leave. Though, God above, I would not be just another patron to take my pleasure and then cast her aside.'

William drew breath to say more, then halted. Hemminges and Oldcastle waited.

William was thinking of Stratford. Its small concerns and shopworn worries seemed remote from him now. If he thought of Stratford at all, then it was to wonder how his children were. How they would marvel at the stories he would tell them of France, of Savoy, of Venice, of waking to the sound of boats knocking at their mooring outside his window, of August heat so strong it lifted the gossamer curtains of his room on air made visible. He might speak of the smell of fish, spices and wine rising through the air and of the sounds of the Venetian dialect wafting up with them. A city so different from Stratford and the damp of Warwickshire, the stink of mud and goats, of petty gossips and mundane business, as to seem not just a different country as a different world. He could see his daughter, Susanna's, face, little mouth in an O of awe, as he spoke of gondolas, of St Mark's Square as the clock struck eleven and the merchants gathered from across the world, Slovenians, Poles, Greeks, Jews, Turks, Germans and all in their traditional show, buying and selling, shouting and talking in as many languages as there were men.

Such thoughts turned to guilt in a moment for he knew that he would not be able to speak to Susanna of the greatest wonder that he had found in Venice, Isabella Lisarro. Oh, but he would wish to do so. To tell Susanna how she might master her own destiny even compelled to obedience to the lives of others. How the life of the mind might roam as freely as a bachelor did, tasting as it willed, where it willed. When he spoke to others of Isabella they smiled and nodded at him, knowing she was beautiful, and he longed to blast their knowing looks down and tell them that it was the poet in her that he loved. That men were not such simple creatures after all and they did themselves disservice to pretend all his interest was swinish and base.

If such country matters had been all his care, then he'd enough in Anne, his wife. Yet it had not been. He and Anne should never have married. He had been too young and stupid to give her her just dessert. He could not tell if he had trapped Anne in a prison of domesticity or given her the keys to her own kingdom. Marriage had seemed to take her to a different place, but not one to which he wished to go with her.

Guilt to stay, guilt to leave, marriage was a bond and a shackle. How then could he say to Hemminges and Oldcastle, leave, when all his living was here, in Venice?

William turned to look at his friends. 'I cannot leave her, for my own sake. I cannot leave this wonder of experience.'

Hemminges sighed and pushed himself up from where he loured over the table.

'Winter has come and must pass before we can travel in ease. We will stay till the spring.'

Oldcastle smiled and nodded. After a moment William did the same.

'But come the spring, we must go.'

'We will talk again in the spring, Hemminges,' said William, taking a bite from his apple at last. He sprang to the door like a schoolboy released from lessons and was gone.

'If we live till spring,' muttered Hemminges at his back.

Outside the House of the White Lion, a man in a hat whose style spoke of Rome worried at his teeth with a pick. When William emerged and walked lightly away, he followed. Hemminges was not the only one who did not wish to wait till spring.

Her arms do lend his neck a sweet embrace

From the balcony of Isabella's house one could see along a narrow ravine of houses to the lagoon beyond. The sun was setting and the canal waters sparkled with Promethean fire, the rose colour of the houses caught the flames and glowed in its turn, the evening was mild and full of sweet scents.

William sat upon a bench on the balcony with his feet upon the balustrade and looked not at the splendours of Venice but only at Isabella. She wore a simple dress and her feet were bare. Shorn of her splendid armour of jewels, gowns, artfully piled tresses, she looked as he imagined Venus would were she to grace a mortal life with her presence. Showing her wonders, by their simplicity, divine.

She spoke out loud a poem she had written. She looked up from her paper to gauge his response. Seeing his look of love Isabella laughed. Her laugh turned to a frown.

'No woman could meet such weight of expectation as lies in your eyes, Will,' she said.

'I know. I thank the heavens they have sent me instead a goddess.'

Isabella coughed and took a sip of wine to soothe her throat and cover her laughter.

'I am no goddess, Will. I break wind as others do.'

'As zephyrs blowing below the violets do.'

'My hair is turned to old, red wires.'

'Copper strands, which as we know, best conduct the heat of passion's fires.'

'My skin that once was cream and rose is turned to curdled whey.'

'The better that it may nourish me, I say.'

'Enough!'

Isabella smiled at the young man before her. Such energy of youth, it would have exhausted her were it not that it gave back in full measure all that it demanded. This boy was both too bold and too wise for her good sense but she would not part from him. At last she was with a lover who did not want her simply to adorn his arm or admire his wit but looked at her as she truly was – and, better, seemed to see her as she wished to be. That was a rare wonder in this world. Isabella wondered at the kind God who had seen fit to send her this reward for her hard life that had been lived in the service of others and always perilously close to destruction.

It was strange, passing strange, that it should have been her old lover, Prospero, the Pope's assassin, that should have brought them together. Prospero, a man she feared and who had given her cause to hate men, to hate their selfishness and brutality, had brought her this lover, a poet, a man with rare understanding and gentle heart. She looked at his dark eyes and thought again, as the first time she had seen them, of their promised wisdom.

'This cannot last, William.'

William did not look at her. 'Hemminges speaks of our return to England. Declares it must be so when spring comes.'

Isabella leaned her head back against the wall of the house and looked along the canal. She thought again of how the lapping of the waters on the walls was the whispering of an enchantment, a promise of magic in the sound.

'Would you come with me?' William asked, his voice so quiet she barely heard it.

'To England? Where would I live, Will? With you and your wife and children? What do? How speak? In Latin or Italian?' She gave a mirthless laugh and shook her head. 'Oh God, Will, this is but a dream, soon we will wake from it and see all dissolve.'

William made no answer. They sat in silence, listening to the evensong of the canal's waters, the tapping of the boats at their moorings. Long minutes passed before Isabella, a great shiver running across her as if she threw off some ghostly touch, spoke again.

'Come inside, the chill air heralds the coming of winter. You men may run hot but we women suffer in cold times.'

'I run hot while you are here. Nor do I fear winter's coming, for you are like a summer's day to me.'

Isabella slapped his arm.

'William the would-be poet, you dare deploy a metaphor so lavish in its uses, so common-hackneyed to the ears of men? A schoolboy might use it in his first effort but you, a full-grown man?'

He crossed to her and grasped her with both hands.

'Scold me for my poor poetry but never doubt that I speak true. Isabella, you are all the good seasons of this earth to me. If you ever left me, then would I be in winter perpetual.'

She reached up and kissed his earnest face.

'Then we must give you more occasion for the practice of your versifying, brave poet, for I could not stay with one who wields imagery so crudely.'

'Occasion for verse of all kinds?' he asked and took her waist in his arms.

'I think, mainly love poetry.'

'That I think requires the most practice.'

Much ado about nothing

'You are alone?' asked Oldcastle, looking up from his lunch. His face was shaped into a mooncalf's look of surprise.

William sighed his acknowledgement. Oldcastle knew well he came alone for William had come to the House of the White Lion at Oldcastle and Hemminges' summoning, parting only reluctantly from Isabella, who had contrived business of her own to attend to.

'Rare, rare happening,' continued Oldcastle. He looked to Hemminges: 'To find the snail without its shell would not occasion more comment than to find our young lover without his love.'

'It is not so,' said William.

Hemminges merely snorted at this denial. Oldcastle held up an imperious hand to stay his companion's mocking.

'We humble friends, we mere ciphers to his company, we must not question the ways of Heaven that we should have been sent this rare visitation. Rejoice, rejoice only.'

'We are often with you, Oldcastle,' William said, shaking his head. He could see that his friend was in good spirits this day and wondered what prompted it.

'Indeed, indeed you are, but when the beauteous Isabella is with you, what eyes have we for you? You are but a cloud that sometime obscures her sun. We wait for wit and poetry from her lips and are too often confronted instead by your punning and Latin doggerel.'

William raised his hands in mocking applause of Oldcastle's speech. 'It is rare I find myself in full agreement with you, Nick. But on this occasion I can say with my whole heart that I too wish she were here.'

'You should not do so,' replied Oldcastle with shocked face. 'Now is your moment to shine. As a candle at noon wastes its light but against a dark background comes into its own, so you, the bright star of your lover no longer obscuring you, may at last be seen.'

'Seen mayhap, but against the surging sea of your words, I think not heard,' William replied.

'Monstrous calumny,' said Oldcastle, 'I offer you praise and you respond with insults, why young master lack-love, master kill-courtesy, you would do well to attend the Queen's Ambassador.'

'Enough,' said Hemminges, interrupting the familiar game between Oldcastle and William. 'To business.'

'Business, what business have we?' asked William.

'Save pleasure,' said Oldcastle.

'Save pleasure,' echoed William.

'I know that for you all days are sporting holidays but since you insist your pleasures require that we stay in the lion's mouth, William, I have decided that we must profit from the stay.'

As Hemminges spoke he steered William on to a gondola waiting outside the House of the White Lion.

'Come, we have an appointment.'

'An appointment? Where are we going?'

'Where?' cried Oldcastle, stepping into the gondola and causing it to rock alarmingly as he sat. 'Where? We are going to where we three belong, Will. We are going to a play!'

I'll make the statue move indeed, descend

Verona

Aemilia crept along the wall toward the palace's private chapel. Tall, in a dress of bright red velvet with a wide train, she was not well set for tiptoeing about like a thief. Thus far she had been fortunate. I am too bold, she thought. God but if I am caught my father shall have me whipped. She had feared she might be late for she had come from an audience with her father, the Duke, and he had held her longer than she'd expected. Of late her father had seemed to her more distract, his worries deeper and their place in his thoughts greater. He had not listened to her so much as spoken at her, of her needful duty to his house, of how she was not free to run wild as she had done as a child, seeking the company of the palace guards rather than her maids. She must show herself decorous, becoming, a fit wife for a good noble family, one that would bring fresh blood and money to her father's line. She'd asked what had brought on this sudden talk of marriage but her father's only reply had been to curse the arrival of a new priest from Rome. An answer that she did not understand and that her father would not make clear. Only the arrival of her father's steward, Rodrigo, with new report of outrages by the growing band of robbers in the country outside Verona had, by her father's instant angry turning to it, released her.

Aemilia cast about to see if any servant passed by and, seeing no one, slipped through the door into the chapel. Moving from the light of the courtyard into the sudden gloom of the chapel's antechamber blinded her.

'Valentine?' she whispered as loudly as she dared. No answer came. The darkness and silence was suddenly a little frightening. She took a breath. A foolish maid, she thought, to be afeared of nothing, of mere want of light, absence of sound. It ill became a woman of twenty years let alone a count's daughter. She should be made of sterner stuff.

'Valentine?'

She called again her cousin's name. The beautiful cousin whose arrival had so changed her view of the court, made it seem at once older, more staid, more set in its ways. She moved from the darkness of the antechamber into the half-light of the chapel proper. Still Valentine made no reply to her call. Was he late to their meeting? Did he not know how hard it was to find even half an hour out of her maid's sight that he should waste half of it being tardy? She tried to let anger at Valentine's lateness push out the frightened trembling in her breast born of the dark and silent chapel and the fear of being caught. It seemed to her so childish. She made herself walk down the aisle, crossing a chequerboard of light and dark; the low winter's sun through the chapel's narrow windows letting in only sharp-edged columns of light between the sepulchral dark of stone and wood. At the far end of the chapel the sun through the great windows, the stained glass depicting scenes from the life of St Zeno of Verona, caught the altar in a halo of light. There was an unearthly beauty to it, motes of dust caught rising in the light like spirits ascending to heaven. Aemilia moved towards the pulpit, to see if from that higher point she could see out over the valley beyond.

'Where are you going?'

Aemilia gave a cry of fear at the sudden voice from the darkness and stumbled back. She turned about and saw a tall figure standing with terrible stillness in the gloom of the transept. The figure stood so still it was as if a statue suddenly came to life and spoke.

'The pulpit is reserved for the clergy,' the voice said.

'I only . . .' said Aemilia.

'Why are you here?' demanded the voice.

'I . . .' Aemilia did not know what answer to give. A lightening of fear and embarrassment was pricking at her fingers and toes. The statue stepped from the transept into the light around the altar and a gaunt face appeared, high cheekbones, pale eyes, and a wolfish look of judgement and dislike. She did not know him. She wanted to ask who he thought he was to bark questions at her but the courage to speak escaped her. His pale eyes were daggers that pinned her in her place.

'Why are you here? Alone and unescorted? Who is this Valentine that you call for to disturb me at my prayers?' the man's demands shot at her.

Aemilia stumbled for an answer that did not betray her. The terror of the strange man's appearance and his coldly uttered demands was with her. A silence fell within the chapel, the questions hanging unanswered, fear rising in her gorge. The man began to advance towards her. Aemilia took a step back, and then the step became a flight and she turned and ran down the aisle back into the darkness of the antechamber and through the door into the courtyard.

The return to daylight returned her calm to her and, immediately, she felt a shame at her own terror and retreat. A hand grasped hers and she cried out once more.

'Aemilia, quiet, or others will hear,' said Valentine.

'Oh, Valentine!' She flung her arms about his neck.

'Not here, sweet, not here, we'll be discovered.'

He grabbed her hand and made to draw her into the privacy of the chapel but she pulled him back and turned and ran, dragging him after her, wanting to put the chapel behind her and with it the memory of the figure whose cold eyes had so frightened her.

Which, to be spoke, would torture thee

Venice

Fat Andrea, Marco Venier's banker and chief rumour monger of the city, patted Oldcastle on the knee and pointed to the wooden stage where the Commedia all'Improvviso was being performed.

'Those, Sir Henry, are the *Innamorati*, the young lovers,' he whispered to Oldcastle. On the stage, a woman dressed in rich clothes, her face heavily painted, one arm flung up across her brow as if about to faint, was singing to a young man whose burnished breastplate and puffed-out chest declared him a soldier. Her voice was high and sweet and clear and it twisted and turned in flights of fancy while her lover responded in more solemn, simpler counterpoint.

Andrea leaned across Oldcastle, heedless of the old man's discomfort at being put so close to a Venetian almost as fat as he, to where William sat with Faustina, another of Marco Venier's circle and almost his equal as a gossip. He grasped William's knee and raised an eyebrow. 'The lovers, Flavio and Isabella, appropriate, eh?'

'Don't listen to that quarrellous weasel, Sir William,' counselled Faustina, fanning herself with vigour though the afternoon was not warm. 'The part is not, of course, named after your own paramour but after the actress herself, the great Isabella Andreini. Venice is fortunate to have her and her company of players. I Gelosi, they are called.'

It pleased Faustina to give William not just his false name of William Fallow but also to treat him as a knight. It was not only the giving of this false title that made William squirm, but Faustina's merciless jibing. Faustina turned to smile at William. 'She is a poet like your own lover.'

William kept his gaze on the stage to avoid Faustina's look. The five of them sat, along with other wealthy citizens of Venice, on raised benches in one of the piazzas of San Polo. A stage had been built on one side, against the wall of a church, and on it were the players. The action upon it changed. The song ended and from the back of the stage stepped a dark-clad, masked figure.

'Pantalone, Isabella's father,' hissed Faustina to William. The dark cloaked figure was dressed in tight red leggings and a red cap, his mask, which covered all but his jaw and mouth, bore two flowing plumes for eyebrows and a great hooked nose. The story was an old one: the young woman loved a man, her father forbade it, the young woman by her cunning got her will. At its end the crowd burst into great cheers and shouts of pleasure.

Hemminges joined them. As they rose at its end he turned to William, 'Clever, clever, did you see? Each player has his part and each moment allows for the business and yet moves on swiftly enough not to pall. They keep the shape but leave in it room for action and speech extempore, to gauge their audience's mood and run with it.'

Oldcastle was less enamoured. 'It was not for me,' he declared, mopping at his brow, which despite the cool day was still dewed with sweat. 'I prefer a well-crafted line to a gabbled rhyme and bumbling pranks.'

William's own verdict lay between the two. 'I thought it cleverly done. That business with the servants was good fooling, the old man taken in by the feigned madness. There is truth in all their figures for all they are drawn with heavy hands. Old men do grow jealous of their daughters and their gold and mad men are forgiven acts that would be crimes in others.'

A pointed cough from behind them interrupted their debate. It was Andrea inviting them to meet the players. 'I have had occasion to employ them in the past and they know I may again. I am sure they will make time to speak to the Ambassador of England. You, my lord, should seize the moment to do so for it is a rare chance. The players come in anticipation of the Carnival and we are fortunate that they do. Not all admire the plays nor that women have a role in them.'

'True, true,' added Faustina. 'Now that we have a new legate from the Pope we must expect the usual contortions from the Signoria to show themselves willing to abide by St Peter's edicts. The plays are an easy sacrifice to make.'

'There is a new envoy from the Pope?'

'Arrived yesterday,' said Faustina, delighted to be delivering news. She looked knowingly at Oldcastle. 'It seems the Pope is not entirely pleased that Venice plays host to so many heretics.'

'If only the heretics did not have quite so much money,' murmured Hemminges, whose eyes sought William's.

'Quite so, quite so,' nodded Andrea, oblivious to this silent parley of the English, 'and thus we must lose a little entertainment so that the godless English money may remain.'

'But for how much longer, Andrea?' chimed in Faustina with a sly glance at the others to gauge their reaction. 'I hear this new Pope's missionaries are to be found simply everywhere now, looking askance on pleasure and searching for heresy under every stone. I hear the most ghastly stories about one who is apparently so eager with the hot poker and the pitchforks that one might think him a devil himself were it not that he moans the name of our Lord each time he presses the iron to your flesh. An Englishman like yourselves, they tell me.'

Faustina took William's arm and pressed it. 'You mustn't worry, Sir William. I shall protect you.' She laughed and moved on to catch up with Andrea.

As they walked to the stage, William whispered to Hemminges, 'You knew of the new envoy?'

'I heard of his arrival but this invitation was chance to discover more from Andrea or Faustina. Or from the players.'

'From the players?' asked William, but there was no moment to hear Hemminges answer. Their short walk had brought them to the players' tiring-house, a tented area behind the stage.

'May I present the Ambassador of England,' said Andrea to the woman who had played the lover and the man who, his mask now removed but his red trousers and cap still in place, had played the part of Pantalone.

'Francesco and Isabella Andreini,' answered Pantalone as he swept into an elaborate bow. 'Of the Compagnia dei Comici Gelosi. We are honoured to welcome the Ambassador of England, Sir Henry Carr.'

William winced to hear Oldcastle's false name said out loud. It was too keen a reminder of the dangerous game that, at his insistence, they still played. Oldcastle was less concerned to be called knight.

'Admirable, admirable,' Oldcastle proclaimed in his most mellifluous voice and William recognised, in its use, jealousy of the players. 'You, sir, were magnificently present on that stage.'

Pantalone responded with a bow more elaborate than the first, though William was not sure what compliment he discerned in Oldcastle's words. They had the shape of one but not the substance. Hemminges, however, was more direct in his praise.

'The piece was marvellous well devised and in the playing of it had as much modesty as cunning. You are the author?'

Isabella Andreini curtsied to Hemminges. 'I am.'

'Does the play have a name?' Oldcastle asked in a tone that hinted of jealousy at Hemminges' praise for another player.

'I call it *Tanto traffico per niente*,' she answered. 'Much ado about nothing.'

'Apt,' said Oldcastle. 'Though if you will forgive me, I thought the lady you portrayed a little too eager to be wooed. In my experience women are more calculating than headstrong. It is the man who must do the wooing.'

'Is it so?' said Isabella, with a glint in her eye that made William wish that Oldcastle would be quiet.

'In my experience,' said Oldcastle in tones of false humility.

'Not in mine, Sir Henry,' answered Isabella. 'You men may say more, swear more, but your show of love is more than will. Why, we have known a woman who gambled all for love of a man.'

'Oh ho, and who was that?' scoffed Oldcastle.

'Vittoria Accoramboni, Duchess of Bracciano.'

William's eyes flicked to Hemminges at the name of the beautiful Roman noblewoman who had incurred the Pope's hatred and against whom the Pope had sent his assassin, Prospero. The woman whose life he, Hemminges, Oldcastle and Isabella had saved almost at cost of their own.

'We had heard you performed at her estate, in Salo,' said Hemminges, not returning William's look. 'The story of the Duchess is well known. Is she as beautiful as they report?'

At Hemminges' question, to William's surprise, Isabella trembled and it was her husband, Pantalone, that answered.

'Alas, sir, we cannot say. We were bidden to her estate as you heard, on our way from Padua to Venice, to entertain her and her servants but—'

Here he too broke off and took a moment to gather himself. The English looked at each other in anticipation of the news that had struck the two players so dreadfully as to take from their mouths even simple speech. At last Pantalone went on.

'Alas, we came too late. The Lady was dead,' he said, and turned to look at his wife before finishing, 'murdered, it seems, by her cousin Lodovico Orsini. The hand of the Pope, uncle to her murdered first husband, is seen in the killing. It is a great scandal and one we were sorry to be tangled with.'

That ever spider twisted from her womb

'Vile, vile, a thousand times more vile than any that lived.' Isabella Lisarro paced the room.

Rain hammered at the windows of Tintoretto's workshop where William, Hemminges and Oldcastle had gathered Isabella and her old friend, the painter, Tintoretto, in conference. December had brought with it true cold and foul news. To the players' tale, the painter could add intelligence of his own.

'They have ta'en him. Orsini is to be tried,' said Tintoretto.

'Tried? What trial needed?' answered Isabella. 'Vittoria was no friend of mine but to die like that and at the hand of one she should have looked to for succour. A murder most foul.'

'When is murder not?' murmured Oldcastle.

'Truly spoken, foul even in the best it is, but this most foul. Foul and unnatural, by a cousin's hand.'

William reached to take her hand and give comfort but Isabella would not be stayed from her pacing.

'There is worse news,' said Hemminges.

Isabella stopped and turned to look at him. Her face that had been hot with anger took on a paler cast of fear. What news could he bring her that was worse than that she had already received?

Isabella despaired. When she had first heard that her old lover Prospero was returned to Venice she had set her will to thwart his vile intentions. She had discovered his target in Vittoria Accoramboni, a selfish, foolish, beautiful Roman noblewoman who was the object of the Pope's vengeance, and Prospero, the instrument of that vengeance. She had sought to warn Vittoria, and when that warning went unheeded had set herself to be the woman's shield. In the English Embassy she had found another of Prospero's deadly purposes but also allies against his machinations.

Now all that strife, that struggle, against Prospero's plots, to thwart the Pope's vengeance against his nephew's killer, Vittoria Accoramboni, Duchess of Bracciano, the terrors she had faced, and the battles she, William, Oldcastle and Hemminges had been forced to fight, was all for nothing. They had thought themselves triumphant when Prospero's servants, even as their blades had been drawn for the killing, had been turned aside to strike against themselves. They had rejoiced when Prospero was condemned to the Doge's prison. Yet still it seemed that monster had struck out. Even from within his cell, he was deadly.

'Well,' said Isabella, 'out with it.'

Hemminges wavered. Oldcastle, seeing his friend's uncharacteristic cowardice, took up the tale.

'The Pope has sent a legate to the Signoria. It seems that the Serene Republic finds it politic to ignore the Pope's actions.' Oldcastle took a swallow of wine against the sudden dryness in his mouth. He feared Isabella's response to his next words. 'Prospero is released.'

She let out a cry of rage. Pain shot through her and she stumbled. William was by her side, holding her. She tried to wave him back.

'Nothing, it's nothing,' she said.

William ignored her protestation and guided her to the bench where Tintoretto sat. The old man put his arm about her. Hemminges approached and crouched before her.

'I saw him leave the Doge's Palace,' said Hemminges quietly. 'It is small recompense but in his limp and crabbed walk were signs full of austere punishments.'

'Where does he stay?' Isabella looked up. Her anger and frustration at the day's news she could still feel as blades within her womb, true pain to add to that her mind felt.

'He did not stay. He walked no more than a hundred paces on Venetian land. From the Doge's Palace to the dock and there on ship, away.'

Isabella groaned again.

'Have you wine, Jacopo?' William asked Tintoretto.

The old man rose and moved to fetch a jug and cups. He returned swiftly and it was tribute to the horror written on Isabella's face that Oldcastle let her be served first and refilled her cup before taking his own draught. The woman they had hoped to protect, killed, the manager of her murder, released and fled from their vengeance. Black day indeed.

A little later, as William and Isabella made to leave that sad conference, Hemminges caught William's arm while Isabella was embracing her old friend Tintoretto.

'With this news we may not wait till spring, Will,' he whispered.

William had no strength for argument. He gripped Hemminges' arm and nodded to him.

'We will speak on it tomorrow,' he answered.

Hemminges nodded in his turn and left Will to return to Oldcastle and pluck from him the jug of wine. Oldcastle looked past Hemminges' shoulder to stare into William's eyes but neither man could hold the other's gaze. There was in that look too many messages to add to the news already had. The morning would be time enough.

Later, when they had walked from Tintoretto's studio back to her house, William and Isabella sat together in silence as the dark drew in. William could see that the rage that had first consumed Isabella at the news of Prospero's release had passed. It was one of the things in her that he admired, her temperate nature. She stormed, she roared, she cried out her pleasure and her pain but she returned to gentle laughter swiftly. Isabella was not one to dwell in the dark places. It was a contrast to his own melancholy that was apt to find something over which to sit in brood. Yet in her silence there was something new, as if word of Prospero's good fortune had planted within her a bitter seed whose poison must be first transmuted before true pleasure could return.

'We were living too richly, Will,' said Isabella at last. 'The gods do not care to be taunted by the sight of too much happiness in mortals.'

'I think the gods care little for the desires of men, pleasure or pain,' answered William.

She turned and smiled at him. He took her hand, grateful for the smile. He was not fooled by it. He knew her too well to think it went deeper than her lips. She and he had had a golden summer but now they had seen that in the cup there was a spider steeped.

'Your pain has passed?' William asked.

'It has,' answered Isabella. 'I think it was a pain of the mind brought on by hearing that Prospero was still living. I had not thought he would leave the Doge's Palace alive, unless it was to pass on to hanging between the columns in the Piazette di San Marco.'

'Nor I,' said William. 'Though by Hemminges' report he has had a cruel time of it there.'

'Cruel enough? Is there punishment enough for one such as him outside of hell?'

'Ay, there's the rub of it.'

Isabella stood up.

'Enough of this melancholic debate,' she said. 'Come to bed. The night is young and we may yet save some portion of it for true pleasure.'

William rose smiling, for now he saw that Isabella's own lips were bowed into a true smile, full, red and welcoming. For a little while longer at least they might forget the world and all the horror that moved within it.

Thy place in Council thou hast rudely lost

Verona

Aemilia lifted her skirts to make better pace as she hurried across the courtyard towards her father's private rooms. She had let Valentine's wooing distract her too long. Her maid met her coming the other way. She threw her arms in the air and gestured silently but most expressively at her charge, her state of disarray, her exposed legs and finally, after briefly clutching at her hair in distress, to the heavens.

'Where have you been, Lady Aemilia?' she demanded. 'Oh God, it is not you alone that shall suffer for your lateness. Where have you been? The new priest sent from Rome, the Englishman, is already in with your father and has put him in a foul temper.'

Aemilia swept on, picking up the maid in her wake and waving down her questions. At the door to her father's closet she paused and took a breath. Her maid took the moment to smooth her mistress's dress and to push her hair behind her ears. Aemilia batted her hands away, turned the handle and walked in.

At once she tasted the poisoned mood; ill-will hung like a haze across the room. Her father's steward, Rodrigo, stood at Duke Leonardo's shoulder. Rodrigo gave the Duke's daughter a chiding look for her lateness as she sidled in and crossed to a seat by the wall, next to the fire. Her father did not acknowledge her arrival. He was intent on the man before him, the priest, Father Thornhill, the Englishman. As she entered Thornhill's eyes turned to her and she shuddered to recognise the pale malice that had so frighted her in the chapel. She hid her shock as she bent to take her seat. So this was the priest that her father had railed against. Why did he wish her to see him now?

'By what authority?' her father demanded of Thornhill.

Thornhill's eyes turned back slowly from Aemilia. 'By the authority of His Holiness.'

Aemilia had seen her father angry often enough that it now passed almost beneath her notice. Duke Leonardo Barbaro sometimes seemed to his daughter to live in a state of perpetual fury at the world. Yet that rooted anger was of the kind that spoke of frustrations and inconveniences brooded upon. It was not fed by anything in the world so much as born of too much choler in the blood. The anger she witnessed in him now was of a different kind, cold, an anger that threatened to burn as a frosted metal does. Aemilia sat quietly and looked to the object of that anger, the priest, tall, thin and with a manner as cold as her father's fury.

'These are not' – her father's hand rapped on the table – 'the Pope's lands. They are mine.'

'I thought they belonged to the Republic of Venice,' queried the priest.

'My lands, priest. Mine. That I owe fealty to the Republic of Venice only serves to remind you that I owe none to the Republic of St Peter.'

Her father did not relish his obeisance to Venice. Yet the north of Italy was a patchwork of such loose fealties and Venice was a powerful protector still, though but a shadow of its former strength.

'We all owe obedience to His Holiness,' answered Thornhill, as if reminding a child of some simple courtesy forgotten. A snake, her father had named him when the priest had first presented himself to her father and demanded his aid in the search for heresy. Railed against him, truth be told. That had been a month past. A little month, and yet such a name this man had made for himself in those few days. A name to be used with children to fright them into bed. Now she saw him for herself and knew him for who he was, she too thought he had an adder's look to him: the stillness with which he held himself, nothing moving save his pale eyes flickering about the Duke's closet. She still felt the shame of her first encounter with the priest, when she had fled from him and his questions.

'Since you came to Verona you have abused the hospitality that I gave to you and your men. You have taken men and tortured them, my subjects,' said the Duke.

For a moment it looked as if Thornhill would speak but instead he simply pursed his lips and said nothing, his eyes roaming back over the room, passing over Aemilia and lingering there an instant, to her discomfort. Nothing could have served to anger the Duke more, the lack of reply only emphasising how little the priest felt that he owed the Duke an explanation.

'You do not deny it?' said the Duke.

'Deny what?' answered Thornhill, his eyes turning back to the Duke, his calm voice a studied contrast to the one that interrogated him. 'That I have searched for heresy in your lands and found it? That I discover here those that conspire against the rule of the Church? Spies? Traitors to Rome? I do not deny it. I proclaim it. Righteousness has slept, Duke Leonardo, and I have come to wake it. As His Holiness ordered me to do.'

The Duke rose from his desk. Aemilia felt the menace of the room grow and she thrilled with both fear and pride to see her father's power. A tall man, broad and dark, the Duke loomed over his desk. 'Mine is the rule here, priest. You will release your prisoners into my control and I will deal with them as I deem just.'

The priest simply shook his head.

'No?'

'No,' said the priest. 'They are prisoners of the Church. Summoned here, my lord, I have come, and so have not yet finished with their questioning. When I have done it may be fit they be released to your control.'

'It *may* be . . .'

The Duke's mouth hung, opening and closing upon itself, as if the foul taste of the priest's defiance could not be fathomed. Father Thornhill held his gaze.

'You would not wish,' said Thornhill into the silence, 'for me to make an ill report of you to His Holiness. This is not a Pope for half measures. There are only those that stand with him, and enemies. He will not let an enemy sit upon the borders of the Republic of St Peter's lands.'

'You threaten?' said Aemilia. She was astounded by how her father's rising tide of anger had been stayed by this Thornhill's lack of regard. She felt the insult herself. Her first fears born of the encounter in the chapel were now o'ershadowed by anger of her own.

Father Thornhill turned to look on her. She was tall like her father but he taller still and his gaze fell down his sharp nose.

'These are the councils of men, child. Quiet becomes a woman best.'

'Not so,' answered Aemilia proudly. 'As I recall it, Caterina Sforza was listened to—'

'Caterina Sforza,' interrupted Thornhill, 'was not a woman but a devil.'

'You will not interrupt me again, priest,' answered Aemilia, eyes blazing, 'or I will show you the same charity that the Lady of Forli showed her enemies.'

'Enough,' called her father. His voice was still rough but a small smile cut his face as he looked at his daughter. He turned back to Father Thornhill.

'The Lady Aemilia speaks with the same pride as her father. You have abused your welcome and I do not bargain with you. I command. Give up your prisoners to my men and then depart.'

'Command? Duke Leonardo,' answered the priest, 'you do not even command the obedience of your daughter who is free to roam your palace, her chastity unguarded, calling for some "Valentine" even in the sanctity of the chapel.'

At Valentine's name the Duke's head swung to Aemilia, the red face becoming darker still, the small smile departed.

'You should think again on the Holy Father's offer, Your Grace.' Father Thornhill rose. His eyes left Aemilia and he looked again on the Duke. 'My prisoners shall be returned to you when I have finished with them. Your pride is nothing to me or to Rome. We seek dangerous men and we will find them. I remind you, Duke Leonardo, those that aid the Church are blessed. Those that stand in its way will have cause for regret, as others, more powerful than you, have found.'

Thornhill did not wait on his release nor look again in Aemilia's direction though she had risen too in anger at his scornful words; he turned and strode from the room.

After the door had closed behind him her father sat back and poured himself a cup of wine. Aemilia strode to the table.

'You let him depart?'

'You were late. Why?' her father answered once he had drunk deeply from the cup.

'He insulted us and threatened us and you let him depart,' insisted Aemilia. 'Why, Father?'

'Why do you think?'

'Is he truly that powerful?'

'Not him but his master. This Pope . . .' Her father refilled his cup and shook his head. 'We have our pride, Aemilia. You did well to remind him of that. Yet my lands are not great nor my men many. This Pope commands armies, spies without number, assassins, and does not fear to use them. Most of all, he commands the obedience of the Church. It is a bold man that defies the Church. The more so since Gregory died and Sixtus rose. Some fixed thing has been stirred in this new Pope's bosom and he will not be calmed. Where once we were left alone now there are agents of Rome at every turn.'

'And this Thornhill is the worst of them,' her father's steward, Rodrigo, added.

'True,' her father nodded.

'Such a beast of a man to wear a priest's robes,' Rodrigo tutted. 'I scarce believe the stories of his—'

Duke Leonardo cut his steward off with a wave of his hand.

'Enough Rodrigo, such talk is not fit for Aemilia's ears.'

'I am not a child, Father . . .'

'I did not say you were, Aemilia. Still there are some matters best—'

'If there is a danger to us,' she broke in again, 'to you, then I should know of it.'

Her father chuckled and wagged his finger at her.

'Ah, there is my little lioness, protective of her own. No, no, there is no danger to us. Thornhill seeks other Englishmen, but not ones loyal to Rome as he is, rather agents of their heretic queen. I told him when he first arrived that he was in the wrong place, eh, Rodrigo?' the Duke added, looking to his steward for witness. 'That he should ask in Padua at the university or in Venice itself, and I told him I would gladly give him horses to aid him in his immediate journey hence. But, no, he wouldn't hie himself off. Others had been sent there, he said, his charge was Verona, and then he set himself to sorting of my subjects for signs of heresy.' Duke Leonardo's smile left him. 'This Father Thornhill is ardent with zeal for his charge. Nor is there mercy in him for those that he considers to have strayed from the path. The men he has taken for questioning . . .'

Her father broke off again with a shake of his head and swirled wine in his mouth and swallowed to take away the taste of Father Thornhill's foulness.

'If he is cruel as you say, Father,' Aemilia pressed, 'the more important that we should show our strength before him now. We let this pass, he thinks us weak, he knows our limit and then he takes again and again. Does not Machiavel say that we must be lions to fight wolves?'

Aemilia saw Rodrigo the steward nod at her counsel but her father shook his head.

'It was to witness how far one might press the claims of one's pride with such as this Father Thornhill that I wanted you here. He will release his prisoners to us, though what state he will leave them in I do not know. We dare not press for more.'

Her father paused at this thought to drain his cup again. It was now Aemilia's turn to shake her head. She paced before her father's desk feeling her own anger growing. This Father Thornhill took her father's subjects and tortured them and they did nothing? How could this stand? Why did her father do nothing about it?

He seemed to read her thoughts. 'He is a dangerous man, Aemilia, and his master more so. The whole of Christendom is caught up in these battles and we must not provoke the eye of the Pope to fall on us.'

'To demand obedience to your law is not to provoke. This priest oversteps his charge—'

Her father rapped his fist on the desk. 'Enough, Aemilia. I command here but to command is not to be free to act only as you wish. Command demands that sometimes a sacrifice be made. Your Machiavel, your Caterina Sforza, they would understand that, mark me.'

A scowl marred the graceful angles of Aemilia's face.

'What was the offer that he spoke of?'

The Duke waved his hand to waft away the question and then gave her a hard look.

'Ah yes, you mind me that still you have not answered my first question, Aemilia. Wherefore were you late? How is it that you give Thornhill power to shame me by talk of Valentine?'

Aemilia blushed. Her thoughts had been too taken with anger at the insolent priest to have prepared an excuse. She stumbled to reply. Her father, not waiting, gestured to his steward.

'Rodrigo tells me you have neglected to attend him. How are you to know our estate if you will not take the time to study it? One day you will have the running of your husband's household and you must know . . .'

'A husband's? Why not my father's? Why not my own?'

Duke Leonardo shook his head.

'We will make a good marriage for you, Aemilia, fear not. A strong man, rich, a good alliance for our family.'

He reached out and patted the hand she had planted on the desk, before gripping it hard.

'As to Valentine,' he said, 'from this time forth be somewhat scanter of your maiden presence.'

'What do you mean?' she answered.

'You know well what I mean.' The Duke slapped his other hand on the table. 'I would not, in plain terms, have you from this time forth so slander any moment's leisure as to give words or talk with the boy Valentine. Do you understand me?'

Chastened, Aemilia nodded her head and her father released the painful hold he had of her. He turned to speak again to his steward and did not see the look of frustration on his daughter's face. Aemilia realised she was dismissed and turned for the door. The moment to speak in praise of Valentine would come. But it was not now. She needed time to think on that campaign. She would win her father round. Of that she was certain.

Condemning some to death and some to exile

Venice

Isabella still looked pale the following morning when they returned to Tintoretto's studio.

'Madonna, you are more lovely in your distress than many in their pomp,' said her friend, the painter. 'Come and sit with me by the window and I will draw you.'

Isabella let herself be taken by Tintoretto into the depths of the studio, between tables strewn with paper and paint, the cloth, the canvas pooling and piled upon the floor. The pain that had come with the news of Vittoria Accoramboni's fate and Prospero's release had not passed but stayed as a reminder of the unhappy news. She moved slowly so as to let her thoughts stay in the place around her rather than fly to fear of Prospero and fury at her failure to protect Vittoria Accoramboni. There was comfort in the familiar space of Tintoretto's studio. She let herself sink into it.

William watched her walk away with her arm on the old man's. Hemminges came up behind him.

'Jacopo will comfort her, Will, come and join us,' he said.

William turned to join him, turning slowly, legs, hips, torso and last his eyes moving, in order to watch his lover as long as he might.

'This news changes everything,' insisted Hemminges. 'Where before we had but fancies now we have hard truths to contend with. The Pope still seeks his vengeance, his agents still prowl the streets looking for their prey and to be English is to be numbered amongst those they hunt.'

'For your own security and the security of those you love we must leave Venice,' said Oldcastle. 'Rumours fly of popish plots, of spies. My God, Will, they speak of tortures and of cruel deaths. These are not stories.' All trace of his usual bantering tone was absent from his speech.

'All so and still I cannot leave Isabella,' said William in answer. 'Of flight, of exile, we have spoken and she asks where she will go and with what hope for the future? Answer have I none. To England? That's a cold and cheerless bier for one born to Venice. To be my mistress in a nook of the Theatre? To learn new languages? To ply new trades?'

William looked up as Hemminges rose and turned away.

'I see you're angry, John. But think, what safety is there on the road to England? The safety that we had as one of Sir Henry's company? Ask Ben Connor or Nate or Watkins if the Pope will stay his hand more readily in Venice or on unregarded roads far from the Signoria's authority?'

'We'll go disguised, not trumpeting our presence with carts and servants,' said Oldcastle.

'As Sir Henry did?' demanded William. All three men knew how that journey had ended. In an ambush and a bloody field of bodies.

'We must to England, Will. You know it,' said Hemminges. 'We were driven to Venice by the bargain our dead master, Sir Henry, had struck. Venetian names for English ones. We now have those names, the agents that work the Pope's plans in England.'

'And have them still.'

'That knowledge is a buried talent. We must carry it to England and set it in the hands of those that would make use of it. God's sake, Will, do you not want to see the Pope's plots undermined? Do you not want that vengeance at least?'

'If we're killed on the road we'll achieve nothing,' said Will. 'Send a letter.'

Hemminges threw up his arms and paced away. Oldcastle shook his head. 'William, William, you've spoken these thoughts before. We have no trusted messenger, we know no cipher into which to place the message if we did, nor do we know to whom we ought to send the message or how to ensure its content is trusted by the one that receives it. It must be us, our witness to the truth of the names we have obtained and how we came by them, the secrecy of our minds the cipher that keeps it safe.'

Hemminges rounded on William. 'You beat the ground to flush excuses forth. Be honest, William. You do not want to go.'

'I do not. I have not hidden that from you, John, that you should call me false now.'

Hemminges made no reply.

The three men sat, not looking at each other. Only the distant murmurs of Isabella and Tintoretto's conversation disturbed the air, too faint to be made out but with the music of laughter in it that was a painful contrast to the taut chord of silence between the Englishmen.

'Here we have friends,' said William at last.

Hemminges snorted.

'He is drawing me you know,' said Oldcastle, with a gesture to where Tintoretto sat, hidden at the far end of his studio behind a forest of canvas.

Hemminges and William looked at Oldcastle in astonishment.

'There is parchment big enough?' said William in awed tones.

'And so much ink in this wide world?' added Hemminges.

'Dogs,' muttered Oldcastle, and then louder, 'The pair of you are merely jealous that in my figure a great artist finds more to like than in you scrawny pair.'

'Much, much more to like,' said Hemminges.

'I doubt not that he needs us for another purpose,' added William. 'As quills to wield. Surely only pens as big as we could capture the magnificence of you, Oldcastle. We will be dipped in buckets and our hairs mark out in ebon ink the shape and form of mighty England.'

'Enough,' said Oldcastle against the sound of William and Hemminges' laughter. Hemminges leaned back to try and frame Oldcastle in his hands but kept having to lean further to fit all in till he tumbled backward from his seat only to spring up and keep moving backward, muttering 'still no, still no' as he moved.

Isabella and Tintoretto returned to find all three still laughing.

'You're recovered?' asked William, seeing his mistress smiling.

'Better to see the three of you in good cheer,' she answered.

William gathered her in his arms and all five travelled from Tintoretto's studio to his house where they ate and drank and spoke no more of the gathering dangers until Christmas had come and gone.

Would you have a love song, or a song of good life?

The twelfth night after Christmas found the three Englishmen together again in revel.

'A song, John, a song, God love you,' roared Oldcastle.

Hemminges waved away the drunken demand. The three men sat, in a square near Tintoretto's studio, on the stone surround of a well. It was early evening, mild and dry. Not so the three men, whose revels, begun at noon, now had them roused and wet with wine.

'Come, a song, John, of England, of our home,' insisted Oldcastle.

'I've no songs like that, Nick,' said Hemminges.

'Yes,' said William, 'let us have no talk of England this day when we are drunk in Venice and with its pleasures. But still, a song, Hemminges! For the love of God.'

'Well then,' said Oldcastle, pouting, 'let the song be a love song or a song of good living.'

'A love song, then,' said William, snatching the jug of wine from Oldcastle as he was about to drain it into his cup, 'you've too much of good living already.'

'Selfish cur,' muttered Oldcastle as he swallowed the dregs of his cup.

William lifted his own cup in recognition of Oldcastle's salute. Beside him Hemminges leaned back his head and began to sing.

O Mistress mine where are you roaming?
O stay and hear, your true love's coming,
        That can sing both high and low.
Trip no further pretty sweeting.
Journeys end in lovers' meeting,
        Every wise man's son doth know.

What is love, 'tis not hereafter,
Present mirth, hath present laughter:
        What's to come, is still unsure.

In delay there lies no plenty,
Then come kiss me sweet and twenty:
Youth's a stuff will not endure.

As such songs will often do, its words, heard in Hemminges' voice, a voice of surprising sweetness in such a solid block of man, brought on melancholy. When Hemminges had finished each man sat in silence with his own thoughts. Oldcastle thought of his youth long past and remembered trysts that had seemed pregnant with possibilities but had passed the way of all things. Hemminges thought of the dangers that surrounded them now and grasped again for blindness to all but the pleasures of the present moment. And William thought of a future without Isabella, the lover he had found at the end of his journey from England and whose every kiss he feared might be the last they would share before their paradise was snatched away from them.

It was in this stupor that Isabella found them. She did not begrudge them their drunken state. All of the little group had been in a sullen mood since the news of Vittoria Accoramboni's death and of that monstrous villain of the Pope's, Giovanni Prospero's freedom and flight from Venice. That sharp pain that had first assailed her when she heard the news had dulled to a tight ache in her gut that did not rise above the worst she endured from month to month but never left her either. She too was in want of release. She only wished she could find escape in wine as easily as the English.

'I find you in the right mood for a pageant, I think,' she said to the three men when they realised her presence and stopped their singing.

'A pageant?' asked Hemminges.

'At Marco Venier's palace, to celebrate twelfth night. The English Ambassador is invited and we accompany him.' Isabella turned to William. 'Did you not tell them?'

'I did, sweet, I did. I told Oldcastle a fortnight past,' answered William, holding up his hands to ward off the sudden sharpness in Isabella's tone.

'He told me,' said Oldcastle, 'but I neglected to pass the message on and then, in truth, I quite forgot it.'

'You surprise me, Nicholas,' said Isabella. 'I Gelosi are to perform at Marco Venier's palace today, at his command.'

Oldcastle gave a grunt. At Isabella's questioning look, William explained that Oldcastle had not cared for the Commedia.

'And what was to like?' demanded Oldcastle.

'Gentlemen,' said Isabella, cutting across the argument. 'Come, you must be up and dressing yourselves if we are not to be unfashionably late. An impoliteness I cannot abide.'

'By all means,' said Oldcastle, heaving himself to his feet, 'let us make haste. God forbid we might miss the start of the play. We will quite lose the thread of the story if we do.'

'Quite so, Nicholas,' said Isabella, taking him by the arm and leading him forth. William and Hemminges, behind her, shook their heads and William was reminded once again that for all that he and Isabella shared there were some kinds of wit that passed her quite by.

Rancour will out; proud prelate

Isabella had not seen Marco Venier since the night of William's wager with Cosimo Tiepolo. She and he had a long history, one that had begun in the usual way for a courtesan and a Venetian nobleman, but that had transformed itself with time and the discovery that they gained greater pleasure from shared thoughts than a shared bed. Isabella was the finer poet and Marco Venier was not fool enough to scorn ability in others because he lacked it in himself. He wanted to share in it and since, in this regard, the whore was greater than the noble then, in this regard, the noble paid obeisance to the whore.

That did not stop him playing his friendship with her to his advantage over the years. Inviting her to his parties and steering her towards friends of his from whose night-time lips might fall words that would profit him when, in turn, Isabella let them drop into his ears. Isabella had understood what she was, though she hated it. Hated that Marco might admire her mind but still sell her body, that his friendship was above all else self-serving and, this most of all, that she was too weak to throw it in his face and cast aside the present pleasures of his feasts, the security his wealth had brought her, the chances for advancement that his company gave.

Marco had in him that same perverse streak of self-interest possessed by all the men with whom she had been close. Not for the first time she found herself wondering what wound it was within her that led her to these men: Giovanni Prospero, who'd had the devil in him; Marco Venier, who was but indifferent wicked and only when it served him; and William Shakespeare, who railed against his own will and yet still let it drive him on. Perhaps it was no wound at all but rather that each of them sought to seize so much of life that to be in their orbit was to be set in thrilling spin.

'Your pain returns?' asked William at her side.

'No, no.' She stroked his arm. 'Just thoughts.'

'Sad ones?' asked William, looking at her furrowed brow and reaching up to smooth it.

'Just thoughts. Good? Bad? It is too soon to say. You are worried?'

'For your safety. Always.'

'For my safety? Have you reason?'

William let out a breath. 'No more than usual.'

Isabella laughed at that. 'You and I have made so many enemies.'

'We have.'

She dipped her head in a small nod. 'We've lived.'

Their gondola pulled up to the water gate of the Ca' Venier and forestalled further talk. The Ca' Venier was one of the oldest palaces on the Canal Grande, its front adorned with spoils from the sack of Constantinople four hundred years before. The early evening was brightened by torches set in brackets that guttered and smoked in a strong wind blowing across the water. Isabella shivered beneath her cloak. 'Let us go in,' she said.

The courtyard of the Ca' Venier was decked with cloth of gold and at its end was built a stage that was itself draped in so much finery that William wondered where the actors might stand. Liveried servants stood at the sides with trays of wine in fine Murano glass while others passed between the guests with platters of food.

Within the centre of the courtyard moved the wealthy of Venice, many of whom William now recognised. To his knowing eye the currents and eddies of this sea of people revealed much about the alliances, schemes and plots of Venice. The Dandolo and the Tiepolo never came too close to each other but, like corks thrust into water, would push suddenly back when each the other spied. Loredan and Foscari came together in waves, spoke and parted, carrying with them murmurs of gossip to others of like mind. On this occasion something disturbed the usual pattern, some rock around which the waters swirled. William looked up. On the colonnaded walkway that ran around the first floor of the courtyard he saw Marco Venier looking down, observing. William followed his gaze and found the cause of the changed waters. From moment to moment the crowd parted enough for William to see a scarlet-clad figure at the centre of the courtyard, surrounded by black-robed men. The papal legate had a florid face, cheeks and nose quite as red as his cloak, his hair as pale as milk, and the combined effect of face and hair was of a strawberry caught with mould. By his side, among the black-robed colleagues, was a face that William felt he recognised but could not place at this distance.

'A strange fellowship for a feast,' whispered William.

'It is Marco's way,' answered Isabella, 'to bring flint and steel together and watch the sparks fly.'

The two advanced to Oldcastle and Hemminges and whispered their warning of the legate's presence. Oldcastle's pallor turned as pale as the legate's hair and he made to depart. Hemminges stepped before him.

'Courage, Sir Henry,' Hemminges admonished. 'The English Ambassador cannot fly from England's enemy quite so swiftly.'

'Here, Sir Henry,' said Isabella, pretending a calm she did not feel herself, as she pressed a glass of wine into Oldcastle's hand. He took it in one swallow and held the glass out for more. Hemminges rolled his eyes at the thought of the time to come, spent guiding Oldcastle along the cliff's edge of courage without letting him fall into unseemly drunkenness. Their thoughts were interrupted by a sharp echo round the courtyard's walls as Marco Venier clapped his hands for his guests' attention.

'Citizens of Venice, honoured guests from every realm, my friends, welcome, welcome. Tonight is the eve of the feast of Epiphany. Tonight the witch La Befana flies across our city bringing gifts to the children and tonight I have for you, my friends, a gift of my own. I Gelosi perform for us in private audience.'

With these words a drum struck up from behind the curtained stage and the assembled guests began to applaud. Two masked figures came on to pull the curtain back revealing the figures of Isabella Andreini and her husband, Francesco, in their players' parts, as Isabella and the Captain. William had thought them gorgeously attired on the last occasion but those were tattered weeds compared to their costume now. Isabella's ruff was a halo of white lace behind her and the dress blossomed out across half the stage. The Captain's breastplate shone in the light of the torches and so many feathers adorned his hat that he seemed more peacock than man.

Their magnificence was undermined by Oldcastle muttering behind William, 'They'll sing now, I suppose.' And when, as if cued, they did begin to sing William heard Oldcastle say, 'There, told you so.'

William did not share Oldcastle's cynicism. He thought both Isabella and the Captain had fair voices and sang in good harmony. Their song was brief and when it was done the two fell into argument, the theme, as ever, love. The crowd took great delight each time Isabella's wit scored against the Captain and when the two left the stage it was to a great round of applause. William watched intently, for the argument on the stage was no simple thing, yet the two players marked its premises and entailments so clearly that even at speed the audience still followed.

'Admirable are they not?'

William and his fellows looked around and saw Marco Venier standing beside them.

'Have you such skilled players in England?'

Oldcastle drew himself up. 'We do and more truthful too.'

'Truthful?' asked Marco Venier.

'Yes, they inhabit the part they play. These merely character it grossly.'

Marco Venier smiled to see Oldcastle's pride pricked. Isabella, sensing that Oldcastle had drunk too much courage, intervened. 'It is a great triumph on your part, Marco, to have secured the performance of so famous a troupe.'

'For that I must thank Andrea's pandering on my behalf, as he will never cease to remind me from this day forth,' Marco answered. 'But not all the excitements of this feast are his doing. Have you yet spoken with the Papal Nuncio?'

'We have not, Marco,' said Isabella, 'nor would we wish to do so since well you know that Rome is no friend of England, or of courtesans.'

'Not so, not so,' said a voice behind her. 'We are friends to all.'

Marco Venier smiled. 'Sir Henry Carr, it is my great pleasure to introduce to you Monsignor Cesare Costa, Nuncio to the Holy See.'

Oldcastle, taken by surprise at the new arrival, shakily gave a leg and then remembered that this was the envoy of the Queen of England's avowed enemy, the Pope, to whom he should not be bowing and hastily straightened himself. His wine slopped from his glass and a great dollop fell into the centre of the circle sending spatters across the legs of the prelate's companions. They remained unmoving, only their frowns deepening.

Marco Venier covered the moment over with an introduction of the others.

'The famous. Isabella Lisarro. I had not expected to meet a woman of such renown in Venice,' said the Nuncio on being introduced to Isabella. His smile in that red face would have seemed almost benign had it reached so high as his eyes and had it not been framed by the scowls of the two clerics beside him. William recognised one of them, that same black crow that had stood beside Cosimo Tiepolo at Marco Venier's former feast, that strangely colourless man whose eyes had glittered with an open malice. He that had first floated the wager. So, much became clearer now, now that William understood it had been no simple private vendetta of Cosimo and Francesco Tiepolo but part of a greater plot, and if that plot came from Rome then it was without doubt to one end – the intelligence the English Embassy had gained in Venice. The names, the names were all.

'I would not have thought the Church so concerned with earthly matters as to know of one such as I,' answered Isabella.

'Oh, Signora, I am told you are known by half the inhabitants of Venice,' the Nuncio replied.

The smile remained but in the cruel jibe at her profession Isabella saw this priest for what he was. She drew herself up.

'I am certain that the Church knows of me,' she answered, 'but had not thought you to have done so, Your Excellency. Then again, your interests may lie in different areas to those that others of your calling profess. The Commedia, for example. I understood the Church condemns a woman on the stage.'

'There are many in the Church that do, but I am of more liberal dispensation and do not scorn to descend into the pit to find the sinners and preach God's word to them. That is perhaps why I have been seen fit person to send to Venice.' The Nuncio gestured to the stage. 'Take these women of the stage. Some of my brothers,' he nodded to the Crow, 'consider them little more than whores, parading themselves for men's eyes.'

'You do not?' asked Marco Venier.

'I consider them also to be great artists,' the Nuncio answered.

'"Also,"' repeated Isabella.

'Yes, of course,' said the Nuncio, deliberately ignoring Isabella's venomed look. 'Of course, all artists are to some extent whores since they sell the better part of themselves, their muse, to others. And others are whores by any measure. But then, did not our Lord preach even to Mary Magdalene?'

'Was not the Pope Nuncio in Venice before you?' asked William to forestall Isabella's angry reply. He would have liked to strike the man for his insults and yet he felt also a strange detachment from what had been said, as if he watched a scene upon the stage. How careful this man was, how considered his barbs and darts. What pleasure did he take from throwing them? How did a man of God come to find in taunting others such obvious entertainment?

The Nuncio's eyes remained on Isabella as he answered William's question. 'He was not. His Holiness' – the Nuncio's tone lent a little stamp to the title, as if to remind them of the need for respect – 'was Inquisitor in Venice, not Nuncio.'

'Ah yes,' said William, who knew the answer already. 'Recalled to Rome at the Signoria's request, I now remember me. Excessive vigour in his duties, was it not?'

'No truth in such story at all,' said the Nuncio, his smile tighter.

'Venice, it seems, does not admire a braggart or a tyrant,' said William.

'Nor Rome a defiant child,' answered the Nuncio. The false smile no longer playing on his face.

'Oh ho, Marco,' Isabella spoke up. 'Do you hear? To the Church we Venetians are but children, to be told the time for bed, to wash our faces, to say grace at mealtimes.'

William witnessed the Nuncio struggle to bring the smile back to his face. 'All are the Church's children, Isabella Lisarro. That is why we call His Holiness the Holy Father. Is it fatherly to let a child dwell in sin unchastened? Only those that repent are forgiven. It is never too late for repentance. That is the lesson of the Parable of the Prodigal Son,' said the Nuncio.

'That son ate of the fatted calf that day, did he not?' said Marco Venier, his eyes on Isabella.

Isabella looked back at Marco and wondered if this meeting was more than just Marco's perverse love of controversy at play. His eyes made appeal to hers. Had a bargain been struck between him and Rome that turned upon the English? What did they have that Rome still wanted? What had Marco promised this Nuncio?

William's thoughts echoed Isabella's but had run on to an answer: the Nuncio sought confirmation that the English knew the names of the spies in England, certainty that they had not yet passed that intelligence on to England. He felt sickness in his stomach. It was one thing for Hemminges to talk of dangers, it was another to be confronted by the net as it tightened about them. To realise that they had already tried to strike through the Tiepolo brothers. That having failed there they were sure to try again. He laughed.

'Something amuses you?' said the Crow.

'Only that I remember a jest of my father's,' said William. 'What were the fatted calf's last words?'

William waited for reply but seeing that none would come, answered himself. '"I hear the young master is returned!"'

William laughed alone.

'It is as foolish to be Rome's enemy as it is wise to be her friend,' said the Nuncio. 'This your little England and her queen will soon find. Why, this very month the kings of France and Spain have signed a truce that will leave the King of Spain free to claim his rightful crown as King of England too. Already he begins to assemble a great fleet of ships to bring his army to your shores.'

The Nuncio looked from face to face and his smile that had wavered returned with full measure.

'Ah,' he crowed, 'this was news to England's Embassy. Such is the strength of England's intelligencers.'

The Nuncio and his two companions exchanged silent looks of delight at the frowns on William's, Hemminges' and Oldcastle's brows.

'He need only cross the Channel,' said Hemminges.

'A few short miles,' said Oldcastle.

'And he will find such a welcome in that voyage from our Admirals Drake and Hawkins,' said William. 'As will light the sky from there to where Your Excellency resides, that you may watch the triumph of his passing.'

'Brave words,' said the Nuncio showing that he, unlike Isabella, recognised English mocking when it came.

'Brave deeds too,' answered Hemminges. 'Rome should remember the fate of those who would rule against a people's will. It ends with knives on a March morning.'

For a little moment the Nuncio said nothing as he gauged the man before him who spoke with such quiet anger and whose gaze did not waver. At last the Nuncio spoke.

'You know Rome's history?'

'A little, enough to profit me with its lessons.'

'Before Caesar there was another dictator, Lucius Cornelius Sylla.'

'A bloody man,' answered William.

'So some say, yet all he sought to do was restore Rome's traditions, to return it to the glory of its earliest days, as His Holiness does,' said the Nuncio. 'When he died, this Sylla, do you know what his epitaph was?'

'One of regret?'

'On the door of his tomb was writ, *Of his friends and of his enemies, he paid them both in full measure.* Those are words to live by, are they not?'

This last to Marco Venier, who bowed his head towards the Nuncio.

The Nuncio and his companions bowed their heads little enough to be insulting and turned and disappeared into the crowd of guests. Isabella moved to berate Marco for making the meeting possible but he too had melted away. Oldcastle drained his glass.

'May we go now?' he said.

No one replied. In silence all four made their way to the gate, leaving behind them the laughter, applause and revels of those that remained behind.

In the gondola that took them through Venice to their home Isabella clutched at William's hand and held it against the pain that griped her guts.

'Isabella, what is wrong?' pleaded William against her silent twists of agony.

'It's nothing, sweet. I am a weak and foolish woman that has found in fear a poison for my stomach.'

She groaned again and her body bent against the pain within her. William pushed her hair from her sweat-dewed brow and felt his own stomach twist. He did not think Isabella weak or foolish or prone to pains that were born in the mind. He feared not the poison of imagination but of a vengeful Pope. Isabella reached up a hand to cradle his cheek.

'Do not fret. This too shall pass.'

All fancy-sick she is and pale of cheer

Isabella's pain did not pass. It grew.

'We must send for a doctor,' insisted her maid, Maria, against her mistress's refusal to countenance such expense.

'I will be well, Maria,' she insisted. 'I am only heart-sick with the late news. Rest, rest will cure all.'

When Isabella had left the room to try and sleep, Maria turned on William. At first she said nothing, simply allowing her expressive look to intimate that she held William responsible for her mistress's malady. William bore her gaze for so long as his will might before exasperation prompted him to confrontation.

'Speak, Maria, I pray you, if you would say anything to the purpose. For well you know I love your mistress dearly and would not see her suffer.'

'Then call for the doctor, Sir William,' said Maria, who had taken to giving William the same false title that Marco Venier had thrust upon him.

'You know of one?'

'I do, Doctor Bellario,' Maria answered with confidence. 'He is known to be a man of experience, particularly in—'

Maria broke off to give William another knowing look. William shook his head in incomprehension.

'It is winter in Venice but that does not mean spring cannot come to the city,' said Maria with a tilt of her head.

'What do you mean?'

'Sir William, you are young but not so young, I'm sure, as to be innocent of what happens when a man and woman come together.'

Realisation came on William and struck him like a vagabond thief.

'You think Isabella is with child?'

'Aye, though whether the child is well or no, I cannot tell. Perchance the pain within her womb is the blossoming of some seed in ground ill-suited to the harvest.'

'It cannot be,' said William but he wondered if it might be so. The thought had come nowhere near him till Maria spoke it and yet now he heard it, he could not let it go. It filled the place of his other fears, fears that he dare not yet speak out loud, that he was the cause of this malady in Isabella.

'To the doctor take you,' said William. 'Fetch him at once. Go, woman, go.'

'The cost?'

'Sir Henry will pay.'

When Maria had scurried from the room William sat and put his head in his hands. He did not know if the thrilling tremor in his nerves at the thought of Isabella carrying his child spoke of delight or fear. William knew himself a selfish man. He railed against it when he might, yet always found himself taking the course that best pleased him. So it had been with Isabella. The vows he'd made to his wife Anne had been parchment bonds against the pull of his strong intent. No harm, he had felt, could come to his wife from this wanton dalliance in a distant land. Had his reasoning changed with thought of a child by Isabella?

What if Maria was in the right of it when she said the child curdled in Isabella's womb and might undo her? His lusts and hers would then have killed her, leaving him unpunished. Unpunished, save that he would have to live with the horror of it and of his part in its cause. What if it was not in this that his closeness to her endangered her? What if Rome had already reached out to strike at him through her? What if Isabella was not ill but poisoned?

His mind was full of fears.

Do you know he promised me marriage?

Verona

The servants shuffled out with the broken chair carried between them. It was rare for her father to be in so foul a temper as to destroy furniture. Usually the worst of it was a cup of wine hurled on to the floor. Aemilia worried for a moment that her father had discovered her continued defiance of his command that she have no more conference with her cousin Valentine. Could he have done so? The two had been so careful since, not risking meeting for more than a moment away from the watchful eyes of her maids. Their enforced separation, she had found, had but fed their desires. Fingers brushing as they passed in the palace gardens had been a communion quite unholy in the thoughts that accompanied it, and such letters he had written her, secreted beneath a broken tile in the arbour of the gardens to be taken out by her and read at night. The more she felt her love denied the greater it had grown. Yet they had been careful. It could not be that which caused her father such rage.

'A whole convoy taken? Tell me again how it is possible?'

Her father spoke to his captain of guards, a man Aemilia admired but did not like. He held himself stiffly before her father.

'They grow bold, Your Grace. It is the winter's privations makes them so. That and there is rumour of a new man among these outlaws, an educated man, who gathers what were before ragged, a crew of patches, into a knitted band. Guides, directs them, that they may strike as one.'

Her father sat down on his chair, newly brought to him by his servants in replacement for the one destroyed. Aemilia thought he looked very old of a sudden. His hands lolled over the chair's arms and his head was slumped. It lasted only a moment. When he looked up there was again the fire of youth in him.

'We must ride out, drive them from the woods.'

The captain and the Duke's steward shared a look, one that Aemilia caught but her father, standing again and pacing before the fire, missed.

'Your Grace, we lack both numbers and the money to hire more,' said Rodrigo.

'And those we have are no longer in the first rank of fighting men,' the captain added.

The Duke turned from his pacing to look at his two officers. His face was red with anger and his brow dented with worries. Aemilia's love went out to her prideful and beleaguered father, whose old age was beset with troubles. Would that he would accept her help in them. Would that these worries did not translate so readily to an anger that, finding itself out of reach of its true target, fell upon those that would aid him in them.

'Go and bring me better news. What lord am I that cannot give safety to his people?'

Rodrigo and the captain bowed and departed. Aemilia crossed to her father and put her arms about him. He reached up and stroked her hair.

'Ah, Aemilia, you were ever a comfort to me. There is so much of your mother's passion in you. I would you'd known her.' He sighed. 'I shall be sorry to lose you.'

Aemilia glanced sharply up at her father. He nodded at her look.

'You are to be married, girl.'

'Father, no.'

Her father pushed her from him. His momentary calm lost again.

'I say yea,' her father roared, then took another breath to calm himself. 'The match is a sound one. For you and for our estate. You are all the heirs of my house and in your fortune lies the safety of many others. You hear how we are beset and want both men and money. Besides you are twenty and that is high time to be married. Count Claudio will make a good husband to you and to this land.'

'Claudio? No.'

'What is this "no", Aemilia, this wretched "no"?'

'Claudio, the Florentine?'

'Even he.'

'Father, he is half your age but twice mine.'

'What of it? A steady and mature hand to guide both wife and lands should I die without issue beside you.'

'His cruelty, Father, oh, I beg you! I have heard such stories of the treatment of his servants, of his vassals . . .' Aemilia felt distress and panic swelling in her breast. She had not thought there would be so little time before her father spoke of marriage and that he should propose Count Claudio! 'And such a face, the blade of a sword across it could only improve it. Oh, Father, and such rumours follow him and how he came by his estate.'

'Ungrateful child, to speak of him thus. No, no,' her father nodded, 'you have the right of it. He is no pampered courtier with hands like a woman and the manners of a lady. He is firm in his rule and does not shirk the stern measure when 'tis needed. The better for it.' The Duke cast his finger out in a wide circle. 'Our position is precarious, Aemilia. We rule at the pleasure of the Signoria of Venice and we are surrounded by enemies jealous of us and of Venice. The Pope wants our lands, Philip of Spain wants our lands, the damnable Duke of Savoy wants our lands, and each has men in numbers that far outmatch that meagre tally I may call upon. God's will, Aemilia, who will fight them if they come? An old man and a girl?'

'Why not? Did not Caterina Sforza defend Forli?'

The Duke roared again, but now with laughter. 'Good child. I see you are mine in bravery at least.' He reached out and pinched her cheek, a gesture that Aemilia could not abide both for the pain of her father's grip and for the way it cast her in a child's role. She smacked his hand away.

'The contract will be made, Aemilia,' her father continued. 'Count Claudio may have the figure of an ox—'

'A dog,' said Aemilia.

'– but he has the courage of a lion.'

'And the manners of a toad.'

'Be silent. I have thought on it much. Count Claudio has wealth and more than that, he has proved himself in the wars. If he be willing, then he will be your husband and my heir unless the good Lord bless me with another child.'

The Duke made to leave but found his daughter danced before him.

'I beg you, Father, let me choose my own husband . . .' Aemilia was in tears. She reached out to grab her father's hand.

'Who would you choose? Some pretty weakling like your cousin Valentine?'

Aemilia looked up with hopeful eyes, 'Why not him, Father? He is your cousin's son and would keep the duchy in the family's hands. Besides' – she clamped her hand on her father's as he tried to pull it away – 'he is a goodly man, educated, wise and graceful.'

Her father finally succeeded in snatching his hand from his pleading daughter's grasp.

'I feared as much. Despite my command, you have let him whisper love words in your ears.'

'Father, he has importuned me with love in honourable fashion.'

'Ay, "fashion" you may call it. Go to, go to.'

'And has given countenance to his speech with almost all the holy vows of heaven.'

'Ay springes to catch woodcocks. I do know, when the blood burns, how prodigal the soul lends the tongue vows. I forbid you his company.'

'Father, no. Please no.'

The Duke strode away. 'You will marry Count Claudio,' he called over his shoulder, 'and there's an end on it.'

Silence that dreadful bell

Venice

The doctor passed William at the doorway and pressed his arm as he passed.

'All things are in God's will. Pray, good sir. Pray.'

William shook off his hand. The wrinkle that rose upon the doctor's face told that this was not the first time the anger, rightly directed at the news, had been sent instead towards the messenger. The doctor would forbear to chide the young man. The news, after all, was bad.

'This corruption of her womb . . .' William began but trailed away.

'It is not uncommon in those of . . .' The doctor paused at the delicacy of his message. 'In those of the lady's profession. I have seen it before. She has had children?'

'Miscarried.'

'That too is of a piece with the other signs that lead to this. I am sorry.'

'You see no sign of poison?' said William. There, he had spoken it. The fear that had lurked in him was in the air.

'Poison?' said the doctor, his voice rising with his brow. 'No, good sir, none of that. Without question it is not poison. You say that the pain has been present for many weeks. I know of no poison that works in that manner. A more mundane blow has struck at the lady. Has she reason to fear poisoning?'

William ignored the question in favour of one of his own. 'What may be done?'

'Little. Prayer, a tincture for the pain. The matter comes to its head. If it is God's will she will recover.'

The doctor waited for William to speak again, to answer his question about the fear of murdering poison. William said nothing, he was thinking how few of his prayers he had found answered in his life. The doctor sighed and moved to leave.

'I shall send my bill,' he said from the door. William waved him away. What did money matter now?

He stepped back into the bed chamber. Isabella sat, propped upon the bed, her hands still crossed upon her stomach. William came and reached for her hand, to hold it. The two lovers looked at each other but William could not hold her gaze. He could not bear the fear in it, nor did he wish her to see his own.

'Maria thought you were with child,' said William.

Isabella barked a laugh.

'She may yet be right,' protested William. 'This physician was too hasty in his judgement. We shall send for others, better. Marco Venier will have names we can call on.'

'William,' Isabella shook her head. 'There's no child here. I know it.'

He made to speak.

'I know it,' Isabella spoke over him. 'Even before the doctor pronounced his sentence, I knew it.'

Again, they fell to silence. A bell began to toll outside. One of Venice's many churches announced some moment, a baptism, a wedding or a death. William spoke over the chimes.

'So much has happened in the few months since I left England, I scarce know myself any more. You are such a great part of that change in me that I cannot bear the thought you will . . .' William's voice fell away. 'I worry that . . . I worry that . . .'

He could not complete his thought, that it was some sin of his had made this canker in Isabella. He had known it too and waited as the physician, with his unseemly fingers, examined Isabella and, nodding, always nodding, turned to him to pronounce his mortal sentence. Why did the doctor not speak to her? Why speak to him? It was not he the physician spoke his tale of death about, nor did he bear the corrupted carbuncle that was the end of happiness. Why speak to him? Curse all physicians. Their only prognostication was unhappiness.

Say he be taken, racked, and tortured

The Veneto

The abbey near Ferrara was small and newly established. It nestled itself in a valley that in the spring was green and verdant and now, in winter, had a snowy stillness and a quiet to it that quite belied the hot hell of torture in its cellars.

'Confess,' demanded Father Thornhill. He was weary of the stink and noise and longed for the fresh air of the courtyard above. But the obstinate merchant would not confess and so he must go on. He thought back to the frustrations of the past weeks. That interfering Duke of Verona had delayed him in his inquisition but only for a while. For the nonce the trail he followed led here to Ferrara and it was politic that it do so since it took him away from the Duke, but there was business left undone in Verona and he would see it done. This time he would not be so humble as the first. The Duke must learn that all kneel to the Church. He nodded to the soldier whose mailed fist began again to beat and blast the ruin of the merchant's face as he had done this hour past.

The man had said little that was meaningful in this past quarter-hour and before that nothing that Father Thornhill did not already know. How quickly he had spoken of his heretic sympathies, of his help to the English at Padua, at Geneva. The man had no spirit at all. That should be no surprise, for he had let the Devil seduce him with this Lutheran poison. Yet of English spies in Venice he'd said nothing. Father Thornhill picked at his nails; perhaps the man knew nothing.

There was an angry hammering at the cellar door. Father Thornhill waved to one of the soldiers, who answered it to the angry face of the Abbot himself.

'What is the meaning of this desecration?' roared the Abbot at the sight that greeted him: a naked man, more dead than living, strapped upside down to a barrel of wine, teeth broken, eyes swollen and shut, blood dripping from lacerations, his voice reduced to pitiful moans where once had been screams, shouts, pleas for a mercy that had not come. Father Thornhill waved to the soldier to stop his blows.

'I asked for privacy, Father Abbot. I would have it still.'

'You will cease this blasphemy within my walls,' cried the Abbot, his face puce with anger, his finger pointing tremblingly at the bloody man.

'What blasphemy?'

'What blasphemy? What blasphemy? Why this, this . . .' The Abbot was lost for words. He gathered himself. 'You will take your men and yourself from my abbey this night.'

'We will go when we are done.'

'You will go now,' declared the Abbot.

'When we are done,' answered Father Thornhill. His voice gave no sign that he thought either the merchant's moans of pain or the Abbot's rage worthy of his concern.

'Escort the Abbot from the room,' he said to the nearest soldier, who responded without pause. The Abbot, lifted bodily from the ground, his feet scrabbling against the soldier's strength, was driven to the door.

'This will not stand,' he cried. 'The Bishop shall hear of this. Rome shall hear of it.'

'Rome already knows,' said Father Thornhill to the closing door. The hammering upon it he ignored. He turned back to the man before him. The soldier held the man's head in his hand.

'He's dead, Father,' said the soldier after a moment's examination.

'Regrettable. Still, we would have sent him to Rome only to have him executed. We save ourselves so much labour.'

'He might have told us more?'

'No. I think not. He said enough. There has been no message, no packet from the English spies by this route. Inform Monsignor Costa at Venice of this at once. If the English spies are still in Venice then they have the names still. Let them be taken with speed.'

And so we add another nail to hammer shut heretic England's coffin, he thought, as he passed to the door to walk out in the fresh air again.

'The body, Father?'

'Burn it.'

Thy grief their sports, thy resolution mocked

Venice

Isabella's pain grew worse.

The doctor sent his bill and William, angry at the price of knowledge without cure, hurled it against the wall and chased the doctor's servant into the street throwing coins at him.

'There's the dignity of spirit I have so much admired,' said Isabella from her bed when William returned.

'I am angry and afraid,' said William.

'I noticed.'

William said nothing. The day had a chill in it and he raked the grate with sharp thrusts of the poker and pulled another log on to the fire.

'Tell me of the child you would have me bear.'

He shook his head: 'I cannot.'

'No. No. I see that. A whim. Distraction only. Then tell me of your children.'

William thought of Susanna and of Hamnet and Judith. How little he knew of his own blood when he strove to know so much of others.

'I cannot speak of them without thinking how little is the time that I have spent with them,' answered William. 'Then I recall how much I am changed by them in all that brief time. And I think of you, Isabella. I think of you and all the changes you have wrought. I would I had the words.'

'You do,' said Isabella with a sudden urgency. 'You do. You think it was your looks seduced me?'

He gave a bitter laugh.

'I do not speak foolishly, William. That time has passed, I think. Each moment precious now,' said Isabella. 'Will you shy from compliments now? May not a dying woman speak freely?'

'Do not speak thus,' demanded William. 'This is but a call to arms. No death knell.'

Her hand clutched at his and her thumb came up to run over the carved face of the gold ring she had given him. The dark cornelian stone set at its heart was engraved with a lance with a pen's tip. It had for many years belonged to Prospero. He had given it to Isabella in honour of her poetry, which he had said could strike deeper than any weapon. She had given it to William in turn, meaning to make of the gift a sign of hope, a sacrament to the way love could be found even in the midst of terrors.

'I love you, William,' said Isabella. 'What a thing, a foolish thing, for a courtesan to say. And I may say it freely. There is no world of aged worry for me now. You will be my end and I may speak without care for what's to come. I love you. I love you. I'll cry it to the reverberate hills, I love you. What a foolish youth you are and still I love you. You will be with me at the end. I shall not pass from this world alone. Think what a thing that is and how few may make so proud a boast.'

'You will not go,' protested William.

'I will.'

William shook his head, denying it, not understanding how she could speak with such certainty of her own doom. 'I would that bell would cease. I cannot think, it frights me with its ringing from any semblance of a plan.'

'A plan?' said Isabella. She reached up and cupped his face and turned it from the window to look upon her own. 'Oh, William. There's no planning to be done. What is to be, will be. If not now, then in a week, a month, a year. Still it will come. The moment itself does not matter. The readiness is all.'

'I am not ready, Isabella,' said William. His voice caught in his throat as he spoke. He did not have the strength, the courage, to hide his fear from her any more.

She cradled him in her arms as his body heaved. 'Oh William, William. Yours is the only readiness that matters.'

Your Grace attended to their sugared words . . .

William's ceaseless pacing in her room at last drove Isabella to suggest a quest: to fetch her a preserve of peaches from the market while she rested. Reluctantly acceding to her wisdom, William left her.

The Campo Erberia was scant of people and those that were there had a subdued air, as if the chill wind that blew through the city had blown away both warmth and joy. Clouds loured over the marketplace and threatened rain, those that were there hurried against its coming.

William felt no such urgency. His step was listless as his spirit. There was a conspiracy against his happiness. Hemminges and Oldcastle sought to drive him from Venice and he defied them. The Papal Nuncio laid his threats against them and he defied him. Now, Isabella was struck down, and his defiance counted for nothing, nothing, against her malady. He was as powerless as a babe in arms.

Such coin as he had was nearly spent, that knavish doctor, that black crow of ill-tidings, having taken all but the last of it. He dared not draw more from the embassy's funds, fearing the strength of his continued disguise as ambassador's man. Yet without funds what action might he take? What physic could he find that might make Isabella well again? What good his power of thought now? The carbuncle in Isabella was proof against his cunning words and those were all he had to offer.

He stopped. Not so. He came at matters too direct. If he had no funds that did not mean others were as poor as he. To Marco Venier would he go, to use such power as his words had to make that man unpick his purse's strings and pour forth physic on to Isabella. Sure, it should not need much work, for was not Marco Venier Isabella's friend? And his?

Resolution made, he turned to the gondolas on the Canal Grande and was at them, his mouth opened to call one for the journey, when he recalled his mistress's quest. To the sound of mocking shouts at his indecision from the gondoliers at Rialto, whose reputation as the most vicious and licentious varlets in Venice was well earned, William hurried back to the Campo Erberia to buy the preserve of peaches. Then carrying the precious package he returned and at last took a gondola.

*

The high walls of the Ca' Venier looked the same to William. The old stone was familiar, as were the tattered banners that decked them, taken from Byzantine and Ottoman ships by Marco Venier's ancestors. All was as it had ever been save in one thing only, there was no welcome here. Two hours he had waited since he'd first announced himself. Now a servant came to send him on his way again. He would not have it.

'Tell him I do not come on my own behalf but that of Isabella Lisarro.'

'I have told him so, sir,' replied the servant who blocked William's way.

'His good friend, Isabella,' William repeated. The little stamps that marked his words bore the emphasis of William's anger and his fear. The servant made no reply.

'Tell your master I shall not leave until I have spoken with him.' William stalked over to the wall by the water gate. 'Here I'll plant myself, tell him.' He subsided to mutters: 'He will speak with me.'

Such uncivil reception he had not thought to find and yet he should have seen its promise. When they had found the Papal Nuncio at Marco Venier's feast he should have thought how strange that was, for Marco Venier was no friend of this Pope, nor Venice inclined to give welcome to one who would be master of its courses. What foul timing, if this betrayal be so, to have Marco Venier gone from them when most they had need of him.

William looked up from his thoughts and saw the servant's angry look. He waved him off: 'Go, tell your master I will speak with him whether he will or no. Though I must stay so long as he may make a post of me to tie his gondola to or build a bench by my support, still he will speak with me before I'm gone.'

The servant turned his head in response to some message from behind. Then, with a sighing and a grimacing show, he beckoned William to him and allowed him through the gate. William's joints, stiff from his watch and his clothes sodden from the rain, moved with ungainly steps into the Ca' Venier but he kept his head held high.

. . . But looked not on the poison of their hearts

'Sir William,' Marco Venier greeted him with no echo of the churlish welcome at the gate in his voice or words. 'I had quite forgot how stubborn a man you are. I do not say a mule for it, but no less an ass.'

'Have we so swiftly turned to insults, sir? Be it so. I have not come on my honour's account but on our friend's behalf.'

'Insult or praise? How often we speak of the same virtue and find our words treated as one or other not by our intent but by the hearer's own thoughts. Wine?'

William shook his head. 'I did not come to speak philosophy with you.'

'Why did you come?' Marco Venier's voice at last showed some hint of anger in it. 'The times are not those they once were. Welcome was not offered.'

'Isabella is sick.'

Marco Venier's face fell for an instant before he pulled it back. 'That is grave news. I am sorry to hear it.'

William's fears began to lift. Whatever had prompted Marco Venier to bar him from the house would not prevent him giving aid to Isabella. He waited to hear that help was offered. The room stayed silent. Marco Venier drank his own wine but said nothing.

'What may you do for her?' William prompted.

'As much as you,' Marco answered.

'I can do nothing more. Such coin I have, it is all spent.'

'I cannot help you.'

'I do not need it. It is your friend, Isabella, needs you.'

'My friend is double-diseased,' said Marco Venier, his own tone a gentle reproof to William's harsh one. 'One plague makes her ill, the other keeps her from those that would have helped her. The first she caught I know not where. The second she caught of you, Sir William.'

William's anger flared like a torch in wind. He strode across the space between Marco Venier and him.

'Then it is a plague of cowardice,' said William. 'You should not fear to breathe the air of those that carry its infection. For I see it corrupts your blood already.'

'You speak as a doctor, but physician, first heal yourself before you seek the cure of others.' He reached up and plucked William's hand from his collar.

William turned and strode to leave. By the door he paused and struck the wall. 'Tell me what has made such a coward of you, Marco Venier.' The strength went out of him and his shoulders fell. 'God's will, she is dying, Marco.'

'Caution is not cowardice, Sir William. When our enemies did play but in a concealed way, then might we make our concealed response. Now they show themselves openly and each blow against them is seen and will be counted, reckoned and revenged.'

'How is it a blow against our enemies to help a poor woman?'

Marco Venier walked across to where William stood. 'My business is in balance, Sir William. My profit comes from holding the scales, not placing weights within them. If I am seen to choose a side, my role is lost. The Nuncio knows I have been friendly with you. The Nuncio knows and makes demands of me, which I in turn resist with that same argument I now give to you.'

'I ask a mote of dust, Marco, and you claim it will set the scales tumbling. You call it choosing a side. As if the Nuncio cares if a whore lives or dies.'

'He does not,' said Marco. 'He cares about your embassy. He speaks of heretics given succour by the state. He looks to see who aids them and counts them amongst those selfsame heretics. You are a plague in the Pope's eyes that passes to all you touch. I must put you from me. Be grateful that I do not do more or seek to win the Nuncio's favour with a gift.'

William laughed. 'I thought in coming here to use such power of language as I possessed to summon you to Isabella's aid. So much a fool am I, and an arrogant fool, to think that if her person was not enough to enchant you that my words might triumph in her memory's stead. Worse, I find that I am but a 'prentice in the orator's art. You have such skill of argument that you have persuaded yourself of this course of treachery, for so we must call it when you turn aside from those that have ever been loyal and loving to you; yes, treachery is the righteous path and not a coward's actions.'

William's words, which had risen in volume and venom, fell back to a hiss. 'The sweet smoke of your own rhetoric comfort you, Marco Venier. While it lasts. For when it and your head clears, you shall have such a deal of sorrow in this moment's remembrance.'

William pulled open the doors to the great room. Two liveried servants blocked the way.

'Let me past.'

'Alas,' said Marco Venier behind him. 'I did not want you here, remember that. Yet having come, what will the Nuncio's spies conclude that I permitted you entry?'

William turned on his heel. Marco Venier had the good grace to look ashamed and saddened by his own words.

'Balance, Sir William. Balance. Admittance speaks of welcome. There must be some sign of rejection to restore the balance.'

The liveried servants clapped their hands on William and began to drag him from the room.

'Come no more for parley, Sir William,' said Marco Venier as he closed the doors on the sight of William being hauled through the corridor, his feet scrabbling for purchase against the rush of events. 'You shall find no welcome here.'

And not Death's ebon dart, to strike him dead

William was thrown into a gondola and rowed out across the wide canal to the Giudecca, away from the heart of the city, and there deposited. Hauling himself up, he had sat in silent anguish on the side of the canal for a quarter of an hour when Hemminges sat down beside him. Hemminges said nothing at all. After another quarter of an hour he picked up a loose stone and skimmed it out across the water of the lagoon.

'You were watching over me again,' said William.

'I was,' said Hemminges. 'I was not the only one to do so.' He nodded towards a scowling figure still standing at the *traghetto* point on the Giudecca, who seeing himself picked out, turned hurriedly and disappeared into the crowd of people gathered to await the ferry's return.

'The waiting time is over,' said Hemminges. 'The playing has begun.'

William and Hemminges trudged through the dark of the city in silence. William felt the weight of Marco Venier's refusal as a stone in his stomach. He had nothing left to give and now it seemed those that might have aided them, nay, say rather those who ought in justice and for the memory of Isabella's wit and good friendship have run to offer her succour in her time of need, no longer cared for that connection. They hid like beetles beneath a log, scurrying from sight at the first tread of the Pope's minion. William's fingers ground against each other.

'We might as well be dead already,' he muttered.

'What's that?' said Hemminges.

'Nothing, nothing.'

William was wondering again how much he might draw on Sir Henry's credit. William and the others had not dared to do so for a month or more. Not since the news of the papal legate's coming to Venice had reached them. Yet, thought William, he might do so now; pay for another doctor to come and see to Isabella. This resolution made his step take on a lighter stride. To act would fend off his sense that he had become but a storm-tossed leaf, blown by fate.

Hemminges put a hand upon his arm. 'Do you hear that?' he whispered.

William stopped and listened. They stood in a small square in the sestiere of Santa Croce. The city was very dark, the moon a thin, crescent bow that shot little light; they were far from the canals and the streets were silent. William strained against the silence and, after a moment, heard what had given Hemminges pause. The shuffle of feet, soft and faint.

William looked to his left and saw that Hemminges had drawn his knife. Hemminges looked past William's shoulder to the shadows of the street beyond. William drew his own blade.

'What think yo—' William began but Hemminges pressed a finger to his lips. The two men stood in the darkness of the square waiting and listening. Minutes passed. From moment to moment William heard sounds but nothing to which he could give a name. Hemminges, it seemed, heard more for he turned to William and pressed his lips close to William's ear.

'Wait for me the time it takes to recite the Lord's Prayer three times then walk, slowly, through the alley there to the bridge ahead,' he whispered.

'What do you fear?' whispered William in reply. The night had taken on many shapes in William's mind and it was only the calm of his friend that kept those fears from spurring him to flight.

'Murder, William. I fear murder,' said Hemminges. With that he pressed William's arm and was gone.

Three times William whispered the words of the prayer, each time his mouth drying as he spoke of those who would trespass against him. Then he screwed his courage to the sticking place and put one foot in front of the other and strode towards the bridge. When before he had fought through Venice's streets at night he had the spur of anger to drive him on. Now he felt only the terrors of the night.

He rounded the corner and the slender light of the moon lit the small bridge across the narrow canal ahead. He stepped out on to the bridge. Three men ran from the darkness towards William. Their faces were swathed in cloth black as their purpose. Swords bared, they swooped towards him as eagles on to prey.

Hemminges came from the darkness and took one of the men in the side, hurling him into his neighbour. The two turned to front their enemy but Hemminges had already knocked the closest man's blade aside and ran his dagger up the sword's metal edge and on to slice through the masked man's arm.

The third man turned his head at the sound of his companion's cry and William, ready for the moment, ran forward. The killer's blade came up and, though William had twisted in anticipation, still its edge cut through his doublet and scored his ribs. With a roar of his own, a heady mix of pain and rage, William thrust his dagger into the shoulder of the man, who stumbled back. William drove on and, abandoning the blade embedded in the man's muscle, dropped slightly, grasped him round the waist and tossed him over the bridge's wall into the canal below. He did not wait to see the man's fate but stooped to pick up the sword the man had dropped when William stabbed him. He raced to where Hemminges now feinted and parried the two blades before him. The narrowness of the street Hemminges played to his advantage, pushing his assailants' blades across each other and stepping always to keep one between him and the other.

William's battle-cry proved too much for the two assassins. At his approach they turned and fled. William skittered to a halt and felt at once the flare of pain in his side. Hemminges reached him and pulled up his shirt to gaze upon the wound.

'A scratch, no more. 'Twill heal. Come, we must go.'

They set off at a pace. Without warning Hemminges pushed William into the shadow of an overhanging arch just as one quarrel slammed into the stonework beside him and another bounced and jumped across the street where the two had been running.

'Jesu, Hemminges . . .'

'Quiet,' Hemminges hissed at William. 'Ahead, Will. Two at least, by the stacked barrels of an inn.' There was a moment of silence, or so it seemed to William, but Hemminges again heard something in the night. William made to peer round the edge of the arch but Hemminges pulled him back.

'Don't be a fool.'

Hemminges looked about him and then, some decision made, he turned to William. 'I will make for the safety of that wall. When they loose, run. We will have but a moment's grace.'

'It is the same men?'

'Who cares, Will? The same. Others. The Pope himself.' Hemminges grasped William's collar and pulled him round to face him. 'When I move, they will loose, then you run. Yes?'

William nodded. He wiped his palms, damp with fear, on his doublet. Hemminges darted from cover, twisted, leapt and rolled. Again the strained, shrill whistle of twisted rope released and the flash of the quarrels in the dark, each flying so close to Hemminges' passage as to seem some aspect of his shadow.

William ran.

Ahead he saw two figures crouched. As Hemminges had said, they hid behind barrels stacked outside an inn, kneeling, cranking at the mechanism of their crossbows. As he closed with them William saw all as if time were slowed. The one closest let his crossbow clatter to the ground and straightened to draw his sword. Too late. William's own borrowed blade went through his enemy's throat and William's charge drove him and the blade on till the hilt struck the man's throat and the blade beyond scraped the stone walls of the inn. William pushed the man back, his hands flapping at the rapier William held. The man lost his footing and fell backward; the weight of his falling body snatched the blade from William's hand. William turned, his dagger set to ward off the second man only to find that Hemminges was on him and dealing with him using short, swift strokes that first hamstrung him and then ripped open his throat.

William stood a moment staring at the man he had surely slain, even if he had breath a few moments longer. It was that selfsame Nuncio's man, the Crow, the colourless man, though his pale face was smirched now with red that poured from the hole in his throat and bubbled and frothed from his mouth. The Crow lay, still kicking, with his hands clawing at the sword through his throat. Hemminges hauled William from his reverie by the arm and the two turned and ran.

Let him depart: his passport shall be made

Not until they had the safety of the House of the White Lion did they pause again. Its door closed behind them and William and Hemminges slumped against the walls of the dark hallway. Their breath came in ragged gasps. After a minute, Hemminges pulled himself to his feet.

'I will rouse Nick. We need take little . . .' He was moving towards the kitchen as he spoke. 'Salarino can call for a gondola at first light to take us to Mestre.'

'I'm not going.' William spoke to Hemminges' back.

Hemminges stopped but did not turn. William raised himself up to his own feet.

'How can you ask that I go?' demanded William. 'Isabella lies dying. You want me to leave her to die alone?'

Hemminges leaned against the hall's wall.

'I do not want her to die alone,' he turned. 'Nor do I wish her to die in company. God's blood, Will, it's the dying I look to avoid. Tonight's events are the writing on the wall. I know you saw him, as I did.'

'The Crow.' William nodded.

'The Nuncio's man, yes? He that stood and glowered at us while his master spoke his veiled threats. We have tarried too long.'

'I cannot go.'

'You cannot stay and live.'

'Then I will die by my lover's side.'

Hemminges' voice rose. 'And leave your children orphans? Jesu, Will, have a care for others.' His fist hammered the wall. 'And there is more at stake than you and Isabella. We must deliver our intelligence.'

'What do these spies' names matter to me next to Isabella?' shouted William in answer.

'Damn the names, Will, I speak of us, of your friends. I need your aid if Oldcastle is to make it to safety. If I am.'

Hemminges stalked back to where William stood silent and grasped him by the shoulders.

'You are overfull of self-affairs, Will. Enough, we can debate no more.' His voice softened. 'Bring Isabella with us. Her safety here in Venice is lost. The thunder's heard and her friends have fled the coming storm. We should flee too.'

'Whither away?'

'Mestre and then on to Verona. We'll shun the canals, take the country roads as we did when we were in Sir Henry's train.'

William shuddered at the memory of that unhappy journey from England and of its bloody ending, the embassy all cut down by the Pope's agents save he, Oldcastle and Hemminges.

'She will not last on that road,' he said, more to himself than to Hemminges. Nonetheless Hemminges answered.

'She will, she must. It is a short journey, a few days. We will have shook off pursuit by the time we reach Verona and may return to the canals from there. Come.'

Hemminges stalked away to climb the stairs to the first floor, the *piano nobile*, where he and Oldcastle's rooms were. William did not follow. He could not do so. He could not leave Isabella and she could not follow them.

The storm is up, and all is on the hazard

As with a storm, whose clouds are seen slowly gathering many miles hence but then upon you comes with the speed of thunderbolts, so the days that followed passed in a clap.

The first day of the Carnival came. The city threw off the cold and the damp, the disappointments of winter were given over to merriment, mischief and masks.

Hemminges did not search William out again. Salarino brought news of his and Oldcastle's departure along with a chest of clothes they had left behind. William told Salarino to send it to England and shut the door on him.

William had not dared to tell Isabella of his meeting with Marco Venier or of his friends' departure. She had not asked after the preserve of peaches she had sent him for or asked why he returned so late. Her strength failed. Her cares turned inward. She sickened quickly.

William waited, listening to the sounds of the Carnival outside, helpless, impotent, and alone.

Sweet love, sweet lines, sweet life!

Verona

Aemilia found him in the walled garden. Despite his mask she knew him easily amongst the aged courtiers of her father's palace. He favoured a Florentine style and Aemilia took a moment as he walked ahead of her to admire him again. To her approving eyes, and to her father's scornful ones, Valentine's doublet sat a little tight about his shoulders, his hose clung a little closely to his calves and his hair, his wonderful, flowing, flaxen hair, swung loosely. The days since her father had announced she would marry Count Claudio had been an agony to her, the more so because her father had at first had her more closely watched and the chance to speak with Valentine had not come. Yet the watch had slackened and now the masks and revelry that accompanied the approach of Martedì Grasso, Fat Tuesday, gave them opportunity.

She looked about to make sure her maid was not near and swept up behind him and pulled him into the dance. Over the sound of music and the laughter of others she told him her grave news.

'Oh, Valentine, what are we to do? I am to be married to Count Claudio.'

'That beast. Never,' Valentine pronounced and pushed her back to hold her at arm's length and gaze up into her eyes. 'I swear it shall not be so.'

How strong he was in his intent, how masterful he seemed in his declaration. She pulled him back to the dance lest they be noticed.

'But how, Valentine? I am promised. Oh, Valentine, I begged him that I might marry you but he only laughed at it. Why? Why are you not ten times the husband in his eyes? Why does he not value your qualities? He thinks only of Claudio's brutish strength, not of your gentle wisdom.'

'You told him of us?'

'No, Valentine, no. As you have urged I told him nothing of our wooing but he knows, of course he knows. I spoke to propose you as a husband.'

Aemilia felt Valentine tremble and marvelled at his passion. She remembered the first time they had spoken, truly spoken, here in this garden, the cousin that had late arrived at court and set all the ladies' tongues to wagging with his good looks and gentle manners. The cousin whose deep blue eyes she had looked on longingly across the dinner table and blushed when he had caught her looking.

In only one thing did she find him wanting, a willingness to speak to her father of their love. Even there she could not fault him overmuch for his pride was understandable. He would not, he declared to her, come as a beggar for her hand but it should be offered to him. He may be poor but he was honourable. He should not have to plead for that which should be given to him by right. She had not pressed him then but now, with her promised to Count Claudio, he must overmaster his own pride and make demand of her to her father.

'The date for your wedding is set?' Valentine asked.

'I know not, I think not. Lent approaches and may create delay. He did not say.'

'Who?'

'My father.'

'Madonna, your father!'

'Yes, my father. Valentine?'

The young man had already pushed away from her and Aemilia watched in astonishment as he scampered away.

'Aemilia.'

With a start, Aemilia heard her father's voice and turned to see him. Masked as they all were, there was no mistaking his size or the still black beard. He took her hand and led her back into the dance.

'Who was that you were with?' her father asked.

She stumbled at his question. 'I know not, Father. I could not tell who was beneath the mask.'

'It was not Valentine?'

'No, sure, Father. You have forbid him my company.' Aemilia again missed the step of the music and her heel came on her father's foot. He cried at the pain of it.

'I am sorry, Father. This unhappy talk distracted me.'

'Really, Aemilia, we must look to your lessons. It will not do for you to be so ungraceful at your wedding.'

They danced on but Aemilia was grateful for her own mask, which hid the tears that welled in her eyes.

Death, that hath sucked the honey of thy breath

Venice

Beyond the balcony of Isabella's bedroom, the sounds of Venice caught in the revels of Carnival were cruel contrast to those of pain within. William strove to give Isabella comfort. Her illness worsened quickly and savaged her mercilessly. Isabella's body was wracked with the most terrible pains that denied her all rest, that made her rend the air with great cries and twist and turn till William thought he would be driven mad by it, by his powerlessness to bring her balm, and still it would not end.

As, day by day, her pain worsened William grew more desperate. He had padded the room with anything that held softness in it so that Isabella might not hurt herself further as she groaned and hurled herself from her bed or bent to vomit the foulness out of her. Gone were the days of poetry and the loving touch, replaced by weeping cries and the raking clutch of her hand on his arm as another wave of agony crossed her. The stench, the horror had been terrible but he had stayed, stayed and stayed. It was now the night before Martedì Grasso, the Carnival had reached its pitch of revelry and Isabella's suffering with it.

The night drew on, long and cruel, with Isabella insensible to all but the pain that tore her. She did not see William or hear his words. She suffered and he was incapable of helping her. All was an agony.

Then there came a minute, in the dark of the night when all outside had at last come to quiet, when she came back to him. For a moment, oh, too brief a moment, she saw him again, the clouds of pain and disease parting.

'Will, you are here?'

'Always.'

'I am so afraid.'

Her hand had reached for his and he had clutched it to him, kissed it, pressed it to his chest and she had smiled up at him, that wondrous smile. Her thumb had run again across the face of the ring she had given him.

'How strange the world is,' she said, looking from its face up to William's own.

A flood of tears came over him and he pushed them away, furious, wanting nothing to obscure the sight of her.

'I love you,' she said.

He could do no more, say no more than an echo of the words back.

Then she was gone again, wracked by her illness once more.

At midnight's toll she had passed into a deep faint and William had rejoiced in it for the calm it seemed to bring her and damned his own selfishness that he longed to speak with her again, to tell her more perfectly that he loved her, how he loved her. He quenched the candle and, sitting to watch over her in the darkness, let her rest.

She never woke. William could not tell the moment that, in his vigil, he had realised she was gone from him forever. His howl had marked it. His howl and echoed howl, his desperate pressing of her hand, his call for her to come back to him, his declaration that it was too soon, too soon, too soon. He could not see for his tears. He should have waked her. He had more to say, more to hear. Oh God, he should have waked her. He needed just a moment more with her. A moment, no more. Come back, be here, be with me. Oh God, he was not ready. He would never be ready.

Maria, called from her rest by his cries, had been in her turn quiet. With gentleness of movement she had guided him, railing, tears falling, broken, from the charnel house to the public room and then returned to see her mistress's body prepared. The awful face of death wiped clean and painted with the false calm of the grave.

When she returned to him William had fallen silent. He sat in a chair and did not move. Nor did Maria speak to him again but, her work done, took herself to her own room. There to weep in private for her mistress whom death had claimed for his own.

The long day's task is done, and we must sleep

William sat in the dark of the great room. Dawn had come and beyond the balcony outside the revels of Martedì Grasso, Fat Tuesday, the Carnival's last day, were already growing to a roar yet William heard them as if from a great distance. In the bedroom behind him lay Isabella, dead.

No, not Isabella. A shell, a body, no more, for in that room and in that body was not the fire of life that had so animated her. William felt himself in turn an empty vessel. The horror of those hours that had passed still marked him. It had been a cruel death.

When the door opened William was still in that chair. His mind was at once so full of thoughts and yet he could not conjure even one to stillness, that it might be examined, interpreted, understood. So, for all the thoughts within him, it was as if his mind was as blank as a tablet.

'Sir William?'

The voice repeated itself two times more before William was pulled back to the moment and its awful truths.

'Marco Venier,' said William without turning round to face the man. 'You've come too late. She's dead.'

'Dead?'

'Aye, dead.'

William heard the footsteps pass to the bedroom and return.

'I am sorry, Sir William,' said Marco Venier.

'Not sorry enough,' he answered.

'This was not my doing,' Marco Venier protested.

William waved his excuses away. What did they matter now?

'I came to warn you both. The Nuncio's men gather this morning. They seek to use the Carnival to hide their acts. They come to silence you both.'

William said nothing.

'Sir William,' urged Marco Venier, 'where is your master, Sir Henry Carr, his man, the dancing-master Hemminges? You all must fly from Venice.'

'Gone,' said William. 'All gone.'

'Then you must go too. Hurry, Sir William, there are not hours but minutes till they come.'

William stood and looked slowly about him, taking in the sight of the walls, the long bench where he and Isabella had sat, the balcony where they had spoken late into the night.

'Maria?' he asked.

'She and her son I have taken into my care already,' said Marco. 'For her mistress's sake, whose Christian burial will also be in my charge.'

William nodded.

'They know nothing.'

'And are the safer for it. I will keep them from harm. I swear it.' Marco Venier grasped William's arm. 'You I cannot protect. You must fly. Now.'

William nodded again. He bent down and picked up a folio from the table and weighed it in his hand but did not move to leave.

From outside the sound of revels was cut by angrier sounds. Shouted instructions to the crowds to part could be heard along with the clatter and clank of metal on metal.

'Come,' said Marco Venier. He pulled William after him and William followed. To leave Venice was nothing to him now. The city was already dead to him.

Act Two

Verona and woods in the Veneto, February to March 1586

My stooping duty tenderly shall show

Verona

Aemilia stood at the back of the hall. She had climbed on to a chair in order to see over the heads of those in front of her, yet, above the disapproving tuts of her maid and whispers of the other courtiers, she could barely hear what commerce her father had with the strange visitors to his court.

'Robbed, I say again, robbed, of wealth, of horse and armour, and of dignity,' declared Oldcastle, turning about with arms spread wide to allow his words and state to be taken in by all those assembled. He finished his orbit facing the Duke. 'Humbly we throw ourselves upon the mercy of your court.'

'Your name, again?' asked the Duke. He was in a poor humour. He'd scarce sat down to breakfast, easily the favourite of his four meals of the day, when servants had called him to his hall to deal with strange new arrivals. The men had been brought before him in a haste by virtue of their tales of banditry in the forests and the Duke had barely been given a moment to speak before the taller, stouter of the two men had begun to declaim the story of his suffering.

'Sir Nicholas Hawkwood, my lord,' replied Oldcastle, performing a deep bow of the kind that always surprised watchers, who assumed no stomach such as Oldcastle possessed would permit such movement at all, let alone that there be so much grace in the performing of it.

'Hawkwood. I know that name . . .' The Duke chewed at his black beard as his mind made a rummage of his memory. 'Was there not a Sir John Hawkwood who led the Compagnia Bianca del Falco?' asked the Duke at length.

Oldcastle had heard of this Hawkwood in London but knew little of him save that he was an Englishman that had come to Italy some hundred or more years before and made a name for himself. When he had suggested to Hemminges their continued disguise he had proposed the name for himself. It had a ring to it that he rather liked, not least for the echo of his own.

'An ancestor, my lord,' decided Oldcastle, inventing the connection extempore and ignoring the slight but audible grind of Hemminges' jaw as he did so.

'And are you of the same profession?' demanded the Duke, a sudden eagerness in him.

'I am,' declared Oldcastle, without the slightest understanding of what he had admitted to. He cared not, for the answer he had given brought out a great smile from the Duke.

'This is good news to make an ill day better.'

The Duke rose from his chair and strode towards Oldcastle. A great bear of a man, he was near Oldcastle's height and the clap of his arm on Oldcastle's shoulder staggered him. 'It has been too long since we had a soldier in my court.'

Oldcastle drew himself a little taller now that he understood more clearly the part that he had taken for himself. A soldier, eh? Well he fancied himself of a martial spirit. The crunching of Hemminges' teeth would not dismay him from the role. The Duke's broad smile buried itself again in his black beard and his frown returned. 'How came a soldier to be robbed?'

Oldcastle told again the story that he and Hemminges had devised on the road from Venice. How they had set forth for England in good spirits and in the company of two squires and a wagon bearing their accoutrements. How they had been set upon by bandits in the forest to the north of Verona, their servants slain and they fled with only their lives. It was a tale to move the heart of the stoniest audience.

Of course, when Oldcastle had first proposed this play-acting to Hemminges it had been intended for the benefit of a simple innkeeper on the road from Venice to Verona. Hemminges had agreed to it only with the deepest reluctance, to prevent Oldcastle from continuing to shamble and pout as they walked along, scuffing his feet and sighing like a sack of wine that was being wrung for its last drops. Hemminges felt a desperation to make haste, to be free of Italy. The burden of the intelligence he held weighed him down and he would be free of it. He feared the secrets that the Signoria of Venice had entrusted to their false embassy. If the dead men that dangled from them did not already speak to their importance the scale of the pursuit roared it. Even in the few days' journey they had made from Venice they had heard constant rumour of papal agents searching for English spies and of the horrors being visited on those that were suspected of harbouring them. More than that, Hemminges wanted to be free of Venice and the remembrance of his friend William and of Isabella, ill, abandoned. Guilt at leaving them behind weighed on him almost as much as the intelligence did. He had vague plans to reach England, to send for William, or to beg aid of Sir Henry Carr's patron, Lord Hunsdon, as the price for the knowledge delivered. He must reach England, that was all to accomplish all else. Yet the more he pulled at Oldcastle to follow with speed, the more Oldcastle, like a stubborn ass, dug in his heels and groaned against the rigours of the journey. Even Hemminges had a limit. Worn down by worry he had relented at last. Now he cursed himself again for his lapses.

Oldcastle was too great an actor. His tale of the robbery had proved too moving for the innkeeper who had insisted, in the teeth of their refusal, that they must pass on the news of this knavish attack on a noble visitor to the Duke Leonardo. At least, thought Hemminges, they had made a rehearsal of the tale and, he noted, performance before nobility raised Oldcastle to the heights of his art again.

'Sure and there were a dozen of them if there was a man. Armed with bows with which they made a terrible slaughter. See here, here, how close I came to my own end.' Oldcastle approached a young lady of the court and gestured to a nasty cut upon his cheek, to which the young lady responded with a gratifying squeak of terror. The cut was one that Oldcastle had made himself while shaving the day before. In Venice he'd had no cause to groom himself, their host Salarino insisting that the dignity of his house required that the English Ambassador receive the service of a barber, and he'd lost the practice of it. In the woods, when Hemminges had spoken up behind him at an unexpected and inopportune moment his hand had slipped and the razor run too deep. He'd sworn then, terrible oaths against Hemminges, himself, the gods and the dullness of the blade. Now he swore again to the Duke, that the crusted line across his cheek marked the passage of an arrow's flight. He was gratified to hear the moan of the audience at his tale, transported by the terror of the thought of so close an encounter with death.

'These bandits plague us, base cowards all, striking at the innocent and the good.' The Duke's hand that gripped Oldcastle's arm clenched in anger at the idea of them, causing Oldcastle to grimace in pain as the fingers ground the muscles. 'It is my care and charge to see to the safety of travellers in my domain. I have failed in that charge to your distress, Sir Nicholas. You shall have welcome in my house until such time as you and I might mete out justice to these recreant dogs.'

Oldcastle made to speak, to beg only the comfort of a few nights' rest before they made for England, but the Duke had turned from him.

'And you?'

'Sir Nicholas' steward, his some-time lieutenant, and his dancing-master, John Russell is my name,' said Hemminges.

'A man of many parts, eh?' said the Duke to this answer. 'And an Englishman, as your master. Seen your share of fighting, have you?'

'I have, my lord.'

'Where?'

'Many places, my lord.'

The Duke looked Hemminges over and nodded. 'A man of few words, that I can respect. The Spartans were of your habit and dimension and for fighting men there were none to match them. Welcome to you also, John Russell. Yes welcome indeed, for I have in mind some small employ for you, dancing-master. If you be willing.'

Her father looked up and about the hall, searching for someone. Aemilia blushed crimson when he caught sight of her standing on the chair and she hastily climbed down. Her father's eye swept on to find his own steward and give orders for his new guests to be housed and clothed and fed. Aemilia thought it wise to depart; and if I am bold, her thinking continued, the arrival of these Englishmen might prove distraction enough to make a meeting with Valentine.

For you and I are past our dancing days

Her father found her again in the walled garden.

'Who was that I saw you with just now? Valentine?' demanded the Duke.

For a moment Aemilia considered throwing her cousin's continued wooing in her father's face. Then she remembered how Valentine had urged her not to.

'No, Father, no. A servant sent to fetch me water.'

Her father looked to where Valentine had fled and then wafted the question away with a hand.

'Daughter, this is John Russell, one of the Englishmen that you were so unseemly curious about.'

Aemilia curtsied and Hemminges bowed in answer. The Englishman looked some thirty or so years old, about Valentine's height, which was to say a little shorter than she, but built like a barn where Valentine was a dovecote. His square, handsome face was weather-worn and his hands had none of Valentine's soft delicacy. Oh Valentine, let your plans to win my father's favour be hastily drawn, she thought, at memory of his hands in hers.

'Master Russell is Sir Nicholas' dancing-master. I realise, Daughter, that I have neglected your gentler instruction. So, I have imposed on Sir Nicholas to lend me Master Russell's services for a while.'

Aemilia looked again at the Englishman, who did not seem built for the dance hall but rather for the wrestling ring.

'Where is your maid, Aemilia?' said her father, looking about with suspicion on his brow.

'Sent for water, Father, as I told you.'

'You should not walk unaccompanied, child. It is not seemly. I shall send your maid to you. Mark you stay in her chaste company henceforth. Master Russell, I leave you to the teaching of my daughter.'

The Duke turned and left them standing in the walled garden. Aemilia looked to Hemminges and he to her, each waiting for the other to speak and move matters on. It was Aemilia who broke the silence.

'What are we to learn?'

'As you wish, Lady Aemilia, the galliard, the pavane, the lavolta.'

'Let it be a galliard, Master Russell,' Aemilia spoke. She wanted to see this rock of a man jump and could not believe him capable of it, so anchored to the ground did he look. Hemminges bowed to her and stepping back began to dance. Aemilia noted, as others had before, the strange division between Hemminges' solidity and the grace with which he moved. He finished the measure with the cadence leap and posed. Aemilia clapped.

'I did you disservice, Master Russell. I had thought that my father sent you less to teach than to watch over me,' she said. 'You have more the look of a guard dog than a dancing-master.'

'Oh, I am both, Lady Aemilia. Your father expects that I shall keep you too busy to stray from the path of chastity, should your thoughts that way incline.'

Aemilia had thought to provoke Hemminges by the frankness of her talk but it was she that blushed to hear the Englishman answer so freely. Hemminges ignored it, clapped his hands and gestured.

'First position please, lady. The leg thus, the hands beginning here.'

And the young woman began to discover, as another youth had done some months before, that there was no schoolmaster so exact and so demanding as John Hemminges.

I have no way and therefore want no eyes

The Veneto

Marco Venier's men had poled William in a barge to the mainland and left him. A day he had walked since then, though he knew not where he had started nor in which direction he had travelled. He walked for want of better purpose and when dusk fell he sat beside the road, pulled his cloak about him and fell asleep.

Hunger woke him as dawn crept in. His joints, stiff and cold, muttered grudges to him as he brought himself to his feet. The day before he had walked without truly seeing. Now the rising sun showed him at the edge of a great wood. He put the sun to his back and trudged on into the forest.

His stomach admonished him for his want of care in the journey but he heeded it not. The sun hauled itself up ever higher, till it stood above the trees and on, till at last it was suspended over him. William looked up at it and thought of the hours that had passed as he made his weary way. Now we see how the world wags, he thought, hour and hour we ripe and ripe and hour and hour we rot and rot. The sun does not care for my passing or for Isabella's. What a deal of pain there has been and stemmed from so much pleasure, a bitter harvest. Was it better to have loved so deeply and so well or to have gentle but unmissed company?

A line from the song that Hemminges had sung so few weeks ago came unbidden to his mind: youth's a stuff will not endure. He longed to see his children again and feared to do so, wondering how they might find him changed. Would he still have love in him or had the wondrous and terrible days with Isabella taken all with their ending? Would it be better not to be than face what he had become?

'Hold there, ho!'

The quiet of the forest was broken by a shout. William looked about him. Having gazed at the sun a minute before now the canopy of the forest cast a double darkness about him and it was a moment before he made out figures emerging from the trees.

'Well met, fellow,' called one to William. 'Where are you going?'

William thought for a moment. 'Truly, sir, I know not.'

His answer was the cause of laughter among the dozen or so men now gathered about him.

'In truth, sir,' the man said, 'we care not. Though we do have a care for the content of your satchel.'

William reached absently down to his satchel and the movement of his hand was accompanied by the sound of the men drawing swords and baring cudgels.

'Gently, sir, your dagger is not needed this day.'

William looked down and saw that his hand in reaching for the satchel had strayed near the blade at his belt. He let his hand drop.

'You are bandits,' he said.

'No, sir, no,' cried the leader. William looked at him more closely and saw a goodly man of fair height, long, black hair tied back by a cord, a lustrous beard that curled about and a suit of buckram over his clothes. 'We are not bandits but bankers, sir,' the man went on, 'and make an audit of these woods and all that's in them. When our audit's done then we make a reckoning.'

He looked about, searching for sign of another ambush to add to their own. There was something in William's stillness that unnerved him. A man about to be robbed should have something of fear or anger or both in him. This figure had none.

'You are alone?' he asked. 'We were sure we heard you speak with another.'

'I spoke but to myself,' said William absently.

'Reckon the man's mad,' laughed another of the bandits.

'Reckon we'll have your satchel and all that's in it,' said a third man, short and with a cast in his eye. This one's voice and look was less polished than the leader's. His words carried less amusement and greater menace to them too.

'Manners, Luca,' chided their leader, watching William carefully, curiously.

'Damn your manners, Orlando,' answered Luca, 'let's be done with this and gone.'

Orlando sighed and shook his head.

'You see, friend? Hunger has made our company mutinous. We, who were already ill-tempered at the world's injustice. But our mood improves with charity. If you would be so kind as to give us your satchel, traveller?'

Without demur William reached up and unslung his satchel and held it out. Much good may it do these thieves. It was as empty of coin as his breast of joy.

'Look at that ring,' spoke up another of the robbers at the sight of gold on William's outstretched hand.

'That you may not have,' said William.

'Hah. Give me the damn ring,' growled Luca, stepping forward and grabbing the satchel from William. He slung it over his shoulder and reached out to grasp William's hand. William's arm was held stiff as an iron poker. Luca's own arm swung out and he struck William across the cheek.

'Give it here, man,' said Luca, 'before we cut it off your corpse.'

William let his arm grow limp and Luca pulled the hand to him and bent to pull the ring from his finger. William's sudden tug caught him unawares and he lost his balance and tripped forward. William slipped behind the stumbling man and pulled him close, drawing his dagger and pressing it to Luca's ribs.

'The ring you shall not have,' declared William. 'I say it, I swear it. If saying and swearing be not believed then try your luck with my dagger's point.'

A cry went up from the other bandits at the sudden change of fortune. One raised his bow to fire but Orlando held up his hand. He was looking at William with an appraising eye.

'That was a fast move, sir, but don't be a fool,' said Orlando. 'There's a dozen men about you will cut you down in a breath. Give us the ring, and then we will take our leave of you.'

'You cannot take from me anything I would more willingly give, except my life. Except my life.'

'Bold words and a rare man, to put so little value on long life,' said Orlando.

'I know not bold, and as for rare, I think my condition rare enough, to have loved not wisely but too well. For life, I value it as I value grief, which I would spare. This ring you shall not have while I breathe.'

'Christ Jesu, the man's distract, have a care, have a care,' squealed Luca, feeling the sharp point of the dagger piercing his clothes and pricking his flesh.

'He seemed to have wit enough when he took your back,' muttered Orlando. He signalled to two of his men to circle round behind William and then turned to look William over.

'This does not seem the moment to speak of love, friend.'

'Why not now?' answered William. 'There always seems another time, and another, until you find that time has wasted you.'

'What have you to grieve over, traveller?'

'One such as you might search the whole world for and never find her equal.'

'Jesus,' growled a bandit with a pocked face. 'Must we listen to this poetic prattle?'

'Hush, Zago,' admonished Orlando.

'Aye, shut your mouth, Zago,' hissed another bandit, a younger man who by his shared look was the brother of the bandit Luca, who squirmed with William's blade at his back. Luca stood as still as he might, his body bent in a sinuous and strained curve, held as far from the press of William's dagger as William's arm about his neck would allow.

Orlando held up a hand for quiet, his eyes watching his men circling behind William.

'She did not requite your love? This is common parlance, man. We've all been in such distress. Myself a dozen times. Even Zago here, and look at his face. That's no cause for murder. Let Luca go, give us the ring and we shall let you pass freely on, I swear it. To be unfortunate in love, come, sir, you know 'tis common.'

'Aye sir,' answered William. 'It is common.'

'Well then, why seems it so particular with you?' said Orlando.

'"Seems", sir? Nay it is. I know not "seems".'

To Orlando's shock, tears welled in William's eyes. 'She loved me well; oft requited me. We shared the story of our lives for a passing moment and then she died. I have never been so alone as to have once been in her company and now to lack it. This ring you shall not have while I live.'

Orlando looked at William's gaunt cheek and red-rimmed eyes. He took a deep breath.

'Here's a pretty pass. I'd not see Luca's throat cut for all Zago's urging. Nor does your story leave me all unmoved. Yet, I cannot be seen to be so lack-willed as to let a man defy me before my companions. And now I see my men are both before and behind you. What to do? What to do?' Orlando's voice turned hard. 'A shame to die for a trinket.'

William shrugged. 'I will not die alone.' He braced himself for the feel of arrows striking his back and it minded him of how Isabella in her anger had once struck at him with a blade, believing him to have betrayed her. On William's hand the gold and cornelian signet ring that Isabella had given him, with the lance with the quill's tip cut into its face, caught the noon sun and glittered. Orlando drew a sharp breath.

'What is your name, traveller?' he asked.

'What does it matter?'

'Call it courtesy,' said Orlando, moving to see the ring better.

'Adam,' answered William. 'Or so you should call me, for like Adam I am an exile from paradise and grieve its loss.'

'Truly name yourself,' said Orlando.

'Adam will serve,' answered William, ignoring Orlando's sharp tone.

Zago rolled his eyes and spat upon the ground. 'Are we to talk all morning? Kill him and be done,' he demanded. 'We've no need of an impatient fool like Luca.'

'Be damned, you hatch, you boil, you . . .' Luca trailed off to a whisper, quite overwrought by the terror of his position. 'Damn you, Zago.'

'Jesus spare us. Kill the god-damned poet,' said Zago and made to thrust his sword at William, who dug his blade into Luca's side and sent up a howl from the man.

'No!' Orlando's blade lashed out and knocked down Zago's own. 'No, impatient rascal!' He pulled his eyes from William's ring. 'That is a ring that speaks of service. Shall we say then that there be some service in exchange for the ring's keeping? What think you, Adam, to such a bargain?'

William nodded. What did it matter to him? What did any of it matter any more?

He's truly valiant that can wisely suffer

Verona

The Duke's palace offered many rooms and Sir Nicholas Hawkwood and his lieutenant, John Russell, had been offered ones that overlooked the road from Venice to Verona and the woods beyond. To these rooms Hemminges retired at the day's end. He eased off his boots and sat heavily upon the bed. His feet ached. A smile creased his face. That young daughter of the Duke was a proud one. She had taunted him for his ugly Italian and his standing in the court but since that first day she had not challenged his skill. Hers was a practical bent, Hemminges mused. If he was to be set over her then at least let her learn from him. Such seemed her thinking and, since it would have been Hemminges' own, he gave it the credit due to one who shared his disposition. She had pushed him so, teach her more, test her. For three days now he had done so. She sweated and moped but Aemilia would not rest. Then, when Hemminges feared for his own strength, she left him to tryst with Valentine.

Hemminges' smile departed. This Valentine he did not trust, still less admire. He could not find in the pale-faced figure, with his airs, his obscure or obvious sayings that he clearly thought the zenith of wit and good fooling, any hook on which Aemilia might hang her admiration. Hemminges shook his head. He need not reason at her love for Valentine overmuch. The young man doted on her and she, in turn, on him. That was enough for her that wanted for soft things in this hard Duke's court.

He eased off his other boot and thought of his conversation with Aemilia that morning. She had been set to race away from his lesson but he had caught her at the gate.

'My lady, a little caution will go a long way.'

She had shook her head as if to deny his meaning but then stopped and smiled at him. 'Master Russell, you speak to me of caution when all I hear from my father are tales of the adventures you and Sir Nicholas have endured, the places seen, the foes overwhelmed.'

'I would not trust all that men say and not one word that comes from Sir Nicholas' mouth.'

'Is't dutiful to say so?' said Aemilia with a shocked smile.

'Maybe not, but true nonetheless.'

'I think you are too modest a man, Master Russell, and too good a man too, to let falsehoods colour the commerce of your business at my father's court. I dare, you dare, both for the thrill of what may be.'

'It is not seemly for a woman—'

'"Seemly", there's a word that's used like a hobble to curb a woman's will. It seems 'tis seemly only that I do what others will of me.'

Hemminges held up his hands at the flare of rage in her eyes.

'If you are caught, Lady Aemilia, it will not be you alone that suffers.'

Aemilia's hand upon the gate paused in the turning of the handle. 'All's well that ends well,' she said but did not let her eyes meet his.

The handle turned and Hemminges called to her back that they would resume their lesson at noon. That afternoon neither had spoken again of their conversation but Hemminges had wondered at its meaning as he watched Aemilia dance.

Now, in his room, having left Oldcastle in carouse with the Duke after dinner, Hemminges strode to the ewer and poured cold water over his hands into the basin and splashed his face clear of the sweat-seamed dust of the day and the fire's soot of the evening. He wondered at himself that he had not told the Duke of his daughter's conference with Valentine. Of course, it served him to stay silent lest the Duke know how little guard of her virtue he made in the face of her stern will. The Duke's anger at him, at Oldcastle, at Aemilia and Valentine, that he feared to think on. For certain, he did not wish Aemilia to face her father's wrath. Pray she is right, and that a successful ending mitigates all sins along the way.

He roused the fire in the grate and threw another log upon it. The room was cold and Hemminges fell back on his bed and pulled the blanket over him and waited for the fire to bite, thinking of the journey to come and the need to return to the road. A long, hard journey before them. A soft bed, a fire, food at hand, these were not to be counted upon on the journey to come. Nor the company of clever women like Lady Aemilia.

Hemminges woke to the sound of the handle of his door rattling and muttered imprecations against the door's makers from without. He was from his bed in the instant and moving to his baldric. Then the door shuddered to the sound of a blow and clapped open to crack and bang again as it swung hard into the wall behind. A great silhouette loomed in the frame of the door, lit from behind by the cast of the moon.

'Jesu, there's a noise,' whispered Oldcastle. 'Still, can't be helped. You're awake, John?'

'If there's a man asleep after that row I salute him as the only greater sot living than you,' answered Hemminges, thrusting his sword back in its scabbard and stamping his way back to his bed.

'Why so angry, John? Why so angry?'

'What o'clock is it?'

'I think it' – Oldcastle paused to suppress a belch – 'eleven.'

'It is past midnight, Nick,' said Hemminges from a nest of blankets.

'Then up, John, up,' cried Oldcastle, hauling at his friend's bedding. 'For truly the wise man is said to rise early.'

Oldcastle succeeded in dragging a blanket from Hemminges' bed and, wrapping himself in it in the style of a Roman emperor, stalked to a seat by the window.

'Have you wine?'

'You have had more than enough.'

'True,' sighed Oldcastle. 'True. By the sweet Lord, the Duke can drink. I may have met my match. Of course I acquit myself in the contest because I had to stay sober enough to speak of the great Sir Nicholas Hawkwood and his adventures. My, but that man has lived.'

'Who?'

'Sir Nicholas Hawkwood, of course, the part I play. I have spoken to the Duke of deadly chances, of moving accidents by flood and field, of hair-breadth escapes in the deadly breach. The more I spoke, the more the Duke loved me for it.'

Hemminges propped his back up against the wall behind the bed.

'You realise that I am supposed to have been this Hawkwood's bosom companion?'

'I do, I do. Rest assured I kept you close in my adventures. The brave and loyal John Russell never strayed far from Sir Nicholas, no matter how close the battle came or how deadly the foe.'

'I meant that if the Duke now asks me of these adventures, what answer shall I give him? I who was not there when you invented them?'

Oldcastle made no reply. He scratched deep within his ear. 'I hadn't thought of that.'

'This whole diversion is a lesson in lack of thought, Nick. If you weren't so damn keen on comfort we might have slipped on quietly. God above, why are we still here? We must be away before these agents of the Pope are upon us.' Hemminges put his head in his hands. 'Yet you must play the lord. You must have wine, warmth and feathered beds and I am too weak a man to drive you on. I tell you, we shall have cold comfort of it if the Duke discover our deception and think a bed of burrs small burden to our rest when set beside hot pincers and the rack.'

'Why speak to fright me, John?' Oldcastle chided. 'No danger of that. Why the Duke and I are closer than brothers of the same birthing and he has given you charge of his only true care, his daughter Aemilia.'

'There lies trouble in its infancy.'

'The girl cannot dance?'

'Not so. Rather she can dance too well and is in a constant whirl of evasions. Thrice in two days have I caught her on her way to a tryst with that Valentine. She is bold, aye, bold.'

'*Oh ho*. Young love.'

'I never knew youth to want for love nor idiocy.'

'Oh, when I speak of love, I do not speak of young Valentine and Aemilia but of young John Russell and Aemilia,' said Oldcastle with a knowing touch to his nose.

'What?'

'What?'

'Truly you are drunker than I thought you, Oldcastle.'

'Of course, quite blind with drink. Yet I hear well enough, that tone of admiration in your voice.'

'A child,' said Hemminges.

'A woman of twenty summers,' answered Oldcastle, 'and comely.'

'Too tall.'

'For you, yes, but not for beauty.'

'A noblewoman, far beyond my reach,' said Hemminges.

'There's confirmation of it,' crowed Oldcastle, 'for what man thinks of his marriage prospects with a woman that he does not desire?'

'I admire her spirit,' said Hemminges, 'no more. For myself and my desires, I desire only to be free of this place before the foolishness now budding comes to fruit. That same spirit I admire will lead her into trouble ere long and we with her.'

'How so?'

'I am set to guard her, am I not? When she strays I will be blamed. We must go on to England, Nick.'

'Would it were so simple, John.'

Oldcastle bent forward and clutched at the hair fraying on his pate. 'Alas, alas the day I was born so great an actor,' he moaned.

He looked up through his brows at Hemminges. 'That we must go? You have my full agreement. But, woe, woe! The Duke is so much taken by my martial prowess, as I have given it over in my speech with him that I am a sword of many battles' honing, and so much filled the part that he sees in me a second Charlemain. Well, to cut a long tale short, the Duke insists I take his yeomen to flush out the bandits that infest these parts.'

Hemminges gave out a groan of his own. His fury with Oldcastle was nothing compared to the fury he felt at himself. Rue the day that ever I allowed Nicholas Oldcastle to lure me to another of his schemes. I should rather have dragged him by his ear past Verona and shown him a bed of stones and scorpions.

'Refuse the commission,' said Hemminges.

'Of course, of course,' said Oldcastle, 'but how, without causing offence?' He paused and danced his fingers across the table while pursing his lips. The fingers stopped and he tapped them and looked to Hemminges. 'Also, he has offered me, Sir Nicholas Hawkwood I should say, quite a deal of gold for the work.'

Hemminges groaned. 'God above, Oldcastle. Now we hear your real reason for going along with this foolishness. What good is gold to a dead man? Oldcastle, you know nothing of war.'

'Nonsense. Nothing to it. Good speech to rouse their spirits, I have plenty of those, then point your men at the enemy and loose 'em.'

'You're a fool, Oldcastle.' Hemminges rubbed his temples. 'We must be gone before Aemilia's fancies find her out, before the Pope's men chase us down from Venice to Verona, and yet, here you have bound us in place.'

'It is a tangled knot, no question of it.' Oldcastle let forth a vast sigh. 'Would that Will were here. He'd have a plan for us.'

'Jesu, aye.' Hemminges shook his head. 'Scarce a week out of his company and already here we are wishing him with us again.'

'Are you sure you have no wine?' asked Oldcastle, casting his gaze about.

Hemminges got up from his bed and snatched the blanket from Oldcastle with one hand while the other, gripping painfully on the old man's arm, guided him to his bed chamber and pushed him to his bed. He stamped back to his own and pulled the blanket over him.

'We leave one trap in Venice only to place ourselves in another,' Hemminges muttered to the wall. 'Which will find us out first, the Pope, the Duke or Aemilia?'

He may not, as unvalued persons do, carve for himself

I need more time, thought Aemilia. My father sets no date for this wedding but it cannot be long coming. How am I to persuade him from the match? How prove to him that Valentine is worthier than he gives him credit?

She hurried through the palace to the courtyard near the chapel where for the last three days she had taken lessons with the English dancing-master, Master Russell. The hour had not yet struck for that day's lesson to begin but she thought that, coming early, she might be released from it sooner, and then in the minutes bought by this she and Valentine might meet and plan. At the corner, where the corridor opened out on to the courtyard, she pulled up short. As she hoped, Master Russell was already there. He was alone. He did not dance but instead practised with a sword. Aemilia pulled herself into the shadow and watched him lunging, twisting, moving the heavy blade in tight patterns, the sword moving either too fast for sight or stopping as if caught by an invisible wall. As with his dancing his movements showed a grace, a subtlety, that his bulk did not augur. Aemilia did not know what he did precisely, but she knew she watched a master at his work.

He sweated with his efforts and, abruptly, at his practice's end, threw down his sword and strode to the far end of the courtyard, pulled off his shirt and dipped his head in a rain barrel to chase the sweat from him. Aemilia felt a thrill pass through her at this unexpected sight. Master Russell was very different to Valentine, a thing of thews and sinew, strong and solid. His broad back and shoulders coursed with muscle, here and there the brown skin was puckered by a line of pink and white that spoke of an old scar. Aemilia suddenly felt her thoughts disloyal to Valentine. She stepped from her hiding place.

'Master Russell, are you ready?' she called, thinking to discomfort him. There was a part of her that thought in his discomfort there would be distraction from her own.

The dancing-master turned at her call. Aemilia had a mocking smile upon her lips but neither that smile nor the sudden arrival of his pupil, alone and unchaperoned while he stood naked to the waist, showed itself in him by any blenching. He dried himself with his old shirt and strode to where a fresh one lay waiting and pulled it on.

'You're early,' he said when he was dressed again. The fresh shirt flung over his still damp torso clung to his body. He pushed his wet hair back from his head.

'Lady Aemilia,' he said, calling her back from her reverie. 'You're early. To some purpose? Where is your maid?'

Aemilia stilled her thoughts. 'I'm eager for our lessons, Master Russell. Though I see now that you might more profitably teach me to fence than to dance.'

'The one you will do often, the other I think never at all.'

Aemilia bristled. 'You think me too weak to hold a sword?'

'I think there's little profit in practising that which one will never do,' answered Hemminges.

The man presumed too much.

'What do you know what I will do? You are a prophet as well as a dancer?' demanded Aemilia.

He walked across to where his sword lay. His foot slipped beneath the blade and with a casual flick he tossed it up into his hand. He walked back to Aemilia.

'Take up the fourth position of the galliard as we have practised it,' he said.

Aemilia made to protest this attempt to divert her back to their dancing lesson but Hemminges simply imitated the pose in answer to her sour look. Reluctantly she set her feet and raised her arms out to the side. Hemminges reached out and grasped her forearm. Aemilia looked at him in astonishment: bar Valentine's stolen moments none had touched her so intimately since she was a child. His hands were callused and his grip was strong.

'Open,' he said.

It took her a moment to understand what he wanted and when she did, he put the sword hilt in her upturned hand. She saw his game at once.

Well, she would show him. Her muscles tensed against the blade's weight. He let go the sword and its point wobbled but she held it out, she steadied it. Hemminges stepped back. Aemilia returned his gaze. She would not fail. A minute passed and the tip of the blade that had fluttered an inch now bowed down and flicked up a foot or more with each beat of her heart. She ground her teeth and her arm burned with the effort. Hemminges walked behind her, she felt his hands on her shoulders.

'Less with the arm's strength, more with the back. Here.' His hands ran down her back to her waist. 'Nor can you hold the weight by tensing of the arm alone. Your body will quickly tire, the sinews tightening, the blood does not flow and the strength fails. Breathe, let the other arm balance you and feel your arm light.'

He stepped aside again, oblivious of her flush of heat at his touch. The sword straightened a moment longer at his instruction but another minute passing, Aemilia could no longer hold it still. Hemminges nodded and Aemilia waited for the mocking comment that would follow. She cursed her own weakness. No comment came. Hemminges made an appraising look and walked over to the courtyard wall where a climbing plant was supported by a cane. He snatched the cane free and walked back to Aemilia.

'Up, up,' he gestured, catching her sword with the cane's tip and raising it. Aemilia lifted it again. Hemminges came on guard.

'Thrust,' he commanded. Aemilia held the sword out toward him. Hemminges did not move as the sword's point came at him, missing him by a foot to the left.

'No, please, with intent, at the heart,' he replied in answer to her feeble effort. Very well, she thought, on his head be it. She pulled her arm back and thrust straight at his chest.

He seemed to move so very little, a shuffle to the side, but as he moved the cane whipped out and struck her blade with a horrid crack and a shock of pain ran up her wrist. The sword fell to the ground.

'Up, up,' he pointed to the sword. She bent and picked it up and held it out before her again; its weight seemed to have grown tenfold since she first held it but Hemminges made no acknowledgement of the sweat that beaded her brow.

'You pull back your arm before the thrust. Your enemy witnesses this prologue, anticipates the thrust that follows and has moved from out the way of harm. Instead, the thrust comes so, direct . . .' He demonstrated with the cane, one moment still, the next the cane at full extension and his whole body's weight behind it. 'Now you.'

Aemilia thrust again, and again Hemminges no longer stood where her thrust had gone, though the movement seemed so small by which he made evasion that she could scarce believe it.

'Better,' he said. He made a series of poses. 'This is the guard, here the first position, here the second position of the hand.'

He made her move her hand across her body, the point of the sword shifting while her hand moved very little. Each time he took her arm and moved it Aemilia was conscious of his closeness, of the strength of the rough hands that held her. That he seemed so uncaring of her closeness was, at the same time, provoking. He turned her waist to angle her body and she felt his chest against her back. He stepped back, took up the cane again and stood before her.

'Defend yourself,' he said. His cane came forward and she moved her hand as she'd been shown, pushing his cane's thrust aside.

'Again,' he said. 'Smaller, smaller movements.'

Aemilia began to enjoy herself. His cane thrust out and she batted it aside. 'No, smaller,' came his instruction. 'Smaller, smaller.' Still the cane thrust out and she moved the sword to push it aside. 'List to me, lady, keep the movements small.'

In frustration at his carping Aemilia banged the next thrust of his cane aside. A further thrust came and she made to meet it but the cane flickered from its path and her sword not meeting the expected blow, her arm came full across her body, the cane flicked down across her hand and with a howl she dropped the sword. The cane thrust out and struck her true in the stomach, winding her, then it whirled about and caught her across the back of the legs, making her cry out again.

'How dare you!'

'What good has your anger done you?' answered Hemminges. His own countenance was calm.

'You've hurt me.' Her hand was hot with pain. The unmoved figure that stood before her provoked her by its very want of emotion.

'I have. You think swordplay is about aught else? There is but one aim – I hurt you but am not hurt in my turn. Your anger is nothing to that purpose. Frustration that I correct you is nothing to that purpose. Your noble state, your woman's weeds, nothing to that purpose. When you sought to learn, then I would teach. When you let frustration show, then I reminded you of that which you would learn – to wound another, to compass by your skill another's injury or death.'

'You're a cruel man, Master Russell,' said Aemilia in a small voice, her shock at his blows departing, leaving only the pain behind.

'Is it cruel to give you what you sought? To take you at your word? You chided me for thinking you weak. You asked to learn the sword and I have shown you what it takes to learn it. Should I be so cruel as to leave you thinking it easy? A game?'

'I did not think it a game.'

'Your swordplay is a serious business?' Hemminges said, and in his scornful tone Aemilia realised that he had taken her demand for teaching as a mockery of him. It made her angry that he could not see why she might wish to wield a sword.

'Why not? Why might I not be serious in my intent?' To her fury her eyes were pricked with tears of frustration. Would no one understand her as she wished to be understood?

'You are a noble lady, not a soldier,' answered Hemminges. His tone had softened at the misting of her eyes.

'I would I were a soldier,' said Aemilia. 'Then might I make my own fortune.'

Emotion took her. Tears, unbidden but unstoppable, came from her then as she thought of how soon she would be married to a man of her father's choosing and how little choice she would be given in what was to follow. She fought to bring herself back under control.

The dancing-master said nothing. He bent and picked up his sword and turned away to let her have her privacy. He put the sword back in its baldric and the cane back in the earth and returned to her.

'Lady, speak to your father,' he said. 'None but he can help you.'

Aemilia shook her head, her throat too thick with tears to make speech.

'I have seen him seek your counsel and follow it,' Hemminges said. 'Why would he not listen to you in this?'

'Why?' said Aemilia, anger giving her strength to speak through her shameful tears before this man. 'I would I knew. I would I knew. He speaks to me of rule and command but offers me none.' She wiped her eyes. 'He has himself told me of Caterina Sforza. You have heard of her?'

Hemminges shook his head.

'A noblewoman, married to the nephew of the last Pope Sixtus, the fourth of that name. Why do you laugh?'

Hemminges shook his head again. 'Nothing, lady, I am just struck by how it is a lesson to be learned: be wary of the wife of the nephew of a pope. Go on, I pray you.'

Aemilia frowned at his strange answer and brushed her cheek of tears before she continued. She doubted Master Russell cared to hear about the Lady of Forli but it calmed her to speak and the thought of Caterina Sforza steeled her. 'Her husband's uncle, the Pope, died and chaos followed. Her husband's palace in Rome was attacked, destroyed. Mobs ran riot through the city, murder abounded. Caterina was with child but she was not daunted. She took her husband's men and she herself seized the Castel Sant'Angelo. She did not yield it until the Cardinals had given her husband the city of Forli to rule and eight thousand ducats. Then when her husband was murdered, she ruled Forli till her son came of age.'

'A mighty woman.'

'Mighty whatever her sex, Master Russell,' said Aemilia fiercely. 'After she fought the Venetians to a standstill they named her the Tiger. Cesare Borgia so feared her command that he offered ten thousand ducats for her capture. When Cesare's army at last stormed her fortress she fought and was captured with a sword in each hand.'

Hemminges nodded. 'She won back Forli?'

'No. She died in exile.'

'Surrounded by those she loved?'

'Alone. Her first two husbands were murdered. Her third died in her arms.'

'Her life was not a happy one, then,' said Hemminges.

'That I do not know,' answered Aemilia. 'But I do know it was her own.'

She curtsied. 'Forgive me, Master Russell. I have quite lost the mood for dancing.'

She did not wait on his reply but turned and left.

Behind her, Hemminges unbent from his bow and watched her depart, her head held high despite a slight limp in her leg. He shook his head and wondered at his own foolishness, to have struck the daughter of the Duke, to have put a sword in her hand. He hit his fist into his thigh. Oldcastle's stupidity in trapping them here had set him in a fretful mood. Aye and faith, but he was provoked. He sighed. Maybe Oldcastle is not the most foolish among us. Maybe he sees more clearly than I do. With that thought he strode back to the water barrel, pulled off his shirt and dunked his head in the frosty water until the cold brought him his good sense back.

O'erstep not the modesty of nature

Valentine allowed a moment after he finished his recitation, holding himself very still, for Aemilia to admire his pose. He had practised it in front of the mill pond and seen in its reflection a rather striking figure, the hand just so, the face tilted thus, the mane of the hair gathered, *la!* The perfect complement to the words of his poem.

'Beautiful, Valentine. It is for me?'

'As are all things, Aemilia, for you are my muse.'

In truth, he sometimes found Aemilia a little frightening. She had a fretful spirit that flared and boiled with unseen heat and he had trouble following her moods. She had come to him in such a mood this day, a fever in her blood brought on by, the Lord alone knew. To his good fortune then that he did not lack imagination, for he had fixed on that spirit as inspiration for his poem.

Besides, beggars could not be choosers and he was a beggar. He cursed again his family, his father most especially, wastrels that had so left him without estate. He had resented being sent to live with his father's second cousin, the Duke. His status as an object of charity had been so clear in the sneering contempt he saw on the faces of all, all, at the Duke's court. Yet his choices had been no choice at all: cur of charity or holy orders in the Church. At least though, there had been his cousin Aemilia at the court, a little tall, a little dark for fashion, but with the most distracting eyes, dark opals, of a black so deep her eyes seemed like a night sky through which meteors flashed. Oh, that was good, he should make use of that line in his next poem. Those stars looked into his eyes now.

'Oh, Valentine, would that we could be together. When will you speak?'

Valentine could not hide a small shudder of fear at the thought of confronting the Duke with his wooing of his only daughter. He disguised it with an embrace, burying his face into Aemilia's neck and breathing in her rosewater scent. He knew he brought nothing to a marriage, save that which women wanted, a fair face, a goodly wit, fine hair. Nothing, in short, to give the Duke any will to let them marry. Yet Aemilia, stubborn

Aemilia, would not be moved by his warnings that the quest was a hopeless one. Aemilia insisted that love and filial piety made its demands and that, before any talk of flight and of secret marriage be entertained, Valentine must first see if lawful permit might be granted.

'And if your father banish me?'

'Then we shall heed the lessons of your verses and I shall join you in exile, beloved Valentine, and we shall live together in the woods as innocents do.'

Valentine closed his eyes and sighed. He might speak in a poem of the freedom of the outlaws but the life of the innocent in the woods sounded uncomfortably close to the woollen shirts, simple food and hard beds that the Church offered.

'Then, beloved, I shall summon up my courage and my art to make persuasion of my love to your father. I pray I do not fail you.'

'Oh best of men,' cried Aemilia, clutching up his hand. 'Fail me? Never. If my father consents we shall be married. Refuses, we shall be happy exiles.'

Valentine rose and kissed her hand.

'I go, your Lancelot, to win this hand or die in the attempt.'

He turned quickly and allowed his hair to fly out and flaunt itself as he did so. First to my chambers, he thought; this doublet and hose are all well enough for wooing but something with a more martial air is needed before I front the Duke. God above, let him be in good spirits. After lunch will be best.

'You should be more discreet,' said Hemminges.

Aemilia gave a cry of fright and struck him on the shoulder. It was like hitting a locked door. A shock of pain ran up her wrist. She stumbled back and looked about her to see if anyone besides the English dancing-master were about, but saw no one save him. He was dressed in a thick coat against the chill of morning and dark shadows beneath his eyes spoke of a sleepless night. She drew her own cloak tighter about her.

'You scared me.'

'I see that,' said Hemminges. 'You grow too bold. You did not think to see who was about before you left off your meeting with Valentine.'

'You were spying on me?' Aemilia said, drawing herself up to use her height to its full advantage.

'I was,' said Hemminges.

Aemilia saw that he answered without shame, and anger grew in her.

'Who do you think you are, Master Dancer, to spy on a duke's daughter?'

'Do you think a duke's daughter so should defy her father, so risk her own honour, as to meet secretly with a young man?'

Aemilia grew angrier still. 'What do you know of it? I dare do all that might become a duke's daughter. So does Valentine. He will today ask for my hand.'

'I wish him good fortune,' said Hemminges. 'And you better.'

He turned away but halted when Aemilia called after him.

'What does that mean?'

'What?'

'What better fortune could I have than marriage to Valentine?'

'A young man that woos without permission? Suborns a daughter in her father's house?'

'Knave. What hope of licence can Valentine have with my father, when he has no lands and no fortune?'

'In saying so, you have answered your own question. As I say, I wish you better fortune.'

'He loves me, Englishman, and there is no better fortune in this world than to be loved.'

'I know many that would deny it so.'

'To them go and offer your advice. It is not looked for here. Yours is a counsel of despair.'

'As honest counsel often is.'

'What do you care that you offer me counsel?'

Hemminges made no reply. The sinews of his jaw could be seen to tighten and release but he said nothing and she would be damned before she spoke again. How dare he presume to counsel her? A foolish thought crossed her mind in answer, that he was envious of Valentine, but she dismissed the vanity of it. Their glowering battle of hard stares was interrupted by commotion from the palace. Hemminges called out to a servant hurrying past for the cause.

'The papal emissary is come again.'

Hemminges cursed under his breath and turned back to Aemilia but she was gone. He hurried on to the hall of the palace. Of Aemilia, the Duke and the Pope, it seemed that it would not be one or other but all at once that brought about his doom.

To seek new friends and stranger companies

The Veneto

William stared up at the canopy of the forest. Three days he'd been among the outlaws now. He was numb, but not from cold alone. A voice called his gaze downwards.

'What's your name, fellow?'

A dark-haired man about William's age, most notable in his ugliness for the wild brow smeared in a single line across his head, sat down on a fallen log near William.

'Forget it,' said Luca, his bad eye squinting at William. 'You'll get no answer from him. He sits and mopes and stares all the long day. As much conversation in him as a hog.'

'Smells like one too,' said Zago from where he squatted by the fire, stirring the pot that hung over it.

'Luca, Zago, Adam, and that there is my brother Tommasso,' said Luca, pointing to each as he sat himself down by the fire to await Zago's declaration that the meal was ready. The men sat in a small clearing that served as Orlando's camp. A stream ran along the bottom and canvas shrouds were strung in the trees, offering poor shelter against the winds and weather of the first days of March.

'Ludovico,' nodded the new arrival in answered introduction.

'What's your story then?' asked Luca.

'Same as yours, I'll warrant,' answered Ludovico. 'Though I'm from Ferrara, south of here. My master turned me off the land when he could not meet these taxations of the new Pope. What living could I earn? What food save that which I would take? Yet that selfsame Pope has driven all away with the sword and the executioner's axe.'

Luca nodded. 'These are hard times that have so many stories such as yours in them. Mine and my brother's would dull the ear in repetition of your own.'

'Mine also,' sniffed Zago at the pot.

'And yours?' asked Ludovico of Will.

'His is a story of love lost and we must not press it from him until the moment ripe,' said Orlando coming up from behind. 'Here there are many stories.' He pointed to Luca with a grin. 'Luca here was dropped on his head as a child and has wandered these woods ever since. He must thank heaven that his brother cares for him like a shepherd with a lamb, though he the younger. Petro here' – he gestured to a man in a filthy habit who was picking at his nails – 'is a priest, or was until he picked a fight with his abbot. Zago here was cook to the Bishop of Mantua, or was it his mistress you cooked for? How is our feast, Zago?'

A mongrel dog had run up with Orlando and now nosed its way about the pot until Zago lifted the ladle as if to strike it. The dog twisted away and William saw that it had only three good legs; the fourth trailed weakly behind it and gave it a strange sideways gait.

'Scant pickings, Orlando, we must fill the pot with better hunting or find some target to aim at for our thieving. Of late, all you have done is add numbers to the mouths we must feed,' answered Zago, and then nodded to Ludovico. 'No offence.'

Ludovico shrugged his shoulders. 'I'll show my worth.'

'Oh, you shall,' smiled Orlando. 'I'm come to tell you that, if Zago's cooking will hold, we might profitably head to the road now and surprise a merchant and his two fat asses.'

Zago was on his feet before Orlando had finished. 'There's the food and nourishment for men such as we. Up, up.' He went about, kicking first at Luca then at Will and then the rest to rouse them at the name of action.

'That is the spirit I so admire, Zago,' said Orlando. 'You are the very devil for thieving.'

The dozen men gathered up such meagre store of weapons as they had and Zago tamped the fire beneath the pot and covered it. When they were ready Orlando pointed the way and they set off. As he passed, Orlando pulled Luca aside.

'Watch Ludovico and Adam, eh? These are new men and yet to be given our full trust. Adam have a special care with.'

Luca nodded and walked on.

Here comes the holy legate of the Pope

Verona

Hemminges reached the hall and squeezed between the gathered courtiers to find Oldcastle standing in the shadow of a pillar, taking as much care as his bulk would allow not to be seen. Hemminges stood next to him, better able to see the scene. The Duke was sat at his great chair, as he had been when Oldcastle and Hemminges had first come to the court. Before him stood a man in priestly raiment, flanked by two armed men. The Duke's own guards stood alert beside him and even if he had not seen the way their hands shifted on the shafts of their halberds, Hemminges would have known the mood uneasy. The Duke's brow, never smooth, was creased deeper than a river's valley and he chewed at his beard as the priest before him spoke his request for lodging for himself and for his men.

The papal emissary was not a figure that Hemminges or Oldcastle recognised. A relief, for Hemminges' greatest fear had been to see Monsignor Cesare Costa or one of his companions gathered in the hall, ready to attaint them. The priest that stood before the Duke was a tall man, thin, and drawn in the face. The most noticeable aspect of him was his hands, which fluttered in ceaseless twitching motion at the end of his arms, arms that hung like dead-weights by his side. The whole effect was like watching two tethered birds struggling to escape. His voice was shrill as a bird's too, but that was not its most noticeable feature.

'The man's English, I'll swear it,' whispered Oldcastle to Hemminges.

Hemminges made no answer, though he thought Oldcastle right and remembered Faustina's rumours of an English priest and of his cruelty. He wanted to hear what was being said.

'We did not look to see you returned so soon, Father Thornhill,' said the Duke. 'Your last visit was the cause of strife. I have sent complaint to Rome.'

Thornhill shrugged. 'I have received no censure from His Holiness. All that I do, I do by his command and to the greater glory of God and the Church.'

'Why are you now returned?'

'Events, my lord, have driven me to return to your court with an unseemly haste,' he said.

'Events?'

'Events, my lord,' repeated Thornhill, unheedful of his offence. 'We will not trouble your lordship a moment more than we must.'

'Would that you did not trouble me at all,' said the Duke.

'My lord, how can an emissary of His Holiness be aught but succour to you?'

Had Oldcastle said these words then Hemminges would have thought the savage humour of his question clear, but in this reedy fellow's mouth the words carried no jesting at all.

'What priest travels with ten men-at-arms?' grumbled the Duke. 'And all wanting lodging, food and provender. Has the Pope such abundance of soldiers that every priest has so many guards about him?'

'I have but nine men, my lord, and I would they were not needed. Alas, there is such a deal of outlawry here about that it was thought prudent to provide an escort. The safe passage of travellers in these parts is your responsibility is it not, my lord? Then I regret I must inform you, even in our coming here we have lost one of our own to those outlaws. We were ten, we are now nine. I thank the good Lord above we are not less.'

'You were attacked?'

'An ambuscade upon the road to the north-west of the city, my lord, where it passes through the great wood. We had not thought that danger would lie so close to your lordship's lodging.'

The Duke's face had taken on an angry red colour as Father Thornhill spoke. 'I know my duties, priest. I have commissioned a noted knight, Sir Nicholas Hawkwood, to clear the woods of this scourge of robbers.'

'Oh Jesu,' muttered Hemminges to this declaration. The priest's head had come up at the English name and, still birdlike, he peered about the hall.

The Duke went on: 'A scourge of bandits, I add, that came upon us when they were driven from His Holiness's lands to mine.'

Father Thornhill briefly turned his attention back to the Duke to answer the implicit charge.

'Thieves such as these, they have no welcome in His Holiness's lands. It is true he beat out those that would abuse his laws and God's, my lord. It is not His Holiness's fault that the anvil was doting when he struck the hammer.'

The sound of shuffling feet made clear that it was not Hemminges alone that heard the offence in the priest's words. The man's confidence, his arrogance, was astounding. The Duke's hand upon his chair's arm had turned knuckle white. Thornhill noticed none of it, or noticing, did not deign to acknowledge it. Again he was looking about.

'You have commissioned an English knight to rid you of the outlaws? I have not heard the name Hawkwood before. Where is he?'

Oldcastle pulled himself deeper into the shadow of the pillar.

'I know not,' growled the Duke.

'He came as one of three? From Venice? Going where?'

'Sir Nicholas, and his lieutenant, Master Russell, have long been in Italy and I do not question them their comings and goings. They are not my prisoners that I may know their place of keeping, but my guests, and wander freely. Nor do I stand here to be questioned by you.'

'A regrettable lack of curiosity,' muttered the priest.

'What did you say?' said the Duke.

'And may we share in your generous welcome, my lord?' Thornhill asked.

The Duke leaned forward in his chair.

'Have a care, priest. These are not His Holiness's lands. Caution that your mouth does not overstep the limit of my patience. You shall have lodging, as I honour the Church. Complete your business and be gone.'

Thornhill bowed and, taking the Duke's words for dismissal, turned and left with the Duke's steward hurrying after to arrange the promised beds.

'Christ,' muttered Oldcastle to Hemminges. 'This bodes ill. What does the priest want?'

'You saw how his head came up at mention of Sir Nicholas? His asking if we came as one of three? It is past question these men are after us. It may be they do not yet have William. He must have fled Venice too.'

'Thank God,' whispered Oldcastle. 'Then is Isabella recovered, for William would not have left her while she was still unwell.'

Hemminges nodded. The urgency of their departure was upon them. The interest of this Thornhill, the way that the Pope's agents pursued them, all spoke to the value and the danger of the intelligence they held. It must be taken to England and yet in this public pronouncement of Sir Nicholas' commission against the bandits, they were shackled more tightly to that task. Again Hemminges wished that William were here and that they might have his crooked mind to call on to puzzle them out of this problem. Though had he been, sure, the priest and his men would have harkened to the three Englishmen for what they were. Better for all, and better for William, that they were separated.

Of breaches, ambuscados, Spanish blades

The Veneto

A cold drizzle fell through the leaves, not hard but enough to cause the men to shiver. Orlando hushed them as they approached the road. He hid them behind a wall of trees from where they could see a way along it; north, the road bent away down into a valley, south, it went straight on into the woods. The men crouched to wait, the first thrill of impending action and haste to the chase replaced by the dullness of the vigil.

William huddled with the others behind the trees. Looking up he saw their branches like bones, too thin and bare to conceal the unloving sky. Truly is the summer gone, he thought, and I do wonder if it will come again. If it does, it will not be such as I have held in my hands and marvelled at. I am a fool, no summer lasts. Its tenure passed, its heat declines and all is turned to greyness by nature's course untrimmed.

A crack of branches on the ground behind them broke off his melancholy thought and announced the arrival of another of their band who had scouted the merchant on the road and came to herald that merchant's close arrival.

Orlando called out in a carrying whisper, 'Listen, gentlemen, as it was before, wait for my command and then fall on them as one. Brook no abuse, yet do not look to give violence. That is not needless mercy on our part but heedful sense: let those that will, surrender. Hush now, he's upon us.'

Round the bend in the road ahead rising from the valley, some quarter-mile distant, could be seen a merchant on his palfrey, behind him two others on ponies and a small chain of asses, laden with goods.

'Luck at last,' whispered Luca beside Will. 'Luck at last.'

Luca turned to his brother. 'Now, remember, Tommasso, hold back. Let more experienced men take the lead. I'll not have your first fight be your last.'

Tommasso nodded but William saw that when his brother turned away again he rolled his eyes and shifted himself to charge. Young fools like to feel their strength, thought William. Old fools think they have it still.

The former friar, Petro, took a large wooden cross from the folds of his filthy habit and kissed it and then turned to either side of him to mutter a blessing over the men, some few crossing themselves in answer.

'Hold, lads, hold,' hushed Orlando as the merchant drew closer. Zago wound the thong at the base of his cudgel tighter round his wrist, Luca kissed the hilt of his old sword with its knocked and pitted blade and muttered a prayer, Ludovico shifted his poniard from hand to hand. They could see now that the men behind the merchant were a guard of sorts, two men in simple leather jerkins, swords slung from the saddles of their ponies. They wore their pot-helms as protection against the rain, which gathered and then sheeted from the brims. Behind them came the asses, the one at the front ridden by a fat man in a filthy cloak, the others laden with tight-wrapped packages were pulled along by a rope from the first. The merchant's train drew level with the copse behind which the little band had gathered for its ambuscade.

'Now! Gentlemen, now!' came Orlando's cry from William's side and the bandits thrust themselves from their hiding places to fall upon the merchant and his men.

A cry went up from the merchant, his horse rearing at the sudden flock of men bursting from the trees like starlings. His guards reached to unhook their swords but the outlaws were crossing the fifty yards between the tree line and the horses too fast. Seeing their numbers and their gain of ground upon them, the guards turned and urgently wheeled their ponies back the way they came. The driver of the asses was whipping his little beast to the same course but it moved slowly, slowly. The triumphant cheer of the outlaws at the rout of the guards rose up against the sound of their fleeing ponies' hooves.

William watched as though at a play, one he did not care for. A flash of blue caught his eye and he turned to see a bird, frighted by the cries, break from its place in a tree nearby and soar for the sky. Luca shouted at him to quit his tarrying and join them and he walked over towards where Orlando now approached the merchant. The man had recovered the horse to his control and now turned it about within the circle of the bandits, his sword drawn and waving about him.

'Come, sir, alight your horse, surrender. No harm shall come to you, as I am a gentleman.'

'Gentleman? *Hah!* Thief, robber! You'll not have me truss myself for your slaughter.' The merchant's voice was high with fear and his eyes darted from man to man. 'Come closer while I keep my blade in my hand.'

'Your insults are uncalled for,' said Orlando. 'I am a gentleman and my word given, I honour it. No harm shall come to you. Look, your men are fled, we have your wares already. Leave off your crowing, give up your horse and walk away.'

Beyond Orlando three of the other outlaws were busy pulling the fat man from his seat on the ass to the ground. Two others struggled to calm the chain of asses that bore the merchant's goods upon their backs.

These two were the first to die.

Riding back up from the valley came the two guards that had fled, but now in company with four others. With swords bared they bore down on the outlaws. The two holding the asses, being closest and tangled with their charges, saw the blades rise to fall on their crowns, then saw no more.

Cries and shouts rose from the other outlaws, scattering to the four compass points.

'Hold, damn you!' Orlando shouted. 'Hold! This merchant is our surety.'

He tried to grab for the merchant's reins but was forced back by the pointing and pricking of the man's sword.

'Hold! We are enough to drive them back . . .' Orlando cried again but his voice trailed away.

His cries of hold were words wasted in the chaos. It is one thing for men, in numbers greater than their foe and with the gift of surprise to offer, to charge down on a fat merchant and his few men. It is quite another to stand against men riding down upon you swords raised to slash your life out of your breast. The outlaws broke and ran for the trees. Another of them died as a sword took him in the back.

William still stood in the clearing, watching. He felt a weight upon him holding him still but no fear. Even among the chaos of the battle his thoughts were not present but far away, in Venice.

Ahead, the mounted men had stilled their ponies and turned them for a second pass. William saw them pointing with their swords at the bandits still milling by the asses. Then one rode for him. He watched his approach calmly. To live or to die; a moment of decision. All felt as one to him in that moment. In death he might be spared the heartache that now weighed so heavily upon him. He might have some peace, some relief from the thousand shocks that were the price of life, the burdens of duty, the contempt of prideful men, the fear of failure. A consummation devoutly to be wished, the peace of the grave. Aye, there was the rub. Who knew if death gave peace or no. Was it the end of heartache or its prolongation to eternity?

A cry bored through these thoughts to the seat of action in his mind. A name was being called. His own? No, but one that meant something to him.

'Run, Adam, run!' cried Orlando and, sprinting past him, he caught William's arm and hauled at it. William, not knowing why he did so, turned and followed hard after. They ran with the sound of hooves closing on them, the drumbeat of the executioner arriving. William ducked under a branch and stumbled, fell, rolled and picked himself up again. Orlando and he ducked and ran through the woods, the branches becoming tighter and more tangled as they went deeper and the sound of their pursuers faded.

Your marriage comes by destiny

Verona

The Duke paced before the fire in his library. He had little time for priests and their meddling ways. Let each man's state of grace be his own affair. Why must these priests be forever going beyond their offices? And why must they meddle in matters temporal? The Duke stopped, plucked up a poker and viciously stirred at the fire with it. Not enough that the Republic of St Peter should have those lands they had already but they must covet more; and where they exercised no temporal power they overstretched their spiritual command to the usurpation of the lawful ruler. This Thornhill was but the latest and the worst of a familiar breed, thought the Duke with punctuating stabs of the ashes in the grate. The greed of the Church needed no proving. If it had then the insulting offer that this Father Thornhill had brought from Rome would be all the testimony needed. That I gift my lands to them in exchange for some paltry indulgence from the Pope? A few Masses said in my honour when I am dead. He had given that suggestion short shrift and at least Thornhill, for all his other offences, had made no mention of it since. Oh but I have been unlucky, in a wife's too early death, in the lack of a son, in a daughter too given to the exercise of her will and too little to the devotion to a father's wishes that is her filial duty. Had I not so loved her mother, I might have married again and had an heir. Oh, would I had a son to leave my land to, then might I give Aemilia all that she wanted. He cast the poker down. Since I do not, married must she be and to the man best suited to the task, Claudio.

'Sir Nicholas, my lord.'

His steward interrupted his brooding to announce Oldcastle's arrival.

'You are well?' the Duke asked on seeing Oldcastle's wan face.

Oldcastle's constitution, unsettled by the Duke's company and the hard drinking that accompanied it, had been further curdled by the priest's arrival. Now summoned to the Duke's presence and mindful of his promised commission, Oldcastle struggled to find his usual cheer. He managed a cough, a pursing of the lips and a wave of the hand, all of which he felt were the movements an old warrior like Sir Nicholas would make to signal both tremendous discomfort and a casual disregard for such pain. The Duke took it so.

'Sit, sit.' The Duke beckoned him to a chair beside the fire. 'Wine!'

The bellowed order caused Oldcastle to start in his chair and clutch at his heart but the Duke did not notice. A servant hurried forward with a jug of wine. The Duke eased himself into the chair opposite Oldcastle, reached forward and rummaged the fire with the poker so forcefully that Oldcastle feared the flurry of sparks thrown up would set his beard afire. At last, satisfied by the blaze, he leant back in his chair and drained his cup in a single swallow.

'Priests, eh.'

Oldcastle made a sound that could have meant almost anything. A most useful sound in his experience since to the audience it conveyed precisely that which they wished to hear. He had prevented many a tavern brawl by its use and, skilfully deployed, caused many an audience to nod in admiration. The Duke did so now.

'Does your man Russell give report of the Lady Aemilia?' the Duke asked.

'That she has a most willing mind to learn and progresses well in her lessons,' answered Oldcastle.

'And of Valentine?'

Oldcastle pretended ignorance of the man.

'An ingrate and importunate son of a dead cousin of mine,' explained the Duke, his eyes upon the fire to which he envisaged condemning Valentine. 'I little liked his father, a drunk, a lecher, who gambled with that which his ancestors had built with care and effort and died a penniless wastrel. Now comes his son, who I, charitable and loving to my family, took in and who repays me with unlawful wooing of my daughter. I will have no such communion beneath my roof.'

'Russell spoke of no such man, and by that I take the Lady Aemilia to have had no communion with him either. Least not while my man has been in her company. For the rest, well . . .'

'Aye, there's the trick of it, for my daughter is no milksop fool.' A little smile of pride crept over the Duke's face. 'If she wants to meet with this

Valentine then she will manage the business. Howsoever I forbid it, she will manage it.'

The Duke poured himself another cup of wine and filled Oldcastle's glass to the brim.

'There has been too little respect for my estate. My daughter, brave in my love of her, defies my wishes for her marriage. And now is this priest returned.'

'The priest?' asked Oldcastle. He had spent many evenings, in many taverns, from London to Bristol, from Paris to Turin, hunting after drinks at another's expense. He considered himself something of a master at the game. Two rules he had for any that would learn his art: first, no man desires to hear any story more than his own, ask him questions and he will answer them, and so his mouth dries and his thirst grows; second, not all are gifted story-tellers but when they falter, as falter they must, and begin to think of turning homeward and taking with them their coin and shared jug of wine, then repetition of their last words, now as a question, will drive them on to the chorus of 'a fresh stoup of wine, Maria'.

'This priest, among the worst of his kind.' The Duke looked hastily up but saw in Oldcastle's encouraging nod a man who shared his dislike of a meddlesome priest. 'Father Thornhill, an Englishman, like yourself, though I think he has lived in Rome for many years. There is a new Pope in Rome, you know this? Little more than a year in possession of St Peter's see, but such a difference a year makes. The signs were there in the name he took, Sixtus, a baleful name. It was the last Pope to have that name that forged in war the Papal States. He is still remembered in these parts, a hundred years after his passing.'

The Duke reached out and again rummaged at the fire with angry strokes.

'This new Sixtus has as covetous an eye. He sends out his minions to stir the land and we may not say aught against them for fear of incurring the wrath of the Church. Well I will not be any man's lapdog, not even the Holy Father in Rome.'

The Duke swung his gaze up to Oldcastle's.

'If a man was uncivil to you in your service how would you treat him?'

'With the lash,' cried Oldcastle, who had the taste of the Duke's mood now. The Duke met his cry with nodding of his head.

'So, so. I also. This priest, lording in my lands, comes questioning. Questioning my own priests, my own men, my servants, my subjects. As if we were some damn heretic Swiss or I some spleeny Lutheran. When I ask him his purpose, what answer makes he? That he will answer to none save His Holiness. Shall I brook such words? Such uncivil tongue in one so far beneath my station? No, I shall not. I did not use the whip but he felt the lash of my tongue. Damn me if he did not glide from it, all untouched. Yet he did go and I was glad to see him do so. Now is he returned and again he is at his questioning and ungiving of his purpose.'

The Duke again drained his glass but this time did not refill it. Instead he set it aside and turned to Oldcastle.

'I did not ask you here to speak of wayward daughters, Sir Nicholas, but of wayward men. These robbers that must be driven from the woods nearby. What men would you need for such a task?'

Oldcastle took a draught of his wine to cover the desperate churning of his brain. All his understanding of battle might be fitted in a thimble with room to spare. How many would seem enough for the task? A dozen? Too boastfully few? A hundred? Too cautious? The Duke looked at him with expectation. His mouth was dry despite the wine. He opened it to answer and was forestalled by a sharp knock at the door.

'My lord, your cousin Valentine craves parley,' announced his steward.

'*Hah*, comes to beard me to my face. Well now, a word for him I have,' growled the Duke. 'With your pardon, Sir Nicholas.'

Oldcastle made a face of understanding that hid his relief at further time for thought. He wished he might speak with Hemminges, who would know what answers he should give the Duke. Oldcastle began to rise from his chair.

'No stay, Sir Nicholas,' commanded the Duke. 'This conference will be the work of moments for I have little to say.'

Oldcastle sat back down, unhappily.

'Admit him,' the Duke ordered, and Valentine came into the room. He was dressed in clothing of more sombre colour than his custom but in sleeves that opened near to his waist and trimmed with ermine, it was not a habit of any practical use and the Duke sneered to see it.

'My gracious lord,' began Valentine, then quavered to see the louring look upon the Duke's face.

'You have been wooing my daughter,' said the Duke.

'I have, my lord, a truer, purer woman this world knows not,' said Valentine.

'I know not either but you shall not have her,' said the Duke.

'My lord, we are in love and would be married with your grace and favour to the match,' stumbled Valentine, who had prepared a speech but now discovered that all preparation is for naught in the first clash of arms.

'Married? How is it that you dare to speak of marriage to my daughter when you have nothing to offer,' the Duke said.

'I have my love, my lord.'

'Love? Love?' scoffed the Duke. 'Do you hear, Sir Nicholas? The fool speaks of love.'

Oldcastle deployed that useful sound again, desperate not to be drawn into the discourse. He buried his face in the cup.

'Will love feed you? Will love defend these lands? What value has love?' roared the Duke. 'I tell you what love gives, trouble. I took you in, penniless child, and fed you, watered you, housed you, clothed you and what repayment for my love have you given?'

'My endu—'

The Duke cut him off with a cry. 'Treachery is my repayment. You suborn my daughter in my own home. My own home!'

The Duke's voice was rising to a thunderous pitch with each spat word as the fears and frustrations of the past days found an outlet. Valentine began to edge his way back.

'I have but one word for you,' declared the Duke. 'Exile.'

Valentine turned and fled the room.

'One word but such a long sentence,' observed Oldcastle, more to himself than to the Duke.

'What?' said the Duke.

'Nothing, my lord, an observation of no merit,' said Oldcastle, lifting his cup. 'To justice severely merited and swiftly delivered.'

The Duke, whose temper had been up, subsided at these words and lifted his cup in acknowledgement of Oldcastle's own.

'Aye, and with it done we may to more important business turn. To purge the woods of thieves – how many men?'

Oldcastle nearly choked on his wine. He'd forgotten he was to lay out his plan. What answer should he give? A score was a goodly company of players.

'A score?'

'Twenty men?'

Oldcastle quailed. Was it too many or too few that the Duke should use that tone? What reply met either challenge?

'More than enough to be certain,' said Oldcastle, praying that it was.

'Good. Good. I feared you would want more,' said the Duke. 'Yet a score is all I have to spare.'

Oldcastle sighed with relief and thought the moment right to proffer a story he'd prepared for the Duke's amusement and launched into it. He did not tell it with his usual skill for half of his mind was with the thought of how to get to Hemminges. By God, he needed Hemminges now, for the two of them must be away from Verona at speed.

Thou great commander, nerve and bone of Greece

The Veneto

The woods were full of mists and disappointments. The men returned to their camp in coughs and spits. They had scattered in all directions from the mounted men's charge and gathered back only slowly, wearily and unhappily.

Zago had rekindled the fire to heat the meagre pottage and the band now ate in silence. Orlando and William were the last to return. Both men's faces were scratched and bloody from their frantic scramble through the trees and bushes but they were otherwise unharmed. The same was true of the rest of the company, save those that had lost their lives in the failed ambush.

William fell to the ground by the fire and sat staring at its low flames. Orlando went to his camp, fetched his bowl and strode to the pot. When he reached it Zago looked up from his stirring, anger drawing lines about his eyes.

'There's none left,' Zago said.

'Give me the ladle, Zago.' Orlando's voice lacked emotion.

'There's none left,' Zago insisted, though he kept stirring. The other outlaws watched and waited. Here was the champion of their complaints.

Orlando met and returned Zago's baleful gaze. 'I did not turn and run,' he said.

'Zounds! And you call me coward?' Zago rose from his squat to outface Orlando, who did not flinch. The others of the band looked on.

'I say that you should not challenge my command,' said Orlando. 'I cried to you "hold". You ran.'

'Against mounted men?'

'Aye, even then.'

'And what preparations had you made against their charge?'

'Sent a man to scout the party, who spoke of only two guards that rode beside the merchant. But that man's past punishment. He's paid a mortal price for his failings. Dead with the rest.'

Zago said nothing. He let his gaze slide away to travel over his fellows, not one of whom rose to match his standing. The only comments were Petro's muttered claim that it was God's judgement against them, a claim he made ten times a day at the least misfortune, and Luca's grim observation that not all that were lost to them had died, that one of their company was taken prisoner. Silence fell again as all wondered if death might not be the better fate than residence in the Duke's dungeons. Orlando reached out and snatched the ladle from Zago's hand, bent and served two spoonfuls of the watery mess into his bowl. He turned to find a seat and as he moved he spoke to the assembly.

'Tomorrow opens up another day,' he said over his shoulder. 'And with new dawns come new hopes.'

William heard these words and thought of another day to come. Tomorrow, he ought to rejoin his friends, Hemminges and Oldcastle. Tomorrow, he ought to make for England with those secret names. Tomorrow, so many things he ought to do and yet he had no will to any of it. Should he have stayed to face the horseman's blade? He had run and now must face another tomorrow and another and another. So creep in the days until the last utterance of recorded time, he thought, full of oughts and must-be-dones and all for what? All our yesterdays but lead us to this fruitless day and promise of a fruitless 'morrow. The story of our lives is but a poor tale, told by an idiot, signifying nothing.

Behind him Orlando sat down next to Luca and asked him his thoughts on the new men.

'For Ludovico, I saw little of him in the mill of it, and for Adam,' Luca said, gesturing at William's still back, 'he was as much use then as he is now. What did you spare him for? You were ever a strange one, Orlando, with strange fantasies, but your care for this one is passing strange. He's nothing but a mouth to feed and by the look of him, half lost to us already.'

Orlando stared at William as he ladled the pottage into his mouth and said nothing.

The cry is still 'They come.'

Verona

The following morning the Duke's breakfast was again disturbed. A merchant came through the palace gates with three bodies added to the loads upon his asses' backs. The Duke came to meet him in the courtyard and was presented with the muddled heap of corpses.

'Robbers, my lord, that would have taken my goods and my life were it not for these men.' The merchant gestured to a group of four mounted men, their faces dusty and sweat smeared, their hands on the pommels of the swords at their sides.

'You come to speak, man, your story quickly.'

Hastily the merchant told the story of the ambush, of the first defeat and then the sudden redemption in the fortunate appearance of the four men. Then he pointed. Standing at the rear of the train of asses was a bound man, crusted blood upon his scalp.

'We took one of their number and it may be that he can tell us more of their place and numbers.'

The Duke clapped the merchant on the back.

'This was well done.' He signalled for the prisoner to be taken away and turned to the men who had saved the merchant.

'To you I owe much thanks,' declared the Duke. 'Your names?'

'Arrigo, Giovanni, Baptiste and Benetto, my lord, all soldiers in the service of His Holiness and sent with message for Father Thornhill.'

The Duke's smile curdled at the news of their office but he kept his welcome for their deeds. They were taken to find food and wine and their horses stabled.

'My lord, these outlaws grow braver,' complained the merchant. 'Where once a simple guard or two was shield enough, now they arrive by the score.'

The Duke nodded at the merchant's words.

'My lord, what will you do?'

'Do?' roared the Duke. 'Do? I will scour them from the woods and have those that still live at the end of it, hanged from the palace walls as a warning.'

A good lenten answer!

The four guards rose quickly from their table as Thornhill entered. He looked with distaste at their plates.

'You break your fast at this early hour?'

He peered a little closer.

'Is that meat?'

'Aye, Father, for we have been broached in battle. Is it not permitted to have meat when the labour demands it?'

Thornhill ignored this special pleading, sat down at the table and pushed aside the bowl of food with the back of his hand. The men did not dare sit again.

'Tell me of this battle, quickly now.'

The four men's leader, Arrigo, hastened to give a good report.

'And?' said the priest when Arrigo was done.

'Father, our companion, Ludovico, was among them as you commanded him. We saw him and he us and, after the general broil when the outlaws were dead or scattered, there came a moment for us to make quick speech unseen. He tells us that there are not three Englishmen within the outlaws' company but there is one strange fellow with an English name and questionable Italian. He will watch him till you command him otherwise.'

Thornhill nodded at this news. He had not hoped of finding the English hidden among ragged outlaws in the forest but it was best to be certain. Look how the overconfidence of Monsignor Cesare Costa had allowed the heretic English to evade judgement in Venice, like eels slipping through an old net. He would not allow the same to happen.

Costa had sworn the English were in Venice on Fat Tuesday and swore they must be there still. If not, then even on horseback they could not have made it so far in so few days. No, either they still hid in Venice, waiting for the hot pursuit to cool, or they had ridden towards Verona.

Thornhill's heart suddenly thrilled with the possibility that he would be the one to catch these English heretics. Then he would know, with a certainty, that he had played his part in bringing England back to the

Church. Blessed be the Lord and the Church that sustains His message. He crossed himself in the closing of his prayer and bent his head.

He scowled at the food before him. It was casuistry such as this, that slipped in 'maybes' and 'ifs' to the clear rules of the lenten fast, that unpicked the simple word of God, which had allowed these Protestants to rend the unity of the Church. A fat king's lusts had been given form and shape and words by fawning, flattering priests. He praised God for this Pope, a strong Pope, that would bring the Church back to its true strength.

Thornhill picked up a spoon and stirred the bowl before him. Venice and its vassals were too liberal. Was not the university at Padua filled with dissenters, with English heretics? Venice, too, by all report, allowed any, even base Moors, turbaned Turks, infidel Jews, to come to the city, if they had gold.

'Throw away this unlenten meat and make a penance of it,' said Thornhill, rising.

The liberality of the world, he thought as he closed the door behind him, is the crack through which seeps in wickedness.

Alack, no remedy – to the greedy touch

The Duke was finally at his breakfast; he brooded over it. This news of robbery so insultingly close to his palace made yet more urgent the need for Aemilia to marry. Then might her new husband bring his charge of men to aid the Duke in preservation of the peace.

'Your Grace, Father Thornhill,' announced the steward, his words followed hard by the priest himself.

'Your Grace, the men who are sent to join me bring further report of villainy on the road,' Thornhill said.

'I know that, priest,' said the Duke, pushing a piece of bread into his mouth and speaking through its obstruction. 'Was I not there when the bodies were brought in? Do you think I know so little of what happens in my lands?'

Thornhill watched the Duke chewing without comment for so long that the Duke became aware of each bite. He really has the most unnatural coloured eyes, he thought. When at last Father Thornhill spoke, it was to admonish.

'My lord does not keep the lenten fast?'

'I keep it well enough for one of my age and labours.'

Somehow the priest's simple disapproving murmur of the lips at this answer was greater insult than any outright condemnation. The Duke's colour grew a darker and more liverish shade.

'No doubt you have the matter of these outlaws in hand,' said Thornhill.

'No doubt? Have I not told you already of Sir Nicholas' commission?'

'Ah yes, the Englishman. He arrived recently?'

'These few days past.'

'That is a rare coincidence for I am in search of some Englishmen. Heretics. Spies. Three men.'

'You suggest Sir Nicholas to be a heretic spy?' scoffed the Duke.

'I know not what he is.'

'Your arithmetic is as poor as your manners, priest. Sir Nicholas and his lieutenant are not three men.'

'The spies may have parted company, the better to evade pursuit.'

'Nonsense.' The Duke shook his head. 'Sir Nicholas is no spy. Why, he has given me proof of his life in every story that he has told. A very Hannibal.'

Thornhill made that same disagreeable murmuring sound in answer.

'I would I might meet with him.'

'A matter for him,' said the Duke.

'My lord might yet arrange it.'

'Alas,' the Duke said, raising his arms in a gesture of disappointment so shallow it might have served as a spoon, 'today I ride to my neighbour to discuss matters touching our two lands.'

'Your Grace refuses to aid the Church?'

'I refuse you, Thornhill.'

'Your Grace should consider how he will answer St Peter when his reckoning comes and how soon that might be.'

The Duke had been taking great pleasure in the visible enjoyment of the food he consumed, stirring his bread in the small dish of honey before lifting it to his lips. Now he pushed his food from him and spoke with a deadly softness.

'You threaten me?'

For a moment it seemed Thornhill would let silence be his answer. He seemed untroubled by the fury which sat on the Duke's brow and showed itself in his grinding jaw, but after some moment he spoke again.

'No, Your Grace. I am sorry if you mistook me. I think only of the Gospel of Matthew, "watch therefore, for you know not the day nor the hour". Your people must look to your stewardship for their safety. You have no heir, all turns on you. A great burden I am certain, one to weary your old age. It is natural in the shadow of that duty that Your Grace rides to propose his daughter's marriage to Count Claudio.' If Thornhill saw the Duke start to hear his secret plans for Aemilia's marriage spoken of as if they were common currency, he did not show it. Instead he steepled his hands beneath his chin. 'But if I may? What benefit does the marriage of your daughter bring? Your title passes from your hands and the hands of your family to those of another and yet you, my lord, see no benefit from it.'

'I shall be dead, priest, and little care for benefits.'

'Quite so,' answered Thornhill, who, uninvited, now drew out a chair at the Duke's table and placed himself within it. 'That is why His Holiness offered to take your lands into the fold of St Peter.'

'You will not speak of this to me again.'

Thornhill spoke on, unperturbed by the sudden crack of the Duke's fist on the table. 'Your concerns now must be not with this life but with the life to come. Your aid to the Church now will be part of the account to come. Think too on what indulgence your lordship would gain by a gift to His Holiness of your lordship's lands. Think what years in purgatory's fires you might allay with His Holiness's own intercession on your behalf? Think too what safety, both of their lives and of their souls, your subjects might thereby gain. Your daughter might still receive a mighty dowry or, if your lordship prefer it, a pension and a place of comfort in Rome. Of course, all this, many years from now – if God, whose church I serve, grace you with long life.'

The Duke's face had turned a colour not seen outside a raw steak and stood up, pointing his finger at the door.

'Get out. Priest, dare you try to sell my bones before I am dead? Get out. Tell His Holiness that my lands and title are not for sale.'

Thornhill nodded. A tilt of his head disclosed that he was saddened by this rude treatment, saddened but not, alas, surprised. He rose and pointed to the table laid before the Duke. 'My lord, at lenten time, food before the noonday is forbidden even to the elderly.'

'Get out.'

It took the Duke some minutes to recover after the door had closed on the priest. He stuffed the remainder of the bread in his mouth and then, through full lips, called for his steward and ordered him to prepare his horse and an escort of men.

'With haste, mark you, with all haste. And have Sir Nicholas come to me. This business of the kites on the road must be seen to.'

The reasons for Aemilia's swift marriage mounted with a terrible urgency. There was much to put in train.

The course of true love never did run smooth

Aemilia had at last slipped her maid's watchful eye and made her way to Valentine's room unseen. She knocked, but no answer came save a sharp cry and then an echoing sob. She entered. Valentine stood by the narrow window, at his foot was a velvet bag, upon his bed were strewn clothes in heaps that Valentine picked up, pressed to his face and then flung back on the bed. He collapsed upon the bed and flung himself back upon the heap of clothes to rail at the ceiling.

'All is lost,' he moaned.

Aemilia rushed to his side, grasped his hand and hauled him up to sitting.

'All is begun,' she said, reaching up to wipe a tear from his fair face and brush back his hair from his brow. She took a deep, shuddering breath for she felt the flutter of fear in her own breast. She let the breath escape; Valentine had dared all for her, she could not now do less than he. If the sentence was exile then it was a sentence she would share. Resolution made, she felt a thrill at it and at the thought of their life to come, in the woods, a simple hut, a stream at its foot, surrounded by fruit trees whose benison was their sustenance. It would be as Valentine had foreseen it in his poems.

'We must make preparation,' said Aemilia.

'Preparation?' said Valentine. 'Preparation? What preparation shall we make for a life of poverty? Which of my clothes shall I wear in the ditch? Which eat?'

'Come, Valentine,' Aemilia answered. She was taken aback by the depth of his distress, which it seemed had quite unmanned him. Had he quite forgotten his own wise words to her in the palace gardens? Very well, she would be strong for both of them.

'You and I are not frightened mice to scurry and hide at the least fright. We will find our way in this world by our own hands.'

Valentine looked down at his hands – long, white fingers stained at the tips with ebon ink. He thought of the comforts of the Duke's court. The ease of his repose here in his room, the scant demands upon his time, the pleasures of the poetry he might write, the food and drink at beck and call. Fat tears began to fall from his eyes and he flung himself back again upon the bed.

'We are undone, Aemilia.'

'Courage,' answered Aemilia, wishing she could in some manner yet pass to Valentine a portion of her own resolve. 'We shall live as innocents do, in the forest, from the bounty of the land and the kindness of strangers.'

'Oh, Aemilia, the woods are filled with brutes. From where shall we take our food? How cook it? What shelter shall we have?' said Valentine from within his burial mound of doublets.

Aemilia looked down at her poet and felt a moment of distaste. She stifled it. Such a shock as Valentine had been given was not to be dismissed without sympathy. Was he not right to raise these worries? Was he not more practical than she, who knew herself much taken with romantic dreams of an exile's bed in a byre of willow fronds and soft moss strewn? He saw more clearly. She had feared her father might be resolute, hard-hearted in his opposition to her marriage to Valentine. Yet she had hoped too, that he would see Valentine was suitable to be both her husband and the Duke of these lands. That he would see that such flaws as he might possess she was, herself, the cure to. Valentine had warned her it would not be so and, as his auguries foretold, so it had come to pass.

She must think. What would Caterina Sforza do? Of course, Caterina Sforza had possessed many allies in her own battles. Yes, it was allies that she and Valentine needed now. Hope sprang in her breast.

'My father loves you,' said Aemilia and ignored the snort from Valentine, 'and he loves me, of that I am certain. We need but absent ourselves a while and our absence shall be as a winter to his heart that our return shall be a summer. A month shall be a season's sporting holidays for us but the sharp salt that admits our marriage to my father's tastes.'

'And for that month?'

Aemilia leaned over and looked at his tear-stained face. She bent and kissed his pale lips. It was the first moment that the two had truly touched as lovers do. His hand reached up to clasp her and hold her to him. They embraced with the fierce passion of youth. All fears were banished then.

Let there be hardships if there might also be this. Reluctantly the two broke apart.

'Trust me,' said Aemilia, her hands still stroking his face. 'Come, make provision for our journey, Valentine, and do not forget to pack your courage. I shall return within the hour and then we depart. Be cheerful, love, all that happens here is that our honeymoon comes before our marriage.'

She kissed him again and left to seek out the ally her mind had fixed upon.

We shall advise this wronged maid

They spoke in whispers.

'Never,' said Hemminges.

'I beg you,' said Aemilia. 'I implore you. If my fortune goes as I hope I shall requite your kindness.'

When the weather promised foul, as that morning it did, the dancing lessons had continued not in the walled garden but in the hall of the palace. It was at the threshold to the hall that Aemilia had pulled Hemminges aside and importuned him for aid: guide her and Valentine to a refuge within the woods a day beyond the palace and be richly rewarded for his help both now and in the future, when Valentine was Duke and she his lady.

'For you and for your Valentine this is foolishness, but for me to aid you in it?' said Hemminges, his eye darting to the hall beyond where Aemilia's maid waited for the morning's lesson. 'No, not foolishness but a capital crime.'

Aemilia got up from her knees and strode over to where Hemminges had retreated.

'Not so, good Master Russell. Not so,' Aemilia begged him listen. 'This is the means by which my father will come to understand the truth of the matter.'

'The truth?'

'Aye, the truth.' Aemilia was certain of it. 'You need not scorn to call it so. He loves me and I in turn love Valentine. When he sees that I will have Valentine with his blessing or no, when he sees that to deny me Valentine is to lose me entire, then he will bend to the marriage as a reed bends to the river's current. His love for me shall to love of Valentine translate.'

Hemminges could not hold back a scornful laugh.

'He will scour the face of the woods for you and when he finds you, he will hang all that are with you.'

In Master Russell's laugh, in the urgency of his words, Aemilia heard the proof of something till now she had not believed: this Englishman's admiration went beyond that of teacher and student. She had been too innocent in her thoughts. Look how she'd been sure her father would understand her love for Valentine. Now, she thought, I see that innocence has shielded me from truths. I have dreamed only of the poetry of the woods and not considered my father's anger when I defy him or the dangers that lie beyond these palace walls. Is this wanton of me? Do I use this Englishman's desires to my own selfish ends? And am I now in search of reasons to stay, to shy from the hardships before me, to hide behind my father's knee at the first scent of danger? No, I am resolved to be no coward. If this be youth in me then it is impetuous to a purpose and that purpose, love. All will bend to it.

'Then he must not find me,' she said finally.

'And how will that be managed?' demanded Hemminges.

'I am determined, with your help or without it, to try the hazard of this course.'

'Why should I not make straight to the Duke and unpack your whole course of action?'

Aemilia stepped close to Hemminges and reached out to stop his retreat. Hemminges looked down at her hand on his arm. 'I did not ask you only for your skill at arms, your knowledge of the camp and field, I beseech you, as you love me, Master Russell. You will not betray me.'

My God, Hemminges thought, am I such an open book that everyone may read my thoughts? As if in echo of that, Aemilia spoke as she took her hand from his arm.

'You are an open, honest man. It is your way and the reason that I trust in you.'

Hemminges looked at Aemilia. Her eyes that made a suit to him were as open and honest as she called him. This was not some flirt-gill abusing his goodwill, relying on his lustier nature to persuade him. She saw a truth that he denied himself. Give any answer that you might, man, he thought, but one cannot hide from one's own stupidity.

'You have the right of it, lady. I will not betray you. Nor, by the love I bear you, will I help you to so foolish a course.'

Aemilia held his gaze for a moment and then turned on her heel and strode away. Hemminges watched her part and cursed every waking moment since he left England to this hour.

'Hold,' he called after her. Aemilia stopped and waited for him.

'What is your plan?' he asked.

'Why do you care?' At the look Hemminges gave her in answer, Aemilia let out a breath of frustration. 'To be gone within the hour with such provision as two, or three, may carry.'

'What need of such haste?'

'Valentine is under sentence of banishment. Its execution stays upon my father's distraction only. We must be gone.'

So, so, thought Hemminges, no wonder then that this should be brought to me so ill-prepared.

'In what disguise will you travel?' he asked.

'Disguise?'

'You think your father's guards will see the Duke's daughter stride from out her father's hand without question? That your maids, seeing you in Valentine's company, arm linked between his and mine, will hold off their shrieks of condemnation?' Hemminges did not wait for Aemilia's reply but turned to struggle for an answer of his own.

Aemilia did not comment that Hemminges had put himself in the story of her escape. She looked to the ceiling in thought. 'I must not be examined too closely. What then if I went in Valentine's clothes?'

'A man? You'd not pass for a man. You are too much the woman.'

'Flatterer.'

'Not a flatterer but a cynic,' answered Hemminges.

'Then see, your cynic's brow need not bend so. I have a man's height and it will not be thought that I should let myself wear men's habit. I will wear my hair in cap, a cowl pulled about my head, my face daub with the stable's grime. Let me be a Sebastian then, a fit companion and page for Valentine. My father's guards will not look to stop Valentine, whose sentence is exile, and we shall be his servants.'

'This is no party game of hoodman-blind we practise here, Aemilia. If we are caught 'twill be the death of me and Valentine too.'

'I know it, Master Russell,' said Aemilia.

Hemminges shook his head. What did this girl know of death, of the dreadful hammering of a heart in the casing of the chest as dangers gathered? What was this course he set himself upon by helping her now? She was resolute, that much he saw, and without his aid went to her certain destruction. But with his help? And what of Oldcastle?

'What if the guards question you? Open your mouth and they will know you false in an instant.'

'We will say that I am English and run mad and cannot speak Italian,' said Aemilia.

'Why English and mad?' said Hemminges.

'Being English I am not known to them. New come with Sir Nicholas, perhaps. Why being mad, to be English too is no addition, for they are all mad there, but 'twill explain my failure to follow their speech as much as answer it.'

Mad Englishmen is true enough, thought Hemminges as he hurried after Aemilia. His mind raced ahead to the woods and their survival there. What perils lay in wait should they pass the test of the guards' observance? Perhaps in the cruel winter of realities Aemilia will see Valentine for the cracked vessel that he is and then might we two return to the Duke with no more lost than a night or two's rough sleeping. This hasty business prevents more careful plan. Or, he realised with a curse, message to my friend. Twice already, the servant assigned to Oldcastle's care while at the palace, Dionisio, had brought messages requiring Master Russell's urgent attendance on Sir Nicholas Hawkwood. There is no helping it, I shall have to resolve this matter, thought Hemminges, and pass message to Oldcastle after. By God, and am I not mad after all? And I had no need of William to fix me in the madness either.

Because that I am more than common tall

Hemminges had not been wrong to think Aemilia too much woman. He groaned to think of the challenge to come. He groaned for another reason too. There was something so oddly lascivious in Aemilia's new attire and what it revealed, that in the moment that Aemilia had re-entered, dressed as a man, Hemminges at first averted his eyes. But they drew back as if called.

If Aemilia noticed his blush or where his eyes went and lingered she affected not to. His were not the only eyes that hung upon her woman's shape, revealed from beneath a woman's skirts. Valentine shook his head, torn between delight and belief in the certainty of discovery. It was only the promise that they would be alone in the woods and the thought of how he and Aemilia might linger in each other's arms that pressed him on when his every will was to abandon this madness and throw himself upon the mercy of the Duke. Aemilia slung a small knapsack on the bed.

'Such jewels as I might safely lay my hands upon,' she said with pride.

Hemminges wished there was cause for further delay but there was none. The three were dressed for travel. He carried their meagre provisions, such as Aemilia could take in haste from the kitchens, gathered in a leather bag that he had slung upon the yoke of his staff, his sword at his side. Valentine was dressed in what might pass in a play for travelling garb but so much of velvet had they to them that there could be no real use in them. In spite of Hemminges' warnings, he would not be dissuaded from their wear. Aemilia had found a linen shirt of her father's and added to them breeches, hose and boots. A loose doublet disguised her sex from the casual witness. Her hair was tucked beneath a cap. Hemminges tossed to her his old cloak, which fastened about her neck and threw further into shadow that which might betray her true person as well as, by its threadbare look, lend credence to her low status.

'Come, come, let us to the postern gate and make our march,' said Aemilia.

Hemminges halted her and came to study her face.

'It will pass?' asked Aemilia.

'Very like if nature had done all,' said Hemminges, dragging her to the basin by Valentine's bed. He filled the basin and pointed. Reluctantly, she dipped her hands into the cold water and scrubbed the paint from her face. It had seemed to her a very little thing she'd added and quite unlike her everyday adornment. When she had finished and her face was plain and red from the cold water and the scrubbing, Hemminges stepped to the fire's grate and reached for ashes that he turned and smeared on Aemilia's chin and cheeks. He stepped back and looked upon his work. A little less the lady and more the scullery-maid now, but a man? He shook his head.

'We're not playing here, lady,' said Hemminges. 'You think men wear painted rhetoric as women do? One look at you and we'd have been discovered.'

He would have spoken on but Aemilia seeing him begin forestalled him. She felt her own courage for the adventure on foot catch at the threshold; any more delay and she was certain she'd stumble back and never escape.

'We go,' she said and ushered Valentine to the door. 'To liberty now and not to banishment.'

Hemminges sucked in his breath, suppressed both words and doubts, and followed.

It was to their good fortune that news of Valentine's sentence had quickly passed among the palace servants. They, too ashamed to look upon the poor, unfortunate exile, no sooner saw him passing than, as if the very look of him would pass on his leprous state, allowed their gaze to slide away. Thus too his companions passed as in a bubble of invisibility towards the gate.

Aemilia's heart quaked as they emerged into the courtyard of the palace to march towards the gate where stood two of her father's guards. Oh God, let us be not discovered, she prayed. She felt her hand tremble and clamped it to her cloak to hide its betraying movement. She willed herself to a swagger. Let my woman's fears lie hidden, she thought.

'Hold there,' called the guard at their approach. 'What's he that travels here?'

'Valentine,' said Valentine in a voice that carried nothing of Mars in it.

'Whither away?' asked the guard and, to the astonishment of all, he was answered by a sob bursting from Valentine's breast and a most unmanly cry.

'I know not.'

The guards did not try to hide their contempt but turned their gaze from Valentine to spare him further shame by being witness to his unmanning. Aemilia felt panic rising in her. Then Master Russell stepped forward to answer them, moving as he did so, between the guards and Aemilia.

'I have the Duke's commission to convey the lord Valentine and his servant from the Duke's lands and there deposit him. I pray you, sirs, delay me not in completion of that commission,' he nodded to the sobbing Valentine, 'lest we be drowned afore it's done.'

'Ay man, it's a piteous commission.'

'Truer words you never spoke, sir.' As Master Russell spoke, his hand was urging Aemilia forward and through the gate. He spoke to the nearest guard in confiding tones, 'God's will I shall be rid of it within two nights but we must hurry if we're to reach our first rest before nightfall.'

Valentine stumbled on with Aemilia at his side and Master Russell, following, raised his cap to the guards as they nodded the three of them through. One by one they bent to pass through the Judas gate and out on to the open road beyond.

'Hold there, ho!' the guard cried from behind them.

Aemilia stiffened and turned at the sound of their discovery. The guard had bent his head and peered through the gate. He called Master Russell back, waving a silken scarf in his hand.

'The little lord has dropped this,' he said.

'Ha, friend,' said Master Russell. 'He'll need that if he keep up this flood of tears.'

Master Russell and the guard shared a laugh before the gate was pulled closed.

It began to rain.

For one's offence why should so many fall

Oldcastle cursed beneath his breath. He had delayed being brought to the Duke's presence as much as he might but he could put off the audience no longer. Where in the name of all the gods was Hemminges? Trust his friend to have made himself absent at just the moment that he needed him most. Surely this audience with the Duke was to put upon him, or say rather upon Sir Nicholas Hawkwood – alack the day he'd ever given voice to that ambitious character – the commission against the woodland rogues that had the Duke in such high temper. Oldcastle's bowels turned to water at the very thought of it. He must have Hemminges' advice: how to flee before the charge was given or, it being given, how to flee thereafter. The fleeing was all. Admittedly flight was not Hemminges' talent, but why then had the man chosen this moment to flee himself?

So far, the Duke had done little but speak dangerous words about Father Thornhill and reveal his plan to marry his daughter at once to a neighbouring lord.

'It is because you of all people have felt the burden of leadership that I dare to speak with a freedom to you that I do not with others.' The Duke led Oldcastle to a table on which sat a silver jug and chalices. The Duke raised an eyebrow at Oldcastle who pursed his lips as if to say, wherefore not? The Duke poured two generous measures of cool wine. They drank and each smacked his lips in satisfaction.

'I must away in haste,' the Duke said.

He leaned in close to Oldcastle and the sour breath told him that the Duke had not waited for his arrival before pouring from the jug.

'That thrice-blasted priest, Thornhill, is sent here to steal my lands.'

'My lord, no,' protested Oldcastle.

''Tis true,' said the Duke. 'He openly spoke of it to me. Such gall. To tell the man you wish to rob that you will do so.'

'You'll never let him,' said Oldcastle.

'Nor will I,' said the Duke. 'See my lands pass to the Republic of St Peter? Be mortgaged out to the whim of the Pope? Never.'

Oldcastle hiccoughed on his wine – for all that they were alone in the Duke's closet, his companion spoke dangerous words. The Duke did not notice Oldcastle's discomfort; instead he plucked his cup from him and set it down, with Oldcastle's gaze mournfully following it. Then, taking him by the arm, he began to lead him down towards the palace's hall.

'Enough of this, Sir Nicholas. I must ask a favour of you. I ride today for the Count Claudio's, he that is to be my daughter's husband. Three days I am to be gone. Leave this priest roaming my palace in that time, stirring trouble and dissent? No.'

The Duke's barked denial made Oldcastle start. The Duke noted his hesitation but took it for a criticism.

'You think me overcautious?'

'No,' hastened Oldcastle in reply. 'No, my lord. You said yourself, you've the proof of the priest's intent in his own speech. Besides, it is not overcautious to send out scouts and set a watch over the camp at night. It is the disciplines of war.'

The Duke beamed at this answer. 'Ay, right, Sir Nicholas, you have the right of it. For it is a war against myself and my lands, though it is not so declared as much. I am heartily relieved to find you of the same mind as I. Yet the battle is not begun. I dare not cast this Thornhill out while I am still weak. When Count Claudio is my heir, when his men are mine to call on, then there shall be a reckoning.'

They entered the hall of the palace and the Duke, still propelling Oldcastle by his grip upon his elbow, brought him to the captain of his guards.

'Here,' said the Duke to his captain, 'is Sir Nicholas Hawkwood. He is to stand in my place in all matters pertaining to the defence of my lands while I am absent.'

Oldcastle's face, which had drooped in shock at these words, hurriedly put on a martial visor as the Duke turned to him. Again, the Duke took his paleness for other than it was.

'I ask too much, I know,' the Duke said. 'Yet I beseech you, Sir Nicholas: let me rest easy these three nights to come knowing that I have you watching over my palace and my daughter.'

He did not wait for Oldcastle's assent. His own words had sparked a remembrance in the Duke.

'Rodrigo,' bellowed the Duke and at his cry his steward ran to his master's side, stumbling slightly in his haste, from where he stood in conference with another servant. 'Valentine, that perfidious child . . .'

'Gone, good my lord,' said the steward, anticipating the Duke's question with a smile. 'The guard at the postern gate reports his departure this hour past. He went, so it is said, tearful and wailing at his fortune.'

'Good. His fate is not near my conscience. Where gratitude and loyalty should have lain in his bosom there rested only a grasping and a lecherous desire. That at least is done.'

The Duke dismissed his steward with a wave and the man returned to finish off the hasty preparations for departure. The Duke turned back to Oldcastle.

'I am grateful beyond measure, Sir Nicholas, for your timely arrival at my court.' He seized Oldcastle by the shoulders and dragged him into an embrace, once, twice, three times kissing him on alternate cheeks. Then, holding him at arms' length, he declared: 'Fortune herself has delivered you to me in my hour of need.'

Oldcastle had decided that he and Lady Fortune would share a few words should he chance upon her and words of no sweet breath but of demand: wherefore should an old man who never did harm to any be so assailed by her distemper? A quiet life was all he asked.

'Rodrigo,' the Duke roared again, causing Oldcastle to blench. Again, the Duke's steward ran to his master's side but his passage was checked by the Duke himself, advancing at speed, and he was picked up in the Duke's wake as he passed. 'All is ready?'

'It is.'

'Then we ride. Adieu, Sir Nicholas, keep my daughter safe and the wolves from my door,' the Duke called and was gone towards the stables, the sound of his called orders to his steward soon fading to an echo.

Oldcastle stood in the suddenly quiet hall alone. Here's a to-do, he thought. Best make of it what I can. First to find Hemminges, and then to find food and wine. On consideration, food and wine first, then John's advice. I shall never hear him out properly if I am distracted by my stomach's growl. He headed toward his rooms, aping the Duke's manner by picking up a servant by the arm as he did so, and sending the man scurrying to the kitchens for food and drink.

In the comfort of his chambers and with the prospect of refreshment on its way he began to feel calm again. After all, he need only pass three days in comfort and good eating and then receive the Duke's gratitude and good favour. He put his feet upon a stool and leaned back in his chair. A knock at the door announced the servant's arrival with a platter of meats and breads and some of that fig preserve that he had grown partial to in Venice.

'Good man, good man,' Oldcastle murmured as the table was laid. 'And if you would be so kind as to find Master Russell and send him to me?'

Oldcastle dismissed the servant. A slice of cured ham on warmed bread and a glass of wine later and his mood had turned from trepidation and despair to good humour and high hopes. A knock at the door heralded the servant's return. The face that answered Oldcastle's cry of entry was pale and trembling. Oldcastle shot to his feet.

'Out with it, man.'

'Oh, my lord, such terrible news,' said the servant. 'The Lady Aemilia is gone.'

'How, "gone"?' said Oldcastle.

'Fled, my lord, with the exiled Valentine.'

'You're certain?' said Oldcastle, now cold with fear.

'Past question, my lord,' answered the servant. 'She has taken some of her jewels too. Her maids have searched the palace this past hour, fearing to make false report.'

Oldcastle clutched at his thin pate. Not two hours passed since the Duke had left him in charge of his daughter and the damn girl had run away. This was disaster writ in words of flame, *Mene, mene, tekel, upharsin.*

'Quick, man, fetch Master Russell to me with haste,' cried Oldcastle. God how he needed Hemminges' counsel and his calm now. Would he had that cunning rogue Shakespeare here too.

'Hurry, man, hurry,' Oldcastle cried, seeing the man did not move.

'My lord, it seems . . .' The man hesitated and Oldcastle, full of fears, roared at him to speak.

'My lord, it seems that Master Russell went with them.'

Oh Jesu, thought Oldcastle as he collapsed to his seat, I am undone, I can bear no more. A knock came at the door and another servant entered.

'My lord,' the servant said, 'Father Thornhill demands audience.'

Act Three

Verona and woods in the Veneto, March 1586

Arise, dissembler; though I wish thy death

The Veneto

The outlaws' camp was sombre. A day and night of rain had cooled the hot mutiny in the men's eyes to sullen embers of discontent. Their leader strode among the perturbed faces and gave the glowering looks no heed.

'Come, Adam,' said Orlando to William. 'Let us leave these oysters to their grim silence. I am sure they have pearls within 'em but right now they speak to me only of slime and salt.'

William couldn't understand why Orlando thought him any different. He'd less to say to Orlando than any man among the company. For the first time in his life William did not feel like speaking and had sat more silent than the surly band, who spoke only to make complaint. He'd passed about the camp doing such business as the day demanded, fetching water and wood for the fire, cleaning a rabbit that Zago had trapped, all without the need for words. There'd been little enough to do and he'd spent such leisure as he had in reading the folio of Isabella's verse he'd taken from her table as he'd left.

In disparte da te sommene andata,
per frastornarti da l'amarmi, avante
ch'unqua mostrarmi a tanto amore ingrata:

Oh, Isabella, I would you had not left me. You have cleft my heart in twain and now I must live without the better part of it.

He'd had a purpose once, or so he thought, but what it was he'd quite forgotten.

'Come, dreamer, up, up.'

Orlando's voice cut through William's thoughts and he pushed himself to his feet and followed after the bandit leader. They passed through the forest with Orlando whistling a jaunty tune. The man gave every appearance of being quite unconcerned either by the previous day's slaughter or by the possibility of being surprised by those who might seek to bring a bandit to justice. At last they came upon a brook and Orlando, without pause, stripped off his baldric, sword and clothes and dove in. He surfaced and threw back the hair from his head.

'Ah, God, but that is cold as Hecate's teat. Jesu, it cleans the soul like a frosty fire.'

He beckoned to William. 'Come, Adam, a man of your name should not shame to bathe in nature.'

He flopped backwards and sculled a little against the current, waiting. William peeled off his clothes and balled them up, laying them on the rock beside Orlando's. He felt the grime of many days' walking and sleeping in the forest and was suddenly desperate to be clean. He took a shallow dive into the river and felt the bite of the cold as his head cut below the water's surface. The current was strong and he warmed himself by swimming against it and up the stream to stand on a shallow rock beneath a drooping willow that stood askant the brook. He looked about him – the afternoon sun cut through the willow's hoary leaves to play upon the water and the reeds. Orlando swam up to join him and drawing near, reached up and grasped a branch of the willow and held it to stay the current's pull from dragging him back downstream. William did not look at him but stared out at the scene, taking its beauty in. This would be a good place to die, he thought.

'I know you are not who you claim to be.'

William did not look over. If Orlando had intended to shock him from his meditation then he was disappointed in William's leaden response.

'Who is?'

'*Hah*, says the philosopher.'

'We all but play parts and tread our brief hour on the stage,' said William. 'You, Orlando, are not who you claim to be neither.'

'And who do I claim to be?'

'The soldier, full of strange oaths, bearded like the pard: you are not making a thievish living on the common road from necessity. You have a reason as do I. My reason's known, but the cause of your sorrow . . .'

William ended with another shrug. He had felt the faintest spark of heat within him, curiosity to know this fellow's story. It was a pale and cheerless thing when set against the furnace that, in the past, was wont to flare within his breast at the merest hint of mystery. For all its shallow heat it was more than he'd felt within him in a week.

'By Jesu, you have the right of it.' Orlando struck the water with his hand. 'I have reason enough for this and more than this and it is that I would speak of to you.'

William shook his head. 'Who'er you think I am, you are mistaken.'

'I know that ring.'

William looked down at the gold ring with its cornelian heart and the strange sigil of a lance with a pen's nib. His head snapped up at Orlando's next words.

'You are the Count Prospero, the Pope's blade.'

There was no passage between the words and the actions. William was upon Orlando in an instant, his hands about his throat, driving the wide-eyed figure under the water and screaming: 'Speak not that name to me. Speak not that name.'

Orlando thrashed against William's closing hands and struggled to find purchase on the slime-covered rocks below his feet, the current pushing him from any footing as William held him beneath the rolling stream. His hands beat at William's sides without force and darkness began to close over his eyes. Suddenly William hauled him up and threw him on the bank where he rolled and coughed and spewed green water on the ground. William stood in the brook still, shivering against both the cold and the sudden flood of anger that had consumed him. He was brought back to himself by the sound of Orlando laughing.

'So, there is still life in you,' said Orlando. 'And there I was fearing you were turning into a statue.'

'Do not call me by that name,' said William.

Orlando held up a hand placatory. 'Never again will it cross my lips.'

Orlando retched again upon the ground. William dove into the water to swim and let the cold calm his thoughts. He emerged and strode to the bundle of his clothes, which he began to unfold. The shirt he took to the water's edge and, squatting, bent to wash some of the salt and dirt from it. Orlando, recovered from his fit of coughing, leaned back against the bank and spoke to the sky.

'That ring, I knew I had seen its seal before. Then when you moved with such dexterity against Luca, well, let us say only that the Pope's assassin's reputation precedes him.'

William carried on beating the dirt from his shirt with hands that thrilled with nameless emotion. Orlando raised an eyebrow at his silence but seemed to take it as proof of his conjectures. Neither spoke for as long as one man might count three hundred. The gentle susurration of the brook in that time was enlivened only by the drumbeat of William's laundry-work.

'Why do I confront you with this character? Not to fright you. I had hoped, here at the river, my sword upon the ground and without any possibility of hidden blade, well . . .' said Orlando, it being his turn now to shrug. 'As you guessed, I was not born an outlaw.'

'No man is,' said William.

'There you are wrong,' answered Orlando. 'Some men have a thief's life thrust upon them but others are born thieves.'

His voice now took on a tone of pride. 'I was born a nobleman and the heir to a fair estate not far from here. My father was a good man but unlucky. Unlucky to have married my mother who died at my birth. Unlucky to be married again to a woman I'll not call Medea for fear I do that lady a dishonour. A woman of great beauty, though not in the flush of May; a Florentine and a libertine. She brought with her a son by her first marriage, the father dead, the son my elder by some years. I'll not say that we were enemies, nor were we friends, but such is sometimes the way with brothers. Rumour spoke of cruelty with his fellows, of privilege demanded of the village girls, but of all that I saw nothing. I was blind to the truth.'

Orlando sat up and grabbed a stone from the bank that he sent skipping into the brook. 'When I was of an age, I left to study at the university in Padua, as my father had done and his father before him. I had been there scarce a year when a letter reached me that my father had taken sick and died. I left Padua at once and rode without rest to my father's castle but arriving, found the gate barred against me and my brother on the battlements, those arms that I should have borne upon his shield. I called for entry but was denied it, words of such foul scorn poured upon my head:

that I was the cause of my father's death, impatient of my estate, that my brother had discovered a plot against our father's life too late. I fled their arrows and by my flight put confirmation on their charges.'

The beat of stone on shirt had ceased. 'Your brother was the murderer?' asked William.

'So I think it. My mother, my second mother, outlived my father not one month more. If the plot was hers she's paid for it, but I think it more probable that my brother, rising to the joys of rule, quickly tired of a dowager's demands and removed her as he had my father. I fled to Padua but my brother pursued me there, laid charge of murder at my door and had me arrested. I pawned such favour as I had to have it let out that in my prison cell I had been taken by a fever and carried off from life. And now a dead man I fled here to the forest.'

'Much cause for revenge.'

'I think so,' laughed Orlando without mirth, 'for I am by a brother's hand deprived of father, mother, lands, and life. Should such a brother live?'

William hung the beaten shirt upon a bough to catch the sun. He squatted again by the water's edge and hurled a stone of his own across the brook.

'A year I have watched and waited in these woods,' said Orlando. 'I have no power to take my brother's keep, nor has he been abroad where I might take my deep revenge. Now the Furies send you to me.'

'Me?' said William.

'You think I spared your life for love of Luca's?' laughed Orlando. 'I need a man that murders, for I have one that I would have murdered.'

'I am no murderer, Orlando. You have mistook me for another.'

'Your price I'll pay when that which belongs to me and to my ancestors is once again within my hands.'

'You are mistook in me,' repeated William wearily. 'It is not want of wherewithal that makes me refuse you.'

'Then what use are you to me?'

'What use to any man?'

Orlando rose to his feet and walked to where his clothes were. He donned them and hung his baldric across his shoulder. William stayed squatting by the river's bank. He did not look round at Orlando or think of the sword now hanging by the bandit's side. Instead he gazed upon the waters and thought again of how the music of their passing over the rocks would sing laments to mark a death.

'Think on it,' said Orlando to his back. 'It is not a murder that I ask but justice.'

'I am not who you think I am. Orlando, I want—' William paused. 'I know not what I want. To go home, perhaps. I have no will to be the instrument of another's vengeance against his brother.'

'Claudio. That is my brother's name. Count Claudio, I should call him now, for so he calls himself.'

'Be patient, Orlando. I have found that the whirligig of time brings in his revenges without more need of human action.'

'My active soul likes not this passive counsel.'

'It's all I have to give.'

'So say you now.'

William heard the footsteps retreating but still did not turn. It was another hour before he'd summoned up the life to dress again and make his way back to the camp. It was a smoked hive that he returned to, the bees drowsy active.

'Luca reports three travellers on the road, unarmed, unhorsed and ripe for plucking,' declared Orlando with vigour.

'Three pilgrims most like, their satchels empty of all but bread I'll warrant,' grumbled Zago.

'Stay then,' said Orlando. 'Prepare the victory feast.'

'With what?' demanded Zago. 'Nettles? Roots?'

'I'll hunt,' said William.

Orlando and Zago looked at him.

'I have hunted before now,' said William.

'Then, by all means, Orion, bring us the fruits of your experience,' said Orlando to the chorus of a scornful snort from Zago.

'You have a bow I can use?' asked William.

Zago gestured to the small stock of weapons that the camp held and William plucked up a bow and a fist of arrows and set off into the woods.

In secret ambush on the forest side

Valentine's heavy gait was the addition of many things. In prime, he was exhausted. They had spent two nights in the woods and he would swear he had seen each hour of darkness toil slowly past while he lay desperate of sleep. No shift of body, no gathering of fronds and moss by a tight-lipped Hemminges, no wrapping of his cloak about him could disguise the poking of rock and root into his tender flesh or stay the shrewd bite of the night air. He was as far from sleep as he was desirous of it and angrily denied his companions' insistence that he had slept and marked the hours of sleep with snores that had prevented sleep in others.

Next to this first he added the damp weight of his soaked garments. He was certain that it had not rained so much or so steadily since the days of Noah's sailing. His velvet was a sodden mess that clung coldly to his body and stained his body with its dye.

For the last, his boots, their soft leather so comfortable at court, had proved quite inadequate to the stony path. They passed on to his feet each pebble, knot and burr that went beneath. When, he moaned, when would this torture end? What byre, what shepherd's hut, what cottage would grant them rest and shelter? Only the sight of Aemilia steeled him to the journey. It was for her sake he suffered now, he her Orpheus, descended to the underworld to rescue her from woe. He trod on a sharp stone and gave a cry of pain. Master Russell called to him for silence. Valentine cursed, but quietly, for this Russell was a fearsome figure, a true Cerberus. Valentine did not like him, not least because his presence prevented him from being truly alone with Aemilia. Each time he had mentioned the matter to Aemilia she had reminded him how little they two knew of such journeys and how much they needed one such as Master Russell. That she was right did not make him happy about it.

Hemminges' own discomfort was not corporeal but spiritual. The constant whine of Valentine's voice bemoaning his misfortune was like the droning of a Lincolnshire bagpipe. Yet still Aemilia would not abandon him. Instead she bent, solicitous to his every complaint, to cheer him and to keep him moving. Hemminges watched and despaired of his first hope, that in the hardship of the woods, Aemilia would quickly falter and, seeing Valentine shorn of the false finery of the court, decide that contract to an older lord was to be preferred to a life spent boiling water in the woods for a pampered prince. No, Aemilia had proved herself of tougher mettle. A corner of his lip turned to smiling for he'd half hoped it might be so. There was pleasure in witnessing her strength, for all that it meant there would be no swift and easy return to the palace of her father.

God's will, Hemminges thought, it was mere days ago I walked these woods in the other direction. A new thought came to him then, one he was reluctant to acknowledge: if Aemilia be of such brazened mettle, then she's no need for me and my protection. I have other duties to attend. I must return to Oldcastle and he and I must go to England. See her safe at some shelter, he thought, then about Hemminges! To England, to our duty, to the giving of these names.

In contrast to Valentine's stumble and Hemminges' stride, Aemilia skipped. She held out her arms and turned about. The rain that had hammered down upon them for a day and night had left and the woods smelt of fresh ivy and moss and damp wood. Her eye caught sight of Valentine creeping unwillingly along, a black slug of velvet, his hair plastered to his face by the downpour. He mustered up a smile for her and her heart went out to him in his suffering. He was not a creature of the woods but of the court. One did not blame the fish for ungainly twisting on the land, the cat for thrashing in the water or the bird for graceless hopping in the mud. Each has its element. Still, she wished he could have shown himself a little more of the stoic in his contemplation of his suffering.

Hemminges, she saw, strode behind alert and untroubled. The casual efficiency with which he had made camp these two nights past was proof of his soldier's skill. Each evening, Aemilia had watched him close and questioned him on each deed, that she might learn the proper disciplines. To rely on others forever and anon was foolish. Who knew how long she and Valentine might be in exile? Valentine's sentence had a dateless limit. Only her hope of her father's love gave reason to believe that sentence would be commuted. She looked on Valentine again. The rain had tarnished his lustre, she had to admit, even as it had made Master Russell's shine brighter.

They managed an hour's silent march before Valentine's voice again rose with complaint. This time in call for food and drink to break their journey.

'I grow faint with hunger,' he declared.

Aemilia signalled to Hemminges who poked about in his sack and pulled out a small leather bag of bread and cheese.

'*Faugh!* Bread and cheese, again. Am I become a mouse?'

'I didn't pack your provisions,' said Hemminges.

'Bread and cheese are eaten by all the heroes of the stories,' said Aemilia brightly. Both men looked at her.

'In stories it may be so,' said Hemminges, 'but in my experience one is better served on a long journey by porridge and a rind of pork.'

Valentine looked to Hemminges and pulled a face of disgust. 'By God's wounds then I am glad you did not pack.' He broke off a piece of bread and of cheese and pushed them both in his mouth as they continued walking. Through stuffed lips he continued his complaints, now blessedly muffled. Aemilia looked across at Hemminges and the two shared a rolling of the eyes and a small grin. Even Valentine's complaining could not quell her delight to be out and free.

They walked on with Valentine's complaints continuing. Their warbling note went on even through the sudden bark for hush from Hemminges. Aemilia turned to look at him, his head lifted like a dog to sniff the wind. Valentine canted on unheedful.

'Good day, gentlemen,' said a gracious voice.

Three men emerged from the woods ahead, blades out. A crackle of stones shifting announced two more stepping on to the road behind. Valentine twisted back and forth to stare at these apparitions with his mouth agape, dripping food. Aemilia drew close towards him. By God, these were the outlaws, they were to be robbed.

'There's no need for alarm, gentles. We wish only to lighten your loads a little.' The vaward of the men to her front, he of the gracious voice, was the one that spoke: a handsome man with a splendid black beard.

'Stop him,' cried a voice behind, harsher and angrier than the first. That cry was prompted by Hemminges, to Aemilia's astonishment, dropping his pack and darting from the road into the woods.

'Oh, coward!' cried Valentine, who had turned as white as the cheese he ate. The blade of the thieves' leader flicked between Aemilia and Valentine.

'I hope to see no such foolish flight from you.'

'None,' swore Valentine. 'On my life, tell us what you will and we shall do it, only spare us, spare us.' His pitiful pleading he accompanied with wringing of his hands. The bandits' leader smiled at the sight.

'There's sense, sir. Hand over your packs, your rings, your purses, and we depart.'

Valentine had scarce heard the end of the speech before he had begun divestment of his wealth on to the ground before him.

'You too, sir,' said their leader to Aemilia.

The first shock of their appearance had passed and now Aemilia studied the bandits. 'You—'

'"Orlando", please,' the bandit leader said smilingly.

'You don't seem overly concerned that my friend has fled.'

'Ah, lad, he'll not get far. There are more than we five in these woods. He'll run but for all his exercise, he'll just die tired.'

As if to affirm his words at that moment a great cry of hurt pierced the woods and Valentine swooned at its sound. Aemilia ran to his side and hauled him to a seat on the ground. She looked up at Orlando, sick with sudden truths.

'We are to die, then?'

Command into obedience: fear and niceness

Verona

'I am told that you command while the Duke is absent,' said Thornhill.

Oldcastle was a wretched man. Rank terror had given him a kind of feverish strength to deny the priest audience that first evening. A night of little sleep and dreams that came full of terrors had left him a hollow reed. A dawn that came without news of either Aemilia or Hemminges' return had snapped him like one. Then, Dionisio, the servant assigned to Oldcastle's care, had brought a message that Father Thornhill again demanded audience.

My God, what shall I do? Oldcastle moaned inwardly. What does this fellow want? Would that Hemminges were here. No doubt he's luxuriating in his adventure with that foolish, headstrong girl hanging off his every wise word. A jaunt, a winter's folly in the woods, while I quake and quail.

Pressed again to admit the priest, he'd strength only to demand that the hearing happen in the great hall of the palace, before witnesses.

Now, confronted by Father Thornhill's pale eyes, the few gathered servants and even the presence of the Duke's captain of guards seemed a slender buckler to put between him and the priest's steel.

'I have the Duke's confidence,' answered Oldcastle and prayed that his voice did not betray him. He'd not dared to take the Duke's seat but had chosen to stand upon the dais in order to have the height advantage. Thornhill had not paused his stride on entering the hall until he stood beside Oldcastle. The priest was shorter by an inch but there was no question of whose stature was the greater.

'You are, sir knight, an Englishman?' asked Thornhill speaking in that language.

'And proudly so,' said Oldcastle.

'As am I,' said Father Thornhill. 'Though I no longer call it home and I have not had cause to speak our mother tongue in many years. You still submit to Rome I trust?'

The waters in which Oldcastle was swimming suddenly teemed with dark, dangerous shapes.

'Dare it be said otherwise,' he huffed.

'To the destruction of all false prophets including that Jezebel of England, Elizabeth?' asked Father Thornhill.

'Of course,' said Oldcastle. 'Why, am I not an exile of King Edward's day?'

Thornhill nodded. The boy king, proud Henry's sickly child, had taken his father's perjuring of Rome and turned it from a convenient trick to a seated purpose. Many English papists had fled the fervour of his rule. Still the boy was dead some thirty years or more.

'You did not return when Queen Mary came to the throne?'

'My ancestors have ever loved Italy and I found I did too,' said Oldcastle whose memories of Edward's reign were hazy and of his sister Mary's uneasy. 'Besides, by then I was engaged a soldier in Italian squabbles from which I've made my fortune. Why I could tell you of some royal fights that I have seen and fought and won and lost, too—'

Thornhill cut across his answer. 'Sir Nicholas, be so kind as to come with me.'

'Why, I . . .' began Oldcastle's reply but Father Thornhill had already begun to stride from the hall and Oldcastle found himself hurrying to catch the priest up. They passed into the corridors of the palace with Oldcastle suffering in his effort to match the tall priest's stride. The two men, like a comet, trailed a tail of men, two of Father Thornhill's men-at-arms and the Duke's captain of guards and, last, a scurrying Dionisio.

'Sir Nicholas,' said Father Thornhill, not looking to the man he addressed. 'Please explain why the Duke and his daughter are fled the palace.'

Oldcastle turned sharply to look at Father Thornhill. How did the damned priest know about Aemilia's departure? Distracted, Oldcastle caught the base of a statue with his hip as he passed and let out a little moan of pain.

'"Fled", Father Thornhill, tush, fie, not so,' said Oldcastle, trying to recover his poise, and with a dismissive fanning of his hand that hid its shaking. The stream of noises from his mouth were coins to no purpose other than the purchase of time. 'What is this talk of flight? The Duke is rode to view his lands, as is his right and duty with this talk of outlaws. As to the girl Aemilia, well, I doubt not your knowledge of the Gospels, Father, yet am I certain that for good reason you know not the whims of women and young women at that.'

Thornhill steepled his fingers beneath his chin as he walked and bent them to gesture that Oldcastle was very welcome to educate him in the matter. Oldcastle's wit, running as fast as it might after a night of sleepless worry and a goodly jug of sweet wine of canary, struggled to keep up with his imagination.

'Why she too is rode to view the lands.'

'To view the—' Thornhill came to a sudden halt. His head retreated on his neck as if his shock at this report demanded that he be positioned to view the giver of it the better. 'Alone? Without her father? Escort? Maids to tend her?'

'My man, John Russell, is with her,' protested Oldcastle.

Thornhill shook his head and moved off again. Their progress resumed, now proceeding from the corridors of the palace to the great courtyard.

'As is her young cousin, Valentine? He that was sent into exile for unlicensed pursuit of her hand?'

'No,' said Oldcastle. 'I mean, yes, he was exiled for overstepping the bounds of his position. But, no, no, to exile he went alone.'

'Is't so?' nodded Father Thornhill.

Despite his nod, it did not seem to Oldcastle that the priest was inclined to believe him. Oldcastle longed for the shelter of his room again and the warm embrace of the wine that waited there. He was no match for this priest whose knowledge of events, it seemed, far exceeded his own. Where in God's name was Thornhill taking them? He struggled to regain control.

'Father, I am delighted that you are so careful of the Duke and his daughter's well-being. The care of young women was ever the Church's concern, of course, of course. I hope you find assurance that all is well.'

Oldcastle would have gone on to move the matter to dismissal but the priest shook his head.

'I do not, I regret. I do not, Sir Nicholas.'

They had reached the far corner of the courtyard where one of the towers on the curtain wall of the palace had its door. Father Thornhill stepped into the dark entrance. Inside was a small antechamber and a flight of stairs descending below the ground.

'I find very little in this domain that gives me assurance and this flight of the Duke and his daughter at my arrival least of all. The Duke lacks control of his own daughter. How can he have control over his lands?'

Oldcastle had no answer to this and it did not seem that Father Thornhill expected one. The priest turned away and for a brief, glorious moment Oldcastle thought the audience might be about to conclude but instead the priest gestured for Oldcastle to follow him down the stairs, the two papal soldiers a step behind.

A faint, unsettling sound could be heard echoing off the stone walls of the staircase, ascending from the darkness below. Oldcastle could not name its source or its nature. Its unreal quality put Oldcastle in mind of the cry of a mermaid.

'Your man, Russell,' Thornhill went on, paying the strange sound no heed, 'you have known him long?'

'Twenty years,' said Oldcastle, remembering when he had first seen Hemminges, solid and strong even at that young age, a boy player then. He'd the measure of me from the off, thought Oldcastle. Where in the name of God is he now?

'He too is faithful to the Pope?'

'As a hound, Father, faithful as a hound. Though in truth I suspect he thinks as much of such matters as a hound would—'

Oldcastle stopped. The sound from below could be heard, louder now and distinctively human. A chill tremor ran through him for he had heard those noises before. Then they emanated from his own throat as the Duchess of Bracciano's men had tortured him in Venice. He looked round. Thornhill's men stood behind, blocking the route up.

'Where do we go?' said Oldcastle.

Thornhill stopped and turned. 'Why to the dungeon, Sir Nicholas. To the prisoners.' He continued on down the stairs. Oldcastle followed, sick with fear at what he was to see.

The steps became a narrow hallway lit by thin grates high above. As they strode along it, chambers either side, barred with iron, revealed bare rooms, empty for the most part, save two. One contained a white-faced man, crouched in the corner of his cell, hands pressed over his ears. In the other the prisoner clutched at the bars and watched Oldcastle pass with eyes as large as an owl's, terror writ in every line of his face. Thornhill paid them no heed. He marched to the wooden door at the far end of the corridor from behind which the moaning came, a moan that as they reached the door burst into a keening howl of pain and terror, and ebbed to sobs. Oldcastle felt his knees shake at the sound.

The door opened on a charnel house. Oldcastle stopped suddenly at the entrance, the two papal soldiers behind him bumping into him at his unexpected halt. Inside the outlaw captured after the raid on the merchant's train was strapped to a table with leather thongs. Another of the papal men stoked a brazier that gave a red glow to the thin light that came from a grate far, far above. The outlaw's naked, grimy body was marked in many places with cruel, red sores where the poker had been applied. The smell of burnt flesh, of vomit and of terror was rich in the stale air. Oldcastle felt himself faint. Thornhill seemed unmoved by the stench in the small room and by the man's piteous mewls. The naked bandit looked half mad with terror and pain.

'Has he provided any intelligence?' asked Thornhill.

'Nothing that we did not already know,' answered the man at the brazier with an appraising look over the mutilated man before him. 'I dare not press him more now. We can try again when these wounds have healed.'

'This must stop.'

'What did you say?' Thornhill swung sharply to Oldcastle.

'This must stop,' said Oldcastle in a louder voice. 'There is no—'

'I did not think to find a soldier so meek,' said Thornhill.

Oldcastle's fear was mingled with horror. Hell had gaped open and he stood at the entrance. He remembered when he had been the one to suffer. He felt his fear turn to disgust, at this Thornhill, aye, at any who would use such methods against another man, but at this priest in particular, whose office should offer succour, not suffering. His loathing for the man stiffened his back. When he turned his eyes from the tortured figure before him to the priest that had wrought the foul deed, it was Sir Nicholas Hawkwood who had in a dozen bloody broils never quailed, never blanched at sight of blood, that looked out at Thornhill and spoke in a voice that could be heard above the cannon's roar.

'The Duke has given no authority to this questioning.'

'I do not need the Duke's authority.'

Oldcastle took a step toward Thornhill and planted himself.

'This is the Duke's prisoner. You will not touch him without the Duke's licence.'

Thornhill said nothing for a long moment. The rise and fall of the sobs of the tortured man came like the ticking of a clock to fill the silence. Oldcastle felt the men behind him elbowed aside by the Duke's captain of guards who finally saw as Oldcastle did and drew breath in echo of Oldcastle's horror.

'Very well,' said Thornhill. He nodded to his man, who thrust the poker back into the brazier and went over to the prisoner, bent over him and gripping his hair lifted his head up and whispered in his ear. The prisoner looked up and weakly shook his head. Thornhill pursed his lips, gestured to his man who began to untie the prisoner, and then brushed past Oldcastle and went up, out of the dungeon, calling back over his shoulder as he went: 'You will inform me the moment that the Duke returns.'

Oldcastle did not answer but turned and strode from the room to follow Thornhill up and out of the dungeon before he'd realised that Thornhill had not made a request but given an order.

Oldcastle hurried up the stairs. Dionisio waited for him in the courtyard. Taking in Oldcastle's pale face and trembling hand he at once ushered him towards his rooms. Foul priest, thought Oldcastle, to question me like that, to show me horrors to fright me. Why if there's anything worse than a cup of sack with lime in it, then it's a meddlesome priest. Ah, sack! There was the remedy for this unsettled stomach of his.

'Wine, Dionisio, and much of it,' he said. He tried to ignore the restless tremble of his hand as he walked.

Across the palace, another master and servant spoke.

'The Englishman knew nothing?' asked Arrigo, who since his arrival now had charge of Father Thornhill's company of soldiers.

'Nothing,' answered Thornhill. 'Less than nothing. The prisoner did not know him. Nor did he give any sign of guilt. The sight of that man's torture would have unmanned him enough if his conscience troubled him. This Hawkwood boasts and he drinks, sins enough, but he's either a dissembler greater than the Devil himself or he's no spy. I think him the old soldier he calls himself. So, if the heretics have not escaped some other way then they are yet to make it this far. They must be in the woods.'

To strike me, spurn me – nay, to kill me too

The Veneto

'We are to die, then?'

Valentine sent up a frantic moan at Aemilia's question, which brought smiles to some of the outlaws' faces and caused others to roll their eyes.

'Only if you give us cause,' said Orlando. 'We are thieves, not murderers, save of necessity. These swords and staves are our untutored rhetoric, they're for persuasion. We can be civil if you are.'

Aemilia unhooked her satchel and threw it to the ground.

'Your purse too, and it please you,' said Orlando.

'There's nought in it but remembrances of my old mother. Let me keep it,' pleaded Aemilia.

'Jesus, not this again,' growled another bandit, far uglier than Orlando and with a cast to his eye.

'I am afraid we'll have all, remembrance too,' said the outlaws' leader with a smile.

'No!'

The next moment was a blur of shouting and cries: Orlando's sudden cry of 'no', his hand raised and staring behind her as she twisted about to see what caught his gaze and saw one of the outlaws, his club raised to strike her down. Then a buzz of wind beside her face and an arrow's shaft took him in the arm and spun him back, with a great cry of pain.

The outlaws scattered for cover against the trees but, not knowing from which quarter the danger sprang, became a flock of hens darting hither and yon. Aemilia stood, rabbit-like, in the road, transfixed by danger. She saw Valentine curled in a ball on the ground, squealing with fear. She saw Orlando edging his way from a crouch to standing to peer about a tree and the hammer's rap as an arrow sank itself, fist deep, into the tree beside his head.

Then a stillness came, broken only by the moans of Valentine and the weeping of the outlaw with the skewered arm.

'Well, goddamn,' said the ugly outlaw with a cast to his eye, to no one in particular. Orlando was shaking his head and muttering from his hastily resumed crouch. He called out: 'Jacopo, Giulio, what is the business?'

No answer came.

'Jacopo! Giulio! What can you see?'

Still no answer came.

'Jacopo, Giulio! Damn you.'

Then a voice called out from the woods and Aemilia recognised it as Master Russell's: 'Are those the names of the two men you set as backers to your ambush?'

Orlando pointed at the outlaw with a cast in his eye and another man beside him and gestured to the woods. They shook their heads in answer until, by angry gestures and hissing imprecations of his own, Orlando persuaded them to venture after the voice. As they departed Orlando struck the tree with his fist in frustration.

'You bluff well,' he called. 'I grant you that. Still we hold the best cards for the game in your two friends.'

Master Russell's voice cried out again but from a different place to where they'd heard it first: 'No bluff. I'd ask the fellow with the red sash and the one with the shepherd's cap to tell you so yourself but they're past talking.'

Orlando scowled and beat the tree again. He pointed to the last two of his company that were not holed with arrows, dead in the woods or already hunting for Hemminges and sent them too after the voice. Orlando's eyes, like a stone skipped on a pond, glanced off Valentine to meet and hold Aemilia's. Aemilia, for whom thought was now finally catching up with action, made to dart away but Orlando sprang in that same instant, grabbed her arm and pitched her to the ground. He dragged her to the cover of the tree and put the point of his dagger to her side.

'Sit still, whelp,' he said in a low voice. 'Your friend has wasted all my manners and good humour with his jesting. I've none to spare for you.'

Aemilia's heart hammered in her chest. Her first instinct had been to struggle but the sharp point of Orlando's dagger had dug into her skin. She looked to where Valentine lay, pale as the moon and wide-eyed as an owl, his mouth gaping and little mewls coming from it. No aid was to come from that quarter. Aemilia's ears strained to hear from the woods. She looked up at Orlando and he down at her and both realised they had the same purpose. Orlando grinned.

'Four to one is fearful odds,' he said.

He stiffened and the grin left him.

'Two to one is better,' said Hemminges from behind him. The point of his sword had tapped Orlando on the head and hovered now behind his neck.

'But best of all is none to one, and so I have it. For all I need do now is run you through the back.'

Orlando did not turn. He remained staring into Aemilia's face, nor did his dagger move from its place in her side. He dug it in a little and Aemilia let out a gasp.

'You cannot kill me fast enough to stop my dagger ending your friend's life.'

'True. I can but avenge the boy's death,' said Hemminges. 'I am sorry for it, Sebastian, but you shall have justice in this life and so, I hope, in the next.'

'No!' screeched Valentine. 'Throw up your blade, Master Russell. I beg you. I beg you.'

Valentine still crouched nearby but his wide eyes were fixed on the brutal tableau before him, Master Russell with his sword held straight out and pointed at Orlando's neck and Orlando hunched over Aemilia, his dagger obscured. Aemilia's breath came in short, scared pants. She could feel Orlando's tremble where he held her.

'Such hasty talk of death and vengeance when we are all yet breathing,' said Orlando.

'Not all,' said Hemminges. 'There's four at least I would not look to dine with again, unless it be in heaven.'

Orlando took a deep breath. 'Let us discuss the matter further.'

'What's to discuss? I kill you, you kill the boy and then I set to killing of the others. If they have not fled yet, as two I think have done. Wiser men than you. Though the one with the arrow in his arm has not crawled far.'

'No,' cried Valentine again, standing at last. 'Let up, let up, I beg you.' It was not clear to whom he spoke.

'None need die today,' said Orlando.

'None more,' corrected Hemminges.

'Yes, yes. You'll forgive me, sir, if I am not in the full grip of logic.' Orlando's frustration, fear and anger showed in his tone. 'Let us say, listen to me, let us say I take my dagger from your friend's side, stand up and we part, friends.'

'I like it not. Let us say instead you drop your dagger now and I forbear to kill you till I have counted so much as a hundred.'

Orlando tilted his head. That sounded like the best bargain he was like to get.

'Two hundred?'

'Drop the dagger, villain, and run.' As Hemminges spoke he edged round the side of Orlando so that the man might see him. Then he took two paces back to show he would not strike in the instant that Orlando dropped his blade. Orlando watched him from the corner of his eye, and hesitated.

It was Aemilia's turn to cry 'no'.

Valentine took that moment to strike Master Russell on the head with a rock. Stunned, Hemminges stumbled and dropped his blade. Orlando leapt towards him as he staggered and grappled him to the ground. The two men rolled and wrestled, Hemminges desperately fending off the dagger in Orlando's hand. Valentine squawked and ran to Aemilia and snatched at her hand. 'Now, fly, fly,' Valentine called as he pulled at her arm, his feet scrabbling in the wet leaves and mud as he sought for purchase against her body's weight. She pushed herself from the ground and Valentine stumbled back at the sudden change.

Aemilia wrenched her hand from his and ran to pluck Hemminges' sword from the ground. She drove it down toward Orlando's back, but as she struck the two wrestling men rolled and the blade missed and slipped and skittered off the rocks where the men had been a moment before. She drew back again but Orlando, seeing her set to strike, threw up his arms and cried for mercy. Hemminges rolled away and sprang to his feet. He took the sword from Aemilia's shaking hand and raised it.

'Mercy,' said Orlando.

Hemminges shifted his feet to thrust but Aemilia's hand came upon his and stayed the blow. She turned to speak to the man on the ground.

'You have a camp?'

The sudden change of tack took Orlando by surprise and Aemilia had to repeat her question before he answered.

'Yes, lad.'

'My name is Sebastian. We three need shelter and food. Will you give it to us?'

'What?' said both Hemminges and Valentine.

'It resolves all. In an instant are we hidden from my father's pursuit, given shelter, given food. No word of us will reach the world to give away our presence.'

'If it's safety that you seek—' began Orlando, battening on hope.

'Shut your mouth,' growled Hemminges.

'We'll be murdered in our beds,' whined Valentine.

'No. I swear it on my life!' cried out Orlando.

'You see,' said Aemilia. 'It's Christian charity to spare his life and doing so, we find ourselves secure.'

'This is a thief, a vagabond, a rogue,' said Hemminges. 'We put our trust in rotten planks to take his word.'

'I am of noble birth, sir,' said Orlando from the ground. 'My word given, is a bond unbreakable.'

'Your nobility is worth as little as the dust you lie in. Besides,' Hemminges turned to Aemilia, 'what of his company, what oaths will they keep?'

'My men will do as I command,' said Orlando.

'I say no. There's no safety in the company of thieves.'

'Whether we join him or no,' said Aemilia, 'we cannot kill a man that's on his back, begging for mercy.'

'Best time to kill him, say I. Then is it easily done.'

'Master Russell, please,' Aemilia begged.

The pattering of Aemilia's heart stilled as she saw Hemminges flick up his blade. He slung it in his baldric again and stalked away. Orlando sighed and slumped against the earth. Hemminges stamped over to pick up his sack and Valentine's. Valentine quailed before him.

'I sought only to protect Aem—' he stuttered before Master Russell cut him off by throwing his small sack to him. The pathetic creature caught it with both hands, which made it impossible for him to deflect the blow that followed. The slap rattled his teeth and knocked him to the ground.

'You're a fool, lad, who should trust where he doubts,' said Hemminges to Valentine, bloody-mouthed and weeping and to whose comfort Aemilia ran. 'Gather your things, we must be away with haste.'

'Your men yet live,' said Hemminges to Orlando over their backs. 'At least I think it may be so if they receive care. You'll find them yonder. Nothing some cat gut and a hot poker cannot cure I'll warrant. If not . . .' He shrugged.

'Come, Sebastian. Come, Valentine. Cease your bleating. This mercy of yours will make for a restless night.'

The third day comes a frost, a killing frost

Verona

Oldcastle, like the ostrich or the fretful porpentine, had stayed hidden in his rooms all that third day, refusing invitations and demands for audience alike. As he sat and drank and picked at food, he thought of the Duke's return, of his anger, of his certain retribution against the man he'd left as treasurer of his daughter's virtue and who had allowed the lock to be picked when scarce an hour had passed. By the bell that rang for the evening meal Oldcastle had been hanged, burnt, racked, boiled in oils and torn to pieces by horses without ever leaving his chair.

The slam of the door came just as he was reaching, tremblingly, for his glass to calm nerves on fire from imagination of cruel deaths.

'Hawkwood!'

The Duke's massy frame filled the door. His hair was as wild as his eyes, he still wore his riding clothes and his crop pointed at Oldcastle. Oldcastle shot to his feet and as the Duke charged down upon him he stumbled back, until the press of the wall beside the fireplace stopped further flight.

'Where is my daughter?'

'Gone,' said Oldcastle.

'How?'

'Valentine,' answered Oldcastle. The many rehearsals of this moment had tortured him greatly but he had his answers ready and he gabbled them out now.

'Why did you not stop him?'

'My lord, recall. He had left before you yourself departed. It was only once you were gone that your servants dared reveal their intelligence, knowing of your great anger at it.'

'Is it so? Well. Well.' The Duke's crop came down to strike against his boot in rhythm with his words, as he paced the room.

Oldcastle eased himself from the wall to put the table between him and the enraged Duke whose crop once more levelled itself at Oldcastle.

'Tell me why there has been no pursuit. Why you proceeded not against these feats so crimeful and so capital in nature.'

'Two reasons, my lord, which to you may seem much unsinewed and yet to me they were strong. The first was that my lieutenant, Russell, whom you know, by cunning made himself of their party.'

'What? Why did he not prevent their flight? We are betrayed, betrayed.'

The Duke sat heavily upon a chair and ran his hands through his hair. Worry for his daughter was writ in his fingers' every tremble.

'Not so, my lord. No. No. Think, my lord, what followed if my man ran hastily to speak of their departure? They put on greater haste and are gone before we can prevent it and now without knowledge of their intended destination and' – Oldcastle paused to lend what next he said a greater emphasis – 'alone, unchaperoned.'

The Duke raged up as he imagined the course of events that Oldcastle set out with his words and saw, in the man's insinuating eyebrow, the frightful implications of his daughter's flight. His anger would have gratified Oldcastle greatly, showing itself a tribute to the power of his rhetoric to paint a scene but, alas, his enjoyment was quite cut short by the piteous sight of the Duke at once tearful and storming against his daughter, hurling whatever came to hand one moment, the next with head in hands.

The thunder receded and Oldcastle peeked out from his place of refuge. The Duke was panting from the effort of his storming and his words came in angry gasps.

'Where?'

'I've yet to receive his sending of his whereabouts,' said Oldcastle, 'but rest assured it comes.'

The Duke did not look comforted. 'I must gather my men, horses, we must ride out. Disaster threatens. My very success with the Count Claudio will be my undoing. The man rides forth to marry within the week. His bags and baggage he sends ahead, that preparation for the wedding feast may be made. His strong purpose, his urgent action, all commend him to me. Now I will present him with an empty wedding bower. My honour, oh God, my honour is undone.'

In distress he clutched again at his hair and more of the furniture suffered beneath his lashing crop.

'I ride tonight. To horse.'

'No, my lord, let me counsel you,' said Oldcastle, coming to the crux of his much imagined argument. 'For you would ride without knowing where and whilst you were absent and your few men with you, what of the priest?'

'The priest?'

'Thornhill,' said Oldcastle. 'Hear my second reason for delay. You had not left the palace long enough for the dust from your horses' hooves to have faded from our sight but Father Thornhill accosted me, bearded me in your great hall with questions about your purpose in leaving, your daughter's flight.'

The Duke was across the room in an instant, pressing close to Oldcastle, grasping him by the collar.

'You told him—'

'Nothing, good my lord. I am not so much a fool as that. Only I said that you were rode to view your estate, your daughter following on a whim, escorted by my man, John Russell.'

'Good, good.'

'There's more. He had taken your prisoner, the outlaw, and put him to the question.'

'What? That damnable outfaced rogue. He presumes upon my command. Absent me a while from this place and I will return to find him lord of my own palace.'

'Curled within like a snail in its shell, impossible to remove,' agreed Oldcastle. Oldcastle's heart still beat a merry pace but he began to have hope that the Duke might yet take his word and the course of his anger be diverted toward the hateful priest.

'My lord, if you depart now in armed retinue so soon after your return . . . Well, Thornhill will make of that what he will and . . . his will tends to the unwholesome for all that he is holy.'

Oldcastle grinned at this last, which he thought rather fine. The Duke paid it no heed, Oldcastle's Italian being a tattered thing whose meaning came mostly through gesture and was not made for punning. Instead, the Duke became lost in thought. He tapped absently on Oldcastle's shoulder with his finger.

'You shall go.'

'My lord?'

'Have you not my commission against these outlaws? We shall say it is that. Then there need be no mention of your true purpose, to find my daughter.'

It was to this Oldcastle had worked.

'Oh wise, my lord, wise. Might I suggest one thought more: let me go alone. Like Orpheus I shall descend into the Underworld and bring back Eurydice, but I shall keep my faith.'

'Madness,' said the Duke. 'Go alone into that nest of vipers?'

'But it must be, for only then may I travel unseen. The soft tread of one man passes unnoticed, whereas the tramp of an army . . .' Oldcastle completed his argument with another of his most expressive shrugs and his head tilted to the side to admire the stratagem. As if to say, do I not speak the wisdom of a Hannibal, a Caesar, a Pompey? He had been particularly pleased with his Orphean simile, which in the imagined arguments of the day had brought a smile to the Duke's face. It failed to do so now.

'Blast it, man,' said the Duke. 'The whole scheme turns on the image of your sweeping the outlaws clean from the woods. You're Hercules and they the Augean stables, not damned Orpheus and his lyre.'

Oldcastle opened his mouth to protest. His plan for escape turned on finding Hemminges alone and the pair making haste for England by such circuitous route as most promised safety. Comfort be damned, he'd had enough of soft beds and thorny problems. What he wanted now was home. Let haste take precedent over luxury. To be trailed by a troop of the Duke's guards would make impossible such a plan. The Duke, however, for whom haste always took precedence, had already turned from Oldcastle and was calling for his captain of guards. He turned to Oldcastle again.

'I had my fill of painful metaphor with Valentine; from a soldier I want plain dealing, not plays on words. You'll ride at dawn. Advantage shall there be in your numbers, your man Russell will thereby know of your coming and convey the message to you where he and my daughter rest. Her found and safe returned, destroy the lousy thieves that infest these woods. If you find them not then join with the Count Claudio's convoy and bring it safely home to the palace.'

At the door the Duke turned to Oldcastle and made a last expressive pass with his crop. 'Bring me Valentine, alive if you can. His head if you cannot.'

And from his bosom purge this black despair

The Veneto

Ahead of her Hemminges strode with angry tread upon the ground. Clouds of leaves and branches shot up as he kicked away obstruction. Aemilia hurried to follow, with Valentine behind.

'That was magnificent,' she panted as she came beside him. 'Such skill at arms, I have never seen its like.'

Hemminges merely grunted and carried on.

'Master Russell, will you again teach me the sword?'

He stopped and rounded on her, his stopping so sudden and so unexpected that Valentine, still moving with his head down, collided with her and sent both stumbling forward. Hemminges looked at them with distaste and shook his head.

'Popinjays playing at adventure.'

'I am not,' said Aemilia, pushing Valentine away so that she might the better confront Master Russell with her sincerity. 'I have studied war. I know my Vegetius and I know my Machiavel and can discourse upon the criticisms of the latter against the former. I have been with my father in his councils. I ride, I am a fair shot with the bow, if I'm to be the master of my own destiny why should I not learn the sword?'

'I'll have no more of this,' said Hemminges. Indecision, a sensation most unaccustomed in his breast, now stuffed it out to bursting. He did not want to thwart Aemilia's will but the same love of her that made him want to give her all that she desired made him desperate of her safety. Her seeming wilful ignorance of the dangers about her was both a source of wonder and of worry. He chided himself for a lovesick fool. There was but one course. 'We must return to your father's palace. This prank is done.'

'Never. I will never return to my father until he gives to me the dignity that I demand.'

'And I cannot,' croaked Valentine. His head still rang from the blow that Hemminges had given him and his jaw swelled and throbbed most painfully. He cared not if the Duke granted him any dignity so long as he would have granted him his hospitality once more. The thought of its loss brought tears to his eyes. Hemminges looked at them both and shook his head again.

'You understand we are hunted? You think these thieves will run from us now because I took them by surprise? Because you showed them mercy?'

'Why not? What do we have that they would want?'

'Oh foolish, foolish woman to say such a thing even if you were not carrying a sack of opals.'

Hemminges dismissed the conversation with a wave of his hand and set off again at a pace. Aemilia considered herself much insulted. Her admiration for Master Russell, which had been growing with each labour he performed, flickered. How dare this servant tell her what she might or might not do? It was only his cowardice that meant they still trudged through the forest when they might have sat by the outlaws' fire and shared their supper. She strode after Hemminges to tell him so.

As she approached he stopped and sniffed the air again, as he had done when the outlaws first surprised them. Aemilia stopped herself and looked about. The afternoon sun was still bright. The trees, bare of their branches, showed themselves all around. What did he see or hear to halt so? Then she heard it too: a cry, a moan upon the wind. Hemminges motioned for her and Valentine to stay. Valentine, his nerves taut already from the earlier fracas, thrilled at the strange keening and with eyes wide with fear shrank to the ground and clutched his hands about his knees, as if he could have shrunk himself into a walnut shell and hid for safety there. Aemilia would have none of it. Ignoring Valentine's frantic waving, she followed after Hemminges. He, creeping ahead, turned and saw her and joined with Valentine in gestures of denial. She set her lips and shook her head. At last, exasperated, he motioned her that if she must follow to do so in silence and set off again after the elusive sound of sadness on the wind.

Ahead, a small bank rose up and it was from beyond that the sound came. Hemminges bent to the ground and crept closer with Aemilia hard behind. They peered beneath gorse bushes and over the edge. A small brook ran below at whose side there stood an old and antique oak tree, roots rising proudly from the bank beside the stream, its canopy bare even as those of other trees had begun to come into leaf. Sequestered within the knot of roots there lay a stag, its side pierced by an arrow, heaving for breath, moaning in pain. Each groaning breath seemed to stretch its hide almost to bursting. From its eyes tears rolled down its nose and down the bank to the black rocks of the brook.

It was not this piteous sight that caused Hemminges' sharp breath. Bent over the stag was a figure, of middling height, gaunt, the face unremarkable save for the dark eyes that quested over the dying stag's body. The man was crying too, for all that his hands held bow and arrows fletched with goose feathers, the same as those in the one that pierced the stag's side. The man bent down to rest his hand on the stag's face.

'Poor deer,' the man said, 'you make a testament as people do. Your tears and mine roll into this brook, giving more to that which has already too much.'

The man looked up and about. 'Where are your friends to succour you in your hour of need? Gone, all gone. It is right. Misery should leave the flux of company.'

As if in answer to his words the far bank was suddenly filled with the spark and jump of feet as a herd of deer raced past. The man stood to watch and cried angrily after them: 'Go then, go, you fat and greasy citizens. Ignore your bankrupt, broken brother here.'

From there he broke into a rant against the tyranny of men who brought with them nothing but death, unhappiness and subjugation. Finishing, he sat heavily down beside the newly dead stag and buried his head in his hands from which closed room emerged the sound of sobbing.

Aemilia shook her head at the mad scene of the hunter weeping over his prey. Outlaws, madmen; the forest was full of incident. Had she but known she would have come earlier to view it all.

Beside her she heard Hemminges let loose the breath he'd held and whisper, 'Oh Will, Will.'

The lunatic, the lover, and the poet

Hemminges stood and called, 'Will.'

The man's head shot up and he stared. 'John?' He got to his feet.

Aemilia could not understand what the man said next for he spoke in a language she did not know, but she saw him turn to address the stag and thought him more clearly mad than any man she'd seen.

Had she ventured that opinion to Hemminges, who did understand Will's English, he might well have agreed with her conclusion.

'I'll not believe it,' said William. 'Yet there you are, John Hemminges I'll call you, friend, companion of my travels. Yet you cannot be here, for sure you are dead with the others. Have we not had this tale before? No matter, it is a good one and will bear retelling. Or is here purgatory and I the ghost?'

He looked down at the stag. 'You see that? The ghost summons me but I'll not go. He may lure me to a place of danger and there take from me my wits.'

William's words had some sense to them but no reason. Hemminges strode down the bank to stand on the other side of the brook from him.

'Will, what . . .' Words seemed to fail him. What question to begin with?

William spoke instead. 'You look well for a ghost. An apparition should not look so plump, think you?' He spoke again to the stag.

'Jesu, Will. Are you mad? I am no ghost. Do you not know me? How come you to these woods? Where is Isabella?'

This torrent of questions William ignored until the last, which seemed to pull him from his reverie.

'Dead.'

With that word William heaved a cry and turned away from Hemminges, his arm coming up to hide his eyes.

'Christ's will,' said Hemminges, his shoulders sinking beneath the sudden burden of the news. 'Christ's will. I am sorry, Will, truly. Her illness?'

'No other hand but God's or so the doctor assured me,' said William over his shoulder.

Hemminges looked about him and seeing no other way, sprang across the brook to where his friend stood. He turned him about and took him in a great embrace that the younger man withstood passively, his arms by his sides, staring beyond him. Hemminges broke his hug and held William at arm's length. He looked gaunt, his pale cheek and hollow eyes, his grief, had added ten years or more to him.

'Tell me what has passed.'

William shook his head. 'I scarcely know and it is a tale of tears and woe to bore with the best of them. Isabella's dead, there's all of it.'

'Will, Will, is there no more?'

'No more but this, Isabella being dead my protection in Venice died with her. I fled, fell in with rogues, and came in search of venison.'

He began to laugh and the laugh soon took him over until he was forced to sit and catch his breath. 'All this way, all this way,' he panted. 'To be again a poacher of deer.'

Hemminges crouched by his unhappy friend and put a hand on his shoulder. William looked drawn and tired. His was not the laughter of happiness but the humming strain of a bowstring too tightly drawn.

'It is good to see you, John,' said William when the breath was back with him.

'And you,' answered Hemminges.

'Who is the woman?' asked William.

Hemminges, puzzled, looked to his friend and then followed his gaze to where Aemilia stood. She had come down from the bank, but the brook was too broad for her to safely vault as Hemminges had done. She waited, watching expectantly. Hemminges could not understand why William called her woman. Her disguise was sound enough for the outlaws' leader at half the distance that William now sat from her. No, it is not her disguise that's broken but poor William's mind, Hemminges thought rapidly. It was better, surely, to maintain the fiction that she was Valentine's page until he knew exactly what occurred here with his friend. He signalled to Aemilia to wait and turned back to William.

'That's no woman, Will, but a lad, Sebastian, a page to the lord Valentine.'

William patted Hemminges on the leg.

'So, so, no woman but a lad, then. And I am Adam!' William pulled Hemminges close. 'But you should know, Hemminges, I am but mad north-north-west. When the wind is in the right quarter,' he looked to Aemilia, 'I know a hawk from a handsaw.'

William walked over to the stag, took his dagger from its sheath and began to dress the beast with swift, clean cuts.

'Will, what are you about?'

William straightened and looked surprisedly at Hemminges. 'Why, preparing this venison for portage.'

'I meant, what are you doing now? Where do you go?'

William's puzzled brow creased deeper. 'I have just said, John.'

'You spoke of the company of rogues.'

'I did, though they are poor players at the part. They know little of their business and their leader would be better at philosophy than at outlawry. Still, I must play my part and that's as huntsman.'

He finished with the stag and stood up. He began to hunt about for a branch thick enough to bear the animal's weight and when he'd found it and shaped it with his dagger, bent again to bind the beast, hand and foot, to the pole. Hemminges peppered him with questions as he did so but he gave them no answer. At the last, when the beast was trussed for carrying, he turned to Hemminges.

'Are you and the lad ready to go?'

'Go where?' said Hemminges, exasperate.

'To the camp, of course. I cannot carry the thing alone. Not easily, at least.'

It seems Aemilia shall have her wish for I am driven to it, thought Hemminges. I can't leave William now he's found. The dusk has come and we've no camp, no fire, no food. Let us hope that they remember Aemilia's mercy.

So pleased was Aemilia to find her plan enacted that she accepted without question that their new fellow traveller was a friend whom grief had made run mad but who was for all that, a friend. But when Valentine learned they were destined for the outlaws' camp after all, he protested shrilly until a stern glance from Hemminges and a scoffing one from Aemilia silenced him. Thereafter he followed, his walk that of a man condemned and resigned to his fate.

As he walked he loudly declared, 'I found myself in a dark forest with the straight path lost to me, alas, how hard it is to say, what was this forest savage, rough and fierce, which to recall is fear.'

And at their front William, hearing Valentine and understanding he quoted Dante, cried out in answer, 'We are not in the forest now, friend. *Abandon hope all you who enter here.*'

'You're smiling, Master Russell,' said Aemilia as she walked beside him. 'That is a look I've not seen on you these three days past.'

His attention drawn to it, Hemminges acknowledged his own good humour. Sure, their position was precarious but William was found and if there was any man in Christendom who might unpick the tangled trap he, Oldcastle and Aemilia all found themselves in then it was William Shakespeare. That is, if he was not truly run mad.

So Hemminges, led by a madman, followed by a woman dressed as a man and trailed by a creature more sodden snail than worldling, tramped to his rest.

Our doubtful hope, our convoy, and our bark

Hemminges' seasoned eye noted two things chiefly as they entered the thieves' camp. First, that there were no sentries set on guard, which was poor discipline and gave substance to Will's claim and Hemminges' own experience that these were new-hatched rogues. The second was that these were a wretched band of starvelings. They'd been met as they approached by one that William had hailed as Ludovico and who'd looked them over with undisguised interest. His had been the friendliest gaze. The rest of the outlaws had watched with grim faces as he, Aemilia and Valentine trooped in with William in the van. They halted by the fire. If William noted the grim looks that followed his companions he gave it no heed. He and Hemminges slung the pole across a frame already set near the fire and when it was fixed William slashed the bindings at the stag's feet to let the body swing free, head down, antlers scraping against the dry leaves on the ground. A mocking applause greeted the completion of his task.

'Fine work, Adam,' said Orlando from a seat by the fire. 'You have brought food and fire alike into our camp.'

William paid him no attention, turning instead to ask something of Aemilia behind him. Hemminges spoke instead.

'You offered us a place earlier.'

'Earlier I was on my back with a sword at my throat.'

Orlando looked unhurt by his encounter. The same was not true for others of the band. The five who had been with Orlando when they had tried to rob Aemilia and Valentine had risen to walk over to the fire. Their bandaged limbs and bruised faces answered for their unhappy look.

'I remember,' Hemminges said.

The low muttering that came from the throats of the men around the fire said that they remembered too.

'Quit your growling,' said Orlando without looking about, his eyes locked on Hemminges. 'The time to play the swaggerer was hours ago.'

He got to his feet. 'Have we had much luck of late, fellows? We have not. We lack the needful skill and discipline. Here is both. They sought our welcome earlier, we should give it now and ask as our price that they teach us how to war.'

This speech did not end the muttering but it did seem to take the venom from it. There was no denying they had proved poor outlaws thus far, nor that Hemminges had ability they lacked and sorely needed. Still all might yet have ended in a brawl, for men that have been hurt have little heed for reason, were it not that at that moment William, who had planted himself by the fire and dragged Valentine to sit shivering beside it, began to sing.

Who doth ambition shun
And loves to live i' the sun,
Seeking the food he eats
And pleased with what he gets,
Come hither, come hither, come hither:
Here shall he see no enemy
But winter and rough weather.

If it do come to pass
That any man turn ass,
Leaving his wealth and ease,
A stubborn will to please,
Ducdame, ducdame, ducdame:
Here shall he see
Gross fools as he,
An if he will come to me.

Aemilia had noticed neither the lack of watch about the camp nor the fact that she was the only woman among them. Her eyes saw with the excitement of an innocent. She saw the company of thieves watch Master Russell pass and interpreted their close attention as born of the same admiration for his skill at arms that she felt. Aemilia came to stand behind Master Russell and Adam. She peeped past them at the bandit leader. He had recovered the poise he had held when first he confronted them in the woods. The dirt and leaves that had marred his hair and face after his wrestling with Master Russell had been washed clean. His hair, still damp, was swept back from his face and glinted darkly in the fire's light. Adam turned to her sharply.

'What was that you said?' he asked.

'Only that I have entered a brave new world,' she said.

'And such creatures in it,' he added with a nod.

When Aemilia's attention was returned to the conference between Master Russell and Orlando she saw at last that theirs was a cold welcome. A circle of angry faces surrounded the little group and looked set for violent action, when the sudden, sweet voice of the madman, Adam, cut across them. The contrast between the song and the mood of the taut circle of men made itself at once apparent, as did the words, which seemed fit to the moment as if crafted for it, for all that they must be the invention of the moment.

It was a little thing but it was enough to break the mood of the moment. Into the gap Orlando slipped his authority. After the second verse had finished, he turned to the gathered group and began to shoo them away.

'Aye, asses, truly. If we are such fools that we would fight each other when we've barely the strength to fight our foes. Go, go to your beds and rest. Tomorrow you'll see fighting enough for any men.'

The men turned and tramped away, some more reluctantly than others.

'What is "ducdame"?' Aemilia asked Adam.

'A Greek invocation, to call fools into a circle,' he answered. He stood and stretched his arms wide and yawned. 'I'll go and sleep, if I can. If I cannot, I'll rail against all the first-born of Egypt.'

With these strange words he made off from the fire to a place nearby, pulled his cloak about him and lay still.

Valentine felt sick. Was it any wonder? He had been on such a swell and ebb of fear these last few moments, he was quite seasick of it. First, he'd had the relief of fire and food promised, then the terror as it seemed they'd be mobbed by vengeful men, and last the odd tension of the mad fool's warbling song that had become, oh strange indeed, the cue for all to sleep.

He heartily wished he'd never spoken to the Duke of his love for Aemilia. He'd been comfortable at the court but striving to better his position, he'd marred what was well. He sneezed. God's blood, would illness now be added to his suffering? Why mock poor fellows thus?

He turned to Aemilia for comfort and tugged at her sleeve. She was pulled from her careful watching of Master Russell and Orlando only after several moments.

'Can we not to bed?' hissed Valentine in her ear.

He noted the look of annoyance that flashed across her face and felt angry at it. Was he not in this hell at her urging? At her insistence had he confronted her father with results all too predictable and harsh. He tugged again at her. Slowly she turned her gaze from the two men's conversation to Valentine.

'Let us rest, Ae—' he began, before a harsh look reminded him of her new name. 'Sebastian. I am a broken reed and must rest.'

Aemilia's despairing gaze suggested that she could not see why his need for rest involved her at all but Valentine was damned if he was going to sleep alone amongst this pack of hyenas. She shrugged in answer and, for want of a better thought, they made their way over to where the madman, Adam, had gone for rest. The ground there proved dry enough if rocky, and though Aemilia lay her head down not thinking sleep would come, the trials of the day saw her asleep before Valentine had finished his muttered complaints in her ear. Valentine's mood grew darker still. He rolled to his side, wrapped his damp velvet about him and shivered his way to his own rest.

Only Hemminges stayed awake, sat by the fire, watching. He and Orlando had spoken after the other men had departed.

'What fighting do you plan for tomorrow?' he had asked Orlando. The outlaw leader turned to him and shrugged.

'I have no plan save action,' he said. 'Your rout of our brave forces is but the latest in a string of failures that have taken the heart from us and kept us from food and treasure. We must do something tomorrow or fall apart in dribs and drabs.'

Hemminges looked about him at the paltry camp. 'Perhaps that would be no bad thing.'

Orlando shook his head. 'I need these men. We've a greater destiny if we can but . . .' He broke off with another shake of his head. He raised his hand in farewell and without more words made his way from the fire to his own sleep.

So Hemminges sat alone by the fire until at last he too rose and went to lie near the others.

That night the quiet was broken by a gruesome crack, the sound of a rock striking rock. It was followed by a whistling of wind and then a howl as Hemminges plied a branch across the calves of the fool who'd tried to murder him under cover of dark. Hemminges had feared such a course when he saw the anger on the men's faces and instead of lying down to sleep had, in the darkness, wrapped his cloak over a rock and stuffed it out with branches, to make it look like he slept. Jacopo, whom Hemminges had struck senseless in the forest at noon, had, at midnight, struck only insensate stone with his own blow. Now Hemminges paid him back with whipping of his tender flesh. The first blow lifted him and set him jumping, the second, the wheel of Hemminges' strike bringing it now across his shins, took him to his knees. Hemminges pulled his arm back to take the fool's head from his body but stopped even before Orlando's shout of 'Hold, enough!'

Jacopo rolled on the ground, clutching at his bleeding shins, groaning and cursing. Orlando, roused, came to stand over him. Hemminges gave the outlaws' leader a cold stare and to it Orlando threw up his hands. 'This business is nothing of my doing.'

Orlando looked down at the moaning Jacopo. 'Jesu, man. Leave off your petty vengeances. It's not good for your health. Hie you to your bed. Go, man, go.'

Another of the outlaws, several of whom had gathered in the darkness to view the matter, dragged the hapless Jacopo to his feet and took him, stumblingly, to his bed. Orlando watched them go before he turned to Hemminges.

'You see, they need action.'

Hemminges only grunted.

A deed of death done on the innocent

Verona

'The Duke has forbidden it,' said Arrigo.

'What do I care for the Duke's orders?' said Thornhill. He paced back and forth in the mean little room given him by the Duke, making Arrigo shuffle out of the way as best he might.

'Father, there is much ill-will towards us here,' began Arrigo but Thornhill turned on him and thrust the parchment in his face.

'They are gone from Venice more than a week,' he barked. 'Do you understand that? What it bodes?'

He turned and hurled the letter from Cesare Costa into the fire. He put a hand on the mantel to steady himself and stared into the flames. I am going to be too late. They are going to escape me. The letter crackled as the fire burnt away words confirming the English spies had escaped from Costa's grasp. At least the fool had discovered that they were indeed travelling separately. One at least had been taken alone by gondola across the lagoon. They must come this way. Thornhill beat his hand on the mantelpiece – they must. Yet, where were they? Too many days had passed. Why could Costa not have discovered this earlier? They might be anywhere.

'What news from Ludovico?'

'None.'

'Get a message to him. I must know if anyone is newly come to join these rogues in the woods.'

Arrigo nodded but wondered how this was to be achieved.

'And we must speak to Sir Nicholas again.'

'Father, he departs this morning.'

'Stop him. Bring him here.'

'He rides to carry out the Duke's commission against the outlaws. Their preparations are made with haste. He may be already gone.'

Thornhill struck the mantel again. How was he to find these damned spies?

Arrigo shuffled in awkward silence trying to think of a way to excuse himself from the room before whatever fire built within Thornhill consumed all in its reach. Occupied with this thought, it was a moment before he realised that the priest was muttering.

'Father?' he ventured.

'Send to Monsignor Costa,' said Thornhill. 'I want from him a detailed description of those he suspects of being the English spies – detailed, you understand, it must be exact in every particular. Tell him to respond with all urgency. We must spread out our net if we are to catch these fish.'

He drummed his fingers on his thigh and spoke half to himself, 'There is something about this Sir Nicholas I do not like.'

'I thought,' said Arrigo behind him, 'that you had found Sir Nicholas to be an innocent.'

Thornhill turned slowly about. His pale eyes were bloodshot and feverish.

'None of us,' he said, 'are innocent. Now go and bring me Costa's reply.'

But, soft! What light through yonder window breaks?

The day had dawned fair and Oldcastle had seen it do so, much to his displeasure.

Dionisio had roused him while it was still dark and helped him to dress. The Duke had offered Oldcastle armour to replace that lost in his reported flight from the robbers, which Oldcastle grimacing to put it on, so heavy was it on his massy frame, now declined as unnecessary, 'against so meagre a foe as the outlawry of the woods'. He'd drawn on the heavy cloak offered him, though, against the anticipated cold of the forest nights, and a brightly polished helm and two steel-backed gauntlets gave him, he felt, a sufficiently martial air to make the absence of a breastplate an inconsequence. He had snatched at some twice-baked bread with ham on it that was offered him and gratefully washed it down with a cup of wine, which he noted with a nod of approval to his servant had not been watered. Then he straightened his back and followed Dionisio from his room, casting a loving glance backward at his bed as the door shut behind him.

In the courtyard of the palace were gathered the Duke's troop of men. A dozen, led by a grey-haired corporal of horse whose grand moustaches drooped like two plumes from beneath his proud nose and made the man look like proud Charlemain as his horse pranced before Oldcastle.

'Your men, Sir Nicholas, stand ready. What is your command?'

Oldcastle, admiring the man's whiskers despite himself, drew in his belly and strutted to his own horse to mount. He placed his foot within the stirrup and made to rise only to realise that the addition of the heavy cloak, helm and gauntlets made grasping of the pommel difficult and graceful rise impossible.

'A little help here, ho,' he called to Dionisio. The man dismounted his own pony and ran to assist him. He did his best to lift Oldcastle's other leg, as Oldcastle commanded, at the count of three. It was a fearful task and Dionisio took several knocks from Oldcastle's sword swinging. At last, with some labour and no grace at all, he took his seat and surveyed his soldiery. For all the corporal's magnificence the others had a careworn look. Their armour was old and pitted and their lances, held at wrist and knee, were tipped with rusting blades. Their faces bore looks of resignation, not excitement. Oldcastle sighed. From beneath the brim of his helm he caught sight of the Duke appearing on the balcony above. Best make a show of it, he thought.

'Soldiers, my brothers in arms, today we make sally to bring your lord's justice to the farthest corners of his realm. Let no man fear us save the outlaw and him . . .' His voice rose to the climax: 'Let him tremble as the dormouse does before the eagle!'

Good enough, he thought. The men seemed largely unmoved and it was a moment before Oldcastle realised that in his nervousness he had spoken in English. Damned if I will repeat it, he thought. The tone is what counts.

'Ride out,' he called and dug his heels into his horse's flank. The beast, more finely trained than those that Oldcastle was used to, sprang to his touch and leapt forward at the canter with Oldcastle clinging and bouncing upon its back. The horse shot through the gate and out on to the road beyond with Oldcastle by the one moment hauling at the reins and calling for the damn thing to halt and by the other flopping forward over its neck as he struggled to maintain his seat. At last he brought it to the trot and then the walk and at last to the halt. He turned its head to the palace where the small troop was now emerging and trotting to join him.

The corporal closed with him and drew alongside.

'Sir Nicholas,' he began, his moustaches pulled back in concern. 'You have a plan?'

'Well of course I have a plan, man,' said Oldcastle indignantly.

'Please, Sir Nicholas, disclose it to me.'

'All in good time, my man, all in good time,' bluffed Oldcastle. 'Is secrecy not one of the six precepts of war? First let us to the woods and make camp. Then we will hold counsel.'

He circled his horse and, more carefully now, set his heels to its side to make it walk on.

'Sir Nicholas,' called the corporal to his back.

Oldcastle sighed and pulled the horse round.

'Enough, man. We must be about our business.'

The corporal shrugged and signalled his men on to follow. Oldcastle in the van felt sweat running from beneath his heavy helm despite the morning's cold.

'Sir Nicholas?' Dionisio called.

He would have to think of some kind of plan soon enough.

'Sir Nicholas?'

If it could be so devised, let it be a plan that allowed him to ditch this company and make for freedom. Dionisio pulled alongside him on his pony.

'Sir Nicholas?'

'Oh yes, Dionisio,' said Oldcastle, the quiet voice at last penetrating a mind distracted by the thought of freedom.

'Sir Nicholas,' the little man said, 'the woods, Sir Nicholas, lie on the other road.'

Oldcastle looked down at the man.

'The other road?'

'To the east, Sir Nicholas,' said Dionisio with an apologetic smile.

Oldcastle looked down at the round face of his servant. Was the man gulling him? He'd ever been kind in his attentions to Oldcastle and his face was open and honest now. They carried on along the road for a quarter of an hour more. Then Oldcastle halted and turned his horse about and rode to the corporal.

'I think that should suffice,' he declared.

The corporal looked at him, confused. Oldcastle nodded sagely.

'Yes, if there be pursuit or spies among the Duke's servants our riding in this direction will have been enough to confound them. Have the men turn about and take us to the east road and the woods.'

The corporal looked at Oldcastle for a moment and then wheeled away to order the troop about and they all set off again back in the direction they had come. At the rear rode Oldcastle and Dionisio. Neither looked at the other or said another word until the woods hove into view.

Our revels now are ended

The Veneto

Hemminges woke to find William already looking over him, knees pulled up and circled by his arms, his cloak wrapped about him like the old hermit of Prague. Hemminges pulled himself upright and leaned against a tree trunk while the blood crept back into his extremities from a cold night spent amidst the roots in the hollow of a tree. He looked about; they were alone and beyond the earshot of others.

'Where are Sebastian and Valentine?'

'Gone.'

'Gone?'

'Aye, gone. Though I am certain they will return,' said William to the strained note in Hemminges' voice. 'Well, almost certain. The tall bristle-bearded woman to the North, the smooth-cheeked boy to the East. Perhaps each went to find a quiet place to bathe? Not much for bathing are our brothers here, save Orlando, who must scrub and scrub at himself until he is pink as a prawn. Still he cannot wash out the stain upon himself.'

'What stain is that?'

William ignored the question, looking instead in the direction that Sebastian had gone.

'Your Sebastian has the look of a bather. Pray Jesu she do not scrub away disguise. Or cause it to be asked why pissing in the brook as the other men do is not good enough.'

'William, what happened in Venice after we left?'

'Little enough.'

'William, I am your friend, be open with me. What passed between you and Isabella?'

William shook his head, muttering, 'Open with you? Open such a box to make of me another Pandora.' His eyes not meeting Hemminges' questing ones, he answered.

'What passed? Little enough and yet a whole world.' He sighed deeply. 'Out went the light and, then, out went the light.'

Hemminges began to rise to go to give his friend comfort, but a look on William's face as he at last returned his gaze made him pause. He sat back down again. There'd been a rockiness in William's eyes that shunned consolation: the soft flesh on the fruit of William's happier days was stripped away to leave behind only the hard and bitter stone.

'I would I could give you a good answer, John, but I've no answers to give, no understanding at all. My days now seem to me to lack all shape and sense. I cannot find a place or reason for her death. I cannot see why I should be given such a love and have it taken away within a year.'

'It is a tragedy.'

'I would it were, John,' said William with venomed voice. 'Yet it cannot be so for the Philosopher tells us Tragedy must have reason, that the last act must be explained by the events of the first. There is no explanation here. This is not Tragedy but Comedy, or so I take it, for all there is seems to me absurdity. She's gone and all that was best and brightest of her gone too. All's cheerless, dark and deadly now.'

'Come, Will, if there is no reason there can you not make one?'

William's answer was a gesture, a player's mummery, a hand that reached and tried to grasp and finding air only, fell limp. Hemminges watched him for a long while. William seemed to feel no urge to conversation and Hemminges, never one to speak where silence would suffice, had no easy words to give him. His own mind was a turmoil. He thought of Aemilia and of his own madness in thinking of one who was so far beyond him. By turns her actions drew his desires on and sent them away again. When she showed herself brave and eager, then he thought her the most beautiful creature in the world. When she showed herself wilful, when she seemed to think only of her own concerns, then he thought her base for all her noble blood. He had no thought for what he wanted of her. Sometimes he thought of asking her to follow him to England. In the same instant he railed against the madness of the idea and thought only of returning her to the safety of her father's court. His mind was not still when it touched on Aemilia. He'd had a calm once that had been his strength and a strength to others. It was lost to him now.

'I am glad to have found you, Will,' said Hemminges at length. 'I need your wits.'

This comment provoked a burst of laughter from William. 'I am mortal sorry then, for I have quite lost them. At least I think I have. Of my five wits four at least are gone. They're not there when I look for them. I wish the fifth were gone too. What is the riddle that you bring me? Perhaps if they're still living you will lure my wits back with the right bait.'

'I pray it is the thornier tangles that your wits find most to their taste,' Hemminges sighed, 'for between our duty to England and to our friend Nick Oldcastle we are caught in such roots and creepers.'

'Duties on duties,' said William. 'Like a watchful god, howsoe'er I run still I remain in their grasp.'

He signalled for Hemminges to go on with a lift of his chin and Hemminges set out the trouble in short swift strokes: how he and Oldcastle came to be disguised, how imposed upon, how they must hurry to England and pass on the deadly burden of these names before they caught a death of them, how he had come to escort Valentine and his page Sebastian in their exile.

'We all must go to England.'

'All?' asked William.

'Yes all. For if the one of us be taken, all having knowledge of the names, then will the extent of that intelligence be known. So may the Pope make plans.'

'What care I for that?'

Hemminges looked shocked at William's reply.

'You? Who have been pursued by the Pope's man? Whose joy in his last days of love was constrained, curtailed, confounded by the Pope's machinations? You most of all have motive strong to discomfort him.'

'And so another plan springs forth from the death of the first. And so and so. I have lost the understanding of it. Here's a riddle for you, John: who is it builds things that last longer than a Pope's plans, a Queen's wishes or a lover's desires?'

Hemminges shrugged his ignorance.

'A gravedigger, for what he builds lasts till Judgement Day.'

Hemminges' intended sharp response to William's playing was cut off by the return of Aemilia and Valentine. Hemminges need not have worried that Aemilia would forget herself and her disguise. He looked in surprise at her head, no cowl or cap covering it: she had hacked at her hair to make of it a man's length. Indeed, Valentine's hair was now its better both for length and lustre. Only a softness to her skin threatened to give away her true nature. They nodded to Hemminges and William as they made their way to the cooking pot to scavenge what pottage remained from the meagre amount there was in opening.

Once passed, Hemminges leaned again towards his friend: 'If not for spiting the Pope then do it for your friends. Oldcastle cannot keep up his forged appearance and when he is discovered he will be killed, and not quickly either.'

'She might pass, she's very plain,' said William, eyes still on Aemilia. Hemminges, despite his frustration that William would not let the problem bite with his wits' gears, bristled in her defence.

'She may not have the gilded outward show that Isabella had, Will,' said Hemminges, 'but the soul inside is as fair. Have a care for others. Yours is not the only suffering in the world.'

'John, you remind me of what I should already know. Love looks not with the eye but with the mind and' – he broke into song –

You that choose not by the view,
choose as fair, choose as true.

The sudden catch ended, he looked from Hemminges to his Sebastian: 'Even a leaden casket may hide a jewel within.'

'It is not my choosing but Valentine's,' said Hemminges a little too sharply.

'Now it is you, I think, has lost his wits to try and gull me so,' said William.

'You're not so out of your wits that you did not see at once through her disguise,' began Hemminges, his frustration building. William held up a hand to stop Hemminges' further protestations.

'Nor you so certain that I am in my wits that you would admit as much at first. Besides,' he went on, 'you promised me good meat to feed my all too shrivelled wits and yet you give me nothing but leavings that would insult a dog. There is no riddle to unpick if what you say be so. Leave the woman here, she is with her lover where she wants to be, and you and I shall take us to the Duke, tell where they are and then depart to England with Oldcastle in our train.'

'That's the counsel of betrayal,' answered Hemminges. 'She will be discovered and . . .' He gestured about him at the knavish company in which a young woman should find herself alone. 'Is your best thought that we should sell them to the Duke?'

'What's she to me or, by your pleading, you? Our cause is England and Oldcastle, is it not? She is a small price to pay for Oldcastle. Why by the size of her next to Oldcastle, pound for pound the exchange is nearly all profit.'

'Must we exchange one for the other? Can you not think how we might save both?'

William shook his head. 'So much pleading for one you claim to think nothing of. I think you have a care for this Sebastian and doubt the quality of her lover. So be it. My proposal solves that too. Let him be taken with these rest and her restored to her father.'

Hemminges shifted in his seat with annoyance. Where was the William of careful planning and cunning thought? He wished he had the power to make his own plans, but he was a blunt instrument and ever had been. His wisdom had always lain in chaining himself to others who might do the greater thinking for him. Now his joy and relief at finding William were curdled by discovery that the old William, whose stratagems had in the past woven selfish desire together with thought for others into a tapestry, had died with Isabella and left only a self-regarding husk behind. He needed William, not singing songs and cursing God, but here and now, his tricksy wits at their most cunning. He had no thought of his own for how to resolve the strands that bound him.

'I can't go and leave the girl here,' he said.

'There's an argument I have heard before.'

'You made it to your own persuasion then, work that same rhetoric now.'

'No.' William's answer was a curt shot of sound. 'No. It persuaded you not then, just as it finds no purchase on me now. Your simple syllogism now lacks a premise, Hemminges. What carried me then was love and that is now dead.'

Where shall we take a purse tomorrow, Jack?

Valentine was reciting a verse as he and Aemilia walked back to the outlaws' camp: a paean to his love that listed out her features and made comparison of them to the stars, the moon, the sky above and cited the hope of seeing them as all that kept him living in the dark woods of the world. William, seeing this, patted Hemminges on the leg.

'Here comes young love now.'

He sprang from his seat on the ground and strode towards them. 'Oh ho,' he said as he approached.

Valentine's voice trailed away as mad Adam bore down upon him.

'Nay,' William said, waving him on with a smile on his face. 'Go on. It is a fair piece and reminds me of another.'

Aemilia laughed. 'A poem of your own, sir?'

Valentine cursed and wondered that she encouraged his madness. William's attention was now wholly on Aemilia.

'Not my own. No, no, a ballad that my father taught me, or was it my grand-dam? No matter. It is about a young man whose lover is lost to him by a curse, transformed into a willow tree. The young man now walks the woods, full of woeful sighs and ballads of his own.'

And with this introduction William began to declaim. Each line began as that of Valentine's but ended in comparison of parts most unseemly, concluding with comparison of his mistress's eyebrow to the beauteous eye of a calf. Aemilia's laughter at it scraped at Valentine's pride and he was glad when commotion from across the camp drew them away.

'You're up, my boys? You've ginger in you?' cried Orlando.

Some of the outlaws scowled for answer but all gathered closer to discover what had put their leader in such good humour on such a grey day.

'We all know that luck has not been with us these last few days,' he said. He ignored Zago's cluck of disgruntlement at this statement and spoke on. 'Well luck is like a tide, it ebbs and flows. It's a foolish sailor that thinks the tide will not turn. Ours has. While you were at your beds I was up and about and so were others. Not an hour from here there strides along the road four fat pilgrims, satchels fat with offerings.'

This was news and the faces of the starved and wretched outlaws shone with anticipation, all save that of Petro. The priest was a younger brother's second son and, as such, fortunate to have been given a vocation in the Church and not abandoned to such fortune as the world might gift him. It was not, however, a role to which he was by temperament suited; he was at root too choleric in temper and too temptable. His oaths daily grated on him and were, as he was wont to say when in drunken remembrance of those days, 'more visible in the breach than in the observance'. Yet he had in him the fear of God and would have been in office still were it not that one morning, when his brother friars had sought to rouse him from a drunken stupor to join in Matins, he had growled and raged and at last struck the abbot of the monastery. He'd fled the promised penance and made his way to the woods, falling in with the outlaws and at last finding in their fellowship a spiritual role that had been lacking in more pampered circumstances.

'I'll none of it, 'tis not godly to rob pilgrims,' the former priest declared.

'As you wish,' said Orlando. 'At this rate you'll be facing St Peter sooner than the rest of us. Those that do not share in the adventure cannot share in its rewards.'

'Fine,' said Petro, whose stomach had always held greatest sway over his conscience. 'I see it is the parable of the talents. Though we should have a care to let them pass on unharmed.'

'Brother Petro,' declared Orlando, 'they shall leave us the better for our meeting. For did not the Lord tell us that those that feed and clothe the hungry and the naked shall be rewarded in heaven?'

Petro nodded. 'That is so, Brother Orlando, in the Gospel of Matthew, chapter 25 it is so written.' He had not expected to be catechised in this manner but added it to the growing list of things he had not expected in his life and yet had come his way.

'I think he also said,' whispered William behind Hemminges, '"Put up your sword for those that live by the sword shall die by it." How rarely that verse finds expression in these days.'

Hemminges did not look round.

'We three shall stay and guard the camp,' said Hemminges.

'Oh ho, you shall not,' said Zago, laughing and shaking his head.

'All in, all one,' said Orlando. 'It was not us that sought your company but you ours.'

'These lads are not yet ready for a fight,' protested Hemminges, pointing at Aemilia and Valentine. Valentine set to vigorous nodding but Aemilia bristled and set her shoulders and would have spoken in her own defence but Orlando spoke first.

'They lack experience,' he said. 'And shall gain it now. Four fat pigeons and so many foxes? No danger, no danger at all. Come Ludovico, do not dawdle at the rear with these new men but lead and show your worth. Come, men, to arms, to arms.'

If he by chance escape your venomed stuck

Verona

'I will have admittance,' Thornhill demanded.

'You shall not,' answered Rodrigo. 'By His Grace's command he will give you no audience. He bids you be grateful that he leaves you and your men with lodging. Your actions to date merit a harsher measure. Ask for nothing more.'

'I tell you I have intelligence touching on the true nature of Sir Nicholas Hawkwood,' said Thornhill.

His voice hissed out between his teeth, the sound of hot metal being dipped in water, he was hot indeed. Angry with himself, with that fool Cesare Costa, with this interfering duke. He blazed. Rodrigo was grateful that the captain stood by his side for Thornhill seemed on the verge of madness. Rodrigo thought it best simply to shake his head in answer. A stillness hung over the antechamber, the only noise the crackle of paper as Thornhill's fist crushed the letter clutched within it. He paid no further courtesy to the Duke's lackeys but turned on his heel and stalked from the room. Behind him Rodrigo's shoulders slumped and it was only the realisation that the captain's had done so too that made him realise how great had been the tension in the room.

'There's one I would not have made an enemy for a thousand ducats,' muttered Rodrigo.

The captain grunted his agreement and turned to make report to the Duke.

Thornhill strode towards his rooms. His fury gave him speed. The letter from Cesare Costa was clutched in his hand. It told a sorry tale of chances missed, of arrogant plotting when direct acts had been needed, of a failure to wield the true might of the Church, none of which Thornhill could forgive. Yet that was not the worst of it, for within it Costa set down what he knew of the English. Three men, one tall and fat, one solid as a block and a third, a young man, handsome in an ordinary way, unremarkable, save that one might know him by the eyes. The last two Thornhill did not recognise but the first, in every detail of Costa's description it was Sir Nicholas Hawkwood, or Sir Henry Carr, or some other name. He had had him in his hands, in the very place of questioning, and let him go. This last he could not forgive himself. How did he deceive me? Thornhill thought. Truly this Hawkwood was a dangerous man, a villain indeed to look so coolly on the torture of another and still to play his part. He must be found with haste, taken with the rest, before he do true harm. Yes, there is God's plan: He lets the first go to lead me to the others.

Thornhill slammed open the door to his rooms and Arrigo, waiting, stood hastily to attention.

'Your man watched Hawkwood leave?' demanded Thornhill.

'Yes, Father. He said it was most strange.'

'Strange, how so?'

'Sir Nicholas rode in commission against the outlaws in the woods yet led his troop of men on the other road.'

Thornhill slapped his leg. Of course, cunning devil, cunning, cunning heretic devil. He led the Duke's men away from the outlaws, away from his friends. Proof of this Hawkwood's deceptions pile in upon themselves.

'And from Ludovico?'

'No news, Father.'

Thornhill sat down at the table, lost in thought.

'Send two men, your best, Arrigo, your best, to follow the road this Hawkwood took. Scout him out, bring me news of his whereabouts with haste. When we know where he has gone then we must be ready to ride at once to take him. At once.'

'I go.' Arrigo saluted and turned to depart.

Thornhill called after him, 'And send again to Ludovico. If message may be got to him, tell him to be ready for our sudden arrival.'

Thornhill heard Arrigo go. Alone in his room a little smile crept to the corner of his lips as he stared at the fire and thought of fires to come.

He will steal, sir, an egg out of a cloister

The Veneto

So changed was the mood of the returning outlaws it was as if they'd departed the camp to attend a funeral and returned with the dead man living again. Whistles as they walked, merry chatter, the clapping of backs, and arms slung across shoulders was their procession made of. Four fat satchels were slung upon the ground and Orlando sprang upon a fallen trunk of tree nearby to direct the bringing of the chest and barrels next.

'All went well then,' said Jacopo, whose injuries had volunteered him to the guarding of the camp.

'Well, friend Jacopo?' said Orlando. 'Well? It was a very triumph!' His cry was met by a cheer from the gathered outlaws. 'For where we thought to fall on four simple pilgrims we found instead a train of them. All chanting like lambs but wanting a shepherd, we crept about them and swept them up in our embrace.'

He pointed to Hemminges. 'There was one of their number, a great bear of a man, that strode at their front carrying a cross, who did not take kindly to our arrival and swung that cross like a halberd but all's too much for brave John Russell, well he deserves that name, who outfaced him as he swung.'

Orlando's mumming of the blows caused him to slip from his perch to the laughter of the outlaws. From his back upon the ground Orlando finished his tale:

'Thus did Master Russell, like an Achilles, a Hector, dart between the blows and bring him to his knees. The which I noted—' But his words were drowned by the outlaws shouting over him '"is the proper place for a Godly man!"'

Orlando looked momentarily discomfited to be spoken over but it passed in an instant and, getting up, he turned and bowed to the men. 'My friends, I humbly thank you. The deed was great, the commentary greater. Nor do we forget young Sebastian who, against the protestations of more experienced men, volunteered to be our bait and our distraction and when assailed stood firm. Here's to the valour of youth!'

Again the outlaws roared their pleasure. The chest was opened and found to contain plate, coin, cups of pewter and some of silver, three candlesticks and a finely wrought lute. Treasure enough for comfort, nay for luxury too. Best of all was this: the barrels being broached held sack, which Luca, who had once worked in a vineyard and considered himself an expert in such matters, drank with great ceremony and pronounced to be good, fresh and ready for drinking. The outlaws joyed in the bounty and loving cups passed from hand to hand.

Aemilia looked about her and felt the excitement of the band join with her own and lift it higher. On their outward march, when Orlando had proposed that she confront the pilgrims and draw their view, she'd felt the tightening in her chest and almost cried off the post but then Master Russell had stepped in, so vehement against it that she, honour pricked, had insisted upon it. It angered her that Master Russell cosseted her so. She had one father already and did not need another.

The sight of the pilgrims' leader, beard tangled, eyes wild, his staff raised above his head, its iron cross set to dash her brains from her head, was an image she would carry to the grave. She'd lifted her dagger above her, knowing it hopeless, that the blow would smash it from her grip, she'd cried out her terror, and then Russell had been upon him, knocking him from his path, the crozier flailing from his hands. It was as though her body had been flooded by joy in that instant as she realised she would live. She'd howled her joy. Russell had not stopped. She'd watched, again in wonder, as he darted across to challenge another of the pilgrims. In a moment all were down or cowed and a great cheer had gone up from the bandits and her voice was loud among them.

Hemminges watched Aemilia, bright-eyed with excitement, be clapped on the back and join with others in retelling the tale of their triumphs. He could not share her pleasure. He was too aware of the dangers that surrounded her.

One of the outlaws, Ludovico, came to sit by him and began to ask him a host of questions about where he came from and where he had learned to fight so well but Hemminges offered only single words in reply. He was not in the mood for conversation even if others were. Out of the corner of his eye he caught sight of William, stood in a sardonic, watchful pose, distant from the others' revels. He made no attempt to join him, standing apart as he had done in the robbery, simply observing. Hemminges wished he had his friend's power of understanding to turn on William himself. Such a deal of pain his friend had suffered, too much it seemed; the iron had not bent but shattered at the blow.

Valentine too was sat apart but his was the look of a man exhausted. He took no pleasure in the shouts of triumph or in the trophies held aloft, for each seemed to him to be another loop in the cord that would become the noose that hanged them all. He'd had riches twice as much as these at his command and tossed them all aside. He felt Aemilia come and sit beside him. He longed to take her in his arms and feel her embrace steady him. When at the court he'd felt his position keenest, his beggar's status and the contempt for the passions that sustained him, poetry, music, philosophy, in Aemilia he had found a willing ear and an uplifting eye. She had not mocked his ambition but given him the wings to think he might fly. Now the sun had seared those wings and he'd tumbled to the ground. He turned to her and her look gave him heart as it had done in the past. He devoutly wished that look would have held longer but Orlando had leapt again to his tree-trunk rostrum and Aemilia's eyes turned to him as he began to speak.

'Now, my friends, are we greedy men? Are we selfish men? Have we in our triumph forgot those who remembered us in our disasters? We have not and we will not. Therefore, let us, when we have reckoned up our booty, give full a half of all that we have gathered here to the poor that dot these woods. What think you of this plan, will you say me, nay?'

To Valentine's judgement the cry of yes had not the force of earlier cheering but it came nonetheless and he saw in Aemilia's moist and uplifted gaze that Orlando's generous spirit had won to him an ardent follower. *Hah!* It is easy to be generous with another's money, he thought, his gloom again upon him.

I must be from this place. I must to the palace again, for I am not of these men's thinking nor of their mettle. He glanced across the company, who were increasingly merry as the barrels drained, until his eyes lit upon Petro, the priest, his matted thatch of black hair hanging over his eyes and almost to his nose, a thing so prominent and bloodshot as almost to demand its own name. The man was luckier than the rest for having his own chalice with which to tap the barrel, rescued from his former abbey as he'd fled.

The sight of the priest turned Valentine's thoughts to the fount and origin of his dilemma, the objection of the Duke to his marrying the Duke's daughter. Why, here was the solution to that dilemma, sottish and sleeping. Return to the Duke with the marriage done. Why not? What matter then for the Duke's approval if, in the eyes of the Lord, he and she were one? The Duke was a practical man above all other things and would bend himself to accommodate the new world that he found himself in. Valentine turned the idea over in his head but could think of no objection to it. What was the worst that could occur? That she and he would be lawful exiles instead of illegitimate ones?

But soft, he must not be overhasty. It would not do to let Aemilia's true state be known, not now, not here among these swinish outlaws, drunk and bawdy and all too dangerous to a maid. He must test the priest against the thought first. If all was propitiate then he and Aemilia might be married before the week was done.

Aemilia watched Valentine stride over to the fire with something of the jaunty step that she had felt on the walk back from the robbing of the pilgrims. Pray God, he is come into better humour by our triumph, she thought. He'd been poor company on their adventure thus far, to her surprise and consternation, for at the palace he'd been the thing that had kept her singing when all about her were merely the bars of the cage that held her. His flights of fancy, his dreams of ambitions mastered, had given her own ambitions wing. Yet how their flight had shown the difference in their natures. He had ventured forth but taken with him a chain about his ankle that ever tugged to pull him back to what lay behind. She, let loose from the confines of her gilded cell, had burst into soars and sweeps and opportunities. She thought how Master Russell had raged when she had proposed herself as the diversion to the pilgrims' caravan but how she had seen in it the chance to show herself more than a pampered child. Had she not been rewarded for it? Had she not seen in Russell's eye a new look of respect for her daring? Had the outlaws' leader not singled her out for praise?

He was an odd one, this Orlando. He stood out from the company that he kept like lustrous ebony among so much ash and cinders. As if thought commanded action she saw that he now came towards her and her heart beat a little faster at his approach. She felt ashamed, since Valentine's approach had not made it do so. Then Orlando was by her, his handsome face smiling at her.

'You've proved your valour today, young Sebastian,' he said. As he spoke he cast an appraising eye over her and combed his beard with his fingers, bright teeth smiling through the black. She did not trust her voice in reply but nodded her thanks for his praise. She wanted to say that he'd seemed more valiant than any but Master Russell and more gallant than all. He'd calmed the women pilgrims, charmed the men – well, all save their leader who'd had to be clubbed to the floor when he would not stop his curses. Yet he'd apologised for its need and promised that charity would guide their use of the money taken and he'd delivered on that promise too. Truly, here was a noble man, for all her father's gilt and chivalry, here was a man that dared all and still found space within his daring to think of others.

Something of her admiring look conveyed itself to Orlando, who blushed. 'You need not look so kindly on me, Sebastian. Three times now I have led these selfsame men to fruitless battles, death and injury our only reward for all our daring. This time we happened on those that trusted in God for their protection and, this time, the Lord provided for we poor villains and not for them.'

'Unto them that have, shall be given,' said Aemilia.

Orlando's blush deepened. For this fair youth's words seemed pregnant with promises and he could not understand the sudden currents of thought and feeling that seemed to swirl about. He spoke lightly to quash the mood.

'That is, no doubt, the consolation that their leader gives to them now.'

'Why are you here?' Aemilia now blushed at her question, blurted out in her headiness at being spoken to so freely and openly by the outlaws' leader.

'Ah, there's a question that calls for more wine than I have yet drunk. What do you say you teach me the best manner to reply by answering it on your own behalf?'

'My story's simply told, sir. I am Valentine's page and his exile's mine to share.'

'His exile?'

'He loved the Duke's daughter and would have married her but the Duke objected to his poverty, reckoning not the value of a true heart and wise mind,' Aemilia said a little more fiercely than she had meant to do.

'What thought the Duke's daughter of the match?' asked Orlando.

'She thought well of it,' said Aemilia. 'Or so it was my understanding.'

Orlando nodded. 'I hope it was so for his sake. His exile was a dear price to pay for an unrequited love.'

'She made the proof of it in her every look and in her pleading on his behalf to her father,' protested Aemilia.

'So, so,' said Orlando. 'I do not doubt it though a woman's love cannot compare to that of a man. A woman's love may be called appetite, no motion of the liver but the palate. That suffers surfeit, cloyment and revolt. Sure and now her lover's exiled she will have pushed away his dish and called for fresh.'

'She will not,' answered Aemilia hotly. 'I know—'

At her breaking off Orlando beckoned her on. That strange heat was in the air again. He could not place its source; perhaps it was the heady wine of their battle won that muddied his thoughts so. He looked at the dark-eyed boy. 'What do you know, lad?'

'Too well the love that women may bear,' said Aemilia, head held proudly up. 'In truth they are as true of heart as we. I had a cousin had a lover.'

'What of her?'

'When her lover was called away to fight in the wars, she took herself off with him. Left hearth and home and comfort.'

'What became of her?'

'She died of her love. They perished both in the wars.'

'A tragedy. As all true love stories are.' Orlando broke his look from Sebastian. He turned to Master Russell's friend Adam who sat nearby. 'There's one that could tell you so. Eh Adam?'

'Life's a woeful tragedy, Orlando,' Adam answered. 'Love is but the tincture that drops in the sadness to our lives. We have love, we fear to lose it, we have it not, all our life is striving to find it. I would we were all stones.'

'By God, he speaks,' said Orlando. 'His words as baleful a sermon as ever I heard but at least he is not turned mute. Come, man, banish melancholy, Adam, and bring forth delight. Today we are triumphant and must make revels. A song, a song.'

'Master Russell has a fair voice,' said Aemilia. Hemminges did not lift his head from where he worked at his venison but shook it in refusal. Aemilia would have none of it. She ran to the chest and took the lute from it and held it out to Hemminges. Only to quell the shouts of the outlaws that he should sing did he reach out and take it from her.

'What song would you have?'

'A love song,' cried Orlando to the echoed shouts of the outlaws. Master Russell struck the strings, paused to tighten the pegs, and then strummed a chord and began to play. The same strong fingers and wrist that played so lightly with a sword now plucked forth sweet sounds and then his voice, honey-rich, joined in. Orlando settled himself to the ground, back to the tree trunk and close to the fire.

'Ah music, the food of love,' sighed Valentine, who had come to stand near Aemilia.

'If music be the food of love,' said Adam from his place outside the circle, 'play on. Give me excess of it, that surfeiting the appetite may sicken and so die.'

His ill-tempered words were a goad to Hemminges, who turned the song from a sweet one to a lively reel. The outlaws stamped their feet and clapped the measure and Luca, who was as expert in his drinking as in his judging of the drink, began to dance, kicking up his legs and singing, hey nonny. Soon half the outlaws were whirling about the camp to Hemminges' playing and the drumming of sticks on the side of the pot and the trees' trunks. Aemilia, caught up in the spirit of misrule that had come over them all, joined in and even Valentine was pulled from conference with a drunken Petro and entered in the dance. Indeed, so full of happiness at the prospect of a future far from the woods was Valentine that he had begun to sing a verse of his own, composing to Hemminges' tune until it became clear that mad Adam was capping each line he sang with a couplet of surpassing foulness, commentary on the young lord's voice that had the outlaws at a roar. Stiff with pride, Valentine had ceased to sing and would have retreated to his bed but that Aemilia, laughing, drew him back into the dance along with the rest. At last only Hemminges, who played for them, and Adam, who would not be persuaded to it for all their begging, were still sitting.

William came to sit by Hemminges. The two players said nothing to each other as they watched the drunken band leap and hop about them. Hemminges' thoughts were all on the lute. His concentration was absolute and in it he found release from his concerns, until beside him William spoke.

'Such display, such wanton spirits and we two the only dour figures among them. Why look you, all are set to revels by your playing. And how generous of young Sebastian, who answering to the need of it there being none present, has joined with Valentine in the measure and taken the woman's part.'

Hemminges looked sharply up, and sure enough, there was Sebastian, in perfect place and time, producing the lady's steps in answer to Valentine's lead.

And to the skirts of this wild wood he came

There'd been no need of another night in the woods to convince Oldcastle he was not made for the soldier's life. He'd been given one anyway and woke feeling much the worse for it. In his youth he'd seen some service in the commotions that accompanied the young King Edward's minority and though his role in the baggage train then had brought him no closer to shot or spear than third-hand report he thanked his youth now for the supply of terms that now gilded over his false standing.

They'd ridden till the sun began to dip towards the tree tops and then he'd commanded his corporal of horse to choose and set the camp, 'as a test of your as yet untried merit'. His Ancient, who bore the Duke's standard, he'd then set to muster of the watch with the same excuse and last, his loyal Dionisio he'd sent to make his own camp. While this activity went on he'd walked about, arms clasped behind his back, nodding at the men as they walked and rubbed down their horses and, on occasion, raising an eyebrow at a cuirass besmirched with mud, a ragged plume or a rust-spotted lance in order to signal his concern at the troops' quality. At last the camp was made and his corporal of horse reported to him that all was in order.

'Very well, then set the watch. I shall retire. Our patrol at dawn continues.'

'Sir Nicholas,' said the corporal, 'will you now unfold your plan to me?'

Oldcastle had waited fearfully for this moment and spent the major part of their ride in contemplation of his answer.

'Plan, man, why the plan is simple: I have considered the matter with great care. I see at once, as you no doubt have done, the closeness betwixt our position now and that as faced Great Pompey when he came to scour the pirate fleets from Roman waters.'

The corporal of horse wrinkled his nose and his whiskers rippled like a pair of nesting mongoose beneath. 'We're far from the sea. I do not take your meaning, Sir Nicholas.'

Oldcastle made a snort of disappointment. 'When Pompey was set to cleanse the sea of pirates he struck at once at all their places of rest, leaving them no refuge or retreat. So shall we also.'

'Pompey had four legions to command, we are a dozen men.'

'They too are few, by the Duke's prisoner's report, divide our force and still outmatch them. Strike as one, we leave them no retreat,' said Oldcastle. It sounded poor even to him but his object was not to impress or show himself a second Hannibal but to give himself a chance to escape by steadily reducing his escort.

'Sir Nicholas, would we not be better served—' the corporal began but Oldcastle cut him off. He could brook no debate to let in doubt about his orders.

'We are best served by obedience to my command,' he said and turned on his heel to stamp his way to where Dionisio had set up a small tent and camp-bed. The thin canvas closing behind him, his trembling nerves at last overcame him and he sat swiftly in his cot. He straightened as Dionisio thrust his head into the tent.

'Sir Nicholas, shall I prepare your supper?'

'Yes, yes, kind Dionisio, I am mortal tired and in need of sustenance.'

'At once, Sir Nicholas,' his servant answered but when he returned he found that Sir Nicholas was so overwrought by the tensions of the day and the exertions of his unaccustomed exercise that he had passed out on his cot and did not stir again till the trumpet's sound announced the dawn.

Oldcastle emerged from his tent to find the camp already full of activity. Seeing him, the Ancient ran to his side.

'The scout reports he has seen a man gathering firewood close by.'

Oldcastle yawned. 'What of it?'

'Why, sir,' the Ancient answered, 'there's no habitation hereabout. This is the part of these woods that the prisoner's report gave us to understand held their camp. He could not give us clear directions nor guide us to it himself, not after his questioning, but if there are any out gathering firewood then it is for that hidden place. If we take the man and put him to the question the base rascals are discovered and may be caught sleeping.'

Oldcastle did his best to smile at this news. His guts churned at it; this action came on too swiftly. There was a real danger that he would find himself involved in a broil and it had ever been a sound and solemn precept of Oldcastle's life, one to which he attributed his advanced age, that he not put himself in the course of harm.

'We must make haste, Sir Nicholas,' the Ancient urged.

'Quite so. Well, sound the tucket sonance and the note to mount,' said Oldcastle. How will I resolve this? He walked swiftly to the lines where the corporal was already in his saddle. Once more with much assistance from Dionisio he made it to his saddle and, leaving the Ancient and four more to guard the camp, the rest set off after the scout's report.

The corporal of horse was in great good humour, as shown by the near lascivious stroking of his moustaches, for with this intelligence gained they might make swift work of the destruction of the outlaws and be on to the tedious but easy business of escorting the Count Claudio's baggage to the palace. The corporal was already spending the Duke's bounty for a job well and quickly done.

Oldcastle's thoughts also travelled forward to what he should do when their quarry was found. If the man did not disclose his comrades' camp at once then Oldcastle feared the demands for hard questioning that would follow. It had been too soon that he'd suffered such a questioning of his own and he still shuddered at its memory and of the more recent sight of that outlaw's broken body in the Duke's dungeons. His own desire to avoid a fight was joined with a will not to see another suffer as he had done and dread at the thought of having to find reason to defy the corporal if he sought it.

The scout rode back towards their party, his hand held low in signal they should halt. He drew level with the corporal and Oldcastle.

'The man's ahead and heavily laden. Now might we do it,' said the scout, his hand gesturing to their front where rose a small bank. 'We must be soft though, sirs. He stands on this bank of the river but if he crosses it, as he might, there's no ford for the horses for half a mile.'

Hope sprang in Oldcastle's breast. He nodded to the corporal and the men began a slow advance, spreading out their horses till there were ten yards between each man, with Oldcastle and the corporal in the centre. They crested the rise. It took Oldcastle a moment to spot their man; he was ahead a quarter-mile, bent-backed beneath a fardel of wood. The river, barely deserving of the title, had been swollen by the recent rains and ran in full spate. It was both a danger and an opportunity to the Duke's men. Its noise disguised their approach but, the far bank gained, the man was safe from all pursuit unless they abandoned their horses, and armed and armoured as they were against a man familiar with the woods, without their horses their pursuit was sure to fail.

Oldcastle saw and understood this all but took a different lesson to the corporal who was signalling to his men to walk their horses slowly and quietly forward. Oldcastle clenched his legs about his horse, offered up his prayers to heaven and spurred his horse to action.

'St George, St George!' he cried as he cantered for the man. The corporal, stunned by the sudden noise and movement, looked about to see what had set his commander to the charge and then cried out to his men to follow. As one they spurred their horses on.

Oldcastle to his horror saw that the man had still not noted their approach.

'Hold!' he cried in a voice that had once commanded five hundred groundlings to silence. He struggled to draw his sword out of his scabbard as he cantered forward and cursed as he nearly cut his horse's ear off in the process. Liberated of its scabbard he began to swirl the blade above his head as he rode on. Come on you blundering ninny, he thought, a dead man would have noted me by now.

At last the outlaw looked up and saw Oldcastle bearing down upon him with half a dozen lances following on behind. He scampered like a hare towards the river's edge. Oldcastle wheeled his horse toward the man, pulling at the bit to slow the horse's stride. His sudden change of course sent him cutting in front of one of his own men as he did so, which caused the man to cry and swerve away so as not to ram his commander in the side. The first man swerving turned the next and the next and thus a ripple of confusion grew.

Ahead, the man, finding a fallen trunk that spanned the river in its spate, scrambled across it and ran on, darting between trees and bushes until lost from sight. Oldcastle reined in his horse at the river's edge and made a show of curses and foul spite at the man's escape. His men gathered slowly behind him as order returned to their ranks. The corporal's face was hot red beneath his whiskers.

'Sir Nicholas, why did you charge? We had him, Sir Nicholas, we had him.'

'You have a willing mind to think it so; did you not see him raise his head at our approach?'

'I did not,' declared the corporal, moustaches lifting and fluttering like pennants caught in the fury of his speech.

Oldcastle smiled sadly in answer. 'No? Well then, my good man, I now understand your hesitation. You were rightly intent on your command for quiet. There's no shame in your distraction and no apology needed.'

The corporal's moustaches fluttered like a bird ready to take wing in protestation that he'd no plan for apologies but Oldcastle waved his lips to close. 'The plan was sound. That we came as close as we did is thanks to my swift charge. Yet plans and swift action are no guarantee of victory.'

Another of the men spoke up: 'They must be close by. No man travels far to gather wood and it was a fair burden he'd got upon his back.'

In answer the corporal spat, 'What good to us is that? He will have given them warning of our approach. We've only half the men here, no surprise to multiply our force's strength and there's a fair chance that riding forth now we will find ourselves the ones are ambushed.'

'Courage, my man,' said Oldcastle in a restful voice and again, as the corporal set to protest that it was not want of courage that made him speak so, Oldcastle waved him down. 'We must return and gather our strength. Send out the scouts again to find where the rats now hide. You forget that we have among their number an ally, my man John Russell. He too will have been alerted to our presence. Have your men be ready for his approach. He will lead us to them now he knows we're here. Do not disguise our passing men, let the path be clear.'

Then Oldcastle for the second time that day set spurs to flank and shot forward, bouncing in his seat, to add to the churning in his guts.

Scout me for him at the corner of the orchard like a bum-bailey

'How far?'

'Half a league, no more, by the river.' Tommasso straightened, heaving for breath from his flight. 'A dozen lances, at least.'

'Cursed spite.' Orlando ran his hand through his hair. 'Go, boy, fetch me Master Russell, Luca, Zago. Make haste.'

The boy hastened away to round up the outlaws. Orlando kicked at some brushwood nearby in frustration. Tommasso would have left a trail a blind man could follow. Their camp would be discovered soon enough. How hard did the soldiers follow on from Tommasso? How long did they have?

'What is all the commotion?' demanded Zago as he approached with Luca and Ludovico by his side; Hemminges was not far behind and trailing him Aemilia and William.

'Tommasso was chased by a troop of soldiers not half an hour ago, a mile or so away, by the river,' said Orlando. 'We must pack up the camp and make haste away to a new and secret spot. Luca, Zago, tell the rest; Master Russell, I need your help with the movement of our bounty of yesterday.'

'You need help with more than that,' said Hemminges. His tone made Luca and Zago hold back. Orlando made a gesture that spoke to his irritation that, at this time of needful haste, his orders were being questioned.

'What is the matter?' demanded Orlando. 'Have you no ears, Englishman?'

'To hear sense, yes.'

'Sense is to fly before armed and mounted men,' said Luca from Hemminges' side.

'And be cut down?' asked Hemminges, rounding on him. He turned back to Orlando. 'You think they followed Tommasso?'

'The boy is brave but he will have set a trail in his haste to report to us,' said Orlando with a shrug. 'It's sense to suspect as much, surely?'

'You conclude too quickly. If you think them near then our hasting away will mean they catch us in our flight, laden with baggage and spoils.

You cannot hide the passage of so many men. Mounted men against men fleeing on foot, heavy burdened?'

All of Hemminges' audience shuddered at the picture that he painted. Hemminges did not stop there.

'We might instead scatter but that's to be taken one by one. How, too, to know where we regroup if we make escape?'

Orlando urged him on: 'Your argument is well made, what then?'

'Stand to, here. Against mounted men close together is best. That small hill yonder' – he pointed – 'the holly and bracken upon it will slow their horses. Let us dart out and be at them as they close.'

As one, Luca, Ludovico, Zago and Orlando looked to where Hemminges was pointing and he watched them shudder again at the thought of the fighting in close quarters to come, the mounted men using their height to cut down at the outlaws, the desperate rush to move past their horses and pull them from their seats, the butchery that there would be on both sides. Better that though than to be ridden down from behind, a lance through the back, a sword across the nape of the neck, the hiss and cold touch of the steel the last sensations in this life.

'Luca,' said Orlando, 'tell the others to gather their weapons and such baggage as they can swiftly take and move to the hill as Master Russell suggests. Go with him, Ludovico. Hurry, man, hurry.' Ludovico studied Hemminges a moment longer before turning and following Luca.

Orlando turned back to Hemminges. 'I pray you are right.'

'I am. A wise man knows to take and use the experience of others,' said Hemminges. He may not have a feel for the plots and stratagems that one needed to move through the waters of Venice, or London for that matter, but he'd an eye for the straight fight. He turned to Zago and, not waiting for Orlando's commission, ordered him to take two men and Tommasso and to scout out the direction from which the soldiers were said to come. Zago grumbled away to his task.

'You supplant me,' said Orlando.

'I've no wish to lead,' said Hemminges in answer. 'It's not by my will that I am here at all. I have a liking for living, though, and, by your leave, I'll freely advise you how I might maintain that state.'

Orlando smiled in answer of his own and held his hands up in surrender. 'I take no offence at it. You were right and I was wrong. Let us all live longer for your honesty and for my lack of false pride. What if Zago reports that the soldiers are not in pursuit?'

'Pray it may be so,' said Hemminges in answer. He'd disposed the men as best he could but mounted men against this rabble of outlaws would be a sorry fight and one he was not sure he'd see the end to. 'Then we have time to make an ordered retreat, disband and make our way to better lives than this.'

Orlando laughed until he saw that Hemminges meant all that he said. 'Man, we'll not shatter at the first blow and split into a thousand useless pieces.'

'Yes, surely,' interrupted Aemilia with a passion. 'Master Russell, we cannot take the first sign of opposition as a signal to surrender? We must make an ambush of these soldiers.'

Now it was Hemminges' turn to laugh. He'd thought Aemilia would have taken fright at the prospect of the battle to come but he'd not credited her untempered metal. She'd not seen, as he had, men dying beneath horses' hooves. Want of imagination or a greater courage than he'd yet allowed her now made her speak of attack when her thoughts should be of flight.

'You mock me?' demanded Aemilia.

'No, no, good Sebastian,' said Hemminges in hasty answer to the sudden flare of anger, 'no insult. But we are thirty men, not one a soldier, and these are men in plate and shield, with horse and lance. It is not courage but a slaughter you propose.'

'Tush,' said Orlando. 'Sebastian has the right of it. If they do not attack us then we must attack them. An ambush set, we might strike them down with arrows and finish them with knives as your English did at Agincourt.'

Hemminges ground his teeth. What had been an amusement to him when Aemilia spoke was now another danger to be faced as Orlando battened to her talk. He opened his mouth to speak sense to Orlando but was cut off by Aemilia.

'That we cannot do,' she said.

'Why is that? It was your suggestion,' protested Orlando.

'We need not proceed by way of slaughter when we might more profitably capture these men and offer them for ransom,' she answered.

Hemminges snorted and turned about in frustration like a dog chasing his tail. He gestured to Aemilia. 'You are run mad. Fight mounted men and kill them is task enough to make proud Hercules blanch, but take them without harming them? And without them harming you in the taking? Impossible. You invite death upon yourself.' He threw up his hands. 'How do you propose to manage this feat?'

Orlando, on whose face a knowing smile ever threatened to play, was now watching the match before him with open delight, the promised arrival of a dozen soldiers not enough to distract from the argument immediately before him. Aemilia's smile came on to join his as she too crossed her arms before Hemminges.

'I've no proposal at all. Yet I have heard it said, it is a wise man knows how to take the experience of others and use it to his own ends. You are our general, Master Russell. You devise our plan,' she said.

'I've enough of this fooling,' said Hemminges. 'To the hill, there. God willing, armed men shall knock sense into both of you.'

He strode away, Orlando, Aemilia and a still silent William following hard on his heels.

Our doubts are traitors

Aemilia was huddled with the rest on the hill while they waited for the men sent out to scout to return and make report. The mood was tense and manifested itself in silence and short tempers. All peered out across the woods, straining to see either their fellows return or the pennants fluttering on the lances of the soldiers that would presage grim fighting and death.

Aemilia felt that tension too, her hand tight upon the small dagger that was her only weapon, but it was mixed with excitement. The air held a crisp scent she had not noted before, the sky's grey was not uniform but streaked with shades and cut with sharp blue, the sound of the wind in the trees was loud in her ears. She felt the danger of the moment and against that feeling life stood out in sharp relief. The routine pleasures of the palace could not compare.

'Sebastian,' said Hemminges in a low voice and beckoned her aside. The two moved to a secluded place near the centre of the circle that the outlaws had formed on top of the hill. They crouched by a tree out of earshot of the others.

'Master Russell,' Aemilia asked, 'have the scouts reported?'

'No,' said Hemminges. His solidity and his sternness steadied her. She wondered if he knew the effect that he had on others, the calmness that standing by him brought, as if his self-control was a rock whose lee harboured ships from the tossing seas. She'd watched him pass by young Tommasso and by a simple hand on the boy's shoulder, steady him. She looked on him with admiration.

'Do not plead to me with your eyes, Aemilia,' he said, mistaking her look for continuation of their earlier argument. 'I have not come to tell you how we might make the impossible possible but to talk of how we three might yet escape.'

'Escape?' protested Aemilia. 'To where? For what?'

Hemminges dragged his hand through his hair and chewed at his cheek. He put a clenched fist against the tree trunk to steady himself in his squat.

'The Duke has sent his soldiers against us. We cannot tarry here to play at outlaws. The game is run, the playing's done and we must make our way back to your father's palace.'

'No, no, no,' said Aemilia. Hemminges lifted his head at her sharp tone. 'Nothing has changed to make my return possible.'

'Nothing? Are armed men nothing? Why speak of "possible"? Our return is a necessity.'

'If the troop attack now then it is too late to show myself for who I am. If they do not, then it matters not.'

'If they do not then we should be away.' The frustration and fear for her safety was writ on Hemminges' face, clear in every line that dug its way across his brow and lips. 'By God, why will no one heed me when I say to run?'

How fortunate she was, she thought, to have someone care for her safety, who kept himself in danger's way rather than leave her to her own courses. She touched his arm and felt him lean into it for an instant before he shied away, looking about to see if they were watched. She drew a breath and stilled herself, as she would do approaching a skittish horse she wished to tame. He was too cautious and for all his dear concern she was tired of being a creature in the care of others; she did not wish to be carried away but to hold the reins.

'List to me, Master Russell. You say it is a thing impossible to take my father's men and ransom them. I say it is not, that it is impossible it be so. I'll not see those men slaughtered. What good would killing them do? Then would my father simply send more men and more and they would be brutal, foreign, caring not for propriety or the law of arms. We'd kill a dog, we'd loose a wolf. No, I will not see these men die. There will be among them some that I have known since my birth. I will not see them killed to preserve my freedom. Yet free I must be, and will be. Tell me then how I may solve this puzzle if not by demanding that the impossible be done? And list, oh list, these men taken, ransomed, have we not opened up a way to grasp my father's thoughts? Into that opening I may send the image of myself as mistress of his realm. I know he does not love Valentine as I do but it is not that which keeps him from blessing our marriage.'

'What then?' said Hemminges. His doubts about her reasoning were not hidden; he was a plain, honest soldier, truly, but she would win him round as she would win her father.

'My father's grandsire was the first to hold his land and title. They say he was a knight most fine, most honoured, thrice renowned: for skill in arms, for manly chivalry and for piety. My father's father died most bravely fighting the Turk at Lepanto. These two giants cast their shadow over my father's rule and set his qualities in the shade. He sees them watching him and senses them judging him. He fears to be the first to lose what they have won. He doubts that Valentine can defend his lands.'

'And is he wrong in that?'

'No. He is wrong in thinking that it falls to Valentine alone to meet that duty.'

'Who else, then?'

'Me.' At his look she raised her voice. 'Stop your scoffing, Master Russell. I will be bold and resolute and prove my worth in this exploit, by taking his men and sending them back to him unarmed and unharmed.'

'Fine intent. The means to it are wanting.'

'There I turn to you, Master Russell. Help me. I will do this, whether you will or no. Help me, I beg of you. Give me this.'

Hemminges shook his head and turned to look at Valentine, huddled nearby but watching him talk to Aemilia.

William watched all three and a fourth, Orlando, whose own eyes circled over the ground beyond the hill, to Valentine, to William and to the two crouched by the tree. What are you thinking? William wondered and caught himself. That is the first care for another's motives that I have had in the fortnight since – he struggled still to name Isabella's death, even in thought. To close his eyes was to see again that dark, foul room where she had screamed in pain for a seeming eternity, to feel again the rage and frustration of her friends' abandonment of her in her hour of need. What had he gained only to lose it? A single summer they had had. Oh, summer's lease has all too short a date.

Hemminges had demanded of him last night why he should be so destroyed by Isabella's death but he had no answer to give.

'You who have such power to understand others' thoughts and feelings? How is it you are so confounded by your own?'

'I do not know, John. I do not know. I see the workings of their souls but they do not touch me. Their motions I grasp in the ventricle of my brain but they've no conjunction with my heart. I am a mirror, the shape and form reproducing but not the heat or breath within.'

'A poet's answer that flatters the speaker and leaves his friends bereft, saving your art.'

He saw how angry Hemminges was with him but it touched him not. If he felt anything now it was not concern for his friend but rage, a sudden rage that Hemminges should allow himself to be so gulled by this girl, moved, manipulated like a puppet to do her bidding. And for what? To serve her in the wooing of that overweening milksop, that antic, lisping, affecting fantasticoe Valentine, that slop of poetry, doling out his suffering in metrical feet. He'd listened to the man complain, mangle Dante, batter words as if they were iron to be beaten into shape and in two nights he'd had his fill. Help her to him? Help their false, shambling semblance of a love? Fie on it, he'd none of it. That was not the story he would write. A different cast, a different plot, a different lesson learned, all changed by but a line here, a line there. He might change it all if he willed it.

William blew out his cheeks, and felt some of the knotted tension that had built within him as he thought of Valentine disappearing on the breeze. How storm-tossed is my mind; one moment becalmed, bereft of motion, the next blown onto rocks I did not know were there. My love for Isabella was the star that stopped my bark from wandering, the compass within, the fixed mark of my understanding. Her death has brought a dropping fog, as black as Acheron, over my mind.

Ludovico crept up to William.

'I do not like this waiting, Adam,' he whispered.

William shrugged. 'That's all there is to life, Ludovico. A long wait for the grave.'

'You know this Master Russell that we should follow his orders?' asked Ludovico.

'I know no man, least of all myself,' answered William. He turned. 'Who knows anyone, truly? Look at you now. Ludovico who tells us he is from Ferrara but who speaks with a Roman accent. Ludovico the farmer who walks with the bow legs of a horseman. Ludovico the simple man who asks so many questions. What do I know of you, Ludovico?'

'There is no need to doubt me friend, Adam,' protested Ludovico. 'At least I am not so prideful as to let my fear hide itself in anger at another.'

William gestured. 'If you want to know Master Russell's plans, enquire of him yourself.'

Hemminges had risen from his crouch by the girl's side and walked to where he could see out over the woods below. Ludovico shook his head and crept away from both. William turned back and saw Valentine slip in beside the girl. Orlando, William saw, watched them still.

At the previous night's revels, Valentine had flattered Petro the priest, crushed away his yawns at the man's stories and topped up his chalice to the brim until the moment had come to ask him if he would be willing to perform a wedding. He was, and boasted of a ruined church not far by, still consecrate, where it might be done. Petro's curiosity to know the intended bride and groom he'd waved away as best he could. It was merely the principle that he wished to establish. This, Petro had not liked.

'A hypothecal marriage has little promise in it, mark you. It is a thing incontro— incontest— uncontist— not to be denied that for success in conjugation there must be two.'

The priest had then held up two fat and filthy fingers, stared intently at them, moving them from one side of his great wall of nose to the other and lifting and raising one until he was certain that there were indeed only two fingers there despite the doubtful evidence of his drunken gaze. Not many minutes later he had fallen into sottish slumber and did not stir even as the dancing began.

That morning Valentine had been at him again before his hammering head had yet been clear, to confirm the truth of the drunken tale of the abandoned church. To stop the pestering youth the priest had taken him to visit it, not an hour's walk from the outlaws' camp. The two had returned to find the camp in the fevered expectation of assault.

'Aemilia,' Valentine began. She gave him a warning look and he huffed but carried on with, 'Sebastian, we must away . . .'

She clutched his sleeve. 'Not yet, Valentine, not yet, but soon. There is a plan, no more than a thought but if it come to fruition, then we may return to my father as man and wife.'

'Let it be so,' said Valentine. 'Do you still wish the match?'

Aemilia made to answer and found herself hesitating. In his question he showed himself again soft and tender to her will, a quality she'd found loving at the court, but it savoured now of a weakness. She'd taken for grief his upset at his exile but he had clung to it and clung to it still, to his unmanning. And worst of all was this Adam. The madman had been at Valentine as a hornet since first they met, ever stinging or threatening so – this pursuit the worse for coming from a lunatic's mouth, for though what he said was madness yet there was meaning in it. Aemilia had thought ill of the cruelly mocking Adam but each of his mocks had brought her back to Valentine's failings. She saw those failings mirrored. Master Russell did not speak of it for others to hear, but by his vinegar regard also showed his contempt for the soft-handed Valentine. His cold glances crushed the tender poet. Nor did Valentine's lustre of the palace still shine so brightly when set against Orlando's. There was a man of action and of romance too. He did not only speak of the freedoms of the woods, he lived them. Where he saw suffering he acted. Valentine wallowed.

She was not sure she wanted the same things now she had desired in the palace.

She saw his hope in the question, though, and was moved by it. His virtue was not strength. So be it, she knew that already. Strength was her virtue and she would show it now, by being firm of purpose.

'I do, I will.'

'They are not coming,' said Orlando.

Hemminges rose and walked over to him, aware of all the eyes that followed him. He looked briefly at William and then addressed Orlando.

'I have a plan.'

'To capture the Duke's men?'

'If it be God's will, so.'

'If it be so then shall we sing: *Non nobis, sed te Deum*. If it be not, then a dirge of different measure.'

Behind Hemminges and Orlando, Aemilia smiled the giddy smile of victory, innocent of its costs. Valentine crossed himself in fear and was not the only one among the outlaws to do so.

Not the king's crown, nor the deputed sword

'The scout has found a trail but dared not go to its end,' said the corporal. 'The villains have sent out scouts of their own.'

'Ah hah,' said Oldcastle. 'Then we have stirred the hornets' nest have we not?'

'To what end, Sir Nicholas, to what end?'

There was a question that Oldcastle struggled to answer even to himself. His hesitation brought out much distemper in the corporal.

'Sir Nicholas, I must know your stratagem, sir,' the corporal stated, standing to attention within Oldcastle's cramped tent to lend dignity to his demand. 'By the Duke's command we are to meet with the Count Claudio's baggage two days from now. I must know your plan, Sir Nicholas, and how we will accomplish all that is asked of us.'

'It has not changed,' said Oldcastle as airily as he might.

'How not? When the situation is now changed.'

'Is it? Is it?' said Oldcastle with a questing look. If he'd hoped to inspire self-doubt in the corporal he failed.

'Yes,' came the answer, and Oldcastle noticed that he was no longer being given his title, however false that title was. Desperate measures were called for.

'We have seen we are near their camp,' he said. 'As I told you, we need only wait for the arrival of my man John Russell. He and I have, in preparation for this moment, laid our plans against it. We wait only for the hour before dawn. At that time, he will make his way from the enemy's lodgement and we two shall meet and he will discover to me how the enemy are disposed, how armed, how numbered and all pertaining to the necessaries of their defeat. Have patience, Corporal. You are too liverish in your judgement.'

The corporal's colour gave support to Oldcastle's own judgement, for he was red and angry.

'And how, Sir Nicholas, will your man find his way to you? In the darkness before dawn? Without prior discussion?'

'That is a matter of secrecy between he and I,' said Oldcastle haughtily.

'Sir Nicholas, I do doubt the merit of this plan. I am patient for all you say I am not. Sir Nicholas, till dawn tomorrow shall I wait but, I say this, and I say it, Sir Nicholas, without intent of dishonour to you, saving your honour, if you have not made parley with your Master Russell by that hour then I shall report as much to the Duke.'

Oldcastle pushed his chin up as high as the low tent would allow him. 'Do so, Corporal. And I have no doubt that when the dawn breaks I shall deserve of you apology.'

'You shall have it.'

The corporal drew himself tighter still, his chin tilted up too so that it would have seemed to one watching that the two men now invoked the witness of the gods on their challenge. The corporal saluted and stamped from the tent. Oldcastle collapsed into his seat. God's will, what a tangled web he found himself in. Still, he'd bought himself an hour, between setting out to meet Hemminges and the discovery that he'd no plan at all but had used that dark hour before dawn to make himself scarce. It was a small window of hope but it must serve to carry all his bulk.

He called for Dionisio and asked the man to pack him a small bag of food. The man looked at him as Oldcastle explained that it was to sustain him in his wait for Master Russell's arrival.

'I should, perhaps, Sir Nicholas, make certain that the packing contains enough to sustain you quite some while?'

'That seems sensible,' said Oldcastle. 'One cannot be certain how long the wait.'

'Quite so, quite so,' said Dionisio.

Act Four

Verona and woods in the Veneto, March 1586

Mischief, thou art afoot

The Veneto

Hemminges crept through the dark of night, edging himself closer to the light of the soldiers' fire. He peered with one eye closed so that the flare of the flames would not leave him blind in the darkness that would follow. It was a small watch the soldiers had set, befitting their small number. One man walked near where the horses were tied, another by the lodgement's north side and the last to the south. All three walked swiftly to their posts, looked out and then returned again to the fire to warm themselves. They thought themselves safe, they were the hunters not the hunted, and they lacked caution in the result.

Hemminges crept a little closer still. If these three men could be quietly dispatched then might they fall on the others and seize them pat. If the camp woke then it would be a different and more deadly matter. Too much turned on these few moments. Hemminges wished he had more courses of action to put before the outlaws than this hazardous one. He'd racked his mind, and there were none. The outlaws were no soldiers to stand and fight at push of pike. A frontal assault could not be borne and Aemilia's insistence that they take the soldiers as a prize had put out of contemplation bloodier, more brutal and safer stratagems. So they were left to the dark of night to give them hope, yet there was hope: the outlaws were not soldiers but some of them were woodsmen and could move with a deadly softness. To this Hemminges trusted now.

The three guards by the fire rubbed their arms for warmth and spoke in low voices to each other, too far and too quiet for Hemminges to hear. Cold minutes passed as he waited, pressed flat to the damp earth. At last the three men set out again for their posts and he steadied himself for action. He closed his eye and let three breaths pass as he heard the guard come closer. He opened both eyes and saw the man, now little more than a shadow beside a tree ten yards away. Hemminges rose to a crouch and began to close upon him. His breath was tight in his chest as he tried to still its sound. A noise from the other side of the camp made the man's head turn sharply but Hemminges had expected it for at this same moment two other men were crouching and moving forward and one among the three of them had to be first upon his prey. By the sound of it, it was not Hemminges who struck first.

'Bernardo?'

Hemminges heard the guard's whispered query toward the camp and then he rose up and in two swift strides was on him, the hood he held in his hands opened and swallowed the man's head whole. He turned and twisted and tightened and felt the man's hands come up to claw at the bag's closing and the muffled grunts from within the leather. The guard's thoughts turned belatedly to the dagger at his belt and he reached down for it, blind hands scrabbling. Hemminges dragged the man back and to his knees. One hand he kept clamped on the tightened thongs of the bag, with the other he pounded the soft ribs of the guard causing shuddering gasps to echo from the cavern of the bag. The hands that had sought the dagger now flailed desperately at the bag's tightening noose then at the fist that crushed the air from his ribs. The struggling went on a minute more, in ebbing waves of effort, and then stopped. Quickly Hemminges loosed the bag and lowered the man to the ground, and the guard's breath came back to him in a shuddering heave. Hemminges turned him on to his belly and with swift movements snared his hands behind him. Roughly, he pushed a rag into the man's mouth and bound it in place. He heard a call like the hoot of an owl and answered with his own. He felt the guard stirring beneath the knee that he had in his back and he leant low to the man's ear and whispered dire warnings of an urgent death if he should make a sound. The man went still. Still too was the night. Hemminges felt his hands tighten on the man's shoulders as he waited for the third call. The wait was an agony of anticipation. All three must fall; it took but one to sound the alarum. Just as he feared all was lost, an owl cried out again from the third quarter. All the guards were taken. Now for the rest.

From the darkness crept the other outlaws, moving towards the tents and sleeping places of the small troop of soldiers. Now in threes and fours they fell on single men and quickly bound them. The outlaws closed on the tents of the officers at the centre of the camp.

Something must have stirred the Ancient. As they approached his tent its side was pulled back and he stepped out, caught sight of the outlaws in the light of the fire and cried the alarm.

'Help, help, we are attacked!' he roared as he drew his sword.

Tommasso, who in youthful excitement had taken the lead, was stunned by the sudden change from silence to roaring noise. The boy shuddered to a halt and gave the most piteous wail, a sound to be heard in the dreams of men long years from that moment, as he looked down at the blade of the Ancient's sword thrust through his chest. Tears sprang to his eyes and he reached out a hand, as if to pull the blade from him, but his fingers clutched at nothing as he fell back. Luca, creeping up behind, saw his brother fall and, roaring, leapt forward to crack his cudgel over the Ancient's skull. The man fell to the ground and the outlaws poured over him, stamping, stabbing and crying out.

'The ropes, the ropes!' cried Hemminges, pointing to the other two tents. It took a moment to understand his meaning but then the outlaws slashed through the ropes that held the tents up and they collapsed on those within leaving them a thrashing misshapen chaos of man and canvas. Now from one tent came oaths and threats and thrashes and from the other moans and pleas and the shape of a man hauling himself to his knees in supplication of mercy.

When order was restored the outlaws were the masters of some eleven soldiers, some more bruised than others, one corporal of horse bound beneath his tent like a furled sail, still sending oaths to the sky. Oldcastle and his servant both looked tremulously about at their captors, and two dead men.

Aemilia stood over the body of Tommasso, Hemminges beside her. Someone had closed his eyes and the Ancient's sharp sword had left no obvious injury on him save that a dark stain covered his breast. For all that, one could not think him merely sleeping for his face still bore lips peeled back in pain as the blade had gone in. The Ancient's body lay nearby, a mangled, broken, bloody thing. Hemminges could see that Aemilia's face, even in the fire's light, was as pale as poor Tommasso's.

'This heavy sight was made by my pleading,' she said to him. Her eyes stayed on the dead boy.

'It was,' said Hemminges. 'There might have been more such as he if another course had been taken.'

'Or none at all,' she said.

'Mayhap none,' said Hemminges. He'd no easy words for her. This was the course she'd argued for and now it was for her to take the good and the bad of it. She shuddered beside him, as if her body threw off a heavy cloak that had been draped across her shoulders, and turned about and walked away leaving Hemminges alone with the two bodies.

Appoint a meeting with this old fat fellow

'Blessed be the day.'

Oldcastle's greatest fears and greatest hopes had met with him within the same hour. Still bound, still on his knees in the centre of the soldiers' camp, he shuffled over towards William.

'William, William, William, is it you? Are you restored to us and we to you?'

How open and clear was the delight on the old man's face to see him, thought William; why then do I feel so little?

'Not so fast, old man,' cried Jacopo, dragging Oldcastle back by the wrists with his good arm and finding that Oldcastle's bulk made for hard work.

'This is my friend, William,' gestured Oldcastle with his head, the only part of him not restrained.

'I know no William, that is Adam,' said Jacopo. 'Now stay where you are put and silent too.'

Oldcastle looked pleadingly to William. The terror in his eyes at Jacopo's menaces moved him where Oldcastle's delight had not. Is it only suffering that I recognise now?

'Foolish, fond, old man.' William came over to Jacopo and pushed him away. He took his dagger out and cut the ties on Oldcastle's wrists. Jacopo began to bleat of traitors, spies and traps.

'Oh hush, intemperate child,' chided William without looking over at Jacopo. 'This is no soldier, this is no danger, this is a good round man, much inclined to drink and good living.'

Jacopo stamped away leaving William alone with Oldcastle who took William in an embrace, tears in his eyes.

'And, by God, I could do with a drink. Fear makes for a terrible dryness in the mouth and I have been afraid this many a day. Cut loose my man Dionisio, Will, he's no more a soldier than I am and has done me good service.'

William went to find Oldcastle's servant and release him.

'Nick, you rogue!'

Hemminges' shout shot across the camp and was followed by a hasting Hemminges who took his old friend in a great hug that left the older man coughing.

'At last we three are together again, glad be the day,' said Oldcastle. Hemminges looked over at William, who was bent over Dionisio nearby, cutting his bonds. Hemminges leaned in to Oldcastle's ear.

'I am not so sure we are. William is changed. Isabella is dead and it has taken something from him. He is not the man he was.'

Oldcastle moaned to hear Hemminges' news. A fresh fat tear rolled down his face and disappeared into his beard. He cried as much for Isabella as for his friend's loss of her. She had been kind to him though she had teased him and he her, and he'd admired her. Why, she had played his games of wit and beat him at them and never admonished him for his excess of humour but forgave him his trespasses against her. He looked over at William and noted properly his gaunt cheek and pale lip. The subtle eyes still roamed unceasingly over all that passed but, alerted to it, Oldcastle now saw they had a dullness in them. The boy had aged a thousand years with Isabella's death.

'God above, mercy on him,' said Oldcastle. He clapped his friend on the shoulder. 'But we must look to what we have, we are joined once more. For England, then.'

Hemminges shook his head. 'The web is too tangled.'

'Not for Will's cunning.'

Hemminges shook his head again. 'He is much changed, Nick.'

'How so?' said Oldcastle but Hemminges was looking past him to the watchful Jacopo, out of earshot, but who studied them and the familiarity with which the two conversed. He began to walk towards Hemminges.

'God's will, John, but we are in a barful strife and must have Will's brain to lead us out of it.'

'There's no rescue to be had from that quarter, Nick. We will speak more anon.'

He broke off as Jacopo approached.

'I will look to this prisoner,' said Hemminges. For a moment Jacopo looked as if he would defy Hemminges but then William came to rejoin them, bringing Dionisio with him.

'Jacopo, Orlando calls for you,' he said as he approached. Jacopo nodded and went with a backward glance to the four men that lingered on Oldcastle.

Oldcastle turned moist eyes on William.

'Will, John tells me that Isabella is dead.'

'There's no more to say,' said William, forestalling any words that Oldcastle might offer. He made to leave but stopped and turned himself long enough to say to his friend, 'I am glad you are with us again.'

He walked away and Oldcastle, astonished, watched him go with his mouth open.

'It is as I said,' said Hemminges sadly. 'He is much changed. Come, I shall acquaint you what I know on the walk to this camp of rogues.'

William walked away from Oldcastle with a catch in his throat. To see the pity in the old man's eyes had near unmanned him; he'd felt his grief's control breaking and fled from the source of his weakness. He could not bear to have his friend speak words of condolence, try to tease some meaning from an event that seemed to William senseless. Unthinkingly he'd crossed the camp and came now to the bodies of Tommasso and the Ancient. Two of the outlaws were digging graves for the men. A third knelt by Tommasso's body, his head bowed, his hand resting on the dead boy's shoulder. Though soundless, his heaving shoulders were testimony to his mourning. He looked up and William saw Luca's red eyes glance over at him.

Petro the priest approached and bent by Luca. 'Do not mourn your brother, Luca.'

'Why should I not when he is dead?' Luca, turning sharply and searching for an outlet for his angry sorrow, spoke harshly.

Petro looked down at the dead boy and crossed himself. 'He is in heaven now, we need not mourn for those that have left this mortal coil to stand before God.'

William wondered at this foolish reasoning. We do not mourn for those that are dead but for ourselves that they are lost to us. If Tommasso is in heaven it is no matter to Luca, who is in hell. William could bear to be around others no more. Their pieties, their reasons, all meaningless to him who longed for a meaning and was constantly offered proof that there was none. He left Luca to his mourning and the others to their work. To care was, in the end, to grieve.

The outlaws led their captives through the darkness to their camp, bringing with them the booty of their victory. A few remained behind, to guard the horses and to finish the burying of the dead. Aemilia was not among them. She marched with the others and cast no backward glance to the dead or the mourning as she walked.

The incense of a vow, a holy vow

Valentine was straining under the weight of half a dozen swords, the outlaws' spoil taken from the soldiers and now to be carried back to the camp. It was still blacker than Hades and, though the outlaws had lit torches for their return, with his arms full of iron Valentine had to make do with what light fell near him from those carrying torches nearby. For the twentieth time in the last ten minutes he stumbled over a tree root and cursed again the ignominy of his position. How little he deserved this fate. His sensibilities were not made for stumbles in the dark. Then, passing by him with a torch, came Aemilia striding through the night with purpose.

'Sebastian,' Valentine hoarsely whispered at her as she passed and then again more loudly when she did not at first take heed of him.

'Valentine.' She came and walked beside him. The swords were in his way and he shifted them about, trying to find a manner of holding them that let him close enough to her to speak privately.

'You are well, Sebastian?'

'I thank you well, Valentine, and you?'

'The better for seeing you and all unharmed. This is too dangerous a business for a woman.'

He sensed rather than saw her bridle at his words.

'Too dangerous for all,' she answered him. 'Or no danger to any. I did not see you in the fight, Valentine, tonight or two days ago when we robbed the pilgrims.'

'"We",' he hissed, 'what is this "we"? You and I are not to be counted amongst these horse-leeches, sucking at the blood of others.'

'What fellowship else have we?'

'What?' Valentine's horror at Aemilia's 'fellowship' made him speak loudly and he quickly shifted the swords in his hands. At the same moment he stumbled again on a tree root and was forced to run forward to regain his balance lest the swords go flying out and increase his clatter. In a fouler mood than he had yet possessed, he waited for Aemilia to rejoin him.

'Aemilia,' he whispered, not caring overmuch now if anyone heard her called by her true name, wanting to appeal to the woman he loved, 'this is madness. When we set forth, our thoughts were only to stay away from your father's house long enough to make him realise that his love for you must make him bow to your desires. We spoke of inns and hot meals and warm baths and a honeymoon. Now, we're stumbling through the dark, one of a band of runaways, wanton servants, villains, outlaws. We cannot continue in this vein, we must return.'

'I told you I had a plan, Valentine.'

'Oh so, and was it that we should engage in desperate fights by moonlight?'

'If you're in this peevish mood, Valentine, I think it best we part.'

'Very well, then,' Valentine declared with all his dignity on muster but as she walked away he called after her, 'Sebastian, Sebastian, we must speak further. Find me in the morning, Sebastian.'

He heard her agreement as she and her light disappeared ahead a moment before his foot caught a root again and he stumbled forward to slam into the trunk of a tree. His cursing was echoed by laughter from others of the outlaws as they passed by. Jesu, he thought as he felt about to pick up the swords he'd dropped, I must be from this place and I will be.

But you'll be secret?

Orlando waved Jacopo away as William approached and then matched his stride to William's.

'Master Russell is quite the soldier, is he not?'

William was grateful for the darkness that hid his face from Orlando.

'He seems so,' answered William. Till he knew better what the outlaw chief desired, he thought, best to keep his answers short.

'"Seems"? What proof more do you desire than his deeds of the last day?'

'The office is not the man,' answered William. 'That he fights well does not make him a soldier.'

'I forget how much you question appearance, Adam, when I should remember your own false facing.'

'I am not false,' William said, his voice harsher than he'd intended. 'I am not the source of other men's expectation.'

'If you are not false, then others are. This Sir Nicholas, he is no knight by his bawling and pleading when we took him. Nor this Sebastian a pageboy for all her shorn hair.'

William heard Orlando name Sebastian for the woman that she was. Where did this go?

'Sir Nicholas is braver than many knights,' said William slowly, 'that much I do know, for all that he does not shy from pleas and bargains for mercy.'

'He knows Russell well and both have English names and speak our language with a grating burr that is not native to it.'

'Perhaps, then, they are English? Come to your purpose, Orlando.'

'You know them too?'

'And if I do?'

'If I recall me, England and His Holiness are not beloved of one another?'

'His Holiness I'm sure loves all men, as befits his office and his faith, and as for England, you speak in generalities. Each man keeps his own thoughts and may have no more in common but that England was the ground that held their mothers when they birthed them.'

'So some from England serve His Holiness and others their Queen?'

William could hear the probing smile in Orlando's voice.

'And some, God knows, serve none at all,' answered William.

The two men walked along in silence for a little while after that. At last Orlando spoke again.

'Have you thought on what we spoke of at the river?'

William did not answer.

'I will have my revenge. I promise you that. I will find my allies where I can. Those that aid me to my revenge will be rewarded. Those that stand in my way . . .'

His unvoiced threat did not touch William. Orlando was to him a toothless lion that growled and paced but, biting, harmed none. Still William said nothing. His silence was an unbearable provocation.

'You think I cannot keep my promise of reward? You give your service only to princes and popes? How came you to this parlous state, then? In the service of a pope.'

'I am not who you think I am, Orlando.'

'Who then?'

Now there was a question. A glover? A player? A poet? A lover? A seasoned traveller rich in secrets and surmises? A foolish boy far from home? What a piece of work is a man; to be so many things in one instant. One might reach out to feel for his form and find him no more than an insubstantial quintessence of dust. Was he the actions of the moment or the motives to them?

From across an age of memory William heard Oldcastle's voice chiding him for asking more questions than a babe of three and Isabella's voice mocking him for wanting all things to be as a poet would have them, chiselled out in elegant lines, the same from every angle, immutable, timeless: 'All things must change, Will, passing through nature to eternity. That is to be welcomed not feared, it is growth. We do not want a love that alters not but one that blossoms outward, enriches, deepens, evermore.' There is no more of evermore for us, sweet Isabella, for you are dead and gone now, for you are dead and gone. He felt the vast and bitter emptiness open within him. It had taken the sight of Luca wailing for his brother's loss to waken him to the truth of his own. Her death was not to be a thing of moments, come and gone again. It was a thing for all time, a pain he would carry with him ever and always.

He's a lamb indeed, that baas like a bear

When they made it back to their new camp and the prisoners had been secured, Aemilia slipped away. She was grateful for the darkness that shrouded her. She knew if she were seen she would be questioned about the paleness in her face, her trembling hand. She needed to gather herself and her thoughts.

She had the sickness of decision in her. Her stomach curdled at what she knew would come with the dawn. She must tell Valentine that she was no longer sure of her love. She'd seen too much of him in his extremity for love to go unquestioned. She'd learned since she left her father's castle that there was more, wonderfully more, to mankind than the twin stars of old soldiers and young cousins.

She kicked at a pile of dry leaves and watched them flutter down, dark shapes falling between the darker shadows of the trees. A red line lit the horizon, the promised dawn. She leant against a tree and let her back slide down to crouch at its bottom. Tommasso's death was in her thoughts. His face staring up at her, its horrified surprise at the turn the day had taken, bloodily inked across it in death. He might have fled the woods and lived but that she wanted to prove herself to her father. Why must her dream of ambition come at the cost of others? What fairness, God, in that? She bent and threw a stick out into the lightening woods.

A sudden shifting sound close by made her spring to her feet and reach for her dagger. The sound came again and she turned in the darkness toward it, in the direction she had thrown the stick. Dagger held before her she crept towards it. From the darkness emerged Luca. He was sat at the base of a tree. His hand was held up in apology.

'I didn't mean to fright you,' he said. 'I only meant to find some quiet. Away from . . .' He waved his hand back towards the outlaws' camp from where the sounds of happiness could be heard. There was light enough to see his face, the tracks of tears white in the moonlight and here and there a russet smudge of blood, his brother's.

'I'm sorry, Luca, for your brother,' Aemilia began but he waved away her consolation. Aemilia was about to move away, to give the man his private grief.

'Stupid fool,' snarled Luca, suddenly angry. 'I'd told him time and again to stay back. He was ever headstrong.' Luca's fist suddenly rang out on the trunk of the tree. 'Always wanting to prove himself, to show his worth to the others. All I wanted was for us to be free of mastery, free of want, to live quietly, bread—' He broke off again, folded his face to rest on his arms and now sobbed into the folds of his sleeve. Aemilia heard his words with the shock of recognition. Was that not her own state? Did she not want to prove herself to others? To her father most of all?

'He was all my family. I've no one left.'

Aemilia moved beside him and bent to place her arm on his shoulders. She opened her mouth to speak but realised she had nothing to say, no comfort to give, she who was the author of the enterprise that had led to his misfortune. She stayed there a moment longer and then Luca wiped his eyes with his arm and muttered that he would recover. He just needed time. Aemilia took her cue and left him.

She walked back through the woods towards the camp full of thoughts.

Come hither, come hither, come hither:
Here shall he see no enemy
But winter and rough weather.

The sudden burst of song nearby had her reaching for her dagger again. This time it was mad Adam that emerged from the darkness. He looked down at the blade, her knuckles white on the hilt.

William smiled. 'Such a topsy-turvy world I have lived in this year. And this the last of many reversals – a lamb, it seems, in wolf's clothing.'

'You scared me.'

'I am sorry for it.' He looked sadly at her. 'How do you fare? You have a brave look about you but, how deep are looks? You are proof of the danger of that reasoning. It's a cruel thing to learn how vile a thing is a man.'

'Get you gone,' said Aemilia.

'A command?' answered Adam. 'Oh my dear child, what do you command? And what use your dagger when you have not the strong arm of friends to shield you too?'

'What means that remark?' asked Aemilia.

'It means you are a fool,' said William in answer.

'I didn't ask for your insults but your meaning.'

'Only a fool looks to a madman for meaning, so I name you again, fool.'

'Get you gone, Adam. I am not in the mood for your games. Find another to taunt.'

'Like Valentine you mean?' William asked.

'I want no more of you,' said Aemilia with a sigh.

'So you say, but it is not clear to me what you do want,' said William. He looked at her with his head tilted as if trying to size up the subject for a painting. 'You who are surrounded by good counsel, why spend your time with a fool? Why spend your time here in the woods, when you might live in comfort in your father's palace?'

Aemilia shuddered with sudden fear. This Adam knew her for the woman she was.

'Are you truly mad, Adam?'

'Truly, I no longer know, Madonna.' His head stayed in that enquiring pose. 'I do wonder if you do know yourself?'

'I would be free, for that I would risk all, and here, in these woods, among this fellowship, I am free. That is not madness. It is purpose.'

'None of us are free, Madonna. Ask Orlando if he is free, or John.'

'I have never seen a man less beholden to the will of others than Master Russell. He is a man who weighs what's right and acts on it.'

'That judgement at least is no madness in you.'

Aemilia looked hard at William, tilting her head in turn to study him. 'Who is he to you and you to him?'

William did not at first answer. He feared he no longer knew.

'A friend, Madonna. A friend I would not see harmed for all the world. You would risk all?' He pointed behind her to where Luca sat. 'There is one who risked all for what he wanted. Gambled, lost, so be it. Yet it was others died for it. Have a care, Madonna.'

Then he bowed and moved off into the dark of the wood, again singing as he went.

Aemilia was left with his strange words circling in her head. Her mood, already black from the evening's blood and the night's tears, was now compounded by a tumult of thoughts. Her heart beat unsteadily to the rhythm of their passing. It took her many minutes to still her breathing and the sun was full above the horizon when she set her feet again for the camp, resolution made. As Sebastian she'd thought she had a freedom she'd not had before, but it had proved a thought as false as her disguise. She would not be free till she did command, and she would be free.

Patch grief with proverbs, make misfortune drunk

The dawn revealed the outlaws' camp to be a patchwork quilt of humours. Bound and huddled together in deep misery were the Duke's soldiers, fearful of their fate, mindful of the Ancient's death and at their core a bruised corporal who scarce drew breath but to utter curses upon the heads of all about him: Sir Nicholas, the night's watch, the creeping bandits and himself, who had trusted others that did not deserve of trust. Bright by their dark misery were the revelling outlaws, their armour burnished by the soldiers' defeat and now demanding greater tests. By the fire, Luca sat still weeping for his dead brother. Orlando, by the fire too, kept his own counsel, his mind full of plots and stratagems, the sound of Luca's tears washing over him but not piercing his buckram suit.

Huddling by a tree far from the fire, shivering and hungry, sat Oldcastle in conversation with Hemminges.

Oldcastle looked over at Hemminges and his shaking head. 'But we might sneak away this night.'

'Nick, you may play the knight but you will never play a mouse. I might make it away but you would wake the dead with your heavy tread. Besides, what of Will? Do we leave him again? Even if we wished to do so, what of the names.'

'These thrice-damned names, I would I'd never heard of them.'

'So, but we have done and there's an end on it. We know they're hunted and we cannot leave even one of us behind that they may be caught. And what of Aemilia? We cannot leave her here among these rogues.'

'So you say, but she is the least of the problems that beset us. She's happier here than I have seen her at the court.'

'It coarsens her.'

'Now you speak to your desires, not hers.'

Maybe so, thought Hemminges, as I have come to love her spirit, I would not see her take a bloody path that turned her boldness into callow disregard. Those were thoughts he did not care to dwell on more, the question of his love, the question of his desires. He spoke of other things to Oldcastle.

'She is among dangerous men. I dare not leave her. Look there.' He gestured with his eyes to where Jacopo watched them. 'This Orlando plays the friend but he has some game greater than to be the beggar king of the woods. Will plays some part in it I think, though what I know not. We too have been taken into it, coin to spend on some matter. He will not let us slip away and if he did I think it would only be because he thinks to make a greater play of Aemilia. Her disguise cannot hold.'

'I am amazed it's held so long as it has,' said Oldcastle with admiration for a novice player's art.

Hemminges snorted. 'I am not sure it has. Orlando has his suspicions, though what it is that he suspects I do not know.' He reached up and snapped a small branch off the tree they sat beside. The same frustration that filled his gesture stuffed out his voice when he spoke. 'I am a blind man in a room of vipers. I do not know which way to turn, which way safety lies. I have not the mind for this work.'

Oldcastle patted his shoulder. 'Nor I. We are simple men, John, caught in crooked times.'

'We're damned,' said Hemminges as he poked the damp earth with the stick.

'William will see the path.'

'William is part of the thicket, not the path through it.'

Oldcastle moaned and put his head back in his hands. He lifted it again, eyes wide. 'We tell them my true nature, then there will be no more foolish talk of ransom.'

'Then they will sell you to the Pope for thirty pieces of silver and a great deal more.'

Oldcastle's chin fell back again to his chest. 'Oh God, truly, we are damned.'

'As I say.'

A cry broke out from the soldiers. Oldcastle and Hemminges looked up and saw the corporal on his feet roaring for order and obedience from those around him. Before them stood the cause of the tremors that ran through them: Aemilia.

'Oh Jesu,' muttered Hemminges, setting off towards them, Oldcastle lumbering behind. His servant Dionisio followed.

'What is the cause of the commotion, Sir Nicholas?' asked the servant.

'I very much fear,' said Oldcastle, 'that someone has been rash.'

I am alone the villain of the earth

Verona

As Thornhill reached the door it swung sharply open and he was forced to step quickly aside to let a crying maidservant scurry past and run off down the corridor. A broad laugh came from within the room beyond. Pushing open the door he stepped in. Count Claudio was sat with one stockinged leg hooked over the arm of his chair; his riding boots, their tops curling limply, sat by the fire, steaming. At Thornhill's entry he turned his head but did not otherwise move. Thornhill waited by the door.

'What do you want?' said the Count.

'I am Father Thornhill.'

'I have no need of a priest,' replied the Count and turned his attention back to the platter of food that the maidservant had brought him.

'All men need the service of the Church,' replied Thornhill.

The Count merely waved a drumstick for reply.

Thornhill struggled to control his irritation. This Count Claudio was now his best and last hope amidst days of frustration and he must be handled gently. Arrigo's scouts had returned that morning, shortly before the Count's arrival with his entourage, to report that there was no sign of Sir Nicholas Hawkwood or the Duke's men.

'You told me that your man had seen Hawkwood head out upon the western road,' he had raged at Arrigo when their failure was told to him.

'They tracked him so in that direction a mile or more but then it seems Hawkwood and the Duke's men turned back upon themselves and their trail is lost amidst the general markings,' answered Arrigo. 'Sure, Father, he anticipated pursuit and disguised his passage. He is as cunning as you feared him.'

'And Ludovico?' asked Thornhill more in hope than expectation. Arrigo shook his head. Thornhill had felt a clutching in his chest at that moment, a fear that he would fail as Costa had, that far from being the cause of England's redemption he would be part of the missed chances that led to its eternal damnation. He had sat heavily in his chair until the clattering sound of the hooves of many horses had stirred him to his feet to hurry to the narrow window and look out on the courtyard below and see the arrival of Count Claudio and a dozen men. New hope had sprung in his breast. He had not waited. He had hurried to find where the Count was lodged.

'Count Claudio,' Thornhill said and walked to where the Count must see him. 'You have spoken with the Duke?'

The Count looked up from his meal but made no reply.

'The Duke has told you all?' asked Thornhill.

'Come to your purpose.'

'You have been shown your bride to be?'

The Count's chewing slowed.

'I arrived earlier than expected. The Lady Aemilia is out, riding.'

Thornhill smiled.

'Cease your riddles, priest. You are of the Duke's household?'

Thornhill shook his head. 'I serve none but the Pope.'

'Ah' – the Count pointed at him with the gnawed bone of the chicken – 'you are the English priest. I have heard of you. You have made quite a reputation in these few months. Well, I'm no heretic, Thornhill.'

'Yet there are heretics hereabouts.'

'For that look to the Duke, these are his lands.'

'I have. He defies me, refuses me audience, seeks to gull me. As he does you.'

The Count put down his meal and waited. Thornhill pressed his suit.

'I suspect much, my lord, touching on your purpose here. I suspect that the Lady Aemilia is not out riding but fled the palace at news of your arrival. I suspect that the Duke has sent out men to find her and has not succeeded. I suspect he has employed the service of an English spy for the task and that this spy betrays him.'

The Count's attention was now all on Thornhill, heavy-lidded eyes holding Thornhill's own pale ones. He spoke carefully.

'Those are grave suspicions. You've basis for them?'

'I ask questions on His Holiness's behalf. I ask them of many people. All answer, some for gold, some for duty, others require hotter persuasion.'

Thornhill paused. 'I can also make questions cease. The questions that surround your stepfather's untimely death, for example.'

The Count stood and strode up to Thornhill. The priest was tall but the Count taller still. He loured over Thornhill and spoke with sullen menace.

'What do you want, Thornhill?'

'Your men, Count. The Duke will not be persuaded to listen to my counsel. I must find a traitor, an English heretic. It must be accomplished swiftly. He has disguised himself as one Sir Nicholas Hawkwood, a mercenary captain. This foolish Duke has been taken in by him and given him a troop of his men to command.'

A knock came at the door and Rodrigo appeared. He took in the sight of Thornhill with a start and then recovered himself to give his message: the Duke sought Count Claudio's company.

'I am honoured to attend His Grace,' the Count spoke over Thornhill's shoulder, then he turned back to Thornhill. 'We shall speak again, Father Thornhill, tonight. You have given me much to think on.'

And let me see thee in thy woman's weeds

The Veneto

Hemminges arrived in time to hear Aemilia say again that she was the Duke's daughter.

'And you know it to be so, Corporal,' she said, pulling off her cap to let such hacked hair as remained frame her face. 'Are you not the man that taught me to ride? Will you deny me now?'

'My lady, it is so. But how come you here? You walk among our captors, those that killed our loyal Ancient.'

Hemminges reached out and pulled at Aemilia's arm. 'What, by the name of Christ, are you about, woman?'

She shook off his arm. 'I am not "woman", Master Russell. You will call me by my title.'

'I'll call you fool, rash, intemperate, headstrong—'

'Enough, I know my business and my state, even if you do not,' said Aemilia. She turned back to the Duke's soldiers, who watched with open mouths. Hemminges, pacing nearby, saw that William too had come to watch and that Orlando and some others of the outlaws had risen from the fire and were making their way over.

'I am sorry that you are shackled here, sorrier still that the noble Ancient died. He did so honourably, in defence of his men, and for that we will a tribute pay when time allows. But now I speak to you as your mistress, will you be ruled by me?'

'To what end, lady? It was but moments ago we took you for an outlaw and now you stand before us, in strange garb, your hair shorn, and with doubtful company. How freely do you speak? For we speak with no freedom at all.'

'My father has decreed I am to marry the Count Claudio.'

'So it is said.'

'He is a cruel and strict master.'

'So it is said.'

'I'll none of him.'

'My lady, your father's will is that you marry him. This is no soldier's business but your own.'

'I am the heir of my father's house. The man I marry will rule there in time. The fate of all that owe my father fealty turns on the choice of him. You cannot wish Count Claudio as your lord.'

There was a general muttering from the soldiers that the corporal quelled with a glare.

'What of wishes, lady? We are soldiers. Our all are orders. So it seems it should be with a dutiful daughter. If you have sway here, let us be freed, then we may escort you safely home to your father.'

'I did not come to speak to you of home.'

'What then?'

'Aye, what then?' growled Hemminges.

'Count Claudio sends his train of baggage for the wedding feast ahead. It was your order that you meet it in these woods as it crossed into my father's lands and bring it safe to the palace.'

The corporal hesitated. He turned and glared at the others in the troop and then lit on Oldcastle, walking free nearby.

'You have told her this,' he cried. 'Traitor, beshrew me, a damned traitor for commander, to reveal our orders.'

Oldcastle protested, 'I never told her aught of it.'

'It's true, he did not. Though it would not have been treachery to speak to me of my father's orders or of my betrothed's plans. Count Claudio's train will be rich with my dowry. I propose that it be taken and I ask for your aid in the task.'

Aemilia's proposal was met with loud cries, laughter from some, shouts of shame from others, thoughtful silence from a few and a look of sorrow from the corporal.

'We are not thieves, lady,' he said with solemn brow.

'Nor are you,' said Hemminges from behind her. Aemilia was not to be dissuaded. She felt a certainty of purpose previously unknown to her. She wanted more than all the world to be the mistress of her own fate. Shorn of false duties save that to her own soul's demands. When she'd learned how soon her father wished to see her married and of the arrival of Count Claudio's train and of how it bore her dowry, it was the further spur and opportunity she needed.

'How can I steal that which is already promised me?' she said to Hemminges, a smile on her lips.

'The train will be strongly guarded. There will be no night-time ambush such as we took these peaceably with.'

'No night-time ambush but the train must pass across the bridge near Tregnano, there might we surprise them.'

'You talk of slaughter. Many will die. These outlaws are not enough to make success of it even if we took Count Claudio's guards abruptly, in full amazement at our attack.'

'I talk of taking what is mine and I speak to my father's men because I need them with me in the action.'

Again, Aemilia's words set up a hubbub among the captured soldiers but now it was joined by talk from the outlaws. Their amazement at Sebastian's true nature was layered over with delight at the thought of this rich train and the capture of the dowry.

'We'll none of it,' said the corporal. His whiskers seemed to bristle at the very talk of it.

'Well I think it sounds like a splendid idea,' said Orlando, coming up behind. His eyes gleamed with a wicked delight. He clapped Hemminges on the back and passed in front of him to make a courtly bow to Aemilia.

'So many mysteries solved, Lady Aemilia,' he said as he straightened. He reached out and took her hand and pressed it to his lips. 'My admiration for your courage, Sebastian, is redoubled. And for your spirit, the measure is not made that could encompass my respect for it.'

He turned to the soldiers. 'Come, fellows, your lady commands you to the action. Why make us ransom you when we might all be the richer at Count Claudio's expense?'

It was clear the thought appealed to many of the troop. It did not appeal to the proud corporal.

'We are not thieves, knave. Are you so base that you think all as cowardly and villainous as you?'

Among the outlaws many were angered by the corporal's words but Orlando merely shrugged at them. He pointed to the corporal and gestured to his men to seize him.

'Do not kill him,' said Aemilia hastily.

Orlando paused and looked down at Aemilia's hand on his arm. She did not take it away.

'He is an honourable man, and does not deserve death because he does his duty.'

Orlando covered her hand with his own. 'Lady Aemilia, I am no callous killer and if I were, your pleas would be commands to me to change my ways. I merely mean to have the corporal taken to his horse and escorted, blindfold that he may not know his route from here, to a place from which he may make his way back to your father. Someone must carry our demands.' Orlando smiled at Aemilia and then looked up at the corporal. 'I can think of no one better to convey them.'

The corporal looked from face to face. Brave he might be, but to have gone from expectation of his death to life and freedom in the passage of a minute would shake the bravest of men. He opened his mouth to speak but stuttered and was hauled away to be set on his horse and sent on his way, taking his noble but unhelpful thinking with him.

'Now perhaps,' said Orlando, 'we ought to speak a little further, Sebastian, for so I'll call you till I see you in your woman's weeds, before we make our plans.'

Ha, ha, what a fool Honesty is!

Such a day of bargaining, plots and remonstrances followed Aemilia's doffing of her disguise. No sooner had Orlando brought her to the fire than Hemminges sought to bring her away again to have more private counsel. This was the first argument, and was settled by expedient of Aemilia planting herself on the fallen trunk of tree beside the fire and refusing to be moved.

That first was vanguard to a dozen more. Should the outlaws attack the convoy of the Count Claudio? Aemilia and Orlando argued so, Hemminges scoffed at their foolhardy talk and spoke of danger and how reward should benefit the dead little. Very well then, should they not seek the service of the troop of soldiers that remained? Aemilia spoke of their certain honesty to her good fortune. Orlando and Hemminges now made common cause in reply against her: the one because such men could not be trusted once they were no longer compelled to obedience, the other arguing against complicity in the corruption of their oaths of fealty to their sovereign lord, the Duke. So, so, all well and good, but could they hope of success without their aid? Aemilia, Orlando and Hemminges, in answer of this query posed, fell upon each other in such a cacophony of dispute, the each professing reasons for their rectitude, that clarity of argument fell victim to the rising passion of their voices.

Then Zago spoke. The man seemed both an angrier and a meaner figure than even his ordinary self, though none but Aemilia and William knew the cause of his distemper or saw the fear that filled him to realise he had importuned, in the surliest terms, the daughter of a lord. Anger and fear informed his speaking now, pointing out that they had already within their possession that which was worth a dowry, namely Aemilia, and they should simply ransom her. Hemminges, now in such a height of passion as Oldcastle had rarely seen him, near drew at that suggestion but sheathed his half-drawn sword again when he realised that this would see Aemilia safe home. He then became the plan's most earnest advocate. Aemilia in her turn raised a great tempest at the perfidy of her brothers of the woods, threatened to take her own life rather than be sent back to her father trussed like a Christmas goose. She lashed Zago across the face with her hand and a general brawl might then have started till, at the last, the idea was quashed for all and good by Orlando's loud refusal to consider such dishonour to the guest rite. He wished, he said, to return to Aemilia's first proposal, to raid the convoy of Count Claudio.

From there, the argument began again, spiralled deeper into the difficulties and dangers of the task, the chance of death, considered high by all and most especially so by Hemminges, whose eloquent description of death in battle brought tears to Luca's eyes at thought of his dead brother, and blanched the face of many among the outlaws.

At this Aemilia, proudly standing forth, spoke to curb their cowardly humour. 'Is it that I, a woman, am more resolute than you? Dare I when men cower? Well then, I'll not insult you, call you cowards, base and fearful, but rather speak in praise of you, say that you are sensible men, wise men, who look to the business as one does a ledger – reckoning profit and loss. Yet I do wonder, when I call my father's men to this deed and march together with them, will you then sit idly by while courage in a woman's form stalks on to glory?'

'Nay,' several cried.

'There's the spirit. I doubted it not. I have seen in you, be you never so base, a noble lustre to your eye. You are those that will dare and dare with me. And with our glory shall come riches, rewards for those that dare, for those that have the courage to show here, to show now, that though they be made of base metal yet they have been forged in the soot and fires of suffering and emerged as steel.'

To Hemminges' surprise a ragged cheer rose from the bandits' throats.

'Don't let pride be a horsefly to sting you from your common sense,' cried Hemminges, but he went quite unheeded under the cheering of the common crowd at Aemilia's oration.

'Which of you is with me?' she called.

Hemminges could only watch, his blood both boiling and freezing, as Aemilia was borne in state to where her father's men now lay in trembling wait, not knowing the cause of the outlaws' excitement. Shorn of their corporal's resolve, weakened by relief at finding the outlaws cheers were for the promise of their company and not for prospect of a crueller resolution of their fate, they proved most willing to accede to Aemilia's plan. She was, they proclaimed, agreeing with her argument, the daughter of their sovereign lord and her command, offering both freedom and riches, had much to be commended in it. Aemilia herself led them in three cheers, at each round of which Hemminges' head stooped lower on his shoulders.

William, sitting by Zago, watched all with his bright eyes hooded and his head dipped. Oldcastle, watching him in turn, wondered at his stillness and if he slept or no but saw him hum or seem to speak aloud some poem as the course of the debate roamed about.

When all was done, Orlando and Aemilia, victorious, turned to planning of the fight to come. Hemminges, slump-shouldered, turned away and kicked the ground as he came to Oldcastle.

'Bloody, bloody, bloody fools,' he said and bent, plucked up a stick and hurled it with main force against a nearby tree where it shattered from the blow.

'Was it not for love of her strong will that you followed her to these woods?' asked William, coming up behind them and witnessing the stick's destruction.

'This is not will but recklessness,' said Hemminges.

'All rivers flood their course from time to time, but drawing back leave richer the land they covered. So may it be with her.'

'For Jesu's sake I liked it better when you were silent, Will. People are not fit for metaphor, they demand plain speaking. The woman is not a river but an innocent. She does not flood, she rages. She is sick with her own freedom and others will catch cold of it and die. As may she.'

William spoke with excitement: 'You see it, then? You see it as clearly as it can be seen.'

William looked from Oldcastle to Hemminges but their faces showed no understanding.

'In plain speaking are we not free to go? These outlaws have quite given over the thought of ransom, their heads are turned by talk of honour gained in the bloody field. Nick they no longer value even at his false worth. And, even if you did not see the dangers in her, Hemminges, you see that this woman no longer cares for your guiding hand. Has thrown it off. Slapped it away. There is no more here for any of us. Let us three then depart.'

Oldcastle was nodding. 'Yes, John, this is a dry company that we keep. I have been foolish in my fancies and I will no more of such foolishness. Let us go now, as you have yourself urged us to do.'

'And watch her die? Watch others die for her?' said Hemminges, shaking his head. 'No, no. I brought her here. I will not abandon her at the moment that she first strays. It is now she needs me most.'

He walked away without saying more and Oldcastle made to follow but then stopped with William's restraining hand on his shoulder.

'Hers is not the only sickness,' William said. 'The illness must run its course.'

'And what medicine shall we apply? William, are you returned to us now? To guide us?' said Oldcastle, looking at his young friend. His searching gaze held hope and trepidation and sadness in equal measures.

'Time, Nick, is the balm for all hurts. Heart's ease, it numbs but it does not cure. The cure's within. I shall give him what he wants. Not what is needful but what he desires.'

He turned his face away and would have left but Oldcastle tried to draw him back. Oldcastle longed to engage his friend, as he had so often done in the past, when in their cups or speaking of some matter conjunctive to their interests they would let wit play on wit and build from it a fire of amusements that blew their thoughts to heaven. Oldcastle felt his loneliness, he who hated that sensation more than any other in the world. Now his friend's face shifted from shrewd to blank in an instant and he could not see where the man had gone within.

'How pregnant sometimes your replies are, William. But are they the happy accident that madness hits on, that reason and sanity could not so prosperously be delivered of?' Oldcastle's eyes still searched his friend's face. 'Will, Will, where did you go and have you yet come back to us? Will, what is the matter?'

But William made no reply save to clasp a hand, too briefly, on his friend's shoulder and then to walk away leaving Oldcastle alone in the forest.

A shrewd knave and an unhappy

Hemminges was not the only one of Aemilia's lovers unhappy at the morning's news. Valentine had risen late and, having risen, remembered his resolve of the night before and hurried to find Petro at the church. He'd left before Aemilia had revealed herself to her father's men and returned to find her the feted Joan of Arc to Orlando's Dauphin, the talk on everyone's lips her plan to seize Count Claudio's convoy. In vain he sought to draw her aside. A crowd of fawning outlaws had surrounded her and when he'd wormed his way to the centre of their sphere she'd waved him away. Redoubling his demand, he'd been interrupted by Orlando putting before her another piece of planning for the raid and she, distracted, had given his plea for her attention no heed at all.

Forlornly, he had sloped away. Wandering from the centre of the camp he'd sat and pulled his commonplace book from its satchel and begun to write: a poem to soothe his soul. His peace had been brief. The madman Adam had come up and taunted him to distraction with idle comments and sharp insults. At last he had sent him away but calm was lost to him. That Adam had a way of saying things that seemed half a fool's mummery and half an augur's prophecy and caused one to brood on him and his proverbs long after he had left.

Looking up he saw where the corporal of horse was being led past upon his palfrey, straight-backed, wrists bound and blindfold. Another who is sent away, Valentine thought. He wandered over, looking back at Aemilia gathered in the tight knot of outlaws as he walked, and thought of his abandonment. Soon this corporal, for all he suffers now, will be back on the couch of luxury while I stay here on a bed of thorns. A sudden thought came to Valentine. He scribbled hastily in his commonplace book.

'You ride to the Duke?' Valentine called to the corporal, coming closer.

The soldier's sneer was all his answer but Valentine did not care. 'Hold a moment, ho,' he said to one-armed Jacopo who led the man. Jacopo ignored him so he ran a little forward and walked close to the mounted man's knee.

'Give my cousin my apology,' said Valentine up to him.

'He'll see you swing for your treachery,' growled the corporal at the simpering voice.

Valentine placed his hand upon the man's leg. 'Tell him, I most earnestly desire his forgiveness.'

'Tell him yourself, on the scaffold,' answered the corporal. Jacopo, embarrassed by the indignity of Valentine's pleading, urged the corporal's horse on to the trot and the two men pulled away leaving Valentine alone again. He sat nearby to begin to ponder on his abandonment and on his treachery when he felt her hand light on his shoulder.

'I am sorry, Valentine,' she said. Her voice was full of gentle regard. 'I was caught in the thrill of our adventure and neglected you who are the cause of it. Oh, Valentine, do you see how we have blossomed in this earth?'

Her eyes were bright but Valentine looked on them with fear for it seemed to him the bright spark of madness. She looked from him to a happier future with only a robbery and a host of dead men between her and its possession.

'This very day we shall seize from Count Claudio my dowry. How little we thought that this might be the promise of our exile!'

Valentine's fear turned to anger. 'It was not to be an outlaw in the woods that we fled.'

'What was it then?' demanded Aemilia. Her smile had gone in an instant and the wolfish look upon her face returned. 'What ambition have you, Valentine? What do you seek for us? Am I not the one that now claims the future for us? Our lives cannot all be poetry and love-making. We must seize what opportunity we can. Even mad Adam understands that: there is a tide in the affairs of men . . . You have heard him say it, heard him set it to song, but have you understood it?'

'I gave no credent ear to the madman, no. Are you sure you are not run mad that you do so? Oh, Aemilia, what is that you say? You were the one that counselled caution and now you throw that off as you throw off your disguise.'

'I have thrown off bondage, Valentine. I will not put the collar round my neck again, not for you or any man.'

'Aemilia, let us from this place. I have arrangements made—' Valentine broke off as Orlando came up to them.

'Aemilia, the men are ready to march and clamour for your wisdom and your words of courage.'

Aemilia looked sadly at Valentine and pressed his arm. He quickly placed his hand over hers to hold her there.

'Promise me that we will meet tomorrow,' he whispered, 'at dawn's first light.'

She pulled away but he held her tight till she made answer.

'Promise me.'

'Tomorrow morning shall we meet.'

He loosed her hand and she turned away to join Orlando and the other outlaws and her father's men. Valentine watched her part, saw how she was in avid conversation with Orlando, saw how she placed her hand on the hilt of the sword she carried now, slung in a baldric and lewdly swaying with her hips. There was a siren's call within these woods that lured her from the safety of his ship to stand at the rail and, heedless of the danger to herself or others, prepare to dive into the wild seas. He must bind her to the mast or see her perish. It was for her own good he acted. No, not so. It was for his own. For he feared that if he did not act now, he would lose her.

The bloody spur cannot provoke him on

Verona

The horse was dead.

The corporal of horse had not been born a harsh man yet he'd ridden his palfrey to its death. Twenty hard miles in half a day he'd travelled, ripping away his blindfold as soon as Jacopo'd left him, setting himself by the sun to head west and pushing his palfrey to the canter. He'd driven it on whenever he could, chafing when it broke into a walk and urging it back to the canter with harsh incision in its hide, and when that failed laying a switch across its back to see it surge forth, until at last, long after the sun had set, he'd reached the Duke's palace. He fell from the horse's back in the courtyard and the horse, lips flecked dry white, the muscles in its shoulders trembling like shaken water, eyes wild with exhaustion, saw its charge delivered, and its heart burst in the instant.

The corporal was brought, half carried between two servants, to the Duke's presence.

'What is it, man?' the Duke had roared at the pitiful sight before him. The corporal was black with mud, streaked with sweat and barely able to stand from his hours in the saddle. 'Where are the rest of your troop?'

Thornhill had full a dozen men amongst the Duke's servants in paid employ. Even had he not, still would he have learned of the disaster that had befallen Sir Nicholas Hawkwood and his men almost at the instant of the corporal's return from the great cry that cannoned out from the hall. The sound of the Duke's rage carried to the farthest corners of the palace.

Thornhill did not wait, but rising from his prayers went straight to the hall. Count Claudio arrived as he did and Thornhill followed so quickly behind the Count that Rodrigo had no chance to bar him entry.

The wall behind Duke Leonardo's throne bore testament to his rage, a great stain of wine blotting over the tapestry of chaste Dian at her bath. The throne itself thrust back, the Duke now paced behind the high table before it and perched upon a stool sat the corporal, head bowed.

'Bloody, bawdy, remorseless villain,' the Duke swore. 'Eat my bread, drink my wine and stab me in the back.'

'My lord has had ill tidings?' asked Thornhill as he entered.

'Ah, the solicitous priest. Who summoned you? Not I,' answered the Duke. 'But then you needed no summoning. Come in carrion black to feast upon the dead. How present you priests are at moments of unhappiness. Yes, yes, I have had ill tidings, priest, as thick as hail they come: the damned Hawkwood and all my men captured; my loyal Ancient dead; my daughter turned outlaw and' – he turned to Count Claudio – 'the Count Claudio's convoy of my daughter's dowry to be taken by these same outlaws. They have turned from horseflies into locusts. What has turned them so?'

Count Claudio was striding toward the battered figure of the corporal. 'What news is this? My convoy to be taken?'

'Aye, my lord, that is their plan.'

Count Claudio turned angry eyes upon the Duke. 'We must ride out, Your Grace. At once.'

The Duke nodded then slumped into his seat. 'Yet how? All those men that I can spare are taken. And where do we ride? Where are they camped?'

'We take mine,' said Claudio.

'A dozen men, too few,' said the Duke.

Claudio looked to Thornhill. The look they shared spoke to the agreements made in the conversations of the night.

'You may have my men,' said Thornhill. 'With mine and those of Count Claudio you are enough.'

The Duke looked warily on Thornhill. 'What is the price of this aid?'

'Only that I be allowed to question Sir Nicholas Hawkwood.'

The Duke was about to answer when Thornhill cut across him: 'Without interference, Your Grace. On my terms and in my time.'

The Duke was too broken by the turn of events to deny him more. It was Count Claudio that answered.

'Your men can ride . . . ?'

'Within the hour,' answered Thornhill.

'Let it be so,' said the Count. 'We ride to meet the convoy on the road and pray we are not too late.'

'Your Grace,' the corporal spoke up. 'There is more.' He reached into his boot and pulled out a small damp square of parchment. 'This message have I for you.'

'A message? Who from?'

'Read, Your Grace.'

The Duke strode round the table and snatched up the paper from his corporal's hand and read. And having read, began to laugh and did not stop his laughter till he, Father Thornhill, Count Claudio and thirty men were in the saddle and riding hard for the woods.

I know not if the day be ours or no

The Veneto

Men had died that night too.

They died in the ambush on Count Claudio's train. Under Hemminges' command, who had been the victim of more than one ambush and laid twice as many more in his youth, the outlaws had set their trap with care, catching the convoy's guard unwary as they crossed a bridge, half trapped on one side, half on the other. For all the care there was in the preparation, it was a close-run thing. When the fighting was over the outlaws had wandered over the field to book the dead and then to bury them: five of their fellowship and one of the Duke's men had fallen before the Count Claudio's men had all been killed or driven off. Aemilia stood by the trench into which the bodies, friend and foe alike, had been put for burial and listened in silence as Petro spoke words over them even as the soil was foisted back on to their still bodies.

Hemminges could not bear to watch any part of it. He stood apart, his back to the grave and revelling outlaws both. He'd put two of the bodies in that grave by his own hand when Aemilia, mad with her own conceits and seeing her small army hesitate at the moment of truth, had charged the column all alone and only Hemminges' swift advance had saved her from the reality of battle. A third had died at Aemilia's sword's point in those same moments. The first man that she had killed. Hemminges had seen the thundercloud come over her eyes as understanding of her deed came to her, as he had seen it fall across the eyes of many a man before who suddenly knew his godlike power to snuff out life as easily as a candle's flame. But then he'd seen the lightning yerk within the cloud, a battle-cry had come to her lips and she'd turned back to the fight.

'What a day, what a night!' Orlando was in great good humour. He came up behind Aemilia and clapped his hands upon her shoulders. 'We must celebrate, a triumph, yes, celebration, with pomp, with revelry. Come, come.'

He pulled her away and ushered her eagerly from the dead towards the carts. Hemminges could hear him speaking as they parted: 'My dear, the splendour of these spoils is past compare. Why yours would have been a wedding so wondrous more men would speak of it than that our Lord attended at Cana.'

Orlando ignored the sharp noise of reproof that came from Petro at this blasphemy. He was too busy showing Aemilia the carts with their barrels of wine, their haunches of meat, and their chests of cloth, furniture and in the last, a small chest that brimmed with opals, pearls and gold coins. Orlando presented it to Aemilia with a bow that, unfolding, became a caper.

'Such a store of wedding cheer was here prepared and now is all of ours. And best of all, it will beggar Claudio. He gave thinking to repossess it all in the fullness of time and so gave generously. *Ha ha!* A fool and now a beggar!'

The other outlaws had joined Orlando in his dancing and even Aemilia's father's men had been caught in the delight of victory. Hemminges watched, a taste like sour wine in his mouth, until he could watch no more and stamped his way back to the outlaws' camp alone. It was an hour before Orlando brought order to himself and then to the others and the captured train could be moved off. Aemilia sat in state on the foremost cart, laurelled Victory on her chariot.

That night Aemilia was giddy with drinking the captured sack, with the lingering wine of action and of death faced and overcome, with the growing sense of her own power. She was sat near to one of the several fires that dotted the bandits' new camp. Her father's soldiers and the bandits did not yet mingle, but there would be time for that, she thought. Till then she did not wish to be seen to favour either group and so sat apart. She pulled tighter around her shoulders the fur-lined cloak she had claimed from the plunder of Count Claudio's train. She watched her comrades, dotted about their new camp, some now sleeping, some slumped in drunken stupor, some in knots of quiet conversation, some few on watch. I will forge them all to my command, she thought.

Orlando walked towards her.

'You are a wonder, Lady Aemilia.'

She looked up at him in surprise. He nodded, as if till that moment he had still doubted the matter but in viewing her had found confirmation of his conjecture. He gestured to ask if he might sit and she smiled her willingness.

'Aye, a wonder, a miracle.' He leaned back against the fallen trunk of tree she sat on and stretched out his legs. His dark hair shone in the firelight and she wondered how he had found time amidst all the business to wash. She suppressed a desire to comb it with her fingers. I am drunker than I knew, she thought.

Orlando was not looking at her but at the fire as he spoke. 'You bravely put yourself in danger and at a moment when courage should fail you, you instead put courage into others.'

Aemilia blushed. Orlando turned and looked up at her.

'Where does this courage come from?'

'I do not know and blush to hear myself praised when I have done so little.'

'You do yourself disservice by refusing my praise. I think you little realise how brave you truly are. Did you not follow Valentine from comfort into hardship? Did you not defy your father's will? All that speaks of courage.'

He shifted further round and gestured at her hose and Aemilia was suddenly aware of how much a man's clothing revealed of her. 'Did you not stand disguised as a man among men? That too speaks of bravery. And in such poor disguise too.'

'Good enough to fool you.'

'At first. It could not last. You are too fair to make for a good man and you dance a woman's part too well.'

Again Aemilia blushed, recalling her eagerness that night and remembering her want of care. At her sudden sad look, Orlando knelt up and put his hand on her arm.

'You should give credit to your own bravery, lady. Admire it as I admire it in you.'

Aemilia said nothing. She did not trust her voice. Orlando's look echoed her own passions. The moment's reflection at her want of care had changed, exultation was in her, for she had triumphed had she not?

Won o'er Master Russell to her command, won o'er her father's men, won o'er the spoils of Count Claudio's train, won o'er all that had been set against her. She cautioned herself against the magic of the night, the wine, the lingering drama in her blood from the actions of the day. Then, a moment, Orlando's head bent to hers and she would not swear that thought played a part in her head tilting down to meet his. No thought at all played a role in the kiss that followed. His hand about her waist hauled her tight to him and hers came up to mingle in his hair and pull him closer still. She felt the muscles move beneath the linen of his shirt; the smoke of the fire and the scent of his fresh-cleaned hair were in the air. She pulled him tighter to her. This was her reward for all her daring and it was honey-sweet.

She broke away, pushed him back as she moved, still saying nothing. After a moment he, silent too, sat beside her.

'I swear your face is so familiar to me, yet I cannot place it,' she said.

'Perhaps you have seen it in your dreams?' asked Orlando.

'Fool.'

They both laughed.

'More wine, Lady Aemilia?'

'Gladly.'

He went to fetch it and she watched him go. He is beautiful, she thought, but so is Valentine. He is brave, but so is John Russell. Am I grown such a wanton that I flit between thoughts of three men? She did not think herself wanton. She thought instead that this was how the butterfly must feel when it is no longer a grub. She had grown wings. She was no longer a child. She smiled at that thought.

A smile stayed on her face the whole rest of that night.

Act Five

Woods in the Veneto,
March 1586

Drugs poison him that so fell sick of you

William lay awake in the dawn's light, his mind examining Valentine as if he were a statue that he held in his hands and turned and twisted to see from all angles: how Valentine longed to be significant to this world and how little he felt his own grace or power trapped here in the woods. What would such a man, such a servant of Mammon, give to be restored to gilded glory? What bargain might he make and have the power to make? As if these thoughts stirred that which they rested on William watched Valentine rise and creep across the camp and shake a rheumy-eyed Aemilia. The sun was still between ground and tree tops and its slanted rays wrote harsh shadows on the forest floor. The rest of the camp slumbered on.

Some men lay where, drunk, they had fallen, others had made it so far as their beds and now remained curled in blankets tight as peascods. The campfires smoked their last; their haze spreading out over the outlaws in their vale seemed Circe's spell that had stilled the camp to silence. The only watch save William's was Jacopo's and his was fitful; to see him nod over the fire was to wonder if he was awake or merely dreamed his sentry's duty.

'Aemilia,' whispered Valentine. He did not dare speak too loudly for fear of waking Orlando, who lay close nearby, too close for Valentine's happiness.

'Huh? Valentine. What o'clock is it?'

Valentine ignored her sleepy questioning and, reaching down, pulled her to sitting. Half by wrestling and half by pleading, he got her to her feet. She rubbed her face with her hands and knuckled her eyes to clear them of sleep.

'Enough, enough, I am awake, Valentine. What is it?'

'Hurry. Come,' he said, taking her by the hand and pulling her after. She was too tired to resist.

William picked himself up from the tree against which he rested and followed.

*

'We are here and none too soon,' Valentine announced an hour later, looking up at the sun.

'A church?' asked Aemilia.

It stood, small and unremarkable, in the centre of a clearing in the wood. There were two or three small broken houses nearby: their exact number could not be counted for each had fallen into the other and bushes, vines and grasses grew across their broken-backed bodies. The church still had its roof though the windows were gone and the lead that held the glass was long stolen. The whole place had a sepulchral air.

'Not just a church, Aemilia.' Valentine walked over to it and stepped across the threshold, and beckoned her to join him. Coming and standing beside him she saw, still sleeping by the altar at the far end, Petro. 'But a priest too.'

'I don't understand,' said Aemilia to the proud, smiling face of her lover.

'He wants to get married,' a voice spoke from behind them and Aemilia watched mad Adam walk from the trees into the little clearing and cross to the church. He looked fresh and rested and, as though to lend an emphasis to the contrast between his state and hers, as he walked he gave a little skip and jumped up and clicked his heels together. 'And a fine day it is for it too.'

'What are you doing here?' demanded Valentine at Adam's unwelcome interruption.

William smiled at him, moved past Aemilia standing by the door and walked down the aisle. Two goats had pushed through a narrow hole in the far wall of the church where once, perhaps, a door had stood but where now the stones hung precariously and ivy wrapped its way from outside over the lintel and up the inward part of the wall towards the ceiling. He walked towards the goats making little clicking noises and holding out his hand as if to feed them. As he walked he sang:

How should I your true love know
From another one?
By his cockle hat and staff,
And his sandal shoon.

'I don't want to get married,' said Aemilia, bringing her attention back from the madman to the lover.

Valentine's hopeful smile diminished even as his eyes grew wide. His lip trembling, he grasped Aemilia's shoulders and gazed at her. 'Do not say I have lost you, Aemilia.'

Aemilia thought he looked foolish, like a mournful horse. She shook her head. She did not want to deal with this now, with Valentine and his pleading, with all the thoughts that his bargaining would throw up, with her guilty remembrance of the passionate embraces of the night. She sought to deflect him.

'Wed here? In a church that is more cattle-byre than consecrate chamber?'

'What does it matter where we marry? It is the ceremony that concerns us, all else is nothing.'

Aemilia could see that Valentine was not easily to be diverted. Her head ached, her heart felt too cramped for its casing. These were the least desired circumstances in the world. William had sat himself down nearby on the shattered remains of a pew to watch their debate and he began a new song as Valentine's pleading grew to a pitch.

By Gis and by Saint Charity,
Alack, and fie for shame!
Young men will do't, if they come to't;
By cock, they are to blame.
Quoth she, before you tumbled me,
You promised me to wed.

'Be quiet,' shouted Aemilia to William, desperate for a moment of quiet in which to think her way out of this bind. 'Are all men fools?'

'Not all, Madonna,' answered William. 'And even among those that are, not all are equal. Why fools are as like husbands as pilchards are to herrings, the husbands the bigger.'

Aemilia threw up her hands. 'It is too early for such merriment. I will see you at the camp, Valentine.'

He reached out and grasped her arm. 'No, Aemilia, no.'

He turned her to look on him. Aemilia sought out other sights, she didn't want this now. She didn't want to have decision thrust on her.

'I love you,' said Valentine. His voice was stretched thin with the urgency of its pleading. 'I love you, world without end, and I wish to marry you. You urged me to that very thing. You demanded that I ask it of your father and, doing so, I was cast out. Now we may make it a fond reality. Here, now. Let us be married.'

'Where is speeding Hymen, Valentine?' called out William. 'For shame, be more temperate. Do they not say a hasty marriage seldom proves well?'

'Oh, Aemilia,' pleaded Valentine, ignoring his chorus, 'let not desire wait on reason but, loving me, be joined with me.'

Aemilia tried to shake off his arm but his grip was as insistent as his voice. She put her hand down to pull his arm from hers and saw his slender figure beneath its soiled silk shirt: it brought her back to another man's arm that had held hers tight with passion of a different kind that yesternight. Shame and guilt burst their banks to cover over all her anger and put in their place a melancholy. She ceased her struggle and lifted a hand to his face, gentle on his cheek. 'We are changed, altered. I am not the woman that I was when I walked into these woods. My desires now are strange to me.'

'I care not.' He clutched at the hand that held him and pressed it to his cheek. 'Love is not love that alters when it alteration finds.'

'Oh good, good, the best I have yet heard from you,' said William from his pew.

'I need to think, Valentine,' said Aemilia. 'Give me time to think.'

'Oh that's never good,' said William. 'No love story begins with that injunction from a lady's lips.'

'Will you be quiet, Adam,' demanded Valentine. He turned back to Aemilia and got down on to one knee and turned his grasp upon her arm into a cradling of her hand with his. 'I love you. Let us be married this day, before the sun is at its highest, let us be joined together and whatever dangers come, whatever challenges we face, let us face them together.'

Aemilia stared down at Valentine. She had once thought him the bravest thing in her life but his gilt was all washed away now. His beautiful hair hung in greasy locks across his brow and his large eyes, into which she had once wished to dive and swim forever, now seemed to her to resemble the empty docility of a cow. He had been tested in the fire and found wanting. Or worse, she had been forged anew in that same fire and their shapes no longer fitted.

'No, Valentine,' she said. 'I do not wish it.'

'You do not? It is the answer to all our woes. Confront your father with the marriage done and none but a churl could spurn his daughter and new-made son then.'

'I do not love you.'

There was a terrible moment of silence that followed these words. Then came a rising of spirit in Valentine, and he rose and roared at Aemilia who backed away from his sudden fury.

'How dare you? How dare you abandon me now? I have given all for you. All. All. To be cast away again as if some fish caught in sport but now too small for your consumption. I will not be so.' His high, angry voice broke and cracked as if in sympathy with his heart and his last words were racked from him as he shook his fist at the woman he loved and who no longer loved him. 'Inconstant woman, was I but a toy to play with?'

And damned be him that first cries, 'Hold, enough!'

A sharp command barked out across the church: 'Enough!'

Hemminges appeared in the doorway, his face a grey, swirling sea of anger. Beside him stood Oldcastle, looking winded and with a sheen of sweat that belied the coldness of the day, and Dionisio, seemingly serene as ever. Hemminges cast a basilisk eye across the scene: Valentine frozen by his shout, fist still raised in anger; Aemilia backed against the wall but staring defiantly at her former lover; Petro stirring by the altar; and William watching it all with a twist of laughter on his lips.

'No need for concern, John,' called William. 'I feared you would be late for a wedding but it seems you arrive in time for a funeral.'

Hemminges looked to Valentine.

'What is this madness, Valentine?'

At Hemminges' words Valentine's rough torrent of feeling that had forced itself out as anger burst forth anew in gouts of tears. Valentine's hands came up to bury his face, he fell back to his knees and shuffled on them towards Aemilia.

'Forgive me, Aemilia,' he cried from the floor, 'forgive me. Oh let us still be married before it is too late.'

Aemilia turned back to him. Behind the weeping Valentine, William had stirred from his seat and was looking intently at the kneeling man. Aemilia took a few steps towards Valentine. She looked at him with pity. 'What is there to forgive? Valentine. I am sorry. I thought there could be more to us but I was wrong. I need more strength than you can offer. I . . . I am sorry. Come, Valentine, take heart, all will be well.'

Valentine fell to the floor. Exasperation warred with guilt within Aemilia. She made to leave.

Orlando appeared at the door, took in the scene and clucked in disappointment. 'It seems such a shame to waste all of dear Valentine's preparation. We have priest, church and bride. If the groom is not to your liking, will you take me in his stead?'

'You?' said Hemminges and Aemilia in the same instant. Orlando patted Hemminges on the shoulder as he passed him and walked towards Aemilia.

'I admit it has been a rough wooing but what are husband and wife but partners in the enterprise of life? If we may find common theme amidst disaster, how much more might we discover when the sweet time of life is with us?'

He drew level with Aemilia and cupped her chin. 'Have we not shown ourselves to be well suited to enterprises and stratagems of great boldness and rare merit? Besides I think you like my look, I know that I like yours.'

'Marry a vagabond thief?' said Hemminges from behind.

'Oh, I am no vagabond but a count, unfairly deprived of my land and title by a villainous brother, my birth as noble as yours. Adam here can vouch to that story,' he answered, without taking his eye from Aemilia. 'And if I am thief, then so is the Lady Aemilia, for she has stolen my heart.'

He bent to take a kiss from her lips but she twisted away to look towards William, who sat still on his broken pew but now with Dionisio and Oldcastle sat beside him. The little servant had unfolded a handkerchief on which a small round of cheese and some dry bread sat at which he and Oldcastle picked as they watched Orlando at his love-making.

'Adam can vouch? Vouch to what?' she demanded.

'Yes, that I too should like to know.' Hemminges had, over the last days, oft told himself that he was no true suitor to Aemilia. They stood in too great distance from each other; the player and the lady, only in a ballad does that end well. It came as a bitter potion swallowed then to see the outlaw king Orlando's assumption of the role and to have it paraded before him. More galling yet, to recognise in Orlando's playing of it the belief that it would be well received. Rather than look on his own bright jealousy Hemminges looked instead at a darker object, William.

Valentine stood again and tried to push past Orlando. 'For God's sake, Aemilia. You cannot be so moon-mad as to want this knave. I beg you, Aemilia, the time is short. Make good your promise to me. Let us be married.'

He gave a little groan of desperation. Aemilia waved him down and kept her look on William but he was looking in his turn at Valentine and his head was tilted in a question.

'Vouch for what?' Aemilia repeated.

William suddenly shot from his seat and ran from the church. Aemilia threw up her hands.

'It is not I that am run moon-mad, but all the men here.'

Luca appeared at the door with Jacopo by his side, both men's faces pale.

'Orlando, Lady Aemilia, armed men are coming, a-horseback.' He pointed out the door. Hemminges strode to the entrance and saw a troop of mounted men spreading out across the clearing, the Duke and Father Thornhill and a third man, heavy-set, dark-featured and menacing, in the van. Aemilia ran over to where Hemminges stood and saw some of the men dismounting by the trees, tie off their horses, draw their swords and advance.

Valentine fell again to his knees.

'Oh, forgive me,' he moaned.

My heart beats thicker than a feverous pulse

Aemilia swung angrily round to confront Valentine.

'"Too late," you said. You knew of this? This is your doing?'

'There is still time,' said Valentine, looking up at her. 'Let us be married, now, in haste.'

His eyes were wild beneath their red and tearful front and he once again shuffled forward on his knees. Behind him Petro had scrambled to the wall and was peering through a gap in the broken stonework at the advancing men. He began to cross himself and moan.

'Oh Lord Christ, forgive us our sins.'

Hemminges dragged Aemilia back into the church and pushed Jacopo along with him.

'Quickly, out the back, quickly. Where is Dionisio?'

Hemminges was looking about but could see no sign of William or Dionisio. He hurried towards the broken doorway where William had been last. Reaching it he peered round the upright of the door and quickly pulled his head back as William came swiftly back round the corner. His face was masked in blood from a shallow cut across his brow.

'No escape there, friend John,' said William breathlessly as he pressed his sleeve against the cut. Behind him were two of the mounted men turning the corner of the church to hem them in from that direction.

'Damn it,' Hemminges growled. 'Where is Dionisio?'

'Draw our swords,' said Aemilia from behind him. 'Let us sell our lives bravely.'

Hemminges rolled his eyes and looked about him for some other exit. He felt Oldcastle tap him on the shoulder and turned to see Orlando backing down the nave towards him. There in the entrance of the church stood the Duke, face red, hair wild.

'Aemilia!' he roared. 'Come here now!'

They retreated into the chancel. Hemminges, Orlando and Aemilia had their blades out, a pitiful defence made more so by the arrival at the rear of the church of men with crossbows. Oldcastle, moving with the swiftness that the terror of these occasions granted him, had scurried to crouch behind the broken altar from where he now tried to beckon William down to join him. William was too occupied with watching the newly arrived Duke Leonardo striding down the nave towards them. He stood with a seeming unconcern at the various swords, quarrels and daggers pointed in his direction. His calm demeanour was a studied contrast to that of Valentine, who cowered almost at the feet of Orlando and Aemilia. Nor had Petro, Luca and Jacopo shown much defiance. The three had backed up as far against the side of the chancel as the rough, cracked stone allowed and Petro now stood with hands clasped in prayer, eyes shut, lips mouthing sacred words as Luca and Jacopo muttered profane ones beside him.

The Duke stopped his advance half-way down the nave and repeated his command, sounding more tired than angry. His face was drawn, the skin purple beneath his eyes where sleep had given them an ill colour.

'Aemilia, for God's sake, put down that sword and come here.'

'No,' she replied and was glad to hear her voice did not betray by its own tremor the quaking within her bosom.

Oldcastle judged the moment ripe to make a pleading on his own account. He pushed his head above the altar's parapet. 'Duke Leonardo, I thank God you are here. Such a deal of trouble there has been.'

He got no further, the Duke's roar cut him off. 'Silence! Traitor, dissembler, I shall deal with you in your turn.'

'This is most unjust, Duke Leonardo,' Oldcastle moaned as he sank back below the stone.

'Daughter, come here,' roared the Duke, his anger back.

'No,' repeated the Duke's daughter.

Two new arrivals to the church walked down the nave to join the Duke, Thornhill and the great, dark figure they had seen riding by his side.

'Claudio,' hissed Orlando, naming his arrival.

'*Count* Claudio,' said his brother with a grin to underpin the title. He made a little tutting sound and wagged his finger at Orlando. 'I was told you were dead.'

'I am. A ghost am I now, come to haunt your guilt-laden conscience.'

'It is not I whose conscience is heavy, Orlando, cruel parricide. I am glad to see you again only that I may also see justice this day.'

His voice betrayed little fervour for justice and the grim grin remained, to his brother's fury.

'Justice?' Orlando shouted.

'Who is this?' said Thornhill to Count Claudio. He spoke disinterestedly and Claudio answered in the same manner, as if they did not stand at the edge of a forest of blades all pointed at the object of their talk.

'This is Orlando, my brother, and, unhappy to relate, my father's murderer,' answered Claudio.

'From Padua I murdered him?' Orlando's reply thrilled with all the anger and fear that seemed wanting in the other two. William, watching, thought it was as if Orlando hoped by his own great emotion he could colour theirs. Ours is a lonely path, thought William, and one in which we wish our cares were held in as high regard by others. They never are.

'Villain! Smiling, damned villain. For one may smile and smile and murder while you smile, at least I see it is so in Verona. You, Claudio, are the murderer and before this day is out it is I that shall have justice.'

Claudio turned his head to the men at the rear of the church without his gaze leaving his brother. 'Kill him,' he ordered.

'No,' cried the Duke beside him. 'You damned fool, you may hit my daughter.'

For the first time an emotion other than amusement crossed over Claudio's face: a look of irritation at being countermanded, a flare of heat on the cheeks at being denied, at being called a fool. Thornhill placed his hand on Claudio's arm and spoke in more soothing terms: 'Too hasty, Count. There are those among these men I would question.'

Aemilia's thoughts at first had all been fixed on her father's sudden appearance and her firm desire to defy him. Then she had seen him and the way darkness rimmed his eyes and worry drew back the corners of his cracked lips and she had felt her child's heart quaver at the sight till his roared command that she heel to him had stiffened her resolve. Then this sudden passage between the brothers had turned her to look between Orlando and Count Claudio. She heard the wretched pain in Orlando's voice as he spoke of his father's murder and, heedless, she had reached out to clutch his arm in sympathy. When Claudio had bid the archers shoot she had tensed against the anticipated blow and heard her father's voice cry 'no' with a relief that near unmanned her. Then realisation that the stay of execution was but temporary struck her and she felt the tension gather in her chest again. Her pulse hammered in her temples. How would this end? She straightened her back and stared at her father. She'd made her choice before now and grown to the truth of it in her heart. If now they were caught then, like the stag at bay, all that remained was to make a proud end.

You must lay down the treasures of your body

'Enough of this,' said the Duke, still glowering at his daughter. He walked towards her, pulling off his gauntlets, quite unnoticing of Hemminges and Orlando and their blades. 'Put down the sword and come here.'

Once again Aemilia shook her head in defiance of her father. He turned and threw his gauntlets at the wall.

'Ungrateful whelp,' said the Duke. 'How sharper than a serpent's tooth it is to have a thankless child. You shame me with your disobedience.' His voice fell quieter but was no less strident in its tone. 'Have you wanted for anything that I should find you so ungrateful now? Have I not given you all?'

'All. All save your respect for my own will.' Aemilia's voice matched her father's for intensity. 'God's blood, Father, why have you schooled me? Let me wander freely in your library? Joined me to your councils? Spoken of your most inmost thoughts to me? Only then to treat me like a ewe that is to be tupped?'

'This,' said the Duke, purple with rage, gesturing at the cowering Valentine, 'this is the ram that you would defy me for.'

'I defy you for no man at all, Father. I defy you for myself.'

Valentine, realising that he was spoken of, got to his feet and tried to present himself more nobly than the wretched figure crumpled on the floor. Neither Aemilia nor the Duke so much as glanced at him and, seeing this, he scuttled backwards till he bumped against the wall beside William.

At the back of the church a new face entered. A stiffening of shock ran through the outlaws as their companion Ludovico walked down the nave and came to Father Thornhill. He whispered in the priest's ear and the priest nodded, his eyes running across Hemminges, William and, after a moment's searching, Oldcastle, peeping above the cracked altar. The priest stepped forward.

'This business is overdone. Let them all be bound and taken for trial.'

'What trial needed?' said Count Claudio. 'My brother's crime is all attested. Let sentence be carried out now. As for these others, are they not outlaws? Let them be executed with him.'

'No, the Englishmen I need alive,' said Thornhill. The priest stared at Hemminges, seeking to make the heat of his gaze sear the soul of the heretic before him. At last, Thornhill thought, I will earn a small piece of salvation for England. 'They must be questioned.'

'Rash, Count Claudio, rash,' rumbled the Duke. 'A trial they shall have, for justice must be done.' He looked across at the outlaws gathered by the altar. 'I swear it shall be so. Put up your swords and make an explanation. No harm shall come to you save that which your actions have deserved.'

'Yes, yes,' said Jacopo, stepping forward. William watched him as he inched forward, his hands wringing, looking up to the Duke from a head bent in penitence. How hope corrupts our judgement, thought William. Jacopo reached out to pluck at Petro the priest's sleeve as he passed, to draw him on to his path. Petro resisted but then allowed himself to be pulled along. Luca cast a forlorn glance towards Orlando and then stepped with the others from the chancel to the nave.

'Get back, you fools,' said Orlando. 'There is no justice offered here, only death delayed.' He turned to snarl at his brother, 'And a lost chance for company on the journey to hell.'

'You are wrong,' said the Duke. 'I have said that you shall have justice and that you shall.' Luca looked again towards Ludovico, whose unexplained entry had unnerved him utterly. His presence promised that there were currents that he understood not that moved and threatened to drag him down. He, Jacopo and Petro shuffled along to where some of the Duke's men stood and, reaching them, they were taken and swiftly bound. Orlando, Hemminges and the rest made no move to join them.

The Duke, exasperate, addressed them: 'Come, you others. There is no flight from here. No salvation in delay. Come, Daughter. What speech must be had between us let us have in private.'

'Spare these men,' said Aemilia, 'and I will come.'

The Duke turned at her promise. 'I offer them justice. What more would you have?'

'I ask for mercy.'

'Justice they shall have, as I am true to my office and my state, and no more.'

'Mercy must temper justice. No ceremony that to great ones belongs, not a duke's robes nor a king's crown nor a marshal's truncheon, becomes them with half so good a grace as mercy does. Oh, Father, show me here your greatness.'

The Duke was about to speak when Thornhill stepped forward and whispered in his ear. The Duke's face let loose a sneer at the priest's words but when he spoke again it was to ask his daughter: 'What recompense for such display?'

Aemilia summoned up her courage, for she had seen that this was the bargain that must come if she were not to see her friends, her brothers, killed. Oh, but I was free. I was free and shall be again, by this hand, I shall. 'I will marry the Count Claudio.'

'Freely?' asked the Duke.

'As willingly as you have given mercy,' answered his daughter.

'So be it. They shall have mercy.'

'And I a husband,' said Aemilia in a voice so quiet only Orlando and Hemminges, standing by her, heard. She put up her sword and made to step forward. Hemminges caught her arm and halted her. He put his head behind hers and spoke as quietly as he might.

'Your father is not alone,' he whispered. 'Whatever promise your father makes can be unmade by those that stand beside him. By God, Aemilia, I'll not see you sacrifice yourself for nothing. At my word, charge left and make for the small door, I'll make what delay—'

Hemminges' words were cut across by a cry.

'Your Grace.'

It was Valentine. He took a hesitant step forward, looked back towards William who nodded at him, and then stiffened, drawing himself up. 'Your Grace, the Lady Aemilia cannot marry the Count Claudio.'

'I would be silent, were I you, Valentine,' said the Duke in a voice tightly ribbed and bounded to keep its anger from overflowing. 'It is for the sake of Aemilia's marriage that you have won some mercy of me.'

Valentine coughed and his own voice was a strangled squeak but still he spoke. Aemilia may no longer love him but he would prove that he had been worthy of her love. He would prove to all gathered here that he was more than a bedraggled poet, to be set up for mockery and cast aside. He would show his worth. 'Duke Leonardo, the Lady Aemilia cannot marry Count Claudio.'

'The bow is bent and drawn, boy,' the Duke warned. 'Make from the shaft.'

Valentine stuttered a moment at the sight of the Duke's anger but gathered himself and pressed on: 'She cannot marry another. She is already married to me. The priest there can vouch for it. We were married this morning. I am your son.'

'Is it so, Aemilia?' demanded her father, his black-rimmed eyes choleric red with anger.

Aemilia was looking as wide-eyed at Valentine as her father was at her. She shook her head.

'Aemilia, come,' said Valentine, a desperate smile upon his face. 'You know 'tis so. As your father knows it was to that purpose that we fled his palace. These men' – he pointed to Orlando and the others – 'may have been outlaws to your rule but they have given succour to your daughter and to' – he hesitated only a moment – 'your son. I cry your mercy now for them and for two lovers who would be lawful joined only.'

Aemilia was still shaking her head at Valentine. What did he think he was at? Valentine was gesturing to her to speak, to support his claim. He knew it false. Their eyes met and she suddenly saw into him. Did he think this would save them? Oh fool, fool. Or, God above, did he think to spare her marriage to Count Claudio? To blunt her father's purpose by drawing his wrath to him? Oh, if so, it was a sudden show of bravery that well became him but, foolish, oh whatsoever his intent, she could not match it.

'Is this so, Aemilia?' demanded her father again.

Aemilia shook her head.

'Please, Aemilia, do not deny me,' said Valentine. The paleness of his face was marked by blooming bright spots of red terror. He saw his gambit fail. He turned in desperation to the Duke.

'It is so, I swear, my lord. It is done, my lord, and what God has brought together no man may put asunder. I know I am not your choice of son but I swear that I shall prove worthy. It was for that reason that I sent the note to call you here, to this church, a gesture of my goodwill, of my obedience.'

'A second treachery,' said Count Claudio. 'First he betrays you, my lord, for your daughter. Then he betrays the daughter for you, my lord. His only constancy is treachery.'

The Duke no longer looked at his daughter. He stared at Valentine as if his eyes would send nails to pin the lad to the wall, his fingers ground against each other in their fists. He began to advance down the nave towards Valentine, speaking as he walked.

'You liar. You ingrate wretch. You wolf's whelp. You cur. You suborn my daughter. You lure her from my care to your own misrule. You sully her good name.'

Valentine sought to back away but the Duke's advance was swift. His foot caught on the step of the chancel and he fell back. The Duke grasped him at the collar of his grimy doublet and dragged him up. Aemilia tried to reach her father and stop him but Hemminges held her fast. No one else moved. Valentine was babbling apologies. The Duke turned and hurled him down the nave. He struck the ground and rolled, cracking his head against a broken pew. The Duke advanced on him again, grabbed him by his long hair and dragged him down the aisle, his feet scrabbling for purchase, his voice howling like a pig being taken for slaughter. The Duke reached the men who guarded Luca, Jacopo and Petro and snatched a rope from their arms.

'Father, no, I beg of you,' Aemilia cried out. 'I cry you mercy. You promised it.'

The Duke was past listening. The barrel had been broached and the rages and frustrations of the last days were spilling out. The rest of the church watched in horrified silence, save Claudio who smiled at it and Thornhill whose eyes never left the Englishmen. The Duke wrapped the rope round Valentine's neck three times and tied it off. He looked up, threw the end over a beam and pulled the remainder to him.

He coiled it in his hands, speaking as the loops gathered in his thick fingers: 'You have betrayed my rule. You have broken oaths of fealty, bonds of family, commandments, laws. Mine is the justice of my lands.'

'His fault was in loving me,' cried Aemilia, struggling against Hemminges' restraining arm. 'Spare him, spare him!'

'Be silent!' the Duke's shouts rose against his daughter's cries. 'Silent. Silent while I command! Mine is the justice of these lands.'

Through the ecstasy of fear and anger that rang the walls of the church the Duke never took his eyes from Valentine, coughing and choking and clawing at the rope tight about his neck.

'His sentence is pronounced,' said the Duke and spat on the mewling figure at his feet. He threw the coiled rope to his men and gestured. 'Haul him up.'

There was a moment's hesitation as his men fathomed out his order. It was a moment too long for the fury boiling in the Duke's breast.

'Hang him up!' he bellowed.

Valentine was hauled up, to his knees, to his feet, to the tips of his toes scrabbling for the floor even as his hands scrabbled at the rope. He made no noise save to choke and caw but the church was filled with the sound of Aemilia's screams, cries, pleas, which lasted till Valentine's feet kicked out their last, and then faded to soft sobs.

Done sacrifice of expiation

The sight of that poor boy, his lolling head covered by his long hair, only his blue lips visible, struck all. A long silence followed the last of Aemilia's sobs that was broken by a shout from Orlando:

'This is your justice?'

He did not wait for answer but hurled himself forward. Three crossbows fired. Two missed, their quarrels slashing past him as he darted forward, to spend themselves in the stones at the rear of the chancel. The third took him in his lifted arm and its force spun him about. His brother stepped forward and his own sword smashed the outlaw's from his nerveless fingers.

'Hold, hold,' Thornhill was crying as his men closed around Hemminges, 'they must be questioned.'

Hemminges' eyes were darting from foe to foe but there were too many. Two men slipped round his side and took the cowering Oldcastle, another put a sword's point to the unresisting throat of William who did not even look at his attacker. His eyes were all for the swinging body and its pendulum creak. Seeing William and Oldcastle threatened, Hemminges cast his sword down and knelt instead to comfort the weeping Aemilia. He had but a moment to do so before rough hands snatched him away. The three Englishmen were herded together and bound.

The Duke strode to his daughter and hauled her to her feet.

'How now, Daughter? Will you be civil and obedient?'

It was not certain that Aemilia heard him. She glanced at Valentine's body. 'Oh wretched, rash, intruding fool.'

'Fool, aye. Come not between the dragon and his wrath.'

'The dragon?' Aemilia looked her father in the eye. 'I name you monster. Monster! What a brave deed. To murder a vain child for your daughter's crime.'

'A daughter's crime? You praise yourself too much. Sure this boy has led you astray. His baleful influence removed, you will return to sense.'

'Even in this,' shouted Aemilia. 'Even in this you will not give me credit, but hand it to a man.'

'What needs this childish rebellion?' The Duke staggered and clutched at his side. He sat heavily down on a pew and reached out a clawing hand to his daughter. 'Have you not been treated well, given clothes and jewels and maids to tend you? Were your silken dresses so poor that you should wear this wanton's outfit? Why repay me with such base coin as peevish insults and revolt?'

'It was not a child's revolt, old man. I am not a dog to be told to sit or heel at your command. Still less a whore, to sell myself for clothes or jewels or maids. I will have my own will. It was you that taught me so.' The passion in her voice died away to be replaced again by tears. 'It was you that taught me so.'

Her father looked at her, heard her use these foul words, miscast his cares for her as baubles put before a bawd, and disgust crept over his face.

'A widow or a maid, she is free to marry now,' he said. He looked to Claudio who was standing over the wounded body of his brother, the malignant grin now a great smile. 'What do you say, Count Claudio? Will you still take her to wife?'

'Gladly, my lord,' Claudio said, thinking of her father's lands. 'We shall see if she prove more obedient to a husband than a father.'

'Come then, away,' the Duke said, turning his back on his daughter. William watched Aemilia's face turn pale with shock at this gesture more than any of her father's angry words. Oh, Aemilia, thought William, there is no rashness like that which comes when love to anger turns. Nor any actions that we more regret than those that follow. The mind cannot bear that change but must forge an understanding of it and comes to think the love was always false and we but deceived then. Too late, too late now for him to return whence he came.

'There is much still ado before the nuptial hour,' commanded the Duke Leonardo. 'To horse. We must ride out and make a rescue of my captured men.'

'You go on, my lord, with the Count Claudio. I shall stay here with these Englishmen,' said Father Thornhill. 'I will escort them to your palace in the morning.'

'No, Father. That will not do. I have promised these men justice and they shall have it. Besides, your men are needed.'

Thornhill did not deign to look over at the Duke as he answered. 'I care not,' he said. 'My only concern is with these Englishmen. The rest is your affair. What was that?'

This last was to William.

'I said, you are making a great mistake, Father,' William replied.

'We shall see,' said Thornhill. His attention was taken from William as the Duke clapped him on the shoulder and hauled him round. The Duke's hot blood, briefly let from him by Valentine's execution, was stoked again by his daughter's ingratitude and had returned to the boil.

'I command here, priest. Those men of yours are needed for the hunt. My men still lie at these outlaws' mercy and I must rescue them.'

Thornhill tried to throw off the Duke's hand but found the old man's grip on his shoulder too strong.

'Unhand me, Your Grace, or it will go ill for you. I am His Holiness's envoy and his affairs are my first duty.'

The Duke grew redder still. 'You threaten me? And with the Pope, is it? The Pope? Damn the Pope. He does not rule here. I do.'

Thornhill turned motionless as the statues that still stood in their niches, high in the church's walls.

'Unhand me now, Duke Leonardo. I work to a greater purpose than your—'

'Greater purpose?' the Duke interrupted. 'Your purpose is to give me your men to put an end to these bandits.'

Thornhill took a long, deep breath. 'A greater purpose, to save the souls of a whole island.'

'*Faugh!*' spat the Duke. 'You speak of souls and I of men's lives. I will rescue my men, now.'

'A whole island,' repeated Father Thornhill. 'What are your few men against tens of thousands? What are your brutish, earthly concerns against the mission of the Church? You lack a fear of God, Duke. You wallow in damned luxury. You eat and drink and rut and think only of your lechery and not of your soul.'

The Duke took a step back and backhanded the priest across the face. 'How dare you speak to me so? Stay here then, and pray if you will, but your men come with me.' He turned and pointed to the priest's soldiers. 'To horse. Count Claudio, your men too.'

Behind him Thornhill was clutching at his cheek. The Duke's rings had raked blood from his face and lip and painted streaks of red across his white robe. Red glinted in his eyes too as he turned to Arrigo: 'Kill him.'

Arrigo did not hesitate. In an instant his blade came out and slipped past the Duke's armour and into his back.

'Oh,' was all the Duke said as he fell to the floor.

Yet so far hath discretion fought with nature

Thornhill looked across at the Count Claudio. The Count had his blade out already and he took a step back. His men backed toward him as those of Thornhill did to the priest. The dead Duke's few men stood in shocked knots of one or two about the church, swords out, eyes wide, hearts hammering, terrified into inaction. Three sets of armed men eyed each other. Thornhill did not move.

'I have not congratulated you on your promised wedding to the Duke's daughter,' said Thornhill to Count Claudio.

'You seem to have put something of a difficulty in the way of marital bliss,' said the Count. 'There will, I think, need to be a funeral before a marriage.'

Aemilia was staring open-mouthed at her dead father as if to cry out at the horror of it, but all her screams had been spent on Valentine's death. She could not comprehend it. The speed with which she'd come to dwell in hell had taken thought from her. Thornhill's mind was not so clouded. He saw with the clear swiftness of a hawk.

'I don't see why it should be so,' said Thornhill. 'Why not a wedding and a funeral in one instant? Let the wedding song be a dirge. You are betrothed. I am a priest. Let the wedding be performed. I will testify to its lawfulness as will His Holiness. We shall add this to the bargain we have already made, Count Claudio. '

'No.' Aemilia at last regained her voice. 'No. All contracts were broken when my father was murdered, priest. I am his heir now and I will not marry.'

Claudio looked at Thornhill to ask his answer to this claim. The priest shrugged his reply and then turned to Arrigo, who commanded his guard.

'God has willed it so,' was all he said, but Arrigo understood. He turned to one of the dead Duke's guards who stood nearest, knocked aside the man's sword with his own and thrust the point up into his throat. His men took their cue and those few the Duke had brought with him were cut down within a minute of their master. The church was become a charnel house.

'The hour is late for a wedding,' said the Count Claudio with a calmness that made a mockery of the bloody slaughter about him.

'Let it be on the 'morrow then,' said Father Thornhill. His own calmness was marbled through with the thought of the inquisition of the English that was to come. It was to them he looked now. Hemminges looking on him with fury written in his brow, Oldcastle staring in horror at the blood that had fallen across his boots, and William, who appraised him, smilingly.

'You smile now, English spy, but you will not smile when I have you back in Count Claudio's new palace.'

'You are wrong on every count, Father Thornhill.'

'You know my name?'

'I know a great deal,' said William. 'Most especially how grievously you have erred.'

'How so?'

'I am no more English than you are Roman,' said William. 'We serve the same master, Father Thornhill, and His Holiness will be most displeased that you have interfered in my work.'

'And who are you?' said Thornhill with a solicitous smile on his lips.

'Ask him,' replied William with a nod to Orlando.

Thornhill looked over at the outlaw's chief, who groaned on the floor with his arm pressed over the quarrel sticking out of his shoulder.

'Him?'

William nodded. Thornhill shrugged as if to say that he would play this little game a while longer and walked over to where Orlando lay at his brother's feet.

'Who is this man?' he asked.

'Go to hell, priest,' spat back Orlando and cried out when his brother kicked his shoulder in answer of his own.

'Keep civil, Brother,' said Count Claudio. 'You speak to the priest who will marry me to Duke Leonardo's daughter.'

'Damn you.'

Count Claudio put his foot on his brother's bloody shoulder and leaned his weight on to it. Orlando cried out in pain.

'Stop, stop,' he babbled as the agony increased and his brother ground his foot against the quarrel's shaft.

'The name?' asked Thornhill.

'Adam, Adam,' cried out Orlando.

'Is that all?' said Thornhill, looking over to William with disappointment. William gestured with his brow that he should ask again. Count Claudio obligingly dug his heel once more into the wound.

'Pray Jesu, stop, dear God, stop,' cried out Orlando. 'His name is Prospero, Giovanni Prospero.'

Thou knowest the mask of night is on my face

Count Claudio laughed at this strange answer but his laughter cut short when he saw the priest had turned pale.

'Is it so?' demanded Father Thornhill, but he spoke neither to Orlando nor to William. He had turned to Ludovico. His spy shook his head.

'I know not, Father. He was called Adam among the outlaws but there was always something false about him. That Adam is not his name is certain. What his name truly is I do not know. I thought him mad. Yet there was a purposefulness to his actions. He stood apart when battle came yet I have seen him work a knife, and heard report of how he is the very devil with a blade. He spoke to me once in a manner that made me wonder if he knew who I truly was. He is no ordinary man. He and this one,' Ludovico gestured to Orlando, 'were often in secret commerce on some matter.'

'Was he not a friend to these two others?'

Ludovico thought a moment before answering.

'He spoke with them, truly. Yet I did not see in them the closeness of friendship. More than that I cannot say.'

William spoke up. 'Two marks I will show you, Father Thornhill, in proof of my claim.' He got slowly to his feet and held out his bound hands before him. There, glittering on his finger, sat the golden ring with its deep-cut sigil. 'Look on this ring. Is this the ring of a poor outlaw? Do you know the seal?'

Father Thornhill's pale face had turned paler still at the sight of the ring. 'And the second?'

'For that we must have private speech for it pertains to the tasks our master, His Holiness, has set us.'

Father Thornhill nodded. He gestured to two of his men who took William by his bound arms and dragged him after the priest as he walked up the nave.

Behind them Count Claudio still loured over his brother.

'Well, well, fortune favours the bold, Brother,' he said. 'Since you live still, you shall live a little longer yet. It will serve me to have your execution publicly made, as a warning.'

He pointed to one of his own men. 'Bind up his wounds and then bind up him and put him with the others.'

'And the Lady Aemilia? And these two, my lord?'

'The knaves put with the others under guard. The Lady Aemilia too. She is a dog that does not yet know her master. Till she does, she must be leashed.'

Aemilia blazed at him. 'Cur! Devil! A beast that wants discourse of reason would not behave as you.'

'Aye, leashed and muzzled too,' said Count Claudio, his grin again upon his face as he looked at the railing Aemilia. 'Tomorrow, when the wedding vows are made, then shall I teach you to love, honour and obey.'

Rather than hold three words' conference with this harpy

William returned from his conference with Thornhill to find the church quiet. Claudio's men had cleared it of the bodies of the dead, which lay in a tumbled heap outside the broken hole in the wall where once a door had been. A fire had been built in the nave around which sat Claudio's men and some of Thornhill's soldiers. The outlaws sat, bound, in a shivering huddle in the chancel, their backs to the broken altar.

Thornhill had questioned him in his guise as Prospero, the Pope's assassin, and William thanked fate that he had found that monster fascinating enough to learn all that he could about him from Isabella and others who knew him. It gave his answers credence. William had seen Prospero, spoken to him, set his mind to understand him that he might wreak his defeat. He took from that understanding and inhabited him now, his manner, his arrogance, his delight in the destruction of others. Thornhill had not met Prospero but he had heard of him – who had not heard report of the Cardinal Montalto's living instrument of vengeance and of his manner? This was the report made flesh. Even the difference in their age William had disguised: his griefs gave his face the weight of years and he'd muddied over the rest with blood from a cut he'd given himself outside the church when he'd realised they were surrounded and disguise needed. All that, when taken with the other signs – the ring, Orlando's naming of him as Prospero, his own spy Ludovico's doubts that he was one of the English party, his seeming madness now explained as a disguise – had been enough for Thornhill, despite his doubts, to grant him a measure of freedom. He had been returned to the others, his bonds cut.

In truth, William thought, it was Thornhill's own belief that this Pope would layer conspiracies on plots on stratagems that made him willing to believe that William was Prospero. We think others as we are ourselves and see in them our own thoughts. Thornhill had remarked on William's coldness at the death of Valentine and Duke Leonardo and seen in that further proof that William was the assassin that he claimed to be. Within himself William wondered at the truth of what Thornhill had observed, for he had felt little at the two men's death. That was a meditation for another day.

William had told Thornhill that he too was sent in search of the English spies and their precious cargo of intelligence, names that would unlock all the Pope's plans for crushing heretic England. William told how he had tracked them to the forest but that the third was missing, separated. Thornhill's gleam of delight at the thought of the imminent questioning of Hemminges and Oldcastle had shone out. William had answered that it could not be here, when so many unknown ears were close to listen. It must be done in private, at the palace of the old Duke Leonardo. Thornhill had licked his lips, dry with desire for the inquisition to come, and grudgingly agreed.

William could barely keep his revulsion from showing itself in that moment. Thornhill's desires were so clear to him though the priest himself saw them not. Thornhill acceded to William's logic because it was in that obedience to cold and calculating thought that the priest restrained his vile passions. Here was a man whose bent knees, cold and sore on hard floors hour after hour, had kept the darkness within from spilling out. Here was a man that looked on the passion of others with jealous eyes and saw in their expression of that passion, be it in rage or in joy, the loosing of that dangerous fount of humours that lay also within him and which he must curb, repress, deny. Did you pull the wings from flies as a boy? William wondered. Did you look with lust on the local maids and find in their revulsion at your clammy touch an echo of your own self-hate?

It mattered not the cause. William saw and understood the man he spoke with and turned him with his words to match his will. He felt he'd understood him from the moment that Hemminges had first spoken of him. Oldcastle's stories had clothed the figure that Hemminges had first sketched. This meeting had only proved a confirmation of the character that William's imagination had already written from his friends' words: this was a man who wanted a purpose, to believe himself part of something greater, something meaningful, more fool him. There's no meaning in this life save that we give it, but I shall give you purpose, though it serve my ends not yours.

Behind William, Thornhill re-entered the church with the rest of his men. Claudio greeted him from his place beside the fire.

'I have set the watch. Too late now to ride for the palace and too dangerous to be abroad in the dark with these bandits about.'

Thornhill nodded and pursed his lips in thought.

'Well, well. We sleep. The morning brings a wedding and then we ride for the palace. Where is the Lady Aemilia?'

Count Claudio gestured to the altar. 'With the rest. A cold night will remind her of the pleasures of a warm hearth.' He laughed but it was not a sound of joy but of cruel pleasure. Thornhill's lip curled with distaste but he said nothing. He looked instead to William and his head bent in the scantest of nods. William, seeing it, walked over to the outlaws and sat down beside them. Oldcastle gazed up at him hopefully. William looked about him – he was out of earshot of all save those bound before him.

'Listen, fellows, mad Adam has a plan.'

She looks for night, and then she longs for morrow

Aemilia heard Adam speak and hope grew in her heart. Over his shoulder she could see the shadows outside the church, one of which was made by her father's body. How angry she had been with him, how furious, the rage within her had seemed too much for mortal frame to bear. Then in a moment he had been slain and all her anger had to sorrow changed. Their last moments on this earth had been filled with fury and with hurtful words hurled at the other in an attempt to break through to the other's understanding. She wept again to think of it. And of that poor boy, Valentine, who she had lured to his death. Was it not so?

'Do not give in to it,' she heard Hemminges whisper to her.

Her head lifted and she met his gaze.

'Do not yield.' He looked from her to William, now walking back towards the fire where Claudio and Thornhill sat. 'It must be so. Sorrow without hope leads on to madness.'

Hemminges wished he had William's gift of words to speak his heart to this woman. He felt the press of Oldcastle's leg on his own and how the old man's thigh trembled with cold or fright. He wished he had that skill some men had to lift up spirits by their words, but it was not his gift. Beside him Aemilia seemed to hear his thoughts.

'Your actions, Master Russell, are my copy and teach me courage. I would I had the words to thank you for your schooling.'

A little part of Hemminges flared with heat despite the cold of night. Ah, but a man can be content, even bound and waiting for his fate. He looked across to William again, a man from whom contentment seemed to have fled. What did it mean that the William who had cast all hope of plans and stratagems in his face when he had begged for them in the woods now spoke of them in the church? Hemminges feared the bargain that the lad had struck with Thornhill and with his own grief.

Oldcastle's mind turned over like a wheel. Here I am again, bound and awaiting the torturer. I should really consider a different course, such wealth of experience is too costly bought. His eyes followed William and he thought of the aimless and immature youth he'd encountered in London. We are all much changed by our journey, but you most of all. Something nagged at Oldcastle's remembrance and the travel of his mind went round and round that missing object hoping to discern its shape. Fear is my axle I doubt not. He tried to still the shaking of his leg and while he thought on it alone it stilled, but his mind turning off again the shaking began again. Oh God, why should an old man's want of comfort bring him over and over again to suffering? What lesson have you, Lord, for one such as I? What I would not give for a cup of sack and a capon.

His thoughts turned to the servant Dionisio who had been with them in the church and had not been seen since the warning of the Duke's approach was given. Has he fled? And safely too? Or is he dead and stacked like cordwood with the others by the door? God's blood, will I wish tomorrow that death had been my fate? He shivered again at the thought of the fevered eyes of the priest. Father Thornhill was not one to care for the body's suffering if he thought the soul was purified by it. I am but a humble, mortal man, thought Oldcastle, what care I for these heavenly matters that I should find myself so tangled in them? He moaned again and looked to William with hope and looking at him felt again the press of that unseen, unremembered thing that nagged at his memory, a thing of vast importance or so his feelings told him, but it was as distant from him as a ghost. Would that I could sleep; sleep would bring it to me. Sleep was far from all of them.

As plain as I see you now

In a story, thought William, a hero might wrestle with a giant and throw him, were that hero half divine, and the Bible might speak of mighty Samson wreaking bloody havoc with no more than an ass's jawbone or bringing down the temple on his tormentors by simple feat of strength. Such is the golden world of heroes, but the iron world of ordinary men calls for more mundane tools to make a fight of things.

Those within the church, all save William, were bound and all, William among them, had their weapons taken from them. No assault from without could hope to save those within before their captors had time to slay them. They must be freed and armed to make defence of themselves. All this William had foreseen, from Valentine's betrayal – captured in the urgency of his speech with the Duke's corporal of horse – to the imminent moment of its revelation at the church, foreseen in Valentine's desperate plea that he and Aemilia be married before it was too late.

William had begun to see clearly again, clearer than before, his horizon heavenly in its sweep. The muddy waters of his grief had cleared to crystal clarity of understanding. He felt his reason noble, his faculties infinite, his apprehension like a god. He felt all this but it brought him no delight, for what had fallen from his eyes to give him this clear sight was pity, pity and hope.

When William had seen Valentine and Aemilia making from the outlaws' camp he'd followed, fearing that Valentine planned to betray Aemilia and them all. Encountering Dionisio, Oldcastle's servant, at his morning business as he passed he'd spared no time for explanations but made him go to rouse Hemminges and Oldcastle and give chase. He'd returned to the lovers' trail – the skills acquired in his time poaching in the forest near Stratford had not been lost to him in a year of travel: Valentine and Aemilia travelled slowly and without fear of pursuit and he had tracked them easily.

When he found that Valentine brought her instead to a ruined church, then he had divined the man's purpose, a wedding. William would know more of this: why Valentine thought Aemilia willing and why now?

Always there were more questions to which he would have answers. To that end he'd made his presence known, that he may hear their talk.

In his words and manner there had been an urgency to Valentine unseen before and that gave William warning of the Duke's arrival. He'd heard the echoed words 'too late' in Valentine's mouth and it was this alone that gave him time to draw Dionisio to him and send him with a message to the outlaws' camp before the net had closed around them. Dionisio would prove true. Even if caught, he might be spared the Duke's wrath enough to slip away at some later point and complete his task. All this had been William's calculation of the instant. Had Dionisio been taken? Did he lie dead, a traitor's reward given him by an angry master? I am, thought William, become a gambler of other men's lives.

The rest had been the crafting of William's mind, extempore. The scene in the church had seemed to him so very like the *Commedia all'Improvviso* that he had seen in Venice. The characters he played with as familiar as household stuff: the angry father, the hypocrite priest, the villainous brother, the noblewoman, the foolish lover and, in William himself, the clown, making mock of them all. How many times had he almost laughed out loud as they played their parts, spoke lines he'd crafted for them from their follies and their desires, each as plain to him as the noses on their faces.

Thornhill had been easiest of all. He so longed to have his goodness noted that he would accept any witness of it, even an assassin, so long as that assassin made good report of him to his master, the Pope.

Yet all had been easy, so very easy.

A man may weep upon his wedding day

'Up, up,' growled Claudio, kicking his still sleeping servant to his feet as he passed to come and stand over the prisoners. 'Morning is come, the wedding hour is nigh and my bride awaits.'

'I'll die first,' answered the bride from her place on the floor.

'Maybe after,' said the Count. He squatted down and placed a hand on her leg and pressed. 'But not before.'

Aemilia spat and the Count laughed as he stood up out of the path of her anger. 'Your father's people must see you by my side and hear the Pope's emissary pronounce us lawfully married. Who knows, Lady Aemilia, with time you may find me a pleasing husband and I may find that you have that in you that keeps my interest.'

Hemminges struggled to rise in her defence only to receive a boot in the chest from the Count that sent him sprawling back against the cracked altar.

'A cold morning for a wedding,' observed William, coming alongside the Count.

'Some seem hot,' grinned the Count. 'And the wedding bed will be warm enough.' He looked down at Aemilia, who drew her legs to her chest.

Thornhill walked over, his hands rubbing impatiently on his robe, trying to bring warmth into the pale fingers. The cold seemed to have leached his little colour from him and his thin skin and sharp bones gave him the look of a cadaver.

'Let the wedding be performed. We must not linger. These Englishmen must be questioned with all speed and it is near a day's ride to the palace if we are not to kill the horses.'

'I am ready,' said the Count.

'There cannot be a wedding while the church is a grave. It is not holy,' said William, pointing to the bodies piled just outside.

'I shall be the judge of that,' answered Thornhill. 'There is no need for any special sanctification to be made. Come, come, make haste.'

'Preparation for the journey must be made. Let these prisoners here perform the burial,' said William. 'It will warm them, eh, Count? And remind them of the consequence of disobedience.'

Claudio was nodding; there was a perverse delight in having the daughter bury the father on her wedding day and the bodies must be disposed of, if the lies that surrounded them were to be hidden.

'Let it be done, Father,' said the Count. 'It need not delay us. Our men may make preparation for departure as these ones work. Then we wed and then we ride.' His leer spoke to the double intent of his words. Aemilia shuddered at them. Thornhill threw up his hands in exasperation.

'Let it be so then, but haste, Count, haste.'

Two loves I have of comfort and despair

'At first light,' said Dionisio. 'That was Adam's command.'

'The madman?' scoffed Zago.

'If he is mad then he is mad in craft,' said Dionisio. 'His instruction was precise. That we prepare to make assault at first light.'

When Dionisio had breathlessly brought news of the events at the church, despair had fallen on the outlaws; no men among them more than those of the Duke's own household who had sided with the outlaws. Dionisio had rallied them, shaming them with their cowardice and herding them towards the church that they might view the field and see how the dangers stood. In the darkness one of the outlaws, an old man of forty winters who moved so silently as to seem more ghost than man, had crept about and brought back the horrid news of the Duke's death and of the capture of the others. The Duke's men changed from fear to anger at this report and clamoured for the fight.

Now Dionisio laid out William's plan of battle. 'The silent among us set themselves in the ruins near the church, the archers in the trees and the Duke's men ready for the charge. Mad Adam will free the prisoners and make assault from the rear at the sound of our battle.'

'God but he asks much trust from us,' muttered Zago.

'That he answered too. If any man has not stomach for the fight, he says, let him depart.' Dionisio cast a steely eye about the gathered outlaws. 'I for one am not so much a coward that I will leave my fellows in their hour of need.'

'Fellows?' said Zago. 'You've been with us less than a day.'

But Zago's querulous comment was growled down by the Duke's men who all swore they would avenge their master.

'Then it is decided.'

So they'd set themselves, three of them making a slow and silent journey to wait in the shadows of the ruined house by the church's front, the finest shots among them climbing the trees to bring down a hard rain of death and the Duke's men waiting, crouched behind the bushes to the front, for the signal to charge.

Dionisio watched and waited with them, a thrill of fear and excitement in him, reminding him of younger days before he'd become a servant, when he had held a sword in the dead Duke's service. A good man, the Duke, who did not deserve to die with a dagger in his back.

The dawn arrived, Dionisio watched as the soldiers came from the church to relieve the watch and to prepare the horses for their departure. Then William had emerged and looked to the trees. To any standing by him he seemed to stretch himself out of the morning's stiffness but Dionisio saw and understood: this was the signal to attack.

'Bid the archers shoot,' he whispered and heard one of the Duke's men move away.

At first he thought his order had not been followed and there was a brief moment when he feared the men had fled in the night or fallen asleep and he felt the terror of failure and what it would mean. Then a whisper came through the trees and the long shafts of arrows bloomed among the soldiers in front of the church and their cries went up, the horses neighing and starting, and Dionisio heard himself cry out, 'Charge! Charge! God for Leonardo!'

And battle was joined.

What ceremony else?

Aemilia knelt by her father's corpse and closed the milky, staring eyes and brushed dirt from his hair and from his face. She wept no tears. They were all used up. His skin was cold as the ground he lay upon, dirt beaded the face she had kissed a thousand times, dark blood that had welled up from his mouth had dried in the crevices that used to deepen in his cheeks when she had made him laugh. She crossed his stiff arms over his chest and kissed his brow.

She and the others had dragged the bodies from by the narrow, broken doorway on to the rough ground outside.

'Bury them,' came the order.

'With what?' protested Hemminges, pointing to the cold, hard ground. A rusted shovel was flung at him and the remains of an old hoe at Luca. The two men began to hack at the ground with the paltry implements, chipping and scraping away at it, making slow progress with bound hands. While they worked Petro, Jacopo and Oldcastle laid the dead more reverently on the ground in preparation for the burial.

From the front of the church there came a shout and the sudden sounds of battle.

The soldiers turned at it.

William appeared through the broken doorway. 'Treachery!' He pointed into the church. 'We are betrayed!' he cried to the soldiers. 'The outlaws attack us.'

Two of the prisoners' guard ran into the church, toward the front. A third reached the opening and felt William's hand on his shoulder.

'Wait,' William said and pointed behind the man to where the prisoners stood. 'You forgot something.'

'What?' he asked.

'This,' said William as he drove the man's dagger, lifted from his belt as he passed, into the soldier's neck and stepped back, dragging it out again across the soldier's throat. Oldcastle stared drop-mouthed but Hemminges had already moved, the edge of his shovel swung in his two bound hands catching a fourth soldier in the jaw and then twisting round and over to crack across the soldier's pate and shatter his skull. The last soldier had drawn his sword and with a savage cut unseamed poor Jacopo, but even as he did so Luca swept his legs from him with his hoe and then Hemminges was on him, finishing him with a strike. Shouts came from the church as the first two guards realised they were deceived and turned, swords drawn, to charge on the prisoners, calling for their comrades to join them in the fight.

They closed and slowed as they did, for now they saw how narrow that gap where the broken doorway was. William stood in it wielding the sword he had plucked from the first man killed. In such a gap, if he were trained to it, one man might hold off an army, for each must come at him one by one. William parried the first blow and swung back, taking the soldier's arm. Thank God for Hemminges' hard lessons now, he thought. Fight as they do on the Ponte dei Pugni, the Bridge of Fists, on the narrow galleys, and these fools who need a field to swing their blades in are done for. We needed a hero out of ancient times to live through this and, look, here am I become Gaius Martius at Corioli, holding back the Volsci in their sally.

Behind him, William heard Hemminges calling for Aemilia to help him cut the ropes that bound him and the others. From the front were the sounds of rising battle outside the church. Then he heard a great shout: it was his own. A cry of delight bursting from his throat, to hear his plots come to their head, to see his scenes play out as he had written them, to feel the exultation of his own understanding and its power.

Then more soldiers appeared, Claudio's men, half a dozen at least, coming in answer to the cries for help from their comrades. William felt Hemminges press in by his side. Blades drove at them, grim, bearded faces beneath their helms, howling their anger and stabbing, stabbing, stabbing. William and Hemminges beat and parried and swung. A man fell, to William's blade or Hemminges', he could no longer tell. The world was a whirl of steel and shouts. He felt the cut that would have maimed him slide instead along his forearm as he twisted and he pulled the man sharply forward as he overreached. Luca's shovel finished him. Another thrust near took his head. There were too many. Even in the narrow doorway their blows took a toll, his arm was heavy, sweat ran down his face. At the rear of the church appeared Arrigo and another of Thornhill's men. They saw the desperate struggle at the door and charged.

Faith, he thought, I have gambled with my own life too and lost.

Wherein, ye gods, you tyrants do defeat

The suddenness of the outlaws' assault had given them advantage. The score of soldiers were caught first by the arrows from the fore and then struck from the side by the men who had hidden in the ruined house nearby. The outlaws, at first equal in number to those outside the church, made what they could of these advantages. Yet the Count Claudio's men and the papal soldiers made war their profession. They rallied and fought back. More came from within the church to replace those that had died in the first moments. The tide of battle turned.

Those three brave men among the outlaws who had crept into the ruins of the nearby house the night before fell to chopping blades and the outlaws began to waver in their attack. All would have turned to rout but Zago, a look of surprise on his face at his own courage, flung himself forward and the battle turned again. Zago fell, a sword cracking his head, but in that moment, when his furious charge had pushed back the line of soldiers, there had been time enough for the old Duke's men to grasp at the reins of their enemy's fleeing horses and mount them. They turned their steeds and charged the line, which broke, the soldiers falling back on the church, and into that place of sanctuary the battle flowed.

William saw the sudden rush of soldiers fleeing from the battle outside and pressed forward. Hemminges on one side and Luca the other, the three advanced. Hemminges' sword smoked with bloody execution. William's own, dancing, pressed and harried at the soldiers and even Luca's clumsy hacks with the shovel now met their target as the soldiers fell back in disarray. Driven now from front and rear, desperate of escape and finding it blocked in all directions, the soldiers' will broke and, as a scale will tip, the battle turned from desperate fight to sudden slaughter. Arrigo found himself alone and had time only to snarl defiance and lift his own sword before William's blade whirled toward him. He made to turn block into backswing but cried out instead as Aemilia darted out from behind William and slammed her small dagger into his side. William took his moment, punched out and caught Arrigo in the jaw with his sword's hilt. He stumbled back and fell and Aemilia leapt on him, wild-eyed with rage, crying out vile curses and slamming home her knife again and again until William hauled her from the corpse.

Claudio still held his nerve. He stood in the centre of the nave and, roaring, laid about him. Hemminges, growling like the Nemean lion, fronted him.

'Now I am not bound, coward, now will you pay,' cried Hemminges, his sword spinning in his hand.

'Base and mean will be your grave,' roared the Count in answer.

This was no duel, no fine and slender swordplay for display. Claudio sought to use his height, his strength, to crush Hemminges but that day, with Aemilia in his mind, Hemminges was valour's minion. Claudio hacked down at Hemminges as if he sought to fell an ox, his blows enough to shatter stone and steel. Hemminges was not there to meet them. He danced and slipped and thrust. For a long minute violence and grace contended until at last, with a cry, Hemminges' sword pierced the Count's side. Hemminges ripped it free. Claudio staggered, fell to one knee and coughed once, a bloody thing, and then, his blade a-whirling, Hemminges struck a second blow. Claudio dropped dead, unseamed from nave to chops.

Courage flowed out of the rest at the baleful sight. Those still standing threw down their swords and cried for mercy. Only Thornhill was unmoved, remaining in the centre of the church, arms spread wide, loud in prayer. Hemminges stepped to him and kicked him in the stomach and with a cry the priest fell back to his knees, retching. Hemminges' sword came up to deal a mortal blow but his hand was caught by William's. For a moment the two men glowered at each other.

'You are not turned executioner yet, John,' said William.

Hemminges stalked away.

The quality of mercy is not strained

The outlaws had lost some half a dozen men, Zago and Jacopo among them. These they buried in the grave that had been made for Duke Leonardo. The Duke's body, at Aemilia's insistence, had been wrapped in linen to be taken back to the palace for burial and lay upon the altar. Of those that had followed Count Claudio only two remained and of the soldiers of St Peter, scarce a dozen men still lived and none without wounds. They were guarded by the outlaws in the chancel where Aemilia and the others had spent the night before.

Thornhill, despite being bound, stood proudly in the nave, disdaining to meet the eyes of any around him. Orlando sat on a pew nearby staring at the bloody remains of his brother.

'What shall be done with this priest?' asked Aemilia.

'Set him free,' answered William. 'Some expiation must be made for your father's death but he is too close to the Pope. That is too powerful an enemy to make so early in your rule, Lady Aemilia.'

'My rule?'

'Your father dead, are you not the heir?'

So it is, thought Aemilia. I have received all I sought. I rule not just myself but others. Such a bloody road I have walked to get here.

'I am.' She called one of her father's men to her.

'You are Francesco?'

'I am, my lady.'

'The Duke, my father, is dead.'

'My sorrow for it and for your loss, my lady.'

'I do not want your sorrow as much as your obedience, which is owed to me as his heir.'

Francesco spoke slowly in answer. 'It is, my lady. And your will?'

She pointed to Thornhill. 'This man is my father's murderer. Take him and hang him from that beam there.'

Francesco looked from her to Thornhill and thence to the beam she pointed to.

'Why do you hesitate?'

The soldier looked to the men about her. Aemilia snarled, 'Is this obedience?'

'This is not wise,' said William, stepping closer.

Aemilia's face became ugly with anger. '"Wise"? "Wise"? I loved my father not wisely but too well, too well to let his murderer go forth.'

She turned back to Francesco: 'I say again, on your obedience, hang that man.' Her voice had grown to a pitch that brooked no further argument.

Francesco turned to his task. Hemminges stepped in front of him to block his way.

'Aemilia, you yourself spoke of the need for mercy in great ones. Let not your rule begin with bloodshed and the making of enemies.'

'Get out of my man's way, Master Russell, or suffer the priest's fate.'

Francesco stepped slowly round Hemminges who still looked pleadingly at Aemilia. William saw his friend's unhappiness but he also saw chains breaking. It had not been the Hemminges of old that he had seen in the woods. Some madness hung on him there as it had hung on William himself. Hemminges, a man of stoic disposition if ever there was, now stood with tears in his eyes.

Francesco reached Thornhill and began to pull him over towards the beam. It seemed that only this movement brought the priest to the reality of his fate.

'Stop, I command you! In the name of the Holy Father, on your faith, take off your hands!'

Francesco continued to drag him to the corner of the church, to the beam from which Valentine had swung. Francesco pointed to one of his fellows to make him a noose but the man shook his head. He shrugged and pointed to another, older man, who slowly got to his feet, picked up a rope and began to tie the knot that would hang Thornhill.

The priest's cries became shriller. 'His Holiness's anger will know no bounds! You make your own graves if you follow this course. Stop, stop this! Stop! *Stop!*'

Hemminges came up to William. 'This must not be. His death's deserved but hanging him, she hangs herself.'

William simply watched. She'd had her warning. It was not for him to make her judgements. He felt his arm taken in a painful grip. He heard the urgency in the whisper.

'I know you have it in you to make persuasion of her.'

William looked into his friend's desperate eyes and shook his head. 'You are wrong, John. I want that glib and oily art to speak and purpose not. I'd see him hanged twice over.'

Hemminges let go his friend and strode again to Aemilia. 'I beg you, not for his sake but for your own. Leave off his execution.'

'My own sake? Should not a daughter want revenge?'

'Should not a ruler be just? Oh, Aemilia, let me speak proudly. You have played upon my love and admiration for you, let that love and admiration counsel you now. When I have loved it was a brave and bold woman that I saw, not one whose rashness overcame her. Where I have admired it was in finding that your boldness was born of a will free and boundless in its vision. Your father was brave, was bold, his will was free as yours is but his bravery turned to anger till anger ruled him; his boldness looked like rashness then and in giving his will rein he gave up judgement. It took justice from him and made him a murderer of his cousin.'

Aemilia looked past him to Thornhill. Hemminges put his hands upon her shoulders and turned her gaze to his.

'I would not see you be a wanton of your desires but grow in them to be the lady of these lands who rules with justice.'

Aemilia shook off his hands and walked from him to the old man who had finished at his knot tying and took the noose from him. She stared a long time at Thornhill. The priest became very still. His eyes closed and his lips began to move in a silent prayer. No more the shrill cries, the orders, threats, no more said at all. Aemilia took her eyes from the priest and looked again to Hemminges. Then she threw the noose to the ground.

Exeunt omnes

'Orlando,' said Aemilia.

'Count.'

'What say you?' demanded Aemilia.

'Count Orlando,' answered the outlaw chief with a smile. He lifted his eyes from his brother's corpse to look on Aemilia. 'For so I am by my father's death and, now, by my usurping brother's.'

He looked across to Hemminges. 'My thanks, Master Russell, for that dear service.' He made a little bow from his seat and winced as his wounded arm was stretched by the movement. Hemminges paid him no heed, he had eyes only for Aemilia.

'Count Orlando, then,' said Aemilia. 'There is much business to be done and little of it done here. Let us to my father's palace and there tell others of the bitter business of these past few days. My father's burial, my cousin's and your brother's too.'

Orlando pushed himself painfully to his feet and held out a hand for her support. He slid his arm over her shoulder.

'All this be done and then, dear Aemilia, I have a notion to your good, if you'll a willing ear incline, what's mine is yours and what is yours is mine.'

Aemilia threw off his arm, making him stumble forward.

'You are much mistaken, Count Orlando, if you think I intend to put on a man's rule having so recently been freed of one. And you would do well to remember that as you are *Count* Orlando so am I *Lady* Aemilia.'

Orlando's smile came back and he held up his hands in entreaty of peace.

'A wonder and a miracle.' He glanced to Thornhill whose pale eyes were tied to the noose that lay on the ground by Aemilia's feet. He looked to Aemilia again. 'I ever shall be ruled by you, My lady. So to your palace let us go.'

Aemilia turned to her father's man, Francesco. 'Take the priest and whip him till he is close to dead. Then set him on his horse with the rest of his men and drive them from my lands.'

Francesco bowed and turned to his orders. Thornhill began crying out against the men that advanced towards him to deliver their mistress's judgement, stern imprecations against their mortal souls, entreaties to their better wills. They dragged him from the church and his voice faded behind the walls. Aemilia made to leave. She drew level with Hemminges. He watched her every movement but she did not look to him when she stopped.

'You and your friends should go.' He put a hand on her arm to stop her passing. At last she turned her eyes on him. 'I shall remember your lessons, John Russell. For them and for many things, I am grateful beyond the power of my words to tell. I am not the foolish woman I once was.' Her own hand rested on his arm as she spoke and he covered it with his other.

'I am sorry for it, for I did not think you foolish.'

She smiled sadly at him. 'Yet more reason why we must part.'

Hemminges watched Aemilia and Orlando leave the church. The air seemed, of a sudden, close about him and he turned and swiftly went outside. He found Oldcastle already there being served a cup of wine by Dionisio, the servant's face still bearing pink blossoms of misted blood from the battle past. William came to join them.

'Now it seems it is at last our moment to depart,' said William. 'Unless that is there is any reason to remain? A lady, perhaps? Or a feathered bed?' He looked between his fellows.

'I shun comfort now,' said Oldcastle with feeling. 'I'd rather a rock for a pillow and a quiet night than this comfort and all the action that must come with it. *Aah*, that is good, kind Dionisio.'

The servant was kneading Oldcastle's shoulders as if Dionisio had not done all the work or Oldcastle far more than cower in a shallow grave till all was done.

Hemminges shook his head in solemn answer of his own. William clapped him on the back and then pushed away Dionisio and heaved Oldcastle to his feet.

'Our thanks, Dionisio. Will you make our excuse and farewell to the rest?'

'I will. Where do you go now?'

'West.'

'I shall say east.'

William inclined his head in thanks for another of the servant's deceptions.

'Our thanks again.'

Dionisio waved them away. 'Such entertainment I have not had in many a long day.'

He saw them off and turned back to go and give his good service to a new mistress.

Woods in the Veneto, March 1586

The future comes apace

The three Englishmen walked past noon in weary silence. Each taken by the need to put distance between themselves and the bloody business of the day, each caught in his own thoughts and regrets. Oldcastle heaved along at the rear, his mind still turning over that missing piece that came to him each time he looked on his friend William. William walked with a jaunty stride, as if a weight had lifted from him. It had perhaps passed to Hemminges. Hemminges' shoulders stooped low. He had found the line between that which he admired and feared was as the razor's edge, invisible.

'You are recovered to us, William,' said Oldcastle when at last they stopped for rest.

'I am.'

'That is good. We have lost Isabella but I would not have lost you, too.'

'I do not think her lost to me. She will live again.' William's mind turned to a poem forming in him, a paean to his lost love. 'An eternal summer she will have.'

Before he could explain his meaning, Oldcastle gripped his friend's shoulder and brought him round to look at him. His grip was crushing and there was concern in his face, which William misunderstood.

'I tell you, Nick, I am well again.'

'I fear it is not so,' said Oldcastle. It had taken him too long to see it, but now he did. He understood that which had worked on his mind and in that understanding was a terror. The old man's face was serious as it so rarely was. 'I fear you are a broken vessel, mended but misshapen.'

William laughed, but Oldcastle's face did not soften.

'We are not playthings, William.'

'I know that, my friend.'

'I do not think so.'

'What do you mean?' William asked.

'Aye,' said Hemminges, 'what do you mean?'

'All this bloody business has been your doing has it not?'

'The plan was mine, you know that, Nick,' said William, brow furrowed.

'More than that, William, more than that. We have been led to this moment by you and all those that died, died in your willing of it.'

'Men died so that we might be saved,' answered William.

'Not all. Some died that you might feel your own power. You have returned to life but not to human feeling.'

William laughed again but his friend still gripped his shoulders hard and did not share in his laughter. Hemminges looked between the two with anxious gaze.

'Is it not so, William?' said Oldcastle.

'What is to deny? That I found a care again and it was for my friends?'

'Such a care. When in the woods Aemilia threw off her guise as Sebastian and nearly threatened all. Who prompted her to it?'

William took a moment to answer.

'I did.'

Hemminges looked shocked, not just to hear that it was his friend had made Aemilia take this rash course but to hear him admit it in such casual terms.

'What of it? I spoke to her of command and of alliances and she rose to my prompts because these thoughts had already found a purchase within her.'

Oldcastle pressed his charge.

'And you having learned of it from my servant, good Dionisio, who was it passed on intelligence of the Count Claudio's convoy to her?'

'I.'

'Was it also your thought to rob it?'

'The thought was all her own.'

'Yet, again, you did prompt her to it?'

Hemminges' face was pale despite the tanning of the wind that coloured it as he worked through again the scenes he'd lived through but not understood until this moment: 'Jesu, and how the crisis that then made forced our hands. My God, William, the dead of that raid will look to you for this.'

'Let them look, they do not touch my conscience. They knew what they did.' He turned to Hemminges and spoke half in vehemence and half in plea. 'I wanted only to free you of the witchcraft of responsibility, to show you the girl's true nature. She cast off more than a man's weeds that day but still, you stubborn fool, you would not leave her.'

Oldcastle nodded. 'And then at the fireside, when we talked of whether the robbery should be made at all and the debate turned from its path, you were there to whisper in Zago's ear and let him turn it back again.'

Hemminges struck fist to palm. 'Valentine! That stupid child, that puppet, it was you that prompted him to that mad confession in the church. You stood by him, you whispered in his ear. What did you say to him? My God, my God, you hanged him, William, sure as if you pulled the noose about his neck yourself.'

William wrenched himself from Oldcastle's grasp and threw down his satchel. He strode angrily back and forth before them. 'Oh list, list, that fool's plan was all his own, laid long before I spoke to him.'

'But it was you, you that gave him the cue to speak and at the moment that the Duke was in his greatest rage.'

'It was his own desire I spoke to him of. And if he'd been right in his expectation I'd have crowned him in that moment.'

'Right in his expectation? You knave,' said Hemminges. 'You knew the Duke's character better in that brief acquaintance than the simple Valentine did in months of knowing him. You knew there was no hope of such an outcome.'

William held out his hand to Hemminges in figure of a question made and demanded of his friend: 'Why shed a tear for a rival gone?'

'"Rival"?' said Hemminges, not understanding.

'Do not forswear your love for Aemilia now.'

'I loved a simple and proud girl, a woman with spirit. And what if she were still the woman that I loved? What value in the death of a rival when I had no hope to begin with?'

'You had hope,' said William. There was great pain in his voice as he spoke. 'We are all fools together, John. We all have hope. At least I did. I thank God such folly is beyond me now. Dead with Isabella's love.'

He closed on his friend. 'You had to see her free, truly free to choose, and see her choose ambition over you. There was enchantment on you and I have broke the spell.'

William turned to look from Hemminges to Oldcastle.

'I never commanded any. I spoke only that they wished to hear.'

'You have done evil.'

William snorted and threw up his arms. 'John, you of all people. To say such childish things. There's nothing good or evil but thinking makes it so.'

Hemminges took in his friend's words with horror writ across his face. He took a step back to look at William and shook his head.

'I see we were wrong,' he said. 'You are Prospero. You are not the player of a part. You are the assassin.'

'Damn you.' William laughed a little – such overblown conceit, to compare him to that assassin.

'Aye, Prospero' – Hemminges' hand came out and pointed in accusation – 'a man who plays with others, who murders with a thought, whose gift is corrupted to misrule. Turn your eye on yourself, William Shakespeare. You who see the minds of others in the turn of their hand, look on your own soul.'

William saw at last that Hemminges was in deadly earnest. 'Damn you to hell,' he answered with a passion he had not felt nor shown in many a long day. 'I never did aught but for our good, that we may be free, that we may flee this place.'

'You are too late. We are lost forever,' Hemminges said.

'*Faugh!* Such drama would shame a boy actor new hatched. The morning will see your understanding clearer.'

'It will not, nor will it see you and I together.'

A quiet fell in the forest glade where a moment before there had been high-lifted, angry voices. William was staring at Hemminges, Hemminges was shaking his head and Oldcastle was looking between the two with tears in his eyes. Not one of them knew what next to say. A kite called from the air above and a strong wind blew gossips through the trees, the rest was silence.

Hemminges turned on his heel and began to walk away to the north. William made no move to follow. Oldcastle's eyes followed Hemminges and then he turned and clapped a hand on William's shoulder and, again, gripped as tightly as he might.

'William, William. What have you done? What have you become?'

The grip became a shake of William's shoulder and then, abruptly, Oldcastle broke away and set off after Hemminges.

After a few minutes the pair were lost to sight among the trees and William was alone. He stood there a good deal longer till at last he reached down and picked up his pack and, pointing himself west, began to walk. As he walked he sang and none saw the tears that coursed his face.

Thy tooth is not so keen
Because thou art not seen,
Although thy breath be rude.
Heigh-ho! sing heigh-ho! unto the green holly:
Most friendship is feigning, most loving mere folly:
Then, heigh-ho! the holly!
This life is most jolly.

Historical Note

The death of Isabella Lisarro is modelled on the terrible recollection of the death of Ada Lovelace from what we must suspect was cervical cancer. For the information I am extremely grateful to John Butler, consultant gynaecologist at the Royal Marsden Hospital and, I am delighted to say, friend of many years.

It is William's fate to have his personal tragedy overshadowed by the political intrigues with which he is now embroiled. In 1585 there is a new pope and he has worldly ambitions. The Papacy in the sixteenth century was more than just a spiritual power, it was a temporal one too. The Pope was the ruler of vast lands in Italy, the Republic of St Peter, the Papal States. Yet with so many demands on the Papacy – to counter Protestantism, to defend against the infidel Ottomans, to guide France towards a Catholic king – it was not surprising that the business of ruling the Papal States went neglected.

So it was that when the Cardinal Montalto succeeded to the Holy See in 1585, as Pope Sixtus V, he found that his predecessor, Pope Gregory, had gifted him a legacy of lawlessness and penury. Banditry was rife throughout the Papal States and order lax among the clergy. The new pope brought order back with a vicious hand. Thousands of bandits were caught and hundreds executed, as were the religious that had breached their vows of chastity. It was contemporaries that claimed there were more heads on spikes on the Pont Sant'Angelo in Rome than melons in the marketplace. Only with this done did Sixtus V turn to rebuilding the Church's finances – through ruinous taxes and the sale of indulgences, among other things.

The Pope's political concerns were many. Two were most pressing: first, the battle between the Protestant Huguenots and the Catholic party in France, the so-called War of the Three Henries. France had a sizeable

Protestant minority whose political leader was Henry of Navarre. That Henry was the heir to the Catholic Henry III, ill and weak and without male issue. The prospect of a Protestant king filled the Catholic French nobility with fear and loathing. Their leader, the third Henry, of Lorraine, Duke of Guise and leader of the Catholic League, set his face against Henry of Navarre's succession. Into this conflict the new pope stepped, unenthusiastically but determinedly. On 9 September 1585 he excommunicated Henry of Navarre, a problem that the pragmatic Henry would ultimately resolve by converting to Catholicism with the famous phrase, 'Paris is well worth a mass.'

Pope Sixtus' other problem was England, the principal Protestant power. In 1570 Pope Pius V had signed a papal bull granting English Roman Catholics authority to overthrow Elizabeth. The focus of those efforts was the placing of Mary, Queen of Scots on the English throne. As a result, from the 1570s onwards waves of Catholic priests and sympathisers infiltrated England. Pope Sixtus V would renew the excommunication of Elizabeth of England and encourage his agents to infiltrate the kingdom to sow dissent, to preach the true faith and to prepare for the invasion of the Catholic fanatic King Philip of Spain. Talk of the Armada begins in 1585 and the preparations have started. The Duke of Parma gathers his forces in the Low Countries and the ships are being built. The Pope has promised vast sums in support of the invasion but only after it lands successfully. That success is doubtful for the crossing of the Channel is difficult and the transportation of so many men hazardous. The success of the venture turns on many things and one of them is that England should already be in flames when Parma lands.

William Shakespeare would have been well aware of these machinations. Simon Hunt, probably one of his schoolmasters at the grammar school in Stratford, later became a Jesuit priest. There are also strong indications that his immediate family may have had Roman Catholic sympathies. Cousins of his mother Mary Arden had been executed for treason in 1583.

The renewal of the excommunication of Elizabeth of England by Pope Sixtus anticipated the coming invasion. Its purpose was, at least in part, to encourage rebellion in her lands to aid the Spanish plot. The names of those in England who might aid that cause are carried now by Shakespeare, Hemminges and Oldcastle.

It may be thought surprising that three players should meet with so much violence in their travels but this was a more brutal age. The murder rate in Elizabethan England was about 1 in 10,000; by comparison, it is now 1 in 100,000. More significantly, murder today is often by someone known to the victim: assault by strangers was far more prevalent then. People went armed and did not fear to use their weapons.

Moreover, players and playwrights lived on the margins of society. There is scarce a playwright in Elizabethan England that is not killed or does not kill someone. Ben Jonson, Shakespeare's contemporary, rival and friend, killed an actor in a duel and would have been hanged for it had he not taken the benefit of the clergy. Jonson already boasted of having slain a Spanish soldier in single combat while a mercenary in the Spanish Netherlands. Christopher Marlowe was, famously, killed in a tavern brawl in Deptford. And one theory about how Shakespeare came to leave Stratford revolves around another murder: in 1587 one of the Queen's Men, William Knel, attacked another actor in the company, Towne, and was killed for his pains with a sword of iron costing we are told 'five shillings'. Knel's death left a gap in the company that speculation fills with Shakespeare joining as they passed through Stratford. Unfortunately for the theory there is nothing to suggest the Queen's Men travelled through or even near Stratford at that time.

And Shakespeare himself was not without the whiff of scandal. In 1596 he was bound over, along with three others, to keep the peace. One William Wayte had accused William of making threats that caused him to fear for his life.

Nor was violence a thing of England only. Among the many remarkable women of sixteenth-century Italy was Caterina Sforza. All that Aemilia tells of her is true and more besides: she was ruled by no man, feared by many and a figure worthy of stories in her own right. If you question Aemilia's role as commander then you do not know how Caterina Sforza, her city captured, persuaded her captors to let her negotiate surrender with the last remaining citadel defending that city. Her enemies trusted her because they held her children as hostages. Yet Caterina, as soon as she was safe behind the walls of that citadel, mounted them, pulled up her skirt and cried out to her enemies that they should kill her children, she had all that she needed with her to make more. They were so terrified that they did not do so – wisely; imagine her vengeance if they had done!

Fortunate then, amid such violence and intrigue, that William should have Hemminges to protect him and teach him. Fortunate too that he should have been to Venice, whose bridge battles, great public brawls between factions of the city, led to them developing a style of fighting well suited to narrow places such as the galleys of Venetian ships. Venetian sword-masters would travel northern Italy teaching their skills.

He will need those skills for he still has far to go and now he is alone . . .

There is a challenge for any writer setting his scene in a time when English was spoken but not as it is today – how to honour that speech and give the book the feel of the time without its archaic nature getting in the way by creating a barrier to understanding. That challenge is greater still when we are familiar with the speech of the time, through knowledge of the plays, without perhaps being comfortable with it. I have tried to use only words that Shakespeare would have known, though I have no doubt that some will have slipped through the net. After all, it is no easy task, for even where we have the same words their meaning has changed over the passage of four hundred years. 'Blurt', for example, now means to speak something hastily and without consideration but then meant something akin to speaking contemptuously about, as in the line from *Pericles*, 'Whilst ours was blurted at, and held a malkin'. 'Malkin', of course, is unknown to us now (it means wench or slut). Such words too I have tried to avoid; I suspect I already send too many to the dictionary, but learning a new word can be a pleasure, at least I hope it may be so.

Acknowledgements

The writing of a novel is not as solitary a process as one might imagine. That it is done at all, let alone done well, is due to the contributions of many to whom I am hugely thankful: All the team at Bonnier Zaffre, including my new editor Sophie Orme and Rebecca Farrell, for once again producing a beautiful book and for eliminating most of my excesses and errors and calmly tolerating me when I stuck my foot down and insisted we keep some "for authenticity".

I am particularly thankful for the contributions of the insightful, erudite and disturbingly youthful Joel Richardson: even if the process of helping me over the various stiles on the path to completion proved so exhausting to him that he upped and left Bonnier for pastures new. (For the record: the score in our undeclared game of "was it Shakespeare or the Bible?" was left only marginally in my favour . . .)

My agent, Ivan Mulcahy, continues to show great patience with me, even gently explaining to me that my editor was right and I was wrong in a way that left me feeling cleverer despite the evidence to the contrary – truly he is as great a salesman as he is a mentor.

My clerks, and in particular my Chief Clerk, Ashley Carr, (who continues to refer to my novel writing as "time off for your book club" and who will not read them on point of principle) have made juggling a very full diary not just possible but a pleasure.

Above all to my family: my parents, whose inspirational love of language has been passed on to me and given me many of the great pleasures of my life, my wife, with whom I am hopelessly and deeply in love and who has, among many wonders, given me my greatest joys in life – my sons Cornelius and Atticus, who show every sign of being as brilliant, hilarious and dangerously clever as their mother.

Last, but very far from least, I am grateful to the generous people who read my first novel and took the time to write to me with kind words and a desire for more of William's adventures. I hope I have fulfilled your hopes.

I can no other answer make but thanks,
And thanks; and ever thanks; and oft good turns
Are shuffled off with such uncurrent pay:
But, were my worth as is my conscience firm,
You should find better dealing.

(Twelfth Night)

Go back to the beginning with the very first Will Shakespeare novel by Benet Brandreth . . .

When he's caught out by one ill-advised seduction too many, young William Shakespeare flees Stratford to seek his fortune.

Cast adrift in London, Will falls in with a band of players – but greater men have their eye on this talented young wordsmith. England's very survival hangs in the balance, and Will finds himself dispatched to Venice on a crucial embassy.

Dazzled by the city's masques – and its beauties – Will little realises the peril in which he finds himself. Catholic assassins would stop at nothing to end his mission on the point of their sharpened knives, and lurking in the shadows is a killer as clever as he is cruel.